S0-CAV-777

DIARY
OF A
WOMAN
IN WHITE

ANDRE SOUBIRAN

Translated from the French
by Mildred Marmur

AVON
PUBLISHERS OF BARD, CAMELOT, DISCUS, EQUINOX AND FLARE BOOKS

This Avon edition is the first publication in English
of *Diary Of A Woman In White*.

AVON BOOKS
A division of
The Hearst Corporation
959 Eighth Avenue
New York, New York 10019

Copyright © 1964 Editions Kent-Segep.
Originally published in French under the title
JOURNAL D'UNE FEMME EN BLANC
English translation copyright © 1969 by Avon Books.
Published by arrangement with the author.

ISBN: 0-380-00075-X

First Avon Printing, November, 1969.

Third Printing.

AVON TRADEMARK REG. U.S. PAT. OFF. AND
FOREIGN COUNTRIES, REGISTERED TRADEMARK—
MARCA REGISTRADA, HECHO EN CHICAGO, U.S.A.

Printed in the U.S.A.

DIARY OF A WOMAN IN WHITE

❧ PART ONE ❧

The Gennevilliers Hospital

❧ I ❧

Night Call

This loose-leaf notebook, with its imitation black leather binding, looks impressive, almost opulent. Yesterday afternoon, in a bookshop on Avenue Clichy, I asked for the most practical kind.

"They don't come any better," said the salesman. He snapped the binder several times to convince me.

As soon as I got home, I opened it on my work table. With childlike eagerness I started to write across the entire width of the first sheet:

FACULTY OF MEDICINE OF PARIS
Thesis for a Doctorate in Medicine
(State Diploma)

and, in the middle of the blank space below:

By Dr. Claude Sauvage

Next November, after my thesis has been "presented and publicly defended," I'll be officially called "doctor." I'm amused when I think that my first name in medical registries and on my nameplate will confuse male patients; they'll be surprised to find out that they're going to have to show their prostate or an embarrassingly located skin condition to a young "lady doctor." But I've got other reasons, better ones, to like my ambiguous first name. . . .

The title page of my thesis, anyway, will be more explicit about my sex, since it will state: "Female, born March 24, 1935, in Louviers (Eure)."

The title will be capitalized:

CONTRIBUTION TO THE STUDY OF THE PHYSICAL AND PSYCHOLOGICAL CONSEQUENCES OF CONTRACEPTION

Then, out of courtesy and gratitude toward Dr. Girodot, my supervisor, I'll add: "Based on work done at the Gynecology and Maternity section of the Gennevilliers (Seine) Community Hospital."

Here, at Gennevilliers, I've just completed the compulsory year of internship which must be done, after course work, in a hospital in a suburb of Paris.

Actually, both the subject for my thesis and advice about presenting it were given to me by Henri Lachaux, the hospital's neuro-psychiatric resident.

I've been on call since noon yesterday, probably for the last time; my year came to an end in June but Morizet, one of the two senior residents of the division, is on three weeks' vacation; he won't be back for another five days, and I'm taking over for him till then.

So I've kept my room at the hospital and between two emergencies this afternoon, I've begun sorting out the notes and observations I've accumulated in the past year, in preparation for my thesis. Using the black notebook, I've copied over the beginning of the introduction. Lachaux helped me work it out:

Contraception can be defined as the sum of the actions taken by a couple, during the sexual act, to prevent procreation, and consequently to influence, by conscious choice, the number and timing of human births.

This definition permits a comprehensive approach to the important problems of birth control today, in a world where, to use an analogy, 80,000 additional breakfasts must be served each morning and yet, of the 80,000 individuals born each day, one out of

10

three will either die before his second year, or, if he survives, will suffer from hunger all his life. However, we don't intend to cope with such vast speculations. They would lead beyond our competence. The problems of the study to which we wish to devote ourselves are those which confront the French doctor today, involving the medical consequences of contraception itself, and particularly the restrictions imposed on him by the Birth Law of 1920. This law was designed to increase the population by severely punishing both criminal abortions and the dissemination of birth-control literature. Economists, sociologists and moralists may find that by limiting ourselves to the medical point of view, we are reducing a subject of enormous general interest to trivial individual dimensions; but our restricted medical viewpoint may perhaps have its own value in the lives of countless couples for whom the risk of pregnancy represents a daily, or rather nightly, obsession. For these couples the legitimate avoidance of this risk can become the saving factor in preserving their home and their love. . . .

I wanted to dramatize the opening statement further; but Lachaux restrained me by reminding me about the three members of the examining committee I'd have to face the day of the defense.

On rereading it, my introduction (even tempered by my adviser's caution) strikes me as explicit and clear. But what delights me most is writing *we* when speaking of myself. Although I can see the humor in this scientifically majestic plural, it also flatters a 25-year-old student using it for the first time.

It's now one in the morning. The day was leaden and stifling, as if a thunderstorm were brewing. The night air coming through my wide open windows has no hint of a breeze, only a smell of hot brick and granite.

The hospital is situated on the northern outskirts of Gennevilliers, surrounded by huge apartment houses, a cemetery and a stadium. Land is probably cheaper here. In back of the hospital, stretching to the Seine along a coal port, is a vast belt of shacks and vegetable gardens. Sometimes they make the air smell almost like the country. But now there's no such breath of air in the warm darkness, only the smell of asphalt and dust-laden smoke, the usual atmosphere of this working-class suburb.

I don't feel sleepy and I don't want to lie down to toss and turn in bed, trying to find a cool spot. I've picked up my pen again; my fingers are moist as I write. I'd really meant this notebook to contain thoughts about medicine and not the inventory of my nearly ended year here. I have no literary aspirations now (although in school I was good in composition and kept a secret diary for months—I eventually burned it). Writing my clinical observations has taught me dry, unembellished phrases, a kind of shorthand of abbreviations and technical terms. And I don't think it's the heat or fatigue that are affecting me; nor am I wallowing in an end-of-school-years/beginning-of-career-problems depression.

No, this nocturnal monologue isn't due to one of those insignificant panics that are always ready to hit you when you're alone; it stems from authentic doubts and guilt. As much as I digress, I always return to the subject which obsesses me, to try to answer constantly recurring questions that I can't keep myself from asking. As soon as you doubt yourself, especially your effectiveness and courage, all paths come back to the same starting point; and then it's not easy to avoid problems and it's even harder to fall asleep. . . .

Tomorrow I'll pull these "non-thesis" pages I'm now scribbling on out of the black binder and tear them up. But it won't be so easy to erase the memory of the surgical abortion I've just performed.

How can I sleep when I keep thinking about it? This abortion wasn't just a routine incident during my turn on call. Even if I can prove in my thesis that the best prevention for abortion is contraception, that the only protection for woman's happiness and family happiness is birth control, it won't erase the fact that at one moment of my internship, I was cowardly about that precise point; and because of my error a 19-year-old woman who has just had an abortion, may die.

About an hour ago, just before midnight, I was straightening out my files when the wall telephone in the residence corridor rang four times—my signal.

I recognized the admitting night clerk at the other end of the phone by her country accent.

"A miscarriage," she announced, "bleeding."

"Temperature?" I asked.

"103."

"I'll be right down."

I hung up. Such a conversation is never very long. Since I have to examine the patient anyway, I ask one or two questions just to get some diagnostic idea, so that I can think about treatment on my way down. At this stage it wasn't very important—I've run almost the entire gamut of tedious cases which an intern on call must handle, but at the beginning I did occasionally glance at the pharmacopoeia or my medical books before I left my room.

The residence is behind the hospital, just beyond the fortifications of 1870 on the outskirts of Paris.

Outside, I inhaled the warm air. A lawn sprinkler was turning with a soft rain-like rustle. I was almost overwhelmed by the contrast between the perfume of the linden trees, the smell of grass, and my airless room. I'd stood here often during the past year, at the top of the three steps, glancing briefly at the geometric shapes of the hospital architecture, the tall streetlights and the gravel-lined cement walks that I was about to step out on. My steps would crunch loud on the gravel, and the bluish night lamps would glow softly through the windows of the buildings.

Wrapped in my intern's cape during the bitter winter nights, or wearing a light white blouse during a spring evening, I'd often looked at the perpetual violet glow of the sky above Paris and tried to tune in on the faraway activity and gaiety of the city. But Paris didn't exist for me any longer. I was here to become a doctor. I loved my temporary room, the depressing buildings and the industrial suburbs with their everlasting smell of soot and factory. My love for medicine was like some inner passion that grows until it devours you completely.

Then I'd rushed along the pathway and hurried to my patients, eager not to delay the moment of initiative and responsibility. At that moment the entire hospital belonged to me.

As I headed toward the admitting office this evening I didn't feel quite so romantic about it; but on my way, by force of habit, I couldn't help thinking about the "miscarriage" awaiting me. A simple hemorrhage would indicate a spontaneous abortion, but with a temperature of 103, it was almost certainly induced. Like almost all women in her situation, the patient would obstinately maintain, contrary to the evidence, that she'd done nothing, and tell me some story of overexertion with a heavy laundry or of falling down the stairs. She'd probably lie even at the risk of death. In any case, there's just one course of action whatever the method of inducing the abortion: immediate injections of antitetanus serum and antibiotics, in order to prevent the two most severe complications. Injections delayed too long after an attempted abortion are often useless.

I'm used to this. Even in this small hospital on the outskirts of the city I've performed one or two curettages every Saturday I've been on duty; women trying to abort hope to rest on Sunday and get right back to work on Monday. And the statistics are indisputable: 2,000 abortions occur in France every day, resulting in as many injuries and deaths as on all the roads of France on a peak vacation day in August. Each year, of 500,000 women who abort, several thousand die and tens of thousands are permanently affected.

I'm going to quote these statistics in my thesis, in tables, curves and graphs but, as I headed toward the admissions office I thought less of the category I'd put this new abortion into than of her link to the immense number of women with unwanted and rejected pregnancies.

How long had my poor patient hoped, growing more and more anxious each day, before she made her decision? How long did she have to wait to feel, with relief and horror, the small lump of flesh slowly slip out amid the blood clots?

I'll have to emphasize all this barbarism in my thesis so that the guilty ones will see what they've done. Perhaps they'll finally change that hideously unjust law of 1920 which provides the same severe punishment for performing criminal abortions (which all physicians denounce) and for publishing birth-control literature, even though freedom of contraception could avert so many tragedies.

I took a deep breath as I entered the building. Septic abortions smell very bad and I hadn't yet become accustomed to the odor.

There was a very young man in workman's clothes in the vestibule, near the door. He started toward me as soon as he saw my white coat but then hesitated, probably surprised to see a woman. I walked over to him.

Men usually supply information without too much hesitation. This one—about twenty-two or twenty-three years old—looked friendly.

I asked: "Are you the husband?"

He cleared his throat anxiously before answering: "Yes, mademoiselle."

"How did it happen?"

"I don't know."

I looked surprised. "You don't know? But I have to know exactly what your wife did so I can treat her."

"No, mademoiselle, I really don't know," he repeated. "She told me to keep out of it, that these things 'don't concern a man.'" Of course, the planning and the danger of the abortion weren't his "business." He only cared about the final result. I shrugged my shoulders.

He noticed my gesture and anxiously asked: "Oh, mademoiselle, that won't stop you from saving her?"

In the narrow examination room the patient was stretched on the table, with her legs spread; the nurse had just about finished shaving her pubic hair. There was a sanitary napkin full of blackened clots and blood at the foot of the table. Even at the door, I recognized the characteristic rank odor.

As I came in, the young woman turned her head. Her pale face was bathed in perspiration. Her beautiful eyes, now ringed with dark shadows, implored me with dignity.

She had on a hospital gown which barely covered her thighs. The slender body and small round breasts of the child-woman contrasted with the maturity of her proud look.

I walked to the table and picked up her wrist to check her pulse. It was beating rapidly and erratically. Her skin was hot; her body shook occasionally with chills.

While palpating the abdomen very gently I began to question her: last menstrual period, onset of bleeding, onset of pain, onset of fever. Beginning of the purulent clotted discharge. Despite the shakiness in her voice, she answered precisely and confidently. Diagnosis confirmed: incomplete septic abortion with hemorrhage. Not very reassuring. Then I asked the difficult question:

"How did you do this?"

No denial but this time she looked away. Of course! She was sworn to silence by the abortionist. Bending over her lovely profile, I explained softly so that she'd clearly understand that my sympathies were with her: "Don't be scared. I have to know so I can help you. I won't get you or anyone else into trouble."

I picked up her burning wrist again. It felt thin and fragile in my fingers. I wanted so much to communicate with her, to show her that I wanted to protect her.

In any case, why would I accuse her when our hypocritical society legally condemns abortions but practices them on a large scale, and when they're especially easy if you have money? I kept talking. The white face contracted with every spasm of pain. She finally turned toward me and told me a story that was tragic because it was so commonplace. One missed period after eight months of marriage and the beginning of an anxious wait. An address supplied by an obliging friend at the shop who'd already had four abortions. The probe inserted by the woman at St. Ouen, and then, deep within her, that nameless pain which each woman describes so badly because it's mixed with too much guilt and anxiety. Then, on the bus trip home, hoping that the jolts would speed the process. Later, when nothing happened but a slight pink discharge, a second visit to the woman, this time followed by a heavy flow of blood and clots, first red, then rust-colored and increasingly malodorous, and a gradually rising fever. This evening, on his return from the factory, her husband, frightened by the bloody napkins, finally persuaded her to go to the hospital.

I slipped on the rubber glove and my fingers explored the moist, sticky cavity, producing a slurping noise. The dark blue eyes looked questioningly at me during the examination. Placenta retention was evident. Fortunately, the abdomen had remained supple; the infection was probably still localized. It was necessary to administer a large dose of antibiotics and intervene immediately. In her pus-filled, and therefore fragile uterus, a steel curette would be too harsh. I decided to do a manual evacuation. To explain that this would be a minor operation, I tried to find that soothing and convincing tone of voice which is surely as old as the first surgeon and his first patient. Yet, as I spoke, her confidence changed to panic.

"You'll put me to sleep, won't you?"

Her small voice was pleading. Why this terror? I guessed the answer. The old story of abortions performed without anesthesia to discourage or punish those seeking

16

them. But were they really just legends, these terrifying stories told by frightened women in hospital rooms? I'm ashamed to realize that they may once have been true. At Gennevilliers, thank God, these cruel practices are unknown or long forgotten, as I explained to my patient. She thanked me with a pathetically brave smile as she was wheeled out on a stretcher to the operating room.

I was jotting down a few descriptive words in the admissions ledger (omitting any mention of an induced abortion) when I noticed that my young patient's name was Mariette Le Hugon, nineteen years old, an operator; an occupation I'd never heard of until recently, when a patient explained to me that an operator is the worker who pieces together the pattern sections cut out by the cutter in a dress factory.

When I reached the operating room, Mariette Le Hugon already had her arms strapped to the table, her legs drawn up and feet fixed in stirrups, thighs widely apart.

The nurse wheeled a table over, covered it with a sterile drape and arranged the bandages and instruments I might need.

While I was scrubbing up, washing my forearms and hands, the telephone rang in the next room. It was the anesthesiologist; she was still at the bedside of the postoperative case and was sorry to have to report that she'd be a few minutes late.

I looked at the young woman. I'd sensed her scrutiny of my every move while I was scrubbing up. Had I reassured her? Or was there an atmosphere of security in the operating room? Her bluish lips and black-ringed eyes began to smile more confidently. But I was afraid that prolonging the wait might frighten her. The thick layer of cotton between her thighs was already red; her body quivered periodically. I was again touched by this young life, so weak and in so much danger.

When I walked back to her, she whispered to me: "You don't remember me, mam'selle, but I remember you. I came to see you last year, in October. For a certificate . . . for the form you need to get married. . . ."

"Of course!" I exclaimed. "I remember you now." But I couldn't admit how unrecognizable her small, serious face was this evening, with its pale cheeks, the feverishly glistening eyes and tight mouth. She looked at me, happy to be remembered.

It was last October. I'd just begun my internship in Gennevilliers and was continually puzzled by my duties. I'd never made out a premarital certificate and both my medical school course and my gynecological textbooks were silent on the subject. What was I supposed to do? To say? To write down? Fortunately the future bride was even more innocent and inexperienced than I. I went to ask the supervisor; all I had to do was fill out the blank form she gave me. . . .

To prove to Mariette that I remembered her, I said: "Of course, you're the one who told me what an operator does. It's the kind of thing you don't forget!"

And we shared a conspiratorial laugh.

I remember that October scene perfectly. Flustered about the matter of the certificate, I kept chatting with my patient after the examination was completed. She had risen to dress and I was studying the delicate features of her face, the fragile contours of her body which would soon be thickened by pregnancy and work.

She was almost dressed when she turned toward me and asked me what to do to avoid pregnancy at the beginning of marriage.

It was the first time a patient had asked me a question as direct as that about birth control. What could I tell her? The nurse had just walked in and was waiting for the consultation to end so she could bring in another patient. In her presence was I going to advise withdrawal, or talk about condoms or douche bags or foamy suppositories or acetic vaginal jelly? I'd already learned that the hospital's atmosphere wasn't receptive to birth control and family planning. In my presence the previous evening, Pascali, one of the interns on duty, had told a mother of eight, distraught by her repeated pregnancies, to "be careful," to avoid at all costs the risks of a ninth birth. When the poor woman asked him about the safest method, he answered her, laughing: "It's not difficult. Send your husband to sleep in the attic or the basement!" And the nurse, seeing the patient's dismay at the advice, had giggled behind the woman's back.

And that was why, because I didn't know what I was allowed to say, because of cowardice in front of that idiotic nurse, and finally because it was late and other patients were waiting for me, I merely inscribed on a prescription blank the title of a pamphlet explaining Ogino's rhythm method.

What effective advice I'd given that morning! Today the young woman comes back to me, seriously infected and nearly exsanguinated. Were it not for the abortionist's probe, the little lump of partly separated flesh which I was about to remove completely would have become one of the numberless "Ogino babies" who swell the world's population, as if thumbing their noses at the method. This poor "Ogino baby" has been rejected before his birth and I'm doubly responsible that he was never born. I'm not very proud of the advice I gave that day.

Mariette kept smiling at me. And, as if to apologize for the trouble she was giving me, she raised her head a little, as the anesthesiologist, who had just arrived, was injecting the Pentothal, and said:

"When I got caught and we knew we couldn't keep the baby, my husband told me, 'Go back to your lady doctor' but I didn't want to. I told him, 'Don't even think about it! The doctor would never be able to help me. She couldn't. . . .' "

Her head fell back. While the Pentothal began to flow through her veins her smile wavered wistfully. The feverish glitter in her eyes began to dim as the anesthetic took effect. She added, in the same meek tone:

"I told him, 'Doctors can't help you until you start it yourself.' Isn't that right, mademoiselle, that they can't do anything before, that they can only help after?"

The injection was completed. Her gaze became fixed and there was a silence broken only by the low, whistling sound of her breath between her teeth. I could begin. . . .

Mariette was still asleep when the operating room orderly lifted her effortlessly from the table, placed her on a stretcher and wheeled her toward the ward. Under the light blanket, her body seemed to have a corpse's ultimate weariness, but her face retained the trace of a smile.

Mariette had been smiling that October morning when she thanked me politely and took her certificate and the prescription. Then she left, the innocent victim of her sex, her soft flesh destined, along with many others, to the abortionist's knife. She vanished into the indifferent crowd, confidently holding a bit of paper on which I'd written the name of a worthless method.

I, with all my dreams of teaching women to use their bodies without fear, I, who for six years have prepared myself without compromise for a profession which would

19

enable me to help other women, suddenly I've come to this tragic dead end, at a mutilated and infected uterus. I've been forced to rake out putrid waste with my fingers, amid blood clots, for an abortion I couldn't prevent! "Before," alas, I didn't know what to do and "after" I could do so little!

Now, back in my room, I'm overwhelmed by distress and weariness. They seep into me as if through an opening in my soul, and obliterate my reason. Am I going to sink to my knees as I used to do when I was a little girl? I haven't prayed in years—it's been a long time since I believed—but now that my will is faltering, I remember once more the naïve prayers of my childhood, the evening prayers that seemed to contain all the promises, but which had only the deceptive softness of a pillow.... Before I can fall asleep, must I say, "Oh my God! Take pity on Mariette and, with her, take pity on me! Let not my entire life be marred by this tragedy. Let Mariette's 'after' not turn into 'too late!' " ...

8 a.m.

I lay awake in the darkness with my eyes open for a long time, hoping for a breath of fresh air, but before it came, sleep finally overtook me, a heavy, troubled sleep that I'd never experienced before.

The phone had awakened me shortly before dawn; a call to the maternity section. I had to lean against the wall as I answered; I was so tired, sweaty and nauseated. When I went back to my room I saw the brown stains on my sheet. I was almost relieved by the discovery. The nighttime emotion I couldn't control, the brutal "hemorrhaging of the soul" was probably due to another, real hemorrhaging; it came from the tears of blood that pious women weep periodically because of the original sin—"the curse"—which to me is the most humiliating and irritating servitude of my sex.

Yet, I've tried for a long time to be honest with myself. Why try to cheat or deceive myself? I know that my confusion last night wasn't due to physiological upset; its cause was neither glandular nor nervous; that kind of moral fever doesn't come from heat or menstruation.

Outside it was still dark, toward the east there was a barely discernible light. A light breeze had come up and I stood still a few minutes and let it caress my forehead.

The maternity call was for a breech delivery. When the

20

midwife talked to me over the phone, she explained that she didn't want to take all the responsibility herself because disengaging the head is often complicated; so she was alerting me a little ahead of time. I had a few minutes before I was due in the labor room so I decided to stop by and see Mariette.

Since the heat wave began, the atmosphere in the ward has been oppressive despite the open windows and the nighttime coolness; there's an ever-present odor of cheap perfume, sweat and fever. Blue shaded night lamps give off a sickly light over the double rows of twenty beds. It took me a few minutes to adjust to the dimness.

Almost all of the women had pushed back their sheets; they slept half naked, sprawled across their beds or else tossing and turning to find a cooler spot. Here and there a snore, a muffled cough or a sigh rose from this group slumber; each woman in this dim shadow was dreaming about her house, worrying about her children or her husband, the unpaid bills, or next month's rent. They fashioned their nightmares out of real miseries.

In the back of the room, a voice cried out: "Bedpan, please."

In the vague light the mass of half-awakened bodies grumbled, stirred, stretched and protested.

Several patients reached out toward their cups of sweetened herb tea and complained that they couldn't breathe because of the heat.

"Pan, please," the voice repeated, more urgent now.

Suddenly dozens of different voices from all parts of the room united in one mass appeal for the pan.

The large white form of the night nurse appeared on the threshold of the room. She was balancing a pile of white enamel bedpans in her arms and began to distribute them in the dark, without turning on the overhead lights. I knew that it was Mme Sandrin because she didn't turn the lights on in the room. The others always switched the blinding bulbs for their own convenience. The patients who recognized her, as I did, called out to her quietly, in friendship. Mme Sandrin, padding silently in her slippers, circulated among the beds, straightening a sheet here, fluffing a pillow there, offering a fresh pot of herb tea.

She recognized me from afar and came over.

"Do you need me, mam'selle?" she asked.

"No, I just wanted to know how the patient who was admitted tonight is doing."

21

"She was asleep half an hour ago, when I passed by last."

Mme Sandrin pulled a flashlight out of her apron pocket—also a piece of individual inititative since the hospital administration only provides a portable lamp, to be plugged in from outlet to outlet. She guided me between the rows like an usher in a movie house.

"There's your patient," she said, focusing on Mariette. She dimmed the flashlight with her fingers.

My post-op was asleep. She looked less sallow, her respiration was more relaxed. A sweat-soaked strand of hair lay on the forehead filled with drug-suffused dreams. She was alone in a bed for the first time in months; she must have groped in the dark for a beloved body, and finding only emptiness, finally curled up with her arms close to her heart.

An old woman lying not too far from Mariette covered her mouth with hands like two fading flowers, and tried to cough discreetly, but the raucous coughs continued and the neighbor in the bed between them murmured nastily: "That was all we needed. Grandma's managed to catch a cold in this heat!"

"Go back to sleep and stop bothering the others!" Mme Sandrin rebuked her.

"I'd like to see you do it!" the crude voice answered. "Every time grandma coughs, she does it in her bed!"

To avoid continuing the conversation, Mme Sandrin shut off the flashlight. We walked away in silence, so we wouldn't interrupt Mariette's peaceful sleep.

"Wait and see" is the basic aphorism of the obstetrician delivering a baby, just as patience is his cardinal virtue.

I realized as soon as I reached the maternity ward that I might be in for a wait. A breech delivery can be prolonged. The fetus, instead of politely presenting a well-flexed head first, which is the ideal position for a child to open the mother's birth canal, had chosen to arrive either feet or buttocks first.

The midwife heard me and came over to apologize for having been hasty about calling me; labor had been in progress for fifteen hours but dilation was progressing very slowly. She suggested an intravenous injection of pitocin in order to accelerate and reinforce the contractions.

I have been taught that the administration of pitocin in an obstructed labor can cause it to become too active and dangerous, so I refused the injection, thinking, "Sorry, old girl, you won't get off early today."

I went into the labor room. The patient was resting between contractions, her eyes closed. She's 39 years old. This will be her first child and for her, even more than for the younger woman, the delivery represents a major event in her life.

I've been checking her regularly in the prenatal clinic for seven months. She dreams of the marvelous little body she'll soon be holding in her arms. She's told me her story; in 1939 she was 18 years old and about to be married. First the marriage was delayed by the mobilization of troops. Then her fiancé was taken prisoner of war in the Saar right at the beginning of hostilities and was held captive for five years. Since 1945 she's been yearning for a child. And now, at 39, after fifteen years of waiting, when she no longer believed it could happen . . .

My patient opened her eyes when she heard me asking the midwife about the baby's heartbeat. Sweat was pouring down her face; she was still panting but for a moment her hands left the bar at the head of the bed where they clenched with every contraction.

Our glances met. She welcomed me with a smile, her face expressing exhaustion, impatience and hope.

I leaned over her and tried to sound encouraging: "Labor is progressing well but it won't be right away. . . ."

"Are you going away again?" she asked anxiously.

"Don't worry. I promised you I'd deliver this beautiful baby myself. I'm just going to sit down next door to wait for him."

A new contraction began. Her face reddened, neck muscles tensed, her mouth, slightly open, grimaced, breathing became difficult and her hands gripped the bar of the bed so hard that her knuckles went white. Her entire body seemed like one intense contraction.

I waited until the contraction was over and smiled at my patient to reassure her before I went out: "Try not to worry. Relax. Breathe quickly, not too deep. I won't be far away."

I usually remain near my patient's bed; I like obstetrics because of the intimate contact with the women, the continual necessity to satisfy their deep instinctive need for protection.

Even though most deliveries have a spontaneously happy conclusion, I even like the moments of waiting that precede responsibility and initiative. When I talk to a patient I try to convey to her the feeling that her security and that of the young life about to be born are my only preoccupations.

But today I didn't have the energy to talk. I was weighed down by exhaustion. While I waited for the moment when I'd have to do my part, I rested in the easy chair vacated by the midwife, so I'd be in better shape when the time came.

During the six years I had supported myself so that I could finance medical school, I was an usher, a tutor, a mother's helper, a clerk in a bookshop, a switchboard operator—I had to schedule everything tightly and learn not to let eating and sleeping interfere with my activities. And, since I had to do without sleep, I learned to will my body to relax completely during the least breathing space. There was no chance of falling asleep here in the midst of "push, push" endlessly repeated to women in labor, amid the wails and cries of the newborn or the continual rushing from one labor room to another; but this morning I couldn't even relax as the gray dawn slowly changed to a grudging, sallow light and finally to a brand-new day.

I felt that the last six years of my life had been in vain. I hadn't allowed myself one frivolous minute, one day of vacation, one single pleasure enjoyed by my contemporaries. I'd entered a man's world, hardened myself and become stubborn; I fought continually against the universally held opinion of female inferiority. I was disappointed in most of the female medical students for not being passionately committed to their tasks, for thinking only of preparing themselves for a respected profession and not of turning society upside down to win, once and for all, a genuine equality of the sexes. In my desire to prove that this equality was possible, at least on an intellectual level, I even reached the point of citing the most bizarre arguments; for example, if you compare the weight of a male and female brain, not to the total weight of the body but to the square root of that weight, you will find rigorously equal proportions for both brains.

And here, in this small world of the maternity ward, where men play no important roles, the women still completely accept the inferiority of their sex. Even the midwives, despite a profession sufficiently rich in risks and responsibility to liberate them, seem to know the defeatism of our sex. I definitely sensed their reservations about me at the beginning of my internship. They openly resisted obeying my orders; I didn't have their confidence. They must have thought (perhaps with some justice) that they knew more about deliveries than I, but their resistance to my authority seemed to stem more from their sensing a specific common inferiority than from technical insufficiency on my part. They were disconcerted, perhaps even humiliated, at taking orders from another woman when those same orders usually came from a male intern.

Do these little midwives at Gennevilliers instinctively feel that the female brain is dogmatic and narrow by nature, that though it may be capable of remembering a lesson, it fixes itself in one position, unable to adapt to a new medical problem or to improve on it rationally, in the masculine manner, by a series of observations and logical deductions? While the female brain can assimilate books, does an original deficiency keep it from ever inventing or broadening anything? And I, always so proud of my intelligence, must I now begin to doubt it?

At 7 a.m. the usual morning commotion began in the hospital.

The night shift had gone, replaced by a new team. Within the white enameled walls, hospital life continued, immutable.

Serving carts brought in hot coffee from the kitchen. The ambulatory patients in their dressing gowns, carrying toothbrush and towel in hand, were filing toward the bathroom. The day nurses scurried about, carrying enemas, tubes and thermometers—the hour of intimate toilets and the taking of temperature had arrived. Most of the women took out lipstick, powder and cream jars from their night tables. Night was liquidated; in the freshness of the morning, everyone cleaned off the last traces of the dark as best she could. Day had returned, and with it the illusions of hope. But the sheer weight of the day would soon bring back suffering and fever. . . .

Never before this morning have all these bitter thoughts attacked me with such force. Why be stubborn? Why fight the prevalent notion that women should be the slaves of men? Why try to transform the world, fight against masculine taboos, hypocrisy, inequality and injustice when these women say they're satisfied? Why continue to study gynecology, so difficult a field? I had decided it would be the point of departure for my crusade to liberate and rehabilitate female bodies. If it's too late now to begin studying something else, shouldn't I give up this harried, difficult life, full of the disappointments and anxieties of the woman doctor, and choose the possibly more practical road of the research laboratory? Instead of talking to women about freedom of conception, why not be the researcher who will perfect a simple, practical, contraceptive method which would protect them, without danger, against the vicissitudes and injustices of love?

Apparently I'd fallen asleep. The midwife awoke me and said: "Fully dilated. But the contractions have slowed down over the past few minutes."

I found it a little difficult to get up. But even this short rest, less than half an hour long, had been refreshing.

The midwife returned to the patient in the labor room. She was moving her stethoscope over an abdomen so enormous and distended that the skin, streaked with stretch-marks, was shiny.

"The child is fine," she concluded.

I slipped on a rubber glove. Proof in hand, I announced to the mother that it was a boy. I added: "Another ten minutes work and it will all be over. From now on everything depends on your courage."

What I couldn't tell her, because I didn't want her to worry, was that now we had come to the most dangerous moment for the child.

Her sufferings seemed to make her radiant. The woman said: "Oh, mam'selle, you'll see. For my little boy, I'll push very hard."

A new contraction began. While I scrubbed up, the nurse's aide brought in a sterile coat which she helped me put on, tying it, bib-fashion, behind my neck and waist. I slipped on a fresh pair of rubber gloves and was ready to begin.

With my foot I pushed a stool toward the woman's legs. They'd been put into white linen boots and lifted into the stirrups. I sat down facing the thighs and the lower abdomen which I smeared profusely with red antiseptic. The tiny buttocks were visible now, covered with greenish meconium.

More waiting ... I remembered the advice of the obstetric supervisor at Baudelocque Maternity Hospital:

"In breech deliveries, be patient and gentle. Not too fast and not too hard. Don't rush in." In order to make us remember his advice, he repeated to us the phrase which has helped the memory of generations of students: "The fetus says, 'Who's the imbecile who's pulling me out by the feet?' " At the same time, lifting his arms toward the sky, he imitated for us, the consternation of the poor fetus about this catastrophic interference. There's no better image to make yourself remember that if you give in to the temptation to hasten the exit too early, you risk extending the child's arms into the uterus and thus blocking its expulsion.

So I kept repeating to myself this morning: "Don't rush in. Patience!"

During my year of internship, I haven't delivered many babies. The midwives do the ordinary cases and Morizet, who's preparing for a specialty in obstetrics, monopolizes the difficult ones.

When I first arrived in Gennevilliers, the only obstetric experience I had was based on three deliveries a year at Baudelocque, when I was still a student, and I hadn't felt very secure about my technique. To avoid any serious errors, I'd glance through the books in my room before going to the maternity ward and rehearse every movement I'd have to make. It was a question of pride. I knew everybody would be watching me and I didn't want to look ridiculous in front of the midwives or Morizet. Before leaving my room I'd shut the books and stand up straight as if I were already under the projector which is lighted at the moment of delivery. The practice helped muster my energy so that I'd be less likely to make any mistakes. The anticipation of being observed by a critical eye somehow helped me regain confidence in myself.

In my first days at Gennevilliers, I'd often needed this preliminary ritual to combat the anxiety I felt during complicated deliveries. Morizet, who was busy elsewhere, couldn't come to help me and I had to rely solely on the midwife. I'd have liked to talk to her in those anxious moments and admit my uncertainties, but I knew that if I lifted my eyes I'd meet a sarcastic glance that would say: "If you're so smart, you don't need our help!"

But now, with the year ended, I've completed my obstetric training quite honorably. A "breech," which is supposed to be a difficult delivery, doesn't scare me any more, and that's fortunate, because I can't expect any support from Mlle Virolleau, the midwife on duty.

We're the same age; she's blonde, rather pretty, always heavily made-up; she's sure of herself, talks very loud and laughs at the slightest excuse just to show her sparkling teeth. She's perfectly trained for her job but she takes advantage of the indulgence of Pascali and Morizet and shamelessly leaves the boring tasks to her colleagues.

Just now, when I was remembering the reluctance of the midwives to obey me as unquestioningly as they obeyed Morizet or Pascali, I was thinking especially of the charming Mlle Virolleau. There's no open hostility, no formal disagreement between us; we've never exchanged really unpleasant words. We simply know that we don't like each other. Mlle Virolleau considered me a conceited, insignificant student, too sentimental and enthusiastic. She's never understood why I insisted last winter that the enamel bedpans be warmed before being slid under the patients' bottoms. Other people's enthusiasms can easily seem ridiculous, and since mine annoy her, Mlle Virolleau likes to make fun of them.

Two new contractions propelled the little behind a bit farther and I'd encourage the patient with each contraction.

"Come on ... That's it ... Very good ... Breathe deeply ... Stop breathing and push ... Bear down on the stirrups. ..."

The perineum bulged, becoming more and more taut with each contraction. It was beginning to whiten in a dangerous way. I would have to do an episiotomy before it tore.

I took a pair of scissors, curved so they wouldn't injure the child; slipped two fingers into the base of the vaginal cavity and, at the height of a contraction (which makes the incision less painful) cut the mother's skin and flesh by an inch and a half with a quick stroke.

The little behind took immediate advantage of this to point more toward the sky, like the tip of a tiny missile; its skin was yellowish under the greenish smear. The pallor meant that all the child's blood was at that moment propelled toward the head. Such congestion of the brain can't be prolonged without risking severe lesions of the meninges. "Not too fast but not too late," the supervisor used to repeat. It is in such moments that it becomes difficult to forbid yourself a hasty move.

I felt Mlle Virolleau looking at me. Did she think that I would be "the imbecile who'll raise the arms of the fetus"?

In order to soothe my impatience to act, I chose to deal with the mother.

"Come on ... Come on ... Keep it up ... Push ... You have to get your child out quickly. . . ."

A new "pain." The behind was pointed more and more toward the sky. With the next contraction the little bundle of flesh, becoming pinker, half emerged as far as the navel.

I put my right hand forward; just as the legs disengaged, the upper body, ejected like a little warm sticky mummy, fell astride my forearm. I hastened to get the pressure off the cord immediately. With my left hand I gently pulled on the bluish, dangling umbilical cord. There! Everything was going well. The little package of flesh riding on my forearm turned brick red. Only one more contraction, and the shoulders and head would emerge with a spurting of fluid, depositing the whole child into my hands like a beautiful ripe fruit.

My tiredness had disappeared completely. A wave of happiness swept over me; I felt like whistling or singing. At the least I wanted to say, laughing, to the midwife: "Wouldn't you say that I'm a good obstetrician?"

But before I said anything, Mlle Virolleau leaned toward me:

"The contractions seem to be slowing down."

Her voice was sarcastic; she was triumphant. The body was partly out but the head still tightly imprisoned in the vaginal cavity. This situation put the child into two dangers: on the one hand, the umbilical cord, which acts rather like a diver's air tube, was for the moment crushed between the hard little skull and the mother's pelvis—which left me only ten minutes to finish the delivery before the fetus was mortally damaged by lack of oxygen; on the other hand, the surrounding fresh air could provoke one or two reflex breaths which would let enough mucus and amniotic fluid into the bronchial tubes to suffocate the child.

If I'd permitted Mlle Virolleau to start the intravenous pitocin drip I could have told her now: "Increase the rate to twenty-five drops a minute and we'll get the uterus started again."

Because of my excessive caution, the driving force had sagged in the middle of its major effort just at the most dangerous moment for the fetus, which is what the mid-wife's mocking glance conveyed.

But did she think I was that inept? This was a case for a "Bracht maneuver"; just as soon as another push would permit me to disengage the arms, I'd be able to complete it satisfactorily.

As in all delivery rooms, a clock hangs on the wall above the delivery table it showed 7:54. The ten-minute countdown toward asphyxiation began. It had to be finished by 8:04. But ten minutes was more than enough. It takes me two minutes to do a Bracht.

Immediately I grabbed the child by the root of each thigh. I lifted him very gently and started to turn him slowly so that his back would face the mother's abdomen. I held the little thighs firmly in my hands. I was conscious of an almost automatic dexterity and also aware of the perfect precision of my gestures. A Bracht as elegant as on the demonstration puppet.

As I gradually lifted the little body, the neck extended over the mother's pubis. I assumed that Mlle Virolleau was following each of my movements attentively. Let her look! I would stop rotating the trunk and the head would release itself. . . . I pulled gently. The head resisted. I pulled harder. The head did not come out. I could feel it blocked.

I didn't dare lift my eyes to the midwife. She was surely smiling. This time, there were real complications. I glanced at the clock: 7:57. I must stay calm. I still had seven minutes. But suddenly, as my eyes turned toward the child, I saw a spasm in the little body. With horror I saw his belly pull in and his chest enlarge because of a contraction of the diaphragm.

As if I myself were suffocating under an air pump, panic cut my breath. This respiratory spasm changed everything. Now I had to go very fast; I couldn't hesitate, I couldn't make a mistake. Should it slide back, the baby might make a totally vain effort to breathe; his nose and mouth were still imprisoned in the vagina, which was filled with mucous matter. And every respiratory attempt would flood the lungs with blood and meconium. If another two or three similar spasms occurred, the child would die of asphyxiation!

All of a sudden this little dark red boy imposed on me a frightening responsibility; he felt leaden in my hands.

For a time—I don't know how long it lasted—I was

terrified. Sweat rolled down between my shoulders. My forehead was icy and my arms slack. I no longer dared look at the clock, as if the fatal minute were already inscribed on the wall. And it was useless to time it. From now on, the danger could no longer be counted in minutes; faced with this paralyzing menace my hands, still clasping the little thighs, refused to obey me.

"Do you want me to push, while you do a 'Mauriceau,' mam'selle?"

Did I understand? Really understand? I looked at the midwife. Yes, it was she who spoke. She looked at me, ready to obey, waiting for my orders.

Through a kind of fog, I heard myself answer, almost against my will: "Yes, of course . . . At once! . . ."

And as soon as I'd taken this in, as if waking up from a nightmare, I felt that my life, for one moment suspended, had started again. My ideas became clear. Even if my vanity suffered, I saw clearly what had just happened: Mlle Virolleau had measured the danger as I did, had seen my panic, and, not daring to give me direct advice, had pretended to offer her help in order to suggest politely the necessary maneuver: the classical "Mauriceau."

There was no time to analyze this unexpected gift as the little body was turning from dark red to blue. Time was very much of the essence. I looked at the midwife, again smiled at her in agreement and immediately had the heady sensation that I would no longer be alone to finish this difficult game. We would win as a team. We began.

Calmly, without losing a second, I slipped my index and middle fingers into the vaginal cavity along the baby's chin; I opened his mouth and pushed my fingers deeply to the base of the tongue. In this way I got a good grip for bending the head, while my left hand, which I placed like a prong on both sides of the neck, would pull.

Only then did I take time out to look at the clock: 8:01.

"Are you ready? Let's go!"

Immediately, Mlle Virolleau, who was bent over the woman's abdomen, pushed gently and slowly through the abdominal wall, in order to flex the head correctly. My left hand and my right hand, fingers deep in the baby's mouth, were moving it at the same time.

For a moment, we meshed our efforts. In vain. Despite the traction, the little skull remained stuck in the pelvis.

"Let's try again! Immediately!" the midwife shouted,

breathless, wiping the sweat on her brow with the sleeve of her coat.

I was also breathless and sweating. 8:02. Only two more minutes! A mad fear gripped me. One awkward move and all would be finished!

Again Mlle Virolleau made a suggestion.

"When you flex the head, you could also try to position it. Like groping with a key to find the hole in the lock!"

I was playing my last card. My entire being was concentrated in my fingertips pulling on the neck and the jaw, as if nothing else existed except this head. I no longer thought of the child—who had turned purple now—or even of his imminent asphyxiation. Blind with sweat, my teeth clenched and my mouth dry, I concentrated on the bony obstacle and tried to find a passageway through with an almost insane obstinacy.

"While I push, try to rotate the head from left to right," the midwife suggested.

Even in my panic, I took in this piece of advice.

While I pulled with all my strength, my fingers at the same time made the little head turn slightly toward the right. Suddenly, in a release so brutal that I felt the floor slip away under me, there was no longer any obstacle. That's it! I almost shouted with joy. Slowly the sticky head slid out. Just in time! I looked at the clock: 8:03, and I smiled at Miss Virolleau to salute our victory.

Two clamps on the cord . . . one scissor cut. Finally this little prisoner who had frightened me so much was liberated. But when I picked up the little packet of purple flesh to show him to his mother, the head—with the wrinkled forehead, flattened nose and puffed up eyes—fell back and rolled gently from one shoulder to the other. No wailing, not even a sigh, came out of the inky blue lips. What I had between my hands was a sad stuffed doll, as inert and limp as a corpse. And yet the child was alive; under the sternum I could clearly see the heart beat.

Behind me, the mother still breathless and panting, was beginning to get worried.

"How is my baby? I don't hear him cry."

Mlle Virolleau, standing near her, was reassuring.

"Mam'selle Sauvage is taking care of him. Relax. He'll be breathing soon."

I turned the newborn over, his head down; the nurse's aide wrapped him in a warm towel and we ran with him to the premature baby room close by. The resuscitating machine was set up on the table. While the assistant prepared a rubber tube, I set the little body down, with his head still lowered. Quickly I poured a little alcohol on his chest and blew on the liquid to stimulate his reflex breathing. No result. Attached to the water trap, the narrow suction tube was ready. I inserted it gently into his nostrils, then into the trachea; with each aspiration I brought out greenish mucus which was blocking my attempts to resuscitate him. Once his air passages were cleared, I inserted a little silver tube into the trachea. Holding the other end between my lips, I began to breathe at my regular rate of breathing.

The little chest rose and fell. I encouraged the breathing movement with my hands. I closed my eyes for a moment, calling on my last reserve of efficiency and energy. My heart pounding, I silently implored a miracle. But what could I promise to obtain it? Whom could I supplicate?

I might have ... I should have ... If I didn't save this child, I'd keep hearing those intolerable words for my entire life. And yet, I'd done my best. But with physicians, results count so much more than intentions or hopes.

I tried to keep up the same breathing rhythm. I watched the second hand on my wrist watch; the irreplaceable seconds could be the last of this little ephemeral life. Three minutes! Would I save him? ... Was it already too late? ... Another four or five mintues, and this newborn, like Mariette's child, would never see the blue ocean and sky.

Nothing else to do but to continue to the end. My temples were throbbing, sweat poured down me. I felt dazed.

Mlle Virolleau came in. Bent over the tube, I couldn't lift my head, but I could see her pink coat. I heard her telling me in a low voice: "The mother's doing very well but she's beginning to get worried."

I was desperate. Was I going to have to face the mother's anxious look, and feel the terrible question in her eyes as soon as I crossed the threshold? I continued the breathing and kept massaging the little chest. Suddenly, the chest, completely still till now, trembled briefly under my fingers. Was I wrong? I didn't feel it again. Ah! This time, no possible error! No sign from the throat but the entire body quivered.

I continued to breathe into the tube a few more times but then stopped and lifted my head. Mlle Virolleau immediately brought an oxygen mask close to the little purple face. With a great raucous gurgle coming from deep within the body, rising only very painfully to the throat, the chest began to rise and fall. The first time the air had not penetrated very far into the lungs.

The three of us, the nurse's aide, the midwife and myself, too gripped by emotion to be able to utter a word, leaned over the little body and watched anxiously. The thorax had become still again. A longer interval between breaths. Six seconds . . . seven seconds . . . eight seconds . . . A second time, a miracle! The chest expanded, the tiny mouth opened toward the fresh flow of oxygen. The entire body underwent a convulsion, a deep quivering of the life restored by the red blood. I pulled the tube out. We didn't dare move, because the real signal of our victory would be the cry. And then, with lungs that would not stop until his last breath, he cried out, sharp, raging, almost demanding.

The horrid nightmare was over. I rested for a moment in front of the table, unable to move, dazed and haggard. Everything seemed to revolve around me, the little body now almost pink, the bronchoscope, the probe, the drapes, the whole room whose blue-painted walls floated in a kind of halo.

Incapable of getting off my seat, I mechanically reassembled all the instruments to replace them in their box. Then, slowly, under the gentle light, my confusion evaporated. My heart calmed down. The joy which overwhelmed me was so strong that I could no longer keep it to myself. I lifted my head to seek a friendly face to share it with.

The nurse's aide was already busy cleaning the baby and preparing to diaper him. While waiting to go back to the mother to deliver the placenta, Mlle Virolleau was putting away the oxygen mask. Probably out of discretion, she did not look at me. There! Incident concluded. Life goes on. In a few moments, both of us would return to the daily humdrum routine. No one would know the dramatic event which had just united us. Now that I was calmer, I would be able to believe that it was a bad dream. Yet, during this anxious half hour a genuine alliance had united

34

me to Mlle Virolleau. I wouldn't leave the delivery room without thanking the midwife. She had suppressed all her grudges in order to help me. I'd swallow my pride to tell her that without her, I couldn't have succeeded.

But before I could say anything Mlle Virolleau told me gently: "Go and show this beautiful young man to his mother."

She put the baby in my hands. Splendidly pink, he was crying and kicking vigorously. As I held the child, I looked once more around the small room which had seen the miracle of the resurrection after the astonishing miracle of birth.

When we entered the room, what better reward for both of us than the joy of the mother? With that beautiful smile of mothers who are hoping and fearing at the same time, she asked:

"Does he have everything he should have? He must hurt. Isn't he crying too loud?"

I reassured her. Yes, he has everything: tiny red fists, clenched with rage, two tiny feet with which he was trying to kick, ears slightly crushed against his skull, but which soon would spread out for hearing, two unfocused eyes astonished at their first blind meeting with the world. Yes, he had everything, this real little man. And if he screamed on entering the world, all the better! With every scream of his little round chest, the cells opened and dilated like sails unfurling under the wind.

Before leaving the wing, I phoned to find out how Mariette was: temperature down to 101°. I was relieved. Outside, the morning sun was shining. I had finally emerged from those frightening hours of the night when we all feel we're becoming cowards. I'd awakened from a nightmare into the light of day. This morning the sun shone for me alone; and it was just for my private happiness that the air was gentle, that the leaves of the linden trees, filled with buzzing bees, were swaying. A new day had started, active and healthy; one of those days when only good things happen.

Last night I helped destroy a new life. This morning, as if to prove that all is renewed, I was able to breathe life into a little child.

And the cries of this newborn baby, who still had some air from my mouth in his lungs, sounded like the most beautiful song of hope.

I took some fruit and a bottle of cold milk to my room. This way, I managed to avoid lunch in the staff dining room. I wasn't hungry enough to face the smell of bad food, noisy service and the ritual jokes I've put up with every day for ten months. Furthermore, probably no one would notice my absence.

In fact, during a meal, everything happened as if someone else were eating in my place; I didn't care what they thought of me, or if their opinions were well founded; I was eating but I wasn't there in spirit. Furthermore my main tormentor, Pascali—"Gorgeous Pascali" as the young midwives and the patients (who are all a little in love with him) call him—lives with me on a footing of a rather benevolent neutrality. Should he continue to call me "The Spirit of Suffering Humanity" or "Our Lady, Holy Virgin, and Martyr"? After all, I'm the kind soul always ready to be on call for him or see his patients and do rounds in his place. At the beginning he used to declare that my looks would discourage even the most lecherous male, and that my nonresponse to jokes was the very negation of a sense of humor. And at that time, when Lachaux suggested, as a thesis topic, a study of the consequences of contraception, Pascali, in the midst of the laughter of all the interns, proposed as my topic "Frequency and hormonal causes of small breasts in well-behaved, dominant-type girls," pretending that I might in my research find a means to increase the size of mine, which he considers too small. During that time, he once inscribed on the dining-room blackboard a want ad, pretending that I was its author: "Wish to meet ideal companion, individualist, who will adapt to strong feminine personality, 25 years old, object matrimony. Hope to beautify with a purple star the sad sky of a sheeplike existence."

I lie on the bed, having drunk my milk and eaten the fruit. The sun beat down on the hospital walls, but my room, which faces north, is bearable; with the venetian blinds drawn it has the coolness of one of those Mediterranean stone houses.

I have my black notebook with me. While waiting to start writing my dissertation, I find a great pleasure in recounting my day. It gives me the chance to put my thoughts in order. I also think that this will be valuable for my thesis because I'd like to make it as powerful as possible.

This morning, because Dr. Girodot, our short-statured "Big Boss," was in Switzerland for eight days at a gynecological conference, and Pascali was operating in his place, I had to do the rounds of the department all by myself. The walk from bed to bed, through two communal wards and the private rooms and cubicles, reminded me of my beginnings as a medical student.

When I first entered hospital work six years ago, I felt I was beginning a heroic adventure. Proud of having been singled out, I felt worthy of the medical experience which, after the completion of my studies, would permit me to be free myself and to liberate other women.

But the experience turned out to be a terrible one for the sensitivities of an eighteen-year-old. From the first morning, with an absurd enthusiasm, I wanted to understand everything and reform everything, all at once. From afar, medicine had appeared to me a precise, orderly, humane science; seen up close, the halls of the charity hospital turned out to be such a miserable and sometimes confusing little world that on some days I thought of leaving it all, as I sensed all around me the immense misery and my powerlessness before those patients who were ever-changing and yet always the same.

The most trying ordeal was the daily passage from one world to the other: there was the morning world, where I came in contact with those who were no longer thought of as human beings, but rather poor bodies preyed on by misery and suffering. There were a thousand lives whose cruel reality couldn't be concealed, and I had to listen with horror to their confused complaints, their shameful stammerings and their cries of hope. There was also the afternoon and evening world, the sandwich or inadequate lunch hastily swallowed, the rushed trip to the medical school, the hours spent in the library and in the dirty, cold attic room. For the nerves of an eighteen-year-old, this was no less a depressing and austere ordeal.

But, having always been a rebel, I didn't think that I was destined for failure. I steeled myself.

Straining toward my long-term goal, I proceeded like a heroic sleepwalker. I came to despise those of my fellow students who had no money problems and thus did not know the supreme joys of achievement. In the morning, most of the girls seemed to lose their feminine sensitivity in this barren and disagreeable novitiate. They appeared more curious than charitable or pitying; they affected the same unconstrained and grating mask as their fellow men students. Maybe they thought that they already were spending too much energy in just holding on, and didn't dare to waste the little which remained to them on superfluous sentimentality. I have never forgotten a conversation which I had at the time with a fellow student; she and I had been assigned to care for the same patient and one morning when we arrived, we found in "our bed" a young woman whom we would have to work up.

Questioning her, we learned that she was twenty-six years old, married for five years and the mother of two children. Her family doctor had insisted strongly that she enter the hospital. After a blood test he told her that she was anemic and urgently needed a specialist's advice. She didn't understand the reason for the hurry; she had only been complaining for the past few weeks of fatigue which she attributed to an increase in work and worry caused by both children having whooping cough. She thought that a little rest would put her back on her feet. As we continued our questioning, we found out that she had lost her appetite, had frequent headaches and also suffered from back pains.

At the end of the account which, despite its banality, I'd scrupulously noted down on her chart, the young woman looked at my colleague and myself:

"This isn't very serious, is it?"

She smiled at us, happy that she was taken care of so promptly. Although she'd just been admitted she was in a hurry to leave the hospital, and as if to apologize for it, she explained:

"My mother, who lives in Cherbourg, has come to take care of the children. So I don't have to worry about that. But you know how it is with a son-in-law and his mother-in-law. . . . It shouldn't go on too long."

Toward the end of the morning, the clinic chief arrived at our patient's bed and read the notes we'd taken. After examining the patient carefully and speaking a few reassuring words to her, he ordered the supervisor to run a series of laboratory tests, and then continued his rounds.

Once out of the room and away from indiscreet ears, he stopped the little procession of students in order to comment on the case; the family doctor had sent the young woman to the department because he suspected leukemia. The diagnosis already seemed to be confirmed.

This was during my early hospital training; I'd never yet seen a case of leukemia, a disease about which I only had rather vague notions, but I did know that the prognosis for leukemia was almost always fatal.

Listening to the chief's diagnosis, I was stunned. I couldn't believe that this terrible disease could be revealed by such routine signs; simple fatigue which could be explained by increased housework, pallor, vague pains . . .

But, as if to confront us with the pitiless reality of the facts, the chief turned to my colleague and myself and said: "Of course, ladies, don't let your patient suspect the diagnosis."

I mustered my courage and asked: "How long can she live, sir?"

"With care, and the medication which we now have, about a year, but not much more in any case. . . ."

At the end of the corridor, the chief dismissed us. As we headed toward the coatroom, I couldn't forget the pale face and the tired but confident smile.

My partner, seeing my preoccupation, asked: "What are you thinking about?"

"The leukemia patient. I tell myself that she doesn't know she's condemned, but that I know it and yet I'm going to continue to go for walks and see the beauty of the sky and the sun and feel the wind. Her death seems so unfair. When I'm a doctor, I'll be tempted to drop medicine if I lose a patient under such horrible conditions."

My colleague had already taken off her hospital coat to reveal a fashionable suit. She pulled her compact and lipstick out of a black lizard handbag. In front of the small mirror hanging on the back of the coatroom door, she was carefully reapplying her makeup. She waited until she finished. Then she moistened her lips delicately in order to make them more shiny and smooth, and answered me somewhat bored: "Listen, if you keep thinking about all this, you can't go on living. . . ."

I'd just put on my old gray duffle coat which I'd worn from my beginning days in high school. For a moment I hesitated over my comment. Would this girl understand if I got indignant? She had no doubt started her medical studies just to be busy, just as she might have gone to art school or rushed around the marriage market. If I spoke up, would I sound pretentious and sentimental? I hated this kind of ridicule. I casually replied: "Those who have some spirit of humanity apparently find it harder to live than others. . . ."

But a male student was approaching and, anxious to put her makeup to the test at once, my colleague was no longer listening to me.

As for me, once the scheduled round was finished, I would come back to the women's ward to question and listen. Despite my youth, the patients seemed to have confidence in me. This direct contact, in the calm light of the wards, filled me with enthusiasm. I never tired of observing the patients or of listening to them, and I had the feeling that I was the only student who appreciated the value of their personal confidences. Others would become excited about auscultation of heart or lungs, or about locating the lower edge of the liver under their fingertips, but locating a soul didn't seem to interest them.

I did find out rather quickly that they were partly right; my psychological investigations couldn't lead me very far without medical knowledge. Evidently the souls and the bodies of my patients formed an overlapping and complex whole. I was baffled when I tried to understand the one without a sufficient experience of life and the other with an almost total ignorance of pathology.

Furthermore, the personal and unscheduled prospecting on which I exerted myself had to be done under rather difficult conditions. Not only did we change hospitals or departments every few months but every morning, the professor, the assistants, the clinic chiefs and the interns escorted us without pause from bed to bed and from room to room, or else, to make the teaching easier, would gather all fifty of us into an amphitheater where we had to cram down theory. When they set us free around half-past noon there was just barely time to hurry through lunch and rush over to the medical school. The next day, the patient whom I had wanted to question would already be in another department, or in X-ray, or the nonresident medical student would be examining her, and the only thing I could do was go away disappointed. Chased away from the patients' bed because we might tire them or because we were in the way, thrown out of the operating rooms as if we were carrying epidemic germs on our hospital coats, we often wondered if we'd end up studying surgery and auscultation by correspondence course.

In the long run I stopped fighting the system, as do most students in their clinic year when they haven't had the time or the courage to prepare for hospital exams. I already led a hard life. I had the double burden of continuing my studies and working at the idiotic part-time jobs that helped to feed me. Even the required preclinical courses, cold and impassive as they were, represented an endurance test. I decided it was wiser to be cautious.

The internship, at the culmination of studies aimed at putting the student into direct contact with the realities of his profession, seemed to me not only a haven after so many difficult months but actually a turning point of my life. Free from financial worries, lodged and fed, I'd finally be able to learn my chosen specialty in depth; so I asked for an assignment in gynecology. And the last ten months haven't disappointed me. In the course of those days, all of which seem meaningful in retrospect, I knew I'd finally reached the very heart of medical practice.

What a wealth of experience there is even in a single morning of internship! This morning, from the time I got to the wards at 9 a.m., until lunch time, I saw more patients at close range than I ever could have seen in a whole trimester of studies.

But the wards and the operating rooms are not my true domain. I'm not like Pascali, who only wants to open, cut, drain, remove and suture; I don't want a career of gynecological surgery. While I've learned to assist at numerous operations and to do a D and C, I'm not interested in fibroids, cysts, tumors, prolapse, pelvic salpingitis and the inflammatory diseases which keep the beds well filled. What I really enjoy are of the consultations with patients.

This morning I did rounds for Morizet, whom I'm currently replacing, and for Pascali who's operating for our absent Chief.

I spent extra time at the beginning with a new admission (fifty-five years old according to her chart), trying to get a more precise idea of her "stomach ache"—most women use this imprecise term for any pain between the knees and the throat. The questioning was long, the examination thorough and I decided that it was almost definitely a fibroid. The woman was sure she had cancer. I explained to her that a fibroid is a noncancerous tumor and doesn't tend to turn into cancer; that it's a benign growth but one that should be removed.

The woman thought for a few minutes, then asked me: "If you operate on me, can I still feel?"

I wasn't paying much attention to her and said absent-mindedly: "Feel what?"

Outraged no doubt by my ignorance, she answered sharply: "With my husband of course!"

I reassured her and then went on to patient in bed twelve, "Mme Twelve," of whom I'm very fond. She's the old grandmother who was reproached so nastily last night for her incontinence. She's over seventy-two, and has meekly borne for years all the miseries that come from what she calls her fallen womb. This is now so complete that her uterus almost shows between her thighs, dragging with it a part of the bladder, pulling on the rectum and causing semipermanent disorders in her functions. The Chief had promised that after his return from Switzerland he'd try to do something for her, but without much hope.

Mme Twelve is ashamed of the work and trouble her infirmities cause: the sheets have to be changed several times a day; and the stench sometimes penetrates the whole room. But she's personally resigned, persuaded that poor people like herself are on this earth only to pay for their neighbors' sins as well as for their own. The sad smile of her old toothless mouth seems to say: "That's how life is. . . . What can you do?"

Mme Twelve symbolizes the submission of women to men and children, to ingratitude and to the injustice of family as well as of the world. I'm sure she's easily frightened by the possibilities of strikes and lock-outs and opposed to any movement of protest or rebellion, that she accepts low wages and wars passively, only fearing the possible dangers for her dear ones, relying for protection on the only things she knows of—weeping and prayer. And yet I love my old Mme Twelve for the frightening patience that has enabled her to produce children, to wipe and feed them, to take care of them and to face accidents, misfortune and unemployment. If you could open a path to freedom to women like her I'm sure they would march courageously, without detour.

Mme Twelve now waits for a cure which is more than improbable. This woman, who in the eyes of all around her is but a cipher, maintains in her corner of the room a healthy air of dignity and goodness, and a kind of grandeur even when her neighbors pretend to hold their noses.

Chance must have been playing games by placing Mme

Doudelette next to her as a contrast. Everybody knows her last name; she never speaks of her husband without repeating with emphasis, as she probably does in her butcher shop, "Monsieur Doudelette." Her great point of pride is to have accumulated, at the age of 39, four difficult abdominal operations. Thus she belongs to the aristocracy of surgical cases. She delights in repeating the opinion the chief surgeon at the Lariboisière hospital had of her case.

"My dear, he told Monsieur Doudelette that I had one of the most painful troubles. Imagine how proud I was!"

She is fat and self-important. Her makeup is heavy and her hair bleached. Installed on her bed, as on a throne of suffering, she gives her advice on every minor event.

This morning when I arrived at her bed, she was barebreasted and had her stocky arms lifted behind her head in an effort to be cool. She was displaying the shaven armpits of the false blonde. The black hair growing out looked almost obscene. Luckily, this was not the day for her dressing and so I didn't have to bend over her abdomen where a rubber drain emerged from the enormous purple bulges of old scars. In a hurry to get to Mariette, I glanced over the temperature chart, concurred with the penicillin prescription, and went on.

My first glance at Mariette's face confirmed the morning's improvement, although her eyes still seemed sunken. Part of her fatigue and fever seemed to have evaporated during her sleep. She seemed surprised to be free of pain so soon. She was no longer uncomfortable, her pulse was slower and more steady and her temperature was down to 101°. Smiling and obediently keeping still, she only turned her head to one side to answer me. Her hair was tousled; the color was starting to come back to her face. But as soon as I reached over to lift the sheet in order to examine the thin body, she recoiled and implored: "Oh! no, mam'selle, no . . ."

I was very sorry to have started the movement. Unfortunately it was too late to stop, especially since Mme Doudelette, behind me, no doubt insulted by the short time I'd spent on her, started to comment on little girls who like to make themselves interesting, and succeed, while great invalids are not even examined.

Barely lifting the sheet, I looked at the cotton pad between her thighs: it was still stained with blood; but the odor was less fetid. Without examining further, I said to Mariette with a smile: "You're doing very well."

As I passed to the next bed, I glanced at Mme Doudelette. Her look of outraged vanity frightened me.

I decided then and there to put Mariette in a private room, even if her case isn't really serious enough to justify it completely; it's the only way to shield her from the unctuous curiosity of her neighbors, allow her to dream, weep, or be silent without having to account to anyone. As soon as I was back in the supervisor's office, I consulted the bed chart. A room would be free at the beginning of the afternoon. I asked that Mariette be transferred to it as soon as possible. That wouldn't give Mme Doudelette enough time to track down my protégé's weak spot and persecute her.

I returned to the ward shortly before 3 p.m. to finish some examinations.

The visitors had already gone by the time I arrived in the building, but they'd left a residual excitement. You could almost see the broad-shouldered men sitting near the beds and smell their tobacco. In their thoughts the women accompanied the temporary bachelors to the Lagriffoul Café, on the small crescent-shaped plaza just outside the hospital fence, near the bus stop.

The private rooms all open off a common corridor near the entrance. I went straight to Mariette's room. The door was open but the white shade was drawn over the window, leaving a dim light. After the uproar of the ward, her room seemed incredibly peaceful and calm. She'd closed her eyes, no doubt the better to enjoy her quiet solitude.

I stood for a moment in the door to look at her. She was resting. Contentment had replaced the tense expression of the morning. Her chest rose and fell evenly, the sheet outlined the graceful line of her hips, legs and small feet. A ray of sunlight bypassed the shade and gilded the tiny rounded shoulders, giving an air of womanly languor to the almost childlike abandon. Seeing this now peaceful body, I felt lighter and almost absolved from my guilt.

I knocked on the door softly before going in—it's a habit of mine to give my patients time to compose themselves. Mariette opened her eyes in surprise, then smiled pleasantly.

I pulled up a chair and sat down next to the bed. Mariette seemed overwhelmed by emotion. I thought it

44

was her gratitude that almost preventing her from speaking; she seemed to have so much to say all at once. I finally understood that she was thanking me for saving her from the repetition of the most unpleasant ordeal of the morning: being put on the bedpan in public. Mme Doudelette hadn't spared her sarcasm this morning on seeing her embarrassment, while her other neighbor explained to her: "You'll see, you'll get used to it, dear; it'll have to come out sooner or later."

Mariette calmed down; from her bed she showed me the splendors of her room. She caught the rope of the shade which hung within reach of her hand, and showed me with childish amusement that she could easily regulate the shade.

Then she said: "It's as nice here as in a private hospital."

Is she aware of the danger she's in because of her induced abortion, or did she naïvely think that she wouldn't die because she didn't want to die? Mariette must have guessed that I was ill at ease because she suddenly became serious again.

After a moment of silence, she quietly asked: "Is it true, mam'selle, that I won't be able to have children? My neighbor, the fat blonde, said so this morning. She said that an abortion brings you bad luck and you stay out of order all your life."

While asking me the question, Mariette's voice remained calm but her eyes revealed her anxiety.

That vicious Mme Doudelette! She took immediate advantage of the situation. She obviously guessed that an induced abortion would cause anxiety and shame in a person like Mariette!

Without leaving me the time to lie—because the true prognosis after amateur abortion is serious: in thirty per cent of the cases there is definite sterility—Mariette continued, with a pathetic quaver in her voice.

"You see, mam'selle, my husband and I decided the way we did because we couldn't do anything else. There was no way to board the baby with relatives in the country where it's easier to raise children. My husband is an orphan, he only has one brother who works in Brest in the arsenal and who already has four children. . . . My own mother is remarried, and my stepfather threw me out when I was seventeen. The months of putting a child out to nurse cost a lot. My husband was just through with his military service when we got married. We wanted to wait at least two years before having a baby, to put away enough money to afford a down payment on a little apartment, and to buy a few pieces of furniture. And then my husband would have liked to buy a motorcycle to go to work. With me in the shop and him in the ball-bearing factory, we don't earn much money yet between both of us. Do you understand, mam'selle?"

"Yes, very well," I affirmed.

What I mainly understood is the unconscious selfishness of the young husband. With masculine casualness, in order to first have his apartment, his motorcycle and maybe his television he asked Mariette to sacrifice this inopportune motherhood. But he let her bear the brunt of the danger and the bad conscience.

Without realizing that I sounded cruel, I couldn't help adding: "I realized this yesterday evening when I talked to your husband for a few minutes, but he also told me that you didn't want him to get mixed up in this . . ."

Did she guess my criticism of her husband's cowardice which left her alone to bear the consequences of a decision they'd made together?

She answered, almost violently: "I had promised. A promise is a promise. . . ."

But immediately recovering a tone of perfect dignity and simplicity: "But then, mam'selle, I love him . . ."

Those few words revealed her entire being. She wasn't looking for sympathy or compassion; she was stating an essential and unique truth: the humble truth of her love.

Mariette fell silent. Afraid that if the silence lasted it would become embarrassing, I took up the first topic which would offer an excuse for her abortion and might make her forget the viciousness of her neighbor.

I knew by experience that for young working-class households the problem of having children is mainly a question of space, so I started to chat with Mariette about her lodgings. I wasn't wrong. Mariette and her husband live in a "hotel." By her description, I recognized the well-known horror of cheap hotels which I'd experienced during my studies: the shaky old furniture, dirty cotton bedspreads, the wardrobe whose mirror has lost its luster, the sink with blackened cracks, the electric bulb hanging without a shade from a tangle of wires, pulleys and weights, and, outside, the small cesspool-like back yard,

46

bounded by a wall so close that you could touch it with a broom.

"The advantage of our room," Mariette explained to me, "is that it's rather large, and it has two wardrobes. That helps. And, by paying extra, the owner lets us cook. My husband has put up a new pink wallpaper; a pale, pretty color. We have to be very careful to keep the walls clean but it's much prettier and lighter. The trouble is that it's expensive. That room costs almost a quarter of what we make, and after clothing, food and carfare, there isn't much left. I should know; I take care of our bills."

She found a way to rehabilitate her husband in my eyes:

"Yves brings me all his wages. He's never even fifty francs short. Only you need at least four or five thousand francs for a down payment on a decent two-room apartment. We've also put our name down at City Hall for public housing but we know very well that we'll never get anything from them. . . ."

She stopped as if to calculate her chances and redo the accounts which she must have mentally recalculated a thousand times. She was touching; her manner of a young woman already enriched by having to cope with a difficult life was in contrast to the innocence of her forehead, over which there fell a rebellious strand of hair. She kept pushing it back impatiently, like a child.

To reassure her further, I told her that I know what it means for a young couple to live in a furnished room. I've already heard the dramatic tale of the room where, even if you have a child, you're thrown out after the first week because beyond that time you'd be on a monthly rental and the landlord couldn't get rid of you so easily. I know the animosity of landlords against young couples; they fear that the arrival of children later on will result in increased use of electricity and water. I know that the couple who show up with a baby at a residential hotel have very little chance to obtain a room even by the day; just as I know how families with many children are persecuted—the landlord cuts off the electricity or the gas, or prohibits visitors in order to force them to move out. I also know through personal experience the total absence of comfort; how hard it is to get any sleep because of the noise, the drudgery of getting the water from the single faucet on the floor, the secret cooking on the kerosene stove, the way two or even three people are

47

crowded into a tiny airless room, the filthy bathrooms for the use of the entire hotel.

I've even learned with amazement that a hotel keeper can prevent a female boarder who gets married from living with her spouse. While the Civil Code forces a woman to follow her husband, there's no law forcing a landlord to accept a new tenant. The young woman who told me this could see her husband only according to the timetable set up for visitors: from 8 a.m. to 8 p.m.!

This story may sound like a bad Courteline farce but I've heard other, more tragic confidences, such as the woman who told me: "I'd like to have a child, but it would be awful to have one in the boarding house, there isn't even enough room for a crib"; or "Living in a hotel, you can't have any children; we can't even manage with what we earn"; or the mother panicked because her husband had been "stupid": "I already have two children. In one room, that's hard enough, and enough for me. When the children grow up, it won't even be possible to use the bidet and keep from having more babies." Only rarely has a woman refusing to bear a child told me that she "wanted to lead her own life." Listening to all these women talk, I've often asked myself if the word "happiness" has any meaning at all if you live in such a house and if, for the young couples forced to live in furnished rooms, happiness doesn't simply mean the hope to be able to leave the hotel some day.

"You see, Mariette," I concluded, "I know about living in hotels and I also know that the baby's crying keeps the parents from sleeping, and that the neighbors complain, the diapers dry badly in a room without fresh air, the milk in the baby's bottle turns sour without an icebox, that many babies die in hotel rooms because of poor hygiene and also many of them die if they are put out to a wet nurse because too many of the wet nurses are neither very clean nor very conscientious. So, Mariette, don't feel guilty! What you've done isn't your fault. You should blame the State: it encourages population increase but doesn't build houses for newborn citizens and doesn't even provide the means to bring them up properly."

A nurse came to the door. She apologized for interrupting me and told me that Number Eighteen was bleeding and wanted to see me.

"Eighteen," Mariette said, "that was the one just across from me. I thought she was paralyzed. She didn't move once this morning. She was just like a statue, except when she was eating."

"She's six months pregnant," I said, smiling to avoid a painful comparison with her own state. "Two weeks ago, she started to bleed and the doctor told her that if she wanted to keep her baby, she had to stay motionless. Since then as you saw, she hasn't even fluttered an eyelash."

"Is she going to keep it?"

"I think so."

Mariette sat up halfway, with a look of hope on her face.

"And I, mam'selle, are you sure that I can have another? You swear?"

"I swear, Mariette, I swear. But only if you rest and let us heal you completely."

Without giving me any time to anticipate her gesture, she grabbed my hand, rapidly put her lips on my palm, then fell back on her pillow.

She smiled with all her love and trust, dreaming of the day she would hold to her breast the little brother of that unhappy embryo who would never see the light of day.

I went back to the patient in bed Number Eighteen. She was upset by the warm sticky oozing that had started again between her thighs. And yet, she said, she had obeyed orders scrupulously, not even daring to speak loudly or turn her head. I reassured her. This submissive patient amazes all the nurses by her obstinate desire to be a mother. They're more accustomed to taking care of induced abortions.

I smiled as I passed old Mme Twelve. Unable to remain idle after having worked hard all her life, she was folding gauze bandages for the nurses. I also listened to Mme Doudelette who explained some of the peculiar aspects of her case to me. I haven't told her but I've decided that the next available private room will be for her; isolated from the others, she'll only be able to vent her nastiness against herself, like a scorpion.

I overheard from a short distance this bit of dialogue:

"Coffee with milk gives me cramps."

"You're crazy to drink coffee with milk! It makes you go to the bathroom!"

"No, it's red wine that makes me go. I get all stopped up with white wine. . . ."

Usually as soon as the Chief enters a room, the patients

shut up, or at least a vigorous "Now, now, ladies! A little silence!" on the part of the supervisor subdues the conversation. It's the same for Pascali's visits. I impress the patients less than either the Chief or Gorgeous Pascali, or else our sharing the same sex makes them think of me more as a woman than a doctor and they bank on feminine sympathy. As I pass through, conversations barely stop—conversations so stupid or naïve or incredible that sometimes, listening to them, I forget the place and my reason for being there.

The passionate chats of the shut-in vary from constipation, on which they are all inexhaustible, to love or recipes. I suppose—and I have to guess since I haven't had the personal experience—that conversations in fashionable beauty salons on the Champs Elysées are just as uninformed. I guess that women, as soon as they're alone together, are attracted by an unknown force; that at the least pretext, an immediate, total need to unburden themselves makes them reveal their past and their most intimate experiences to each other.

In the hospital, the patients seem to want to re-create their daily lives. By discussing all their daily preoccupations, they doubtless make themselves believe that they're at home, in slippers and bathrobe, or lingering at the grocery, thirsty for news, gossip, or silly talk. To be sure, above all it's a way to kill the long hours, to make the time pass a little faster.

I soon learned that I was mistaken. The hospital doesn't disguise any cancer, physical or moral. And if, from afar, in their beds, the patients look as alike as those little tenement houses which you can recognize only by their number, from up close they all resume their individual identity: each one, forced to suffer by herself, at the same time wants all the others to suffer with her. I quickly discovered that a hospital ward is not always a place of rest, and that one Mme Doudelette is enough to turn it into a place of torment by her envy and cunning malice. I've also learned very quickly that evil proliferates easily on human ground while the seed of goodness has trouble germinating in it.

During this past night, for example, during the hours of disillusion and fatigue, the goodness in my patients appeared totally "irrecoverable" through some constitutional defect. But at other moments, when I'm more optimistic, I ask myself why and how these women to whom life has

50

shown so little pity, could be kind toward each other; paradoxically this idea gives me courage again. To re-create woman with the intention of liberating her from her harsh fate, to give her back her dignity by freeing her from her slavery, no longer seems such an unworthwhile enterprise in those moments.

Today, thanks to Mariette's apparent recovery, my afternoon has been optimistic.

I saw my "breech" of this morning in the maternity ward. The mother was lying on her bed, calm, quiet, glowing with happiness. The newborn lay in the metal crib at the foot of the bed. He looked like a large white cylindrical worm with a red, wrinkled head. He was crowned with black fuzz and showed two little clenched fists; he screamed when I began to undress him. Once liberated, he started to move his legs. To show the mother that she had produced a healthy and lively baby, I held him up on the bed; as soon as he felt the blanket under his feet, he attempted three or four steps.

"You see," I laughed, "he's already walking! He's coming to say hello!"

The mother tenderly held out her arms to shelter the little being just emerged from the nest of her belly. He seemed to want to return to that lukewarm refuge of which, according to Freud, we keep a subconscious nostalgia until death.

11 p.m.

"It's already ten after eight! I'm hungry! Do we have to keep waiting for Pascali or can we eat?" Lachaux asked. (He's the neuro-psychiatric resident on call in Medicine.)

"Let's give him till a quarter after," I said.

"Hardly anyone for dinner any more," Lachaux said. He pulled up his chair, glancing at the three settings. "You can tell it's vacation time." Anna, the cook, kept the shutters closed all afternoon to keep out the heat which permeates the bricks. When we arrived she opened one shutter. Most of the dining room is obscured by shadow so that you can't see the obscene drawings on the wall. The outdoor light touches only the edge of the table, where our three settings are placed on the sheet which doubles as a tablecloth. The heavy hospital plates, thick glasses and tin forks reflect the rays of the setting sun.

Despite Anna's precautions it was almost as hot in the

dining room as outside. You could still smell the cigarette butts and fried foods of the lunch hour.

Lachaux had disappeared into the medical school at about two or three p.m. today to do some research so I wasn't able to discuss with him certain thesis passages which he'd suggested to me. So I went to the dining room this evening partly for psychiatric advice for my thesis, but mostly for the pleasure of chatting with him. Lachaux is practically my only friend among the interns. We've never needed too many words in order to understand each other.

He conceals strong individuality under an almost insignificant exterior. The other interns, though different in looks and personality, are really all of a kind. Lachaux is almost ugly with his thin freckled cheeks, nearly albino white hair and pale blue eyes. They give him a slightly vague, sleepy look. But his forehead is high above an aquiline nose and gives his face a certain nobility. The first time I lunched in the interns' dining room and Pascali started his jokes, my eyes met Lachaux's; since that day I've sensed a continuing bond between us. Two or three days after that first meeting I went to see him about a patient in his section; I found him sitting on a stool in the consultation room talking to a little boy about eight years old, who was installed in the easy chair.

After the examination was over I mentioned my surprise. He explained, smiling: "If you want to establish contact with a child, first you have to take off your adult uniform. With me on the footstool, and him in my chair, the roles are reversed and the questioning becomes easy."

I was impressed by his level voice and calm, kind look. It had obviously aroused confidence in the child.

I've often gone back to see Lachaux. I feel less strange with him since he's so different from his colleagues; it seems to me that we're both of the same breed, that we have the same concept of medicine. I feel that he can teach me things that the other interns seem incapable of feeling, and consequently of teaching to me. . . .

"Ah! Here are the two conspirators! And they're so darling, waiting for me!" Pascali made his noisy entrance and dropped into the treasurer's chair, the place of honor at the end of the table.

"Oh! Damn being on call. I'm totally dehydrated! How about a drink?"

Without waiting for our answer he turned to the door of the kitchen.

"Anna, the whiskey bottle, water, ice, and three large glasses!" Fat Anna hurried to please him, partly because Pascali as treasurer rules the interns' dining room but mainly because he always gives his orders in a bossy but charming tone which neither nurses, nor midwives, nor patients can resist. Patients especially seem to like being pushed around.

Pascali has the air of a young cock in the middle of a chicken coop. It suits him. He doesn't wear a shirt under his white short-sleeved coat and when it's unbuttoned because of the heat, it reveals a muscled torso with beautifully tanned skin and a long muscular neck. His self-confident bearing radiates ambition and the joy of living.

Well established in his chair, satisfied with himself and with his day, he poured the whiskey, added water and ice, and after having swizzled his own glass to mix it, drank with evident pleasure.

"That's better! I thought you might be waiting for me but I got held up by old Lagriffoul. He injured his hand with a sliver of glass on his counter. While I was putting a clamp on it he told me that he's going to use as a motto for his bar 'You're better off here than on the other side of the street,' since he's located in front of the hospital and right next to the cemetery. He was delighted with his idea. Then he asked me: 'How are your deliveries coming along?' I tried to be funny and answered: 'No chance of unemployment with all these men who work for me!' But the old guy gave me a wicked wink like an old crony and corrected me: 'You mean to say all these little men who work *for us*!' These people from the Auvergne, they're so clever! . . . Anna, please bring on the food, I'm starving!"

Pascali glanced at the hors d'oeuvre and served himself first according to the treasurer's tradition, then handed me the heavy earthenware platter and added, especially for me:

"Incidentally, this afternoon I got an ectopic pregnancy. The diagnosis was almost certain but there was a slight doubt, so I took advantage of the Chief's absence to do a peritoneoscopy.

He laughed briefly, in his smug fashion, then went on:

"I was a little hesitant because the Chief doesn't like it very much when you use his personal toys, especially when they're new. But this was too tempting and my motive was

53

good. I told the woman that a peritoneoscopy, despite its complicated name, is a very simple examination; first you blow into the abdomen with air injected through a small hole and then through another small hole you insert a kind of thin periscope which permits you to look at the interior of the abdomen without having to cut it open. I also explained to her that as a diagnostic measure this is a painless examination, simple and interesting for her."

"You should have added: 'And especially interesting for me!' " Lachaux said ironically.

"Never lose an occasion to train yourself, old boy. That's my principle! And ever since we've had the apparatus the Chief has reserved all the peritoneoscopies for himself. I wasn't going to pass this one up. As soon as the woman said yes and, since she hadn't eaten, I went right to it! Anesthetic and then a trocar cut in the belly close to and under the rib. When I plunged the instrument in I felt it going clear through the peritoneal wall: it gave like the skin of a drum. As soon as the optical apparatus was placed in the abdomen I saw that I was right; it was definitely an ectopic pregnancy. The Fallopian tube was swollen and blackened where the embryo was implanted, and there was a bit of blood on the end of the tube."

Pascali seemed delighted with his accomplishment. He added in a sarcastic, mysterious tone:

"And you know what I also discovered? On the left, an ovarian cyst. Her chart showed that she's complained for several years of pains in the lower abdomen. As soon as the diagnosis was confirmed, I operated on her and took advantage of the opening to take care of the ovary. So she'll have no more abdominal pains."

And, this time definitely ironic:

"And the funniest thing about this story, my good friends, is that you two have been treating her for eight months and she's always had the same pain!"

He paused a moment and then concluded:

"Evidently psychotherapy and kind words are insufficient to dissolve an ovarian cyst! I don't believe in that psychosomatic gynecology that you two preach. The proof is that the insertion of the peritoneoscope into the abdomen of your patient told me immediately why you were losing time with your little talks. I helped your good little woman more in three minutes by operating on her ovary than you would have by psychoanalyzing her for three years."

54

"You believe this as categorically as you're stating it?" Lachaux asked quietly.

"Sure!"

"In that case, if you can spare five minutes, would you like me to explain our point of view to you?"

"Go ahead," Pascali said with generous skepticism.

"Let's look at your first argument," said Lachaux, his usual calm manner, learned from dealing with his mental patients, contrasting with his colleague's aggressive tone:

"Sure, if you see the woman only as a mammal, if a patient for you is merely a uterus, two Fallopian tubes, two ovaries, a whole mass of viscera, just a red blob, because you know its anatomy very well, if you only care about what can be seen, palpated, cut, taken out, resewn, everything's simple, or at least relatively simple: in fact, like work done by a superior plumber. You have no sympathy or antipathy toward your patient. Furthermore, with your hands, your scalpel and the extra vision you get from your abdominal peritoneoscope, you can in many cases make an excellent diagnosis and give equally efficient treatment, especially since you also operate very well."

Pascali, pleased with the compliment, thanked him with a shake of his head. Lachaux ate another mouthful before proceeding.

"But if you admit that the organs in that abdomen belong to a human being, then everything changes. It's easy to write a prescription to take care of ordinary diseases or operate when all signs are clear. It's much more difficult to disentangle the threads of life, trying to get at what could make a patient blush or cry, not to be content with one interview and an even briefer examination and not to yield to the ease of laboratory tests which are becoming more and more ubiquitous and anonymous."

Pascali was busy extracting a bone from a cutlet but Lachaux's words apparently seemed so extravagant to him that he put down his knife and fork and interrupted.

"You don't really mean to make me believe that you have to go all sentimental about your patients, like English old maids with stray cats? Furthermore, I've been taught to diagnose appendicitis, ovarian cysts, and ectopic pregnancies, not to be a lay confessor."

He went back to his food and concluded, most amiably:

"If you want my opinion, nine-tenths of the women we see in gynecology are hypochondriac, and more or less crazy. That, incidentally is why if you look at them from a distance, they end up looking all alike as if you saw them through a dirty glass."

"No," Lachaux answered gently. "They're neither all odd, nor all alike. But they're all tormented by worry about their abdomen because that's where there's always a risk of some growth or disease or of a pregnancy. They have sexual anxieties. It starts with little girls' penis envy and continues with fear caused by the first menstruation and the awakening of sexuality. And sexual feeling is too often inhibited by incompetent educators or idiotic parents. Then comes the psychic trauma of deflowering which is equally often done badly by an incompetent lover or husband; and for many of them it ends with the exaggerated desire or the exaggerated fear of pregnancy and so on ... and if woman suffers in so many ways in her genital region, it's surely because the deepest aggressions against the essence of her femininity occur there. A young girl who has been deflowered without love will suffer subsequently from a pain in her lower abdomen rather than from a nervous cough or from migraine."

Pascali laughed indulgently. "Suppose you're right! In that case, what can we do? Transform me into a priest in a white coat to try to get their abdominal-sentimental secrets out of them?"

"Maybe it would be better to try to begin with that, with the patient whose ovarian cyst you removed. You probably didn't rid her of her pain."

Pascali banged his salad bowl down on the table as if to underline his surprise.

"Now you've got me. Why would she continue to suffer if the diseased organ is removed?"

"Because there's a reason you're not taking into account as the basis of her pain. It also brings her certain benefits; maybe consciously by permitting her to refuse sex or obtain vacations or even the bittersweet advantages of a hospital stay thanks to the instrument of a well-meaning surgeon. Or unconsciously because this well-organized pain makes her the center of worry in the family. It's a way of holding on to a neglectful husband, of eliciting concern from children who are usually unconcerned and is, on all occasions, an excellent means of blackmail. But the great— the second great reason for a lasting pain, which was legitimate at one point, is that it lasts and is even implanted more deeply as long as the psychic cause that provoked it hasn't disappeared. Thus the patient you operated on today will probably—very probably—begin to suffer again after your operation. She'll remain frigid and continue not to love her husband; she'll be able to annoy him while she goes on suffering, to refuse sex with him and castrate him indirectly. And I can predict with virtual certainty that she'll stop suffering as soon as she no longer *needs* to suffer. . . ."

"So after all this, the only thing I can do is to lock up my instruments in a drawer and practice the laying-on of hands with psychoanalytic cures!"

To show us that he was ready to abandon surgery, Pascali laid his bare forearms and open hands on the table, as a joke.

We all laughed, then Lachaux confidently replied:

"Don't do one or the other! Simply try to identify a bit more with your patients; not pretending, but really sharing their thoughts and trying to understand their happiness or unhappiness. . . . You like card games, look at gynecology that way. It's a marvelous poker game, with its share of intuition, daring and chance, and is much more efficient than merely handling the peritoneoscope and other instruments."

The corridor telephone rang. Anna answered it and came back to the door, announcing: "It's for you, Dr. Pascali, long-distance."

We all know that Pascali's girl friend is vacationing in Cabourg. She phones him every night. Pascali got up with the nonchalance of a young man who is loved too much.

"Do you know," Lachaux asked him, "that in psychoanalytic terms excessive use of the telephone is considered a sign of anxiety-laden sexual overexcitement and that endless conversation indicates a feeling of being emotionally unattached?"

"She should be anxious," Pascali replied acidly. "If she continues her politely phrased telephonic complaints, I'm going to drop her soon!"

All the way from the phone he sounded annoyed. The conversation with Cabourg must have been tempestuous. He hung up and came back, sighing with irritation.

No sooner had he sat down, than the telephone rang again.

Anna came back to announce: "It's for you again, Dr. Pascali. They're calling you from Admissions."

He grumbled and got up.

Anna came to clear the table. She brought me an envelope.

"This is the inventory for your room; Administration sent it over this afternoon. You have to turn it in before you leave."

"A hospital administration is very strange," Lachaux remarked. "It makes each intern sign an inventory for pieces of furniture which altogether wouldn't fetch more than two hundred francs in the Flea Market, but blindly trusts him with forty patients. And when he leaves, it carefully checks to see if anything's broken but lets him go without bothering to find out if he's hurt or helped his patients."

"That compensates for medical school," I said. "Remember how the man in charge of anatomy lab kept telling us to save the human material because of the shortage of corpses? Here the human material doesn't have to be hoarded. There's too much of it."

"I think the hospital does know its patients. For all the time that it's crowded them in, fed them badly and mistreated them, it's learned that most of them will survive. . . ."

We were silent for a moment, then Lachaux said, almost echoing my own thoughts:

"Pascali's by no means the most dangerous. He doesn't understand much about the psychology of his patients but at least when he operates on them, he doesn't kill them."

The phone rang again. Since it wasn't for Pascali, Anna merely shouted from the corridor:

"Dr. Lachaux is wanted in Medicine Three."

Lachaux got up and smiled.

"I don't think we're going to discuss your thesis today."

Some other evening I might have waited for Lachaux, or have even accompanied him to Medicine Three. Then we would have gone back to his room or mine to talk until his next call.

But today I felt too nervous and tired so I returned to my room. I'd left the window open. I stayed in the darkness for a while, to savor the gentleness of the night with its shimmering stars and the yellow blinking of the streetlights.

In the half shadow my open notebook looked white on the table. I lit my desk lamp. I was tired, but I was curious to look through the pages I'd written in less than twenty-four hours. Since I started to write in this note-

58

book, enough things have happened to make the D and C of last night seem far away. In rereading my entries I reexperienced my various moods, and especially my joy about the improvement in Mariette's condition. It seemed to me that seeing my thoughts of the day written down in this notebook gave them more precision, the way you can visualize the course of a fever better by its chart.

That's why I also recorded this evening's conversation before going to bed. I didn't feel sufficiently self-confident to tell Pascali what Lachaux told him. But I know Lachaux's ideas so well—they've become mine—that I'm sure I've repeated them accurately here.

Now I'll take a shower; I need one to relax after this sweaty, torrid day.

I've read in Alexander that "menstruation is a badge of femininity borne joyfully by mature and fulfilled women but painfully by infantile or masculine women." I'm neither mature, nor fulfilled, nor infantile. I must be in the masculine category. Does the tension-laden fatigue I feel tonight indicate a revolt against my sexual fate, even though I know that it's a normal body function and not the "curse" that most women call it?

Whatever the answer, in ten minutes I'll turn off my lamp and hope that I'll soon be asleep.

⚜ II ⚜

Consultations

Thursday, July 11th, 12:30 p.m.

Consultations with patients, as I've said before, are my
domain, a kingdom Pascali has surrendered to me without
opposition, not for a horse but because it means he can
spend more time in the operating room.

There were fewer consultations today because vacations
have begun so I finished a little earlier than usual and
went up to my room before lunch to rest for a minute. In
this July heat one solid morning of examining pregnant
women leaves me exhausted. However, when Pascali says
I've made the gynecological examination much too detailed, I have to admit he's right.

Here again our ideas are opposed; for him pregnancy is
a kind of female military service, more exactly a voluntary enlistment since coitus in the nation's service isn't
obligatory yet. He set up an efficient system for his examinations, like a barracks infirmary or an army board of
examiners. So he could work faster, the patients would
wait their turn, all half undressed, in the middle of an
incredible hubbub. ... He sped up the procedure even
more by installing two examination tables side by side,
separated only by a curtain. On each table one patient
would succeed another without interruption. There was
always one woman waiting, thighs spread and abdomen

bared, and listening to his questions during her neighbor's examination.

I had some trouble modifying this assembly-line gynecology, because Pascali's mechanization was convenient for the nurses. It simplified their work.

I'm sure that what irritates me most about Pascali is this indifference toward pregnancy, which can be a joy or an ordeal for every woman.

In his favor, I must admit that many of our patients listen to confirmation of their pregnancy with an air of smug satisfaction, almost like setting hens, and others reveal their mercenary thoughts by asking immediately about the amount of the state baby bonuses. But how can he ignore the radiant happiness of other women, those who display serenity and quiet joy throughout their pregnancy, lying on the table, their hands protectively spread on their abdomens?

There are still others for whom a pregnancy is a disaster. Two cases this morning.

Mme Michelon is one of my oldest patients. Her chart reads: "Housewife, thirty-nine years old, six children." Her last child was born three weeks before I arrived at the hospital. As often happens after numerous births, the delivery had been difficult and the placenta badly placed. Mme Michelon came to see me right after, about the effects of her difficult delivery, but she hadn't been back for three or four months, since she'd asked me how to avoid a new pregnancy after the baby was weaned. She thought six children in eight years of marriage was enough of a burden.

Her unwillingness to undergo a seventh pregnancy is certainly understandable. Her husband is a simple bricklayer who drinks a bit too much. They have a three-room apartment for a family of eight. Her sixth pregnancy seems to have completely taken away her youth, leaving her a faded face, stretch-marked belly and swollen breasts. I tried to help the poor woman with everything I'd learned about contraception.

As I said in my notes on Mariette, contraceptive techniques are completely ignored in our gynecological textbooks. The French books dealing with the matter do so only indirectly because of the 1920 Birth Law and its clause about the crime of disseminating birth-control literature. I had to read English or American books in the school library. At least they were perfectly clear. There's no point in prescribing diaphragms to my patients (they're forbidden in France), so if the woman appears to have some sense of planning and especially if her periods are regular, I tell her about the rhythm method, but always warn her that it's not completely reliable.

When Mme Michelon asked me for advice, I tried as best I could to explain to her the possibilities of the rhythm method, but once more I encountered the almost complete ignorance most women have about the facts of the reproductive process and the menstrual cycle.

Mme Michelon also told me that she didn't need to understand since her husband categorically refused to allow her to take any precautions when he came home half drunk and ready for sex once a week.

I asked her to send her husband in to see me and tried to reason with him. I couldn't. He's not nasty, but he has an alcoholic's personality. He stared at me with a glazed look, his eyes yellow and bloodshot. He could only find one excuse. "It's not my fault. The second I put my pants over the chair, she gets pregnant." Sobered and a little awed by the hospital environment, he promised me he'd take the precautions I suggested, but I felt I was wasting my time. When he gets home drunk at night, will he be capable of restraining himself?

How can a doctor avoid feeling depressed and indignant at his impotence when he thinks of the undesired children, progeny of chance, born uncalled-for to women who are less fortunate than the females of the animal world—at least they can rest outside of mating time. I know that some of these children will be helpful either to their parents or to society. Though they're not welcomed at birth, the love and sacrifices they'll inspire afterwards will strengthen their family ties, but when I think of the misery and pain I see every day because of unplanned motherhood, I'd have to be unfeeling, blind or mad to resign myself to it.

When Mme Michelon's husband left, still smug about his virility, I suspected there would still be endless nights when the poor woman would have to submit to him. And then this morning she told me she hadn't had a period in two months and was nauseated every morning.

An experienced patient, she installed herself on the table. As she placed her feet in the stirrups I noticed the enormous varicose veins in her legs. The slip she pulled up to expose her abdomen was made of cheap cotton and carefully darned.

As I examined her it was obvious she was about two and a half months pregnant. I looked at her; she apparently discerned my sympathy because she said immediately, "Another one, huh?" I nodded my head, saying nothing.

She raised her head as if to ask me something, then let it fall back.

"What am I going to do?" she finally asked.

She was probably thinking about the abortion suggestions neighbors give each other, wormwood, permanganate, soapy water, lead lotion, or perhaps about finding an abortionist. Did she also think about the tiny being in her flesh who was already feeding off her, taking her iron, her phosphate, and her calcium, impoverishing her blood a little more, making her live through weeks of nausea and sickness. As the poet says, "The flower must wither to give its fruit."

The best I could do to lessen the damage caused by the unexpected parasite was to give her a prescription for the drugstore and to sign the first sheets of the social security form; small interim help that will do no good once the child is born. As for her husband, he'll guzzle some more red wine and drink to the health of mother and child.

Mme Michelon took the forms that will turn her into a modest pensioner of society for a few months. She thanked me with a wistful smile, then sighed as if she were thinking of impossible hopes or regrets. It was already clear that she was resigned to having the child.

Mme Michelon was followed by a young woman with her mother-in-law. I had to persuade the mother-in-law that a maternity girdle would not choke her future grandchild.

Then came a young man who wanted me to hypnotize his fiancée (whom I'd examined eight days ago) to find out if she'd had previous relations, and to brainwash her so she'd be faithful. I had trouble dissuading him from his plan: he'd already prepared a list of questions he wanted me to ask her.

I announced to the next patient that she was pregnant. When she stepped off the examination table, her eyes were shining with happiness. Her husband looked almost drunk with joy. As they left the husband asked me if intercourse during pregnancy would harm the child. I told him no but suggested positions that were better adapted to his wife's condition.

They were followed by a young woman with the heavy tread and thickening waist of four month's pregnancy.

For her too the first child is a wonderful adventure. She told me at once, with great pride: "He's been moving for the last eight days."

I examined her, then listened to a description of the movements; sometimes she felt the roundness of the head, sometimes the baby would stretch and then curl up into a ball, sometimes she'd be startled by its kicking feet.

From the way she speaks of her child, you can see that he already has a personality and a will of his own. Even before his birth, this little male in her belly—she has no doubt it's a boy—is already an adored tyrant.

My last patient was a young woman I'd never seen before. About twenty-five, ordinary features, no makeup, hair cut very short. She was dressed rather severely in a white, long-sleeved shirtwaist blouse with a Peter Pan collar, pleated skirt with black and white checks. She carried a novel in her hand. I could read the title, *Uneasy Conscience* by Suzanne Allen. She wasn't wearing a wedding band.

I picked up her chart; the nurse had put down "secretary" for occupation. She sat down opposite me, quite calm. Her eyes seemed to express pride and reserve. She answered my questions crisply, discouraging any nonmedical queries. Her case seemed quite simple; she hadn't menstruated in over two months and wanted to know if she was pregnant.

I asked her to step up to the table. Everything she did, the way she pulled up her skirt, climbed on the footstool and spread her thighs, expressed aggressiveness and pride.

I told her she was about three months pregnant.

I've noticed that the human face has only a limited range of expressions showing despair. But this girl's expression was new to me; at lightning speed, her face showed panic, fury, distress and defiance. She seemed ageless. Then she regained self-control; only her eyes trembled, almost imperceptibly. She sat up silently, stepped down from the table, smoothed the pleats of her skirt and, still silent, stood next to the desk while I filled in her chart. While I was writing, I asked myself what I could say to this woman who had already, I was sure, decided to have an abortion.

When I looked up her face was pale and expressionless.

An abortion after three months, especially one performed illegally, is often fatal. All I could do for her was to advise her to be careful or even to abstain next time. But as soon as I opened my mouth she stopped me with a curt sentence: "I only want a diagnosis, doctor."

Her eyes certainly weren't asking for pity. Though she was pale and her temples were moist with perspiration, her face was hard and closed.

She thanked me, took her social security form and left. I didn't dare say anything.

What could I have said? In her eyes I was the enemy. My white coat, my speculum, my syringes and my probes were proof that I was part of an illogical and cowardly system. I could warn her of the danger of an abortion but, because of my fear of an unjust law, I was leaving her to the frightening talents of the abortionist who was now her only hope.

I was silent as she left. Words of friendship or sympathy would have been an insult to this girl. But I'm ashamed when I remember how relieved I felt when the door shut; I immediately decided that since I knew nothing about this patient who was too proud to see me again, or anything about the motives which drove her to an abortion, it would be easier for me to forget her.

2 p.m.

I ate lunch in the dining room.

The hall is empty at dinner because so many people are on vacation, but at lunchtime it's crowded. It has the usual background noises: dishes banging, laughter, shouts and obscenities.

I suspect that the Gennevilliers interns, out of the nonconformists' conformism, try to keep up the tradition of the medical student who's as crude as he is learned. They look as ridiculous when they make their silly jokes as when they boast of their astute diagnoses or operating prowess; "I discovered . . . I decided." They tell you how wonderful they are and then end up believing it.

Interns by divine right, and men, later on they'll form the elite, assuming they're not that already. According to them, the rest of humanity, patients especially, is composed of nobodies and incompetents. This makes their superiority and exploitation of others perfectly legitimate.

65

My opinion of the interns as stupid bourgeois isn't a political one. As Lachaux says, I'm more fanatic and rebellious than revolutionary—I agree with Bebel that "women and the proletariat are both oppressed"; I believe it all the more since proletarian originally meant "maker of children." In ancient Rome, a proletarian was a poor man who was considered useful only if he had a large family.

I don't like my bourgeois colleagues. I've been as fanatic as Lachaux says I am since childhood. I've never taken anything lightly, and I've always acted according to my beliefs.

But all through my training I've met the same acceptance of the established order that I hated as a child, when I discovered that even though adults pretended to disapprove of lies, they didn't hesitate to use them as soon as they had a reason to.

In the staff room I do what I used to do as a defense against the arbitrariness and stupidity of grownups. By nature, I've always had difficulty in relating to other people (my schizophrenic side, Lachaux says) and when I was small I used to withdraw mentally, even from my family, though I was physically present.

I do this at Gennevilliers too. I eat, listen and keep to myself as much as possible. At meals, except when I can find a place near Lachaux, I sit near the end of the table so that I only have one neighbor. That gives me a symbolic half freedom. All I have to do to be completely free is turn my chair a bit.

Lunch was less animated than usual today. A lot of people are away, including Lachaux. But tonight there'll be the last party of the year, first for intern Rouzeau, who's just presented his thesis, and then for me, since I'm leaving. Pascali wanted to have a masquerade but no one was enthusiastic so he said we'd have a "really good dinner" and bring our own laughs.

Coffee was being served, in the usual thick cups, when Anna called from the door:

"Mam'selle Sauvage, there's a call for you on the outside phone."

I rarely get calls from the outside; and was surprised to hear an unfamiliar female voice:

"Claude?"

"Yes, who's this?"

The voice went on laughing: "Is that how you greet an

old friend? Don't you recognize me any more? Arlette! Well, after all this time, I guess it *is* a surprise."

The amused tone was so much like the voice of long ago that I immediately remembered the lovely face, blonde shoulder-length hair and big eyes. That was how Arlette Faulmier looked at fifteen when we were best friends at boarding school in Evreaux.

It was my turn to laugh. I imitated the nasal voice of our study hall teacher:

" 'Mam'selle Sauvage and Mam'selle Faulmier! Stop talking or I'll keep you after school!' . . . Where've you been all these years?"

"Just now, Casablanca. It's too long to tell on the phone. I need your advice. When can I see you? It's rather urgent."

"Right now, if you're free. I don't have anything until my afternoon rounds. But how did you find me?

"Through Alberte Apple. Remember her? The one who used to tag along after us? The one they put between us in study hall and the dormitory to stop us from talking?"

Another face came to mind, round, with myopic eyes and thick glasses, with heavy lips that sputtered when they passed our messages. Arlette went on without waiting for my answer:

"She's teaching at the Jules-Ferry Lycée. I ran into her in the subway two days ago. Remember how jealous she was of me because she worshiped you but I was your best friend? She keeps tabs on you even now. Anyway, see you soon."

Lunch was over so I went back to my room. I tried looking at it through Arlette's eyes. Until now I'd never realized how ugly and dirty it was. When I first arrived I didn't try to decorate it—no flowers or pictures; I didn't even try to hide the countless stains and scratches on the walls. I've looked at them a thousand times without their bothering me. But I couldn't let Arlette see it in such a mess so I cleaned it up a bit and sat down to wait for her.

A strange friendship had linked Arlette and me during the three years at the Lycée.

We shared enthusiasms about authors: Rimbaud, Kafka, Sartre, Camus, Simone de Beauvoir. We had reading orgies that left us dizzy, gorged with images, drunk with words and ideas. I had my greatest intellectual stimulation the last year, reading everything, classwork and unassigned books, with unlimited hunger.

And I kept being disconcerted by what I discovered. I had wanted to be a boy ever since I could remember. I hated dresses; they were awkward and got dirty too quickly; I didn't want to play with dolls and refused to play house because I didn't want to be the mother. I always chose the violent games and forced myself to play as hard as the boys, and then I suddenly learned in natural science class that one tiny chromosomal change would have made me male.

I also discovered when reading Jean Rostand that all sexual dissimilarities come from infinitesimal hormonal differences, that I was a woman essentially because of the hormone estrogen while the chemically related hormone testosterone would have made me a man. I also learned that estrogen gives women their external femininity and the quality of their emotions; so estrogen is a necessary precondition for love, if not the only one. I told myself that if morality is all in the glands, love is only a hormonal contamination of the blood.

Arlette and I were upset for weeks at the idea that love was only Nature's way of insuring the reproduction of the species and not the beautiful platonic myth of one being, separated into two by the wrath of Zeus, each part searching all over the world for the other in order to recover the perfect union. After our first shock we looked down on our fellow students who were always confiding in each other about their little crushes on the boys who came to pick them up on our days off. Later we read Kirkegaard's sentence: "What a misfortune to be a woman! And yet the real misfortune of being a woman is not to comprehend that it is one!" And we would congratulate each other for the perceptiveness that let us cut free of the pack.

In our childish enthusiasm, our future seemed set. Our classmates, accepting their unfortunate femininity and that official version of prostitution called marriage, would submit to their husbands, have children and become matrons, but we two, relying faithfully on each other, would prepare the way for the woman of the future. To liberate her from her slavery, and let her shape her life freely, we would dynamite, piece by piece, the oppressive world of men.

How? Our plan was simple: since I'd been so excited by my first contact with physiology, I'd study medicine. I was sure that I'd quickly discover laws of human parthenogenesis that would liberate woman by enabling her to produce children without male sperm.

Arlette would study for a degree, like Simone de Beauvoir, to become the spokesman for my discoveries and their philosophic implications.

Graduation time arrived. We both got our diplomas at seventeen. We took leave of each other on a Friday early in July, on the platform of the Evreux station. We made a date to meet in Paris on November 1st to start our university studies. Arlette didn't yet know that her father, who was the postmaster of Acquigny, had just been assigned to Algiers at his own request and that he'd kept the news from her so she wouldn't worry about it while she was preparing for exams. After we found out about the catastrophe, we corresponded all summer. Our resolution remained unshaken; each of us would work on her own, then . . .

I don't feel like finishing the phrase that I broke off when Arlette arrived. After describing our oaths of eternal friendship I don't like going over the details of the way our relationship dwindled away. I'm sure that nothing binds us to each other now except some old memories of snickering boarding-school girls and Alberte Apple and the teacher from Poland we called Popiska. It's one of life's greatest ironies that you can live in constant intimacy with someone for three years and then, when you're separated, realize that life goes on just the same without them and that you don't even miss the person you thought you couldn't live without. The Arlette of today is a stranger to me.

When she first appeared at my door, graceful and radiant, she hugged me the way she used to. In school, she used to embrace me on the slightest pretext; she'd take my arm or my hand when we walked across the courtyard. I usually rejected that kind of female mannerism, but I accepted her public show of affection because it irritated our fellow students and because it was a way of defying those teachers who kept looking for what they called "excessive friendships."

I learned all about the intervening years in less than half an hour, even with digressions like "Oh, that happened in '55, you wouldn't understand, I'll explain . . ."

Arlette had been studying literature in Algiers for two

years when she met a law student from Oran, just finishing his military service. Three months later they were married. She showed me a picture of their engagement party; a background of ships and piers, the two of them leaning against a white railing. He was dark and looked very masculine. He held a short pipe in his hand. She was leaning on him tenderly, the picture of charm and femininity. After his army discharge, Gilbert (that was the paragon's first name) joined an insurance company which sent him to their Moroccan agency in Oujda.

As soon as she was away from my influence, Arlette had quickly discovered that men are the masters of the world. Even if all careers are officially open to women, marriage is still the best one. Once she met her prince charming she didn't hesitate long. She gave up her studies and her ambitions for a career, and instead chose a husband destined to be a success.

She sat on the edge of my couch, completely at ease, her legs tucked under her, an elegant, well-bred young woman. Her hands gestured gracefully as she talked about the past and her life in Morocco. The first three years in Oujda were rather depressing, and things got worse when the war in Algeria began. Young Michael was born after one year, and then two years later, in 1958, came Jean-Pierre. Then her husband was sent to the Casablanca office and life was easier. They got their first car, went out more, spent weekends in Agadir, Fedala, Marrakech. Finally, three months ago came the unexpected promotion to the company's head office in Paris.

The long story of the young bride and mother, and the description of the not-quite gilded cage she'd chosen, enchanted by the bars, struck me as perfectly insipid. I was sure that a new friendship between us was impossible; we no longer had anything to say to each other and I only managed to hide my indifference by chattering.

Arlette concluded her Moroccan interlude and finally came to the reason for her visit.

"Alberte Apple told me that you'd stopped seeing each other a long time ago but one of her close relatives corresponds with your mother, and Alberte said that you were specializing in gynecology. And that's why I'm here . . ."

In the two or three seconds before she launched into her story, I thought she too had come to see me about a little problem. But no.

70

"You see, even though Gilbert has an excellent job, and he's being promoted very fast, I have to work at least for a while. You live in the hospital and have no family burdens so you can't know how the high cost of living in Paris is. It's frightening. I was lucky enough to find a job, though, through a colleague of Gilbert's. I like it and it's right up my alley. I just started working for *The French-woman*, the woman's weekly. You do know it?"

"Sure," I said. "My patients read it. We have stacks of back issues in the waiting room."

"I'm working with the group who edit the social and medical columns and give legal advice. Readers' mail, lonely hearts, et cetera. I've been there four days. The other editors seem nice enough but they're all professional journalists and I'm an amateur as far as they're concerned. So I have to manage on my own. Gilbert introduced me to one of his company's lawyers who's being very helpful about legal matters. I thought you could do the same for me on the medical side. I can get along on my own with the lonely hearts but I'll need help in the other areas."

I was tempted to get out of this by inventing some excuse, the way I'd managed to discourage Alberte Apple's friendship. But Arlette looked at me with the same pleading gaze she'd used in school when she wanted something from me.

"You're lucky," I finally said. "I'm supposed to be on vacation now but I'm still here subbing for an intern who's due back any day. When can you spend a morning or afternoon at the hospital?"

"Tomorrow? The magazine goes to press Thursday night so I'm supposed to be free on Friday. The house-keeper comes in at eight. She'll take care of the children so I can be here at nine."

She glanced quickly at a tiny golden spherical watch hanging from a bracelet, and said, in a businesslike tone, as if already nothing could be done at *The Frenchwoman* without her:

"I've got to get back to the office. It's almost closing time."

I walked her to the entrance, I in my rough hospital coat and flats, she swaying silkily as she stepped on the gravel in her high heels.

She hugged me good-bye in front of Lagriffoul Café. A bus for Paris was at the terminal. As soon as Arlette sat down, the bus conductor, looking at her, rang the bell as if dedicating it to her.

I did my second rounds and stopped by to see Mariette. The antibiotics have worked. Her temperature is down to normal. She was aglow with impatience because I'd promised her this morning that if the fever was over, I'd let her go home in four or five days. I confirmed my promise and was delighted to see how happy it made her.

Three rooms down, isolated like a quarantine case, was Mme Doudelette, all self-deprecating charity: "A room to myself is much too much," she said. She felt guilty when she thought about the women who were more seriously ill than she and were still in the ward. She'd be perfectly happy to go back to her old bed. . . . I was firm; four operations as exceptional as hers and the opinion of the head surgeon of Lariboisière about her case demanded special attention. She can take advantage of her private room without guilt. It's not a favor. She has a right to it.

I noticed copies of *The Frenchwoman* in the wards, spread out on the beds or being read by the patients. The salpingitis case in Bed Nine checks the horoscope page eagerly; it's more reassuring than the temperature recorded on her chart. Her neighbor, a housewife, was so engrossed reading about the glamorous life of Queen Elizabeth that she hardly lifted her eyes to answer me. Maybe she was consoling herself for her own poverty-stricken existence, physical miseries and daily worries by thinking about people privileged by beauty and power.

Several of the younger patients were huddled around a transistor, listening to a popular song about birds and dreams of love and moonlight, sung in syrupy tones by a female vocalist.

What do they find in all this? What hope? Who'll make these poor girls with their bovine souls understand that the poetry is only a camouflage for male desires that makes them fall into their arms? Will Arlette's advice teach them that life isn't like the movies?

When I returned to my room, there was a faint but persistent reminder of Arlette's perfume. The fragrance was just right for the new Arlette—fresh, young, not openly provocative but with a subtle attraction.

She'd no doubt chosen it among all the others to make the closest match to her personality, so that it would be unique like her clothes and her makeup. How funny!

Arlette's concerned with making herself unique as soon as she's become as conventional and false as all the others, as soon as she's achieved the supreme success—catching a husband. Arlette, intelligent and sensitive, joining the herd of "eternal slaves" because, as a young patient of mine who'd been deserted after three years of a bad marriage told me sadly a few days ago, "It's impossible for a woman to live alone."

Must it be a tragedy for women to live alone? The only girls I went to school with who are still single must be Alberte Apple and I.

1 a.m.

The "good dinner" was even more depressing than our ordinary lunch. Seated at the long table was the usual assortment (Lachaux claims that any staff room will contain a girl-chaser, a cynic, a pedant, a prankster and one conceited bastard), interspersed with nonmedical guests, who seem delighted at the simple-minded, crude medical jokes and that peculiar feeling of sadism a hospital atmosphere offers to the uninitiated because of the proximity of sick people. The guests were the ones who sang the dirty songs the loudest. The single interns brought a few pretty girls along, all with faces heavily made up to show how "liberated" they were. Pascali had changed from his upper class girl from Cabourg to a redhead, all curves, dimples and milky skin. She wore a low-cut green silk dress that clung to her like a tank suit.

Because we were celebrating my leaving as well as Rouzeau's handing in his thesis, Pascali, seated at the head of the table, sat me at his right, facing his beautiful date. So I had to keep looking at that disgustingly feminine face during the entire meal. Her breasts were exposed by the dress. They were so full that they embarrassed me almost as much as her dress and perfume did. She looked vain and stubborn, as well as stupid. "That's what makes her so attractive," Pascali would have said if he weren't so busy being host.

Lachaux sat on my right, but when such a magnificent redhead is around, it's obviously impossible for a man to look elsewhere. Even when he was talking to me he didn't take his eyes off her. He, with his albino coloring, and I with my sallow complexion, both of us in hospital coats, must have made a rather uninteresting couple. Yet at one point the redhead gave us a curious and somewhat hostile look, then leaned over to Pascali and, still staring, asked him, "Who's the light-haired character and that nothing girl he's talking to?" Pascali's answer, half lost in the noise, sounded like: "The hospital virgin and the seminarist. You won't be able to defrock him, he's chaste."

She leaned back and laughed dramatically, looking provocatively at Lachaux from under half-closed lids.

The party props were distributed. A handful of confetti fell on the redhead, and some of it got into her eyes and mouth. Pascali began to help her get rid of it and Lachaux raised his voice as if he were continuing a conversation:

"Yes, the observation of male baboons, chimpanzees and others has shown them to be polite about sharing their banana rations with females when they are in heat and are able to excite them unusually; on the other hand, the rest of the time the female has to be content with scrounging and peels. . . ."

Then, he looked sneeringly at Pascali, who was still harvesting the confetti.

"And, according to Valensin, sociability at rutting time is often expressed in monkeys by defleaing, even if there are no fleas. This is one of the first forms of wooing. You also find the delousing communion among the most primitive men; for example, among the Sirionos of South America, it precedes intercourse. . . ."

General laughter greeted this tirade. Pascali looked at Lachaux with some hesitation, then afraid of appearing ridiculous, he laughed loud with the others and plunged his hand into his neighbor's bodice, shouting:

"Defleaing and caressing are the two nipples of love. Kiss me!"

The girl threw us a last venomous glance then looked away for good.

After the chicken, the dinner started to lag lamentably; Rouzeau said that the hospital administration had fattened the chicken with female hormones to reduce sex in the residence hall, but the joke didn't last long.

Pascali started singing obscene songs. Everyone came in on the chorus as if that proved their virility. But it was too hot and the chorus soon faded into silence. Three or four couples wanted to dance and started to move, hoping to drag along the others, but they got breathless and sweaty so fast that they didn't persuade them.

Pascali ended the party at 12:15, the usual time. Doors

74

slammed shut under my windows and the hall was quiet again. But there were giggles from nearby rooms. They would become sighs and creaks in a few minutes.

I lay down on the bed, not really sleepy, and looked at the dark blue of the starry night through my windows. The air hadn't cooled down yet. My head ached; too much noise, too many songs and especially too much punch. I had to drink it before dinner: I couldn't refuse the farewell drink and Pascali kept his eyes on me while I swallowed about a third of the glass.

Is it because I'm not used to alcohol that my temples throb, and my knees feel weak and I'm so irritable? Or is it Arlette's visit and the depressing memories it revived? Or the redhead laughing when she tried to humiliate me? Yet I did have the small pleasure of seeing Lachaux come to my aid and annoying her.

I guess I should have stayed with Lachaux for a while instead of locking myself into my room, overwhelmed by the stifling heat and my loneliness.

I know that I'm tired from too much exhausting tension, too much work. I take refuge in my work like those fanatics who aim for a first in school and are afraid they'll lose if they stop for a second.

"It's impossible for a woman to live alone," my patient told me. I'm sure this is Arlette's excuse too. As if life isn't always a solitary adventure. As if you don't have to draw a circle around yourself to prepare for battle and forbid yourself to go out of it.

When I first flopped down on the bed I was still dressed. I got up to wash and studied my face in the mirror over the basin.

The redhead had some reason to make fun of me; hollow cheeks, dull skin, shadows under my eyes, my hair oily and plastered down. I suddenly saw, superimposed on my face, Arlette, with her glowing smile, the radiant redhead and even the ordinary prettiness of the interns' overly made-up dates, I guess that loneliness, which usually refreshes me, can make me feel horribly frustrated when I drink a bit.

But why not be honest? No sense losing sleep and energy by playing games with myself. Should I be jealous of Arlette's beauty, of her love, coming and going, smiling and sure of herself, in a paradise that excludes girls like me? And why keep thinking about the redhead? Am I going to be jealous of a limited petty woman because of her animal ways that make men admire her? What do we two have in common except menstruating thirteen times a year? I looked at myself in the mirror and said: "Be reasonable. The punch isn't making you edgy. It's your period reminding you that in spite of yourself you're a woman like Arlette and the redhead and those girls sighing with pleasure in the other bedrooms. Haven't you learned by now from other women that the flesh exists and that it's demanding and difficult to silence?"

I know only one way to escape from indecision. Work. Like a nun who fasts to avoid the devil's temptation.

But most of all, I still have my pride.

Friday, 6 p.m.

Arlette showed up on time, chic, smiling and perfumed. I'd borrowed an apron and smock from Anna. I handed them to her.

She was surprised. "Where are you taking me?"

"To my consultations. I'll sit you down in a corner and you can listen. It'll be the best way to learn."

"But I don't want to start studying medicine!" Arlette protested, laughing. Despite her smile, I had the feeling that direct contact with patients might frighten her a bit.

She slipped on the smock and tied the apron strings around her waist. When I wear it, the uniform looks impersonal. On her it immediately became graceful and snow-white, as if she were a movie star playing the part of a young female doctor.

It was so hot outside that I knew the hospital would be a furnace by noon.

As we walked along the buildings, Arlette glanced, half curious, half frightened, through the windows, at the patients napping in their beds.

On the way, I told her that I thought her job on the magazine was something like the old family doctor's, who was both friend and adviser and who was consulted about all the important events of the family.

"The family doctor's dying out," I added, "and being replaced by the specialist who's psychosomatically oriented, the kind of doctor who tries to untangle the diseases which come from the stresses of modern life. He's the only specialist who *listens*; listens as often and as long as necessary so that the patient develops confidence in him and can open up and reveal the cause of his conflicts.

Eventually a friendship develops between doctor and patient which makes the doctor's suggestions meaningful."

"Is that what you're going to do?" Arlette asked.

"Yes, but I'll orient myself toward gynecology. As a woman and a doctor I'm ideally situated to study female problems, and husband-and-wife problems, and try to find solutions. When you start answering readers who work and keep house, you'll see what their lives are like. The husband only has to cope with his job but it's double slavery for the wife, and her physical and emotional energy are used up very quickly. You'll also see how a couple's sex life is affected by this kind of life."

I was so carried away by the subject that I didn't realize Arlette might take this generalization as a comment on her own life. But as we walked she turned and looked at me with annoyance. Did she think I'd become petty? I stopped talking. When I fell silent, she said, rather acidly:

"If a woman works, why is her life a double slavery instead of another step toward equality and liberty?"

It was my turn to answer sharply:

"Because the husband always directs the couple's life, despite the apparent equality. Take your situation; you followed your husband from Algiers to Oujda, from Oujda to Casablanca, from Casablanca to Paris. And, incidentally, the law would have made you do so. If your husband's career demands it, you'll follow him to Mazamet or Lille and drop what you've started in Paris. So where's your equality and liberty?"

She looked at me, astounded.

"Forgive my talking to you like this," I continued more softly, a little ashamed of myself. "These problems are very important to me. And they're almost the same for you, though you're married, as for me even though I'm single, because even a woman who's determined to live alone can't be entirely free, not even free to dress as she pleases."

I looked at Arlette. We were wearing the same smock and apron, but she was tripping along gracefully in her high heels while I clumped along in my flats. I added:

"The independent woman who doesn't want to be dominated by men, or even to give in by flirting with them, stands out like a freak among other women. Men let her know very fast that her nonconformism lowers her in their eyes. And women who want to be both feminine and

77

independent are also in a fix because they've had the bad luck to be born in a period still dominated by men."

Almost timidly, as she used to do back at school when she wanted to ask me something which might make me angry, she said: "But you've made your choice?"

"No," I answered. "I didn't have to choose. I just kept to what I'd always decided: to remain alone, without fear or hypocrisy, without compromise, and earn my own living so I can do as I please. I haven't changed."

I almost added: "Besides, it's not hard to be independent when you're poor and plain."

Luckily, we reached the maternity ward just then. We had to cross the waiting room. I counted the patients with one glance. About fifteen, less than usual. Conversations stopped as we passed but picked up as soon as we closed the door.

"When will the last patient leave?" Arlette asked.

"Not before half-past twelve, I'd guess."

"Why don't you give them staggered appointments?"

"I wanted to but the director wouldn't allow any change in regulations, even though I told him the waiting room ought to be called the patience room. The staff would raise a fuss. Signing in stops at nine a.m. and it's just too bad for someone who's late."

Arlette looked at the desk and the equipment: examination table, boxes of rubber gloves, enamel tray with the speculum and forceps, the glass case filled with instruments. She seemed uncomfortable.

"Sit down on the chair next to my desk," I said. "I'm going to call in the first patient."

"Won't she be embarrassed by me?" she asked, as if hoping she could escape.

"Just keep quiet and look interested. Patients are more or less like children. A couple of physicians intensely occupied with them reminds them of their two parents bent over their child."

I dismissed my last patient at 12:15. Toward the end, despite the partly open window, the air was so full of sweat, breath and vaginal smells that it had become unbearable.

At first I was worried that this session might be a poor one for the kind of lesson I wanted to give Arlette. But in Gennevilliers any morning would be suitable. Even though it was vacation time, Arlette, sitting silently at my side, had witnessed a generous sampling of nerves in shreds, family tragedies, worries and vices. Each patient seemed to have brought her full burden of miseries with her.

So at least Arlette learned before she answered her first readers' letters that those women don't live in her circumscribed middle-class world; that they don't all know the magazine atmosphere with its ghosted actors' autobiographies and trumped-up family problems, set forth in 300,-000 copies; that they suffer from real troubles, from conflicts between the spirit and the flesh, from problems of prejudice, inadequate education, religious guilt, and false shame. Even if the passage from her world to the other has been too harsh for her this morning, she must understand before she begins her correspondence that these two worlds coexist; that next to hers, with all its technicolor illusions, is the other one made up of bitter reality.

The sun was beating down on the building as we walked out. Arlette looked as if she were about to faint.

There's a small square with a few benches under the linden trees to the right of the maternity ward. It's set up for the patients and at lunch time it's deserted. I took Arlette there instead of going to my room. She seemed unsure of her feet as she walked, then fell onto a bench and sat there expressionless, eyes shut, mouth half open. I said softly: "Rest a while. We have time."

Even in the shade of the linden trees, with their fragrance of orange blossoms and vanilla, the light was bright. My friend's eyes stayed closed. As I'd looked at my own face in the mirror during the night, I leaned toward hers to compare it with my memories. She opened her eyes, smiled at me as if amused by her momentary weakness and asked quietly:

"How can you stand listening to them? All those faces and stories. It seems endless. I couldn't take it."

"You'll see, when you start answering your mail that the main thing is to start out conscientiously. You'll develop a strong stomach as you go along, and you'll be able to dig deeper and understand better. The women who'll confide in you by mail will be in real trouble. You won't get any confessions from happy stable women. If you do your job well, you won't feel the need of reading detective stories anymore."

"But I'll have to play detective, won't I? I noticed this morning how your patients try to conceal things and how you keep questioning them until you get to the truth. Why do they lie to you if they come to see you of their own free will?"

"That's what happens as soon as you get involved with sex. Medicine is full of lies and mistakes: patients cheat on a diet, forget to take their medicine, don't tell their doctor that they've consulted a specialist. An analyst would tell you that the doctor represents the image of the authoritative father, so the patient's delighted to disobey him. And when you get involved with genital problems, you're working in an area that nice people don't talk about. You saw this morning that the lower class patients don't have any false modesty. But I had trouble even with them in the beginning. Sometimes they'd get mad. Now they understand that I'm not snooping when I question them. The thing that's helped most is that I'm a woman and so they're less ashamed to talk to me than to a man."

I was hot and thirsty and had a raspy tongue from talking for three hours. I didn't feel like going on. But Arlette asked:

"Why are they so reticent, especially today? Wherever you go people talk about sex, Freud, psychoanalysis and complexes. The papers and novels and the movies are full of it, and it's even in *The Frenchwoman,* though it's rather conservative and timid."

"You're forgetting the power of middle-class conformity and its firmly ingrained sexual taboos. You'll never find a middle-aged, middle-class mother telling you she likes to have her clitoris stimulated. It would be some emancipated young woman who thinks of love as a physiological act, purely chemical and so lacking in feeling that it leads her to insensitivity."

Arlette sat up a bit more. She seemed to have rediscovered that interest in arguing that she'd had six years ago when we discussed things in the school courtyard during recess. The linden trees there gave off that same fragrance of vanilla and orange blossoms.

She asked: "At least, this new kind of woman must be sincere in presenting her problems?"

She fell silent, nibbling her lips as she used to do in school when she was involved in a discussion. Caught up by my old desire to convince her, I said:

"That would be true if women of all ages didn't exaggerate. They make up whole novels about their failures. The approaches differ according to how much education they've had, what they read, and whether they stress their

80

emotions, hormones or the psyche. Most of them dramatize to make themselves and their sex problems more interesting. But to be fair, I should tell you that some of their deceptions are unconscious, not deliberate."

A breeze rustled through the linden trees, then the silvery leaves became motionless again in the torrid air.

Arlette asked: "What kind of lies? How can I detect them in my mail?"

"They're almost always the same. They forget the number of their sexual experiences. They deny masturbating and are quite likely to deny adultery. You noticed how difficult it was to make them answer those three questions? They'll deny several affairs and a premarital pregnancy completely. They've never heard of masturbation. And a frigid woman doesn't count adultery because she takes a lover in the hope of awakening her senses just the way she'd take medicine. But their myth-making really reaches its peak when they start describing sexual feelings."

Arlette frowned.

"If the ones who are frigid don't feel anything what can they tell you?"

"They have plenty of information. Even the woman who counts the flowers in the wallpaper while her husband makes love to her knows what to say; her colleagues in the office tell her, with exaggerations, what they feel, or else what one has to pretend to feel to flatter the partner's self-esteem. Remember that blonde woman? Short, about twenty-one. The third or fourth patient. The one who said she was frigid and didn't want to bring her husband in? She only became anxious after a girl friend described to her the ideal emotions in intercourse. But if she hadn't learned it from her friend, she'd have found out from movies or novels. Her pleasure may really be minimal— the female orgasm has never been clearly defined—but in the past, when people didn't talk about paradise and the pleasures of sex, she'd probably have been quite content. Nowadays all the women want to compete for the sensuality record."

"Why didn't she want to bring her husband in?"

"Probably because she lied to me about him. She told me she loved him. I doubt that she does but it would take several interviews before I could find out. On the other hand, she said she helped support her husband's mother. That's probably true. A bit later, she acknowledged that she doesn't get along with her own mother. The only young women who support their mothers-in-law are those who detest their own mothers, which proves the principle that you need a good hatred to stabilize a family's harmony."

Just then, a wasp brushed past Arlette's mouth. She pulled back and wiped her lips with the back of her hand. I remembered how she'd always been afraid of insects and smiled. But she ignored my look and continued soberly:

"What do you do to keep them from lying?"

"First of all, you listen patiently without interrupting, because you can learn from a patient's digressions; interruptions merely annoy her. And you don't ask direct questions. Take an oblique approach. If you ask a patient if she's been unfaithful, she'll deny it flatly. So you say 'You're a very attractive young woman. I'm sure you've been told this?' It's easy enough for her to agree and give you the cue to ask 'Is there anyone special right now?' And then you may learn that her husband's best friend won't leave her alone, which is half an admission."

"Do you think there'll be a lot of frigidity problems in my letters?"

"I'd say one out of three pretty young women you pass on the street, happy as she may look, is frigid."

"One out of three?" Arlette exclaimed unbelievingly.

I started to laugh. She was so obvious. She blushed and looked down like a schoolgirl caught saying a dirty word.

"Yes," I said, "one out of three at least, and I think those are optimistic statistics. But you'll have to be careful because you'll get letters from the false frigid types who will hint that their reactions are normal but that their husband is somehow deficient, either because he ejaculates prematurely or because of some other impotence. These ladies write you hoping you'll tell them to change partners because they're afraid to do it on their own. For heaven's sake, don't advise it. If they fail, they'll hold you responsible for their unfaithfulness and accuse you of immorality. So leave them the responsibility and the initiative."

"But I'm supposed to answer. What do I say?"

"Keep it sensible. When the wife works, and also has to cope with an overcrowded home, little money or a mother-in-law in the house, sexual harmony is hard to achieve. You can't find your readers larger apartments, get them raises or remove the mother-in-law but if you explain that overwork, overcrowding and lack of leisure affect the sex life and cause frigidity, you'll help eliminate their anxiety about their sex troubles, even if you don't help the actual difficulty. But be very careful in your choice of words."

Arlette didn't seem convinced. I added:

"Frigidity is a shield for lots of women. It protects them from a number of troubles. Are you going to tell some woman who complains about being frigid that she's narcissistic and infantile and doesn't really love her husband, or that she'd be better off with a more vigorous man than her husband who's a clerk? What good would you do her if you inspired her to leave home with nothing to fall back on? As her adviser you should help your reader understand her life. Don't distort it by romantic illusions. Help her cope with life as it is. Then her husband will seem less shabby and clumsy; the apartment will look a little better and the children will get fewer slaps."

I could see that Arlette was disappointed at this modest program; she felt the same disappointment I'd felt when, as an ardent novice in the hospital, I wanted to reform everything all at once.

I went on persuasively:

"That isn't much, in fact it's very little, but when you get to know the problems of most households you'll feel that it's better than nothing. There will be ladies who sign themselves "Sick and Frightened" or "Desperate" and who'll write you mostly to see their "case" in print so that their friends and neighbors will recognize it and talk about it, but you'll find many women with real anxiety and problems. They feel alone and defenseless against stupidity, a dull routine life, ignorance and selfishness, and their married life has become slavery. And you can help free these women from the resentment they have against life, men, and against themselves. They write you only to find some freedom. . . . If you answer them as an honest friend, you'll keep them from brooding endlessly over their troubles and making their lives even more stifling. You'll give them back some serenity."

I looked at my watch:

"Almost one. We did a lot of work this morning. Let's go have lunch." I jumped up, smiling, and gave my hand to Arlette. But she took her compact out of her smock and said:

"I must look awful. Give me a second. I haven't even powdered my nose since this morning."

My pleasure instantly dissolved. The self-conscious gesture was certainly from the new Arlette. She'd thought of the interns we were going to lunch with and wanted to polish her armor before she faced them. She opened her lipstick and studied her lips in the compact mirror. Then, sure she was attractive, she began to smile again.

The patients were probably baiting their traps for the afternoon visitors just the same way.

I was upset. I turned away so Arlette wouldn't guess what I was thinking if she looked at me.

The dining room was still empty. As we passed the kitchen, Anna called out:

"Mam'selle Sauvage, you just got a package."

She handed me a dressmaker's carton. There was a letter tucked under the string.

I opened it in my room and read it, then explained to Arlette:

"It's from a patient I treated for menstrual cramps. She made me two dresses to thank me. She's a seamstress."

"Let's see, quick!" Arlette said.

She was so curious that she untied the string immediately, opened the box and pulled out two linen dresses. She waved them in her hands and said:

"They're darling. And just the colors in style this summer. You'll look charming in them. Which one are you going to try on first?"

"I'm not charming at all. I'll write my patient to thank her but I won't try either of them on."

Arlette ignored my tone and ran to the washstand, took my comb from the table and came back.

"Do be nice. Let me try. Just changing your hair style slightly, a drop of rouge and powder, and you'll look charming in one of these dresses. You always had beautiful eyes."

She pretended to run the comb through my hair.

I was tempted for a minute. Why not show myself that I'm not as old-looking and clumsy as the girl I see in my mirror? Arlette saw my hesitation and insisted.

"Please! Don't be so silly. Not even a pretty girl could get away with your hair-do and bushy eyebrows and pale cheeks. It would be all right if no one used makeup, but when you're the only one who doesn't set her hair and do something to her face . . ."

She handed me the dresses again. They were light and colorful. I was about to say yes. Then, with a slight effort

I shook my head. I rejected the image of a prettily made-up Claude in a summer dress the way you discard a bad photograph. What's the point of giving in? Why risk getting mixed up? I don't want to know Arlette's secrets. I don't need them for what I've chosen to do.

Our dining room seating arrangements are informal. An intern can bring anyone he or she wants to a meal. If his colleagues are already seated, the intern and his guest walk around the table greeting the others until they find two empty seats.

Lunch hadn't started when we came back to the dining room so I had to make some introductions. I was careful to say that Arlette was studying literature at the Sorbonne because calling her a journalist might have caused too much interest.

The interns straggled in, sweaty but relaxed. Pascali arrived shortly after we did. He looked at Arlette curiously and came right over to us. When we sat down, he placed Arlette at his right and me at his left. The others pulled chairs out noisily and flopped down where they stood. There are no fixed places.

There's always a certain vulgarity in Pascali's talk but he put on an act of candor and honesty for Arlette. Of course, as soon as he heard that she'd been in my office all morning he couldn't resist making mild fun of my advice to couples "just breaking in" or to "older couples in for a retread." He didn't take his eyes off her as he spoke. She kept smiling, more because she sensed the handsome intern's admiration (his naked chest was visible under his carelessly closed coat) than because the conversation was funny.

She even managed to recapture her old girlish giggle at some of his stories. She must know how it suits her, showing her teeth and her pink, glistening tongue flirtatiously.

Pascali had to leave right after lunch but he made it clear that my charming friend would always be welcome. He looked knowingly at Arlette when he told her he hoped she'd be back soon.

Lachaux had come in late and was sitting at the other end of the table. When people started leaving after coffee, I signaled him to join us.

As he came over, Arlette whispered to me without

moving her lips, the way we used to do in study hall:
"Funny-looking, isn't he?"

I answered the same way: "He's intelligent and kind.
And he's taught me how to understand patients."

Lachaux sat down in the chair our "bursar" had just
vacated. There's an amazing contrast between Pascali's
animal perfection, which makes him an aristocrat of beauty, and Lachaux's pathetic ugliness.

Since we were alone at our end of the table I explained
that Arlette had asked me for help in her new job.
Lachaux listened and watched her. His pale eyes in his
pale face made him look almost asleep.

Then I told Arlette what Lachaux had done for me this
past year and what she could expect from him if he
agreed to help her.

She'd been indifferent until then but she immediately
put on her dazzling smile.

The waitress made a great commotion about clearing
the table. I suggested we go to my room.

Pascali had made Arlette laugh during lunch about my
"pubic relations" contraceptive advice, but I thought that
she'd certainly have to give similar counsel to her readers
and that she should be told how important it was.
Lachaux would be better than I at making her understand.

So, as soon as we were back in my room, with Arlette
installed on my couch and Lachaux on the chair, I asked
him to outline the major psychological arguments in favor
of birth control, the way he'd had me do for my thesis.
His face instantly became animated, as if he'd just awakened.

He began with Freud's famous statement that defines
"any sexual activity which renounces procreation and
seeks pleasure as an independent goal" as perverse. This
led into the point of view of the people who are opposed
to birth control. They believe that its methods are especially harmful to the woman who deeply needs to be a
mother.

He went on to list the objections of Catholic Psychiatrists to the different methods of birth control: the artificial and technical aspects, the mechanical or chemical
means that transform the partner into a simple instrument
of gratification; the frustration and lack of satisfaction for
the woman in intercourse interrupted by withdrawal.

"These are," he explained, "arguments you can't contradict even if you're totally in favor of birth control. For example, Simone de Beauvoir emphasizes that the pleasure a woman gets from sex is largely because of a kind of magic spell which demands complete abandon; if words or movements go against the magic of caresses, the spell is broken."

He went on to point out that it's precisely this need for spontaneity, for total abandon, for absolute fusion in love, that provokes conscious or subconscious resistance to birth control in many women, especially if it is up to them to choose a contraceptive and be responsible for using it.

"Because of their religious education or their idealism," he said "this 'cheating' may make certain scrupulous or delicate women feel guilty. And the old bourgeois moralism makes others think that mechanical or chemical contraceptives are instruments of forbidden pleasure or illicit relations."

After having gone over the arguments of the opponents of contraception, he came to the argument of its defenders. One of the most important ones is that the fear of pregnancy causes frigidity. Again he cited Freud, talking about Catholic couples who practice continence because of traditional belief rather than a strong personal faith. In their case, "the libido, finding its way blocked, will try to escape in a direction where it can spend its reserve of energy!"

"A 'direction' which is," he said, "rarely that of morality, and which is very likely to result in a neurosis."

During Lachaux's explanation, Arlette relaxed on the couch, fanning herself with a magazine, only asking questions about the precise meaning of some psychiatric term. She was evidently much less interested than in the morning or during our conversation under the linden trees.

I didn't understand this change. Was it the heat? Was she tired? Was our "lecture" too complicated for her? It seemed to me that Lachaux had explained things at her level very intelligently, with patience and easy persuasiveness that long practice with mental patients has given him.

After he'd finished an objective presentation of each side's arguments, Arlette only asked, in a tone of polite social interest, "And what is your opinion, doctor?"

No doubt Lachaux felt her indifference. He answered:

"I believe that no method of contraception can be used without psychological inconvenience, at least by some people, or without the risk of creating as many frictions and conflicts for the couple as the absence of contraception. But I also believe that these inconveniences have been greatly exaggerated."

"And you, Claude, what do you think?" Arlette asked in the same polite voice.

I was hurt by this obvious fiasco. Nonetheless I made an effort to put some feeling into a discussion that I thought was important.

"Oh!" I said vehemently, "I'm much more positive than Lachaux. What I've seen here every day for a year has proved to me that the official prohibition of efficient contraceptives (which women can use freely in America, England and over half of the world) leads to abuses that are much more serious—both qualitatively and quantitatively—than their free and organized use. It's true that sexual dissatisfaction of coitus interruptus or the fear of withdrawing too late, or the simple fact that each sexual act is risky because none of the contraceptives now in use is a hundred per cent safe, may lead to numerous cases of frigidity. But with the prohibition of all female contraception, the ghost of pregnancy is always there, and you end up with much more frigidity. According to some recent statistics, nearly eighty per cent of the women haunted by the fear of pregnancy were frigid, but only forty-nine percent of the others were. But the use of contraceptives must be free *and* organized. There has to be a minimum of advice and instruction to make them really effective. There's no other way to eliminate their clandestine, deceitful aspect. That's what makes them psychologically harmful."

Arlette continued to listen to me distractedly. I tried to catch her interest the way I would have if we'd been talking at school.

"You remember in our last year at school when we read in Léon Blum's book on marriage that it is neither more difficult nor more shocking to find out that you cannot have children than it is to have them? We thought he was right. With what I've learned by now, I'm opposed to the methods of birth control that date back to the time of the Bible or Hippocrates. But now that man has made such immense progress over Nature. I'm even more opposed to a morality and laws that make pregnancy unavoidable. Just as a rationally desired pregnancy is acceptable, so pregnancy for a woman "caught' by Nature in spite of herself is revolting! The universal conspiracy of silence is also revolting, the refusal to see the obvious distinction between women who reject motherhood for selfish reasons (and how much more elastic morality is when it comes to male selfishness!) and women who would accept motherhood with joy if it weren't an unbearable burden for them. Since the State considers motherhood a kind of female social service and issues anti-birth-control laws to subdue the rebels, just like hauling deserters before a court martial, I affirm with all my strength the right of refusing pregnancy, just as I affirm the rights of women againt the laws of society and the species."

Lachaux stood up with a smile, and said to Arlette:

"You see how extreme Claude is. It doesn't matter where you're concerned, but let's pray that she'll be able to be more moderate when she defends her thesis."

Then, looking at his watch:

"You'll excuse me? I must go. If I can do you a favor in any way, don't hesitate to let me know. I'd be delighted to help you."

"Your friend is intelligent and very nice," Arlette declared languorously after he left. "And you," she added with more warmth, "you're just the same as always . . . so passionate, so completely dedicated."

I almost said that it was simply that I hadn't changed my mind in those six years, that I'm still trying to accomplish my task and to keep my word in everything, large and small.

The two dresses were still lying on a corner of the couch. Dropping the subject of contraception, Arlette again tried to charm me out of what she calls "my stubborn desire to make myself ugly." But when I refused as emphatically as before, she didn't insist.

The afternoon was becoming painfully long. The air had a dusty summer taste. I did nothing to keep Arlette back when she looked at her watch and cried:

"I have to go. The housekeeper will be waiting for me."

She looked at herself in the mirror for one last time, as if to make sure that she still had her charm after a long, tiring day; then came toward me to thank me. I was sitting down at my work table. Arlette looked at the heap of folders for my thesis, all clearly titled, and my note cards, carefully arranged in piles.

Looking at all my papers and documents, couldn't she

realize how impolite, or even hurtful, her lack of interest in Lachaux's presentation seemed to me? For a moment she was silent. She was obviously hesitating. Should she say she was sorry or say nothing? She looked thoughtful, as she had in the morning, then she said:

"I'm sorry if I seem awkward or stupid, but there's something I don't understand. All these patients that I've watched you devote yourself to—sometimes you talk about them compassionately, and sometimes you seem faintly contemptuous of them. . . ."

I thought our talk was over. Was I going to have to start it up again? I didn't feel like it. But I didn't want to refuse to talk about it altogether.

"Yes," I answered, "I do have a little contempt for them, because if they really wanted to, they could free themselves, instead of choosing to live in misery; I also pity them because men have become their oppressors so deliberately. Remember that sentence in Sartre that we loved so much: 'Half victims, half accomplices, like everyone . . .' I pity women because they're victims of men and I try to help them, but I resent their being accomplices of their own unhappiness."

"And you think that you can change the nature of women—what men who dislike us call the 'eternal feminine'?"

Without knowing it—or maybe just because she knows me so well—Arlette had put her finger on the very question that's most painful for me; the question I ask myself over and over: Will men and women be really free and equal someday?

I didn't want to answer it now. Some other time I might explain to her what my hopes are for women. Today she showed interest too late. I only wanted her to leave. I said, quickly and drily:

"You know me, I've always had a passion for lost causes. So winning or losing the battle doesn't matter very much to me if I know that the cause is just. And in the present case, I didn't plan to be heroic. I didn't choose my battlefield in the beginning, or rather I didn't imagine it the way it is. Now that I'm on it, I can't desert—I have a common cause with women even if most of the women I'm fighting for are more like fat cows than proud amazons. Once you become aware of women's problems— the kind that you saw today—you can't keep on living the life of a selfish privileged woman who doesn't care."

The dryness of my speech must have showed that I

didn't want to talk about it any more. Arlette probably felt it because she didn't insist. She kissed me, thanked me again, and said good-bye.

After she left, I folded the present from the grateful seamstress back into its box and put it on the top shelf of my closet so I wouldn't have to think about it again. I did it to blot out the image of Arlette, indifferent to Lachaux's explanation and waving the two little dresses at me to tempt me to become her sort of woman. But thinking about it, I began to understand the difference between her reactions in the morning and in the afternoon.

Between the painful succession of faces and bellies she'd been so upset with in the morning and the lecture on contraception that she'd listened so absentmindedly to, had been lunch. Under Pascali's admiring gaze she'd become a beautiful, desirable, happy woman again, and again that became her one interest.

Arlette like most women, "half victim, half accomplice"! ... That's her life. I'll never accept it.

9 p.m.

After Arlette left, I felt nervous. I was irritated with everybody. Her last question had touched me to the quick and I hadn't kept on talking only because I feared it would end in reproaches or a quarrel. Can the woman of the future, the one I'd like to liberate, who will be responsible and equal to man, be born after thousands of years of masculine domination? After looking at Arlette's example, I was tempted to say a shameful, bitter "No!"

This morning I'd been too preoccupied with my friend to have the time to go through the wards. So my second round this afternoon was much longer. I ended up at the private rooms. I made sure to visit Mme Doudelette. Once again she asked me to put her back into the ward and again we acted out the same little comedy: she pretended to be filled with unselfish charity that prevented her from enjoying such unusual comfort without guilt; and I pretended to be so awed by her high-mindedness, that I was happy to keep her in her privileged position.

My last visit was with Mariette. After so many indistinguishable, stupid faces, and especially after Mme Doudelette's bloated face, it was a joy to finally see hers— innocent but marked by harsh experience—with its simple, wholesome look, and giving an overwhelming impression of candor and courage.

When I came into the room she was half asleep. Because of the heat, her woolen blanket was pushed down to the foot of the bed. The sheet barely hid her young body at rest. Looking at this body, barely saved from death, I felt pity for its uncertain future. I wanted to protect her, to take away all pain, all unhappiness forever.

She probably read some of the tenderness and pity in my eyes when I tapped quietly on the glass panel of the door and woke her. For a few seconds she had the softly astonished look of the convalescent, but as soon as she recognized me, she gave me a smile full of confidence, a young, free smile that put dimples in the corners of her mouth.

I looked first at the temperature chart at the foot of the bed. Mariette was watching me; she suddenly became serious again.

"Ninety-nine point five," I announced, "like this morning."

I noticed the panic in her eyes, and added quickly:

"In this heat and for an evening temperature—it's good that it isn't higher."

Immediately she became peaceful again. She even smiled, and, like a happy little girl, she cried:

"Then, mam'selle, you still promise that I can leave in three days?"

I promised again very formally, since convalescents can never be too happy. The same thought made me ask her without even thinking:

"When you leave the hospital, where will you go for a rest?"

Mariette seemed amazed by the question.

"Home," she finally answered. "To our room at the boarding house!"

Her voice implied: where do you expect me to go? And she looked so astonished and so sweet that I gulped:

"Would you like to come with me to the country? I'm going to visit my mother in Normandy in three days."

For a few seconds Mariette was dumfounded. Emotion and gratitude seemed to have taken away her voice, or else she didn't quite understand what she had just heard. Out! . . . Out in three days! No more bed, no more fever, shots, hard mattress, and damp pillow! A summer dress again, the outdoors, the sun on her face—all that was wonderful enough! But, by some miracle, there would be even more—the green of forests and meadows, white clouds blown by the wind through a limitless sky—things so marvelous and vast that she didn't even dare imagine them yet! ... And suddenly, she finally understood and started to clap her hands like a child, and burst into a radiant smile.

When this explosion of joy had calmed down, I explained to her that my internship would be over in two or three days at the latest and that I'd promised my mother to spend a few days with her before looking for a job as a summer replacement for a doctor to earn some money during July and August.

Mariette listened to me so seriously that I was really touched. I asked her:

"Did you see *Nez de Cuir* at the movies?"

"Oh! Yes, mam'selle. With Jean Marais. He had on a mask, but you could recognize him anyway. He was still very handsome ..."

"Well! My mother lives in the Ouche country near the place where they filmed *Nez de Cuir*."

"Does she live in a castle too?" Mariette exclaimed, wholly carried away by her imagination.

"No, not in a castle. My mother is a widow living on a very small pension. She lives in a house that she inherited from a brother of hers who died last winter. Since my mother hadn't been on speaking terms with him for a very long time, I've never been to his house and I don't have any idea what it's like. My mother moved there from Louviers this spring. It's not very big, but I know it has a yard."

"I could sunbathe?"

Mariette looked at me, her face brimming over with plans for the country—walks, and swimming, and picnics.

At one point she stopped, to take a sip of lemonade. She grimaced slightly as she swallowed.

"What's the matter?" I asked.

"Nothing," Mariette answered quickly. "It's my wisdom tooth. When I get out, I'll have to go to the dentist."

I went to fetch a tongue depressor. Opening her mouth, Mariette made another face. I found the culprit and examined the gums, but I noticed nothing abnormal there or in her throat.

"Good!" I concluded. "An aspirin if it hurts during the night, and tomorrow I'll ask someone from the dentistry department to take a look at you." I gave her a slight, reassuring tap on the cheek to let her know that I didn't think the pain was anything important.

"Now I'm going to say good night. When your husband comes to see you, ask him whether it's all right with him if you come with me."

She looked very serious.

"He's sure to say yes, because I'll enjoy it. He's been so worried about me for the last five days. He says that all that happened is his fault. He wanted to ask my forgiveness but I wouldn't let him, because you promised me that I could have children in spite of the miscarriage. Then he told me 'You'll see, everything will be better when you get out of the hospital. We'll save our money and as soon as we can move out of the boarding house, we'll have another child.'"

Her eyes were shining. She smiled with all the sweetness of her gentle soul, smiled at her fate, her duties, her worries, her love. And she repeated, "He's sure to say yes, and then I can come and rest at your house. The two of us get along so well together!"

Since Lachaux wasn't dining in, I ate some fruit in my room, despite Anna's protests: she thinks I'm on a diet to stay thin, and predicts the direst consequences.

Then I worked a little on my thesis. This turned my thoughts back to Arlette. Why had I replied in such a complicated way when she was about to leave, since I didn't want to answer her question thoroughly? I could have said, very simply, "The only certainty is in my profession, well done, and in everyday work."

That would have been enough of an explanation for my stubborn perseverence.

Midnight

"No! It's not possible! It isn't possible!" But it's useless to keep repeating the words I write on the unprotesting page, as if they were a protest or an exorcism—nothing keeps my reason from facing the unavoidable evidence: Mariette has postabortion tetanus. For the last few minutes I've known that Mariette has almost a fifty-fifty chance of dying.

Around ten o'clock I turned off my light, but I couldn't fall asleep. My head ached. Was I going to have this exhausting insomnia forever? My eyes stared into the darkness and I thought about how soft the nights in Normandy would be. I imagined Mariette in her room, lying and staring at the ceiling like me, unable to sleep because she was too happy. She had smiled so happily when she heard my invitation! And how enthusiastic she'd been—the little city child planning her country adventures! Talking about her plans had made her so breathless she had to take a drink. Amused, I remembered her graceful gesture toward the night table to take the glass of lemonade. But at the same time, I thought of the little painful grimace when she drank. Then I felt a hesitant, uncertain anxiety which changed slowly to an awful, imprecise foreboding: a diagnosis which my mind still refused to accept. . . .

For a moment my brain was still; then, with a sudden click, the medical reflex came into play: the pain and the difficulty in swallowing was not an accidental wisdom tooth, it was lockjaw, and the first sign of it in a casualty or in a woman who has had an abortion makes you suspect the onset of tetanus.

That's the evidence; that's the logic. What sort of emotional blindness could have made me misunderstand it? No doubt Mariette's happiness had misled me. The diagnosis was obvious, but deep inside me I refused to accept it—the first of the refusals that have been pursuing me for an hour. . . . At that point I couldn't definitely discount all hope of having made a mistake. I kept repeating to myself; in medicine you can never be sure!

But at the same time in the back of my mind I felt the wave of horror become more and more precise and sure. If I still obstinately refused to deny its reality, it was because there's a moment when the spirit has to rebel in the face of a great injustice.

I couldn't rest. I got up, turned on my light again and opened a medical textbook to the chapter: "Tetanus." The text was coldly precise: before you can eliminate a diagnosis of tetanus, you must review the other causes of spasm of the jaw muscles: arthritis of the jaw bone, tonsillitis, impacted wisdom tooth, inflammation of the bone and the gums of the lower jaw.

Now that I was alert to the possibility of tetanus, it was my duty to reexamine Mariette. I got dressed again. As I passed Lachaux's door, I almost knocked, then I remembered that neither he nor Pascali was sleeping in the dorm tonight.

In the main building the air was heavy and oppressive. Avoiding the wards, I went directly to the office.

In the office, the night nurse—a volunteer—was knitting, and without stopping to explain I told her that I was going to room Number Three. Only the night lights were burning in the corridor.

Mariette's room was dark. From the door, I could only vaguely make out the bed, but a slight sigh in the shadows showed that Mariette was asleep. For a few seconds, I hesitated to cross the threshold. . . . But behind me I heard above the snoring from the wards, a rapid click of heels, then the noise of the electric switch. The whole corridor was lit up immediately. The night nurse had put aside her knitting; now she was on guard.

Mariette woke with a start, sat up and put a hand to her eyes; the nurse was already there and had turned on the overhead light. Mariette, disheveled and weak with sleep, looked at me, vaguely surprised. I made my voice as natural as I could and explained:

"I was just passing by. I wanted to say good night to you."

Then I added kindly, "It's very hot in your room. I bet you're thirsty and would like something to drink."

I filled her glass with lemonade and offered it to her. She took it with both hands, the way a child grasps its cup, and started to drink, immediately she made the same face as in the afternoon. After three or four swallows, she put the glass down, saying:

"It hurts when I swallow. . . ."

Then she put her hands to her neck. Two teardrops shone in her eyes and she looked as if she was about to burst into sobs. It was an effort to ask:

"Does it hurt more than this afternoon?"

"Yes," she answered, sniffing back her tears.

"And did the chewing bother you this evening when you were eating?"

"Yes, a little."

"Good!" I concluded, smiling reassuringly. "We'll have to take another look at that naughty wisdom tooth."

I asked for the flashlight and a tongue depressor and I reexamined the teeth, the gums, the throat, and palpated the glands without discovering anything. After each test, I saw with consternation that another chance to find a symptom which would count out tetanus had disappeared. Then I made Mariette lie down flat in bed, and put my hand softly under her neck.

"That's funny," she said, "since I took that drink, my tongue feels prickly and my mouth tastes like pepper."

And, as I tried to flex her neck, she instantly added the words I was afraid to hear:

"Your hand hurts me."

My world trembled. No more possible doubt! My vague horror had become a certainty, a reality, a horror which could only be called tetanus.

The stiffness of the neck, the peppery taste in the mouth—these two symptoms had changed everything. They had just liberated the forces of evil: now, large and menacing, they prowled around the room. They, not the night air, were moving the curtains as they passed.

I leaned against the head of the bed for a few moments, incapable of saying a word, feeling the horror growing inside me. What saved me was Mariette's look—like a frightened little school girl—and her anxious eyes watching me under the hair that stuck to her forehead. All at once I recovered the convincing tone, the patient words, the reasonable, deceptive arguments I'd used so often—though I never put so much tenderness and pity into them as during this horrible night.

I leaned over Mariette and kissed her good night quickly before I left her—alone again in the humid night, alone with her destiny, poor passionate little soul, so full of love and so close, maybe, to death.

Outside the building I had to lean against the door to get some air. A faint wind had come up. The shadow around the maternity clinic had the sweet heady smell of the linden trees. The sky was deep blue and perfectly clear. But this evening, what could even the most beautiful summer night mean to me?

I started toward the dormitory, and as I walked, I reviewed every sign which I had noted, evaluating them, comparing them. They were all classic and all pointed to a diagnosis of tetanus. With one exception—the peppery prickling of the tongue. That sign must have struck me because it's not usually described in the textbooks. Where had I read about it?

As I went up the stairs, I thought I remembered the reference. I pushed open the door and turned on the light in a small room. There, piled up on open shelves, is a disorderly mixture of incomplete packets of periodicals and old medical texts which makes up the dormitory library.

I had to go through dusty piles of periodicals and dig among heaps of books before I finally found the book I was looking for under an encyclopedia. I recognized it at once by its gray cover and its frontispiece—a golden hourglass on a red circle. That was the sign the editor had chosen for the cover of *Fatal Abortions* by Professor Henri Mondor.

I drew a chair up to the table and cleared a space among the jumble of papers that littered it. I found the passage immediately. This book was where I had read about the small, rarely noticed symptom that Mariette had pointed out. Professor Mondor underlined its diagnostic interest because it appears very early.

Then, leafing through the pages, I reread the description of a typical tetanus case. "The patient's intelligence is not affected, but she answers questions with difficulty—she speaks through clenched teeth, she points to her throat, which feels as if it has been caught in a vise, she complains of an insatiable thirst. The head seems nailed to the pillow; breathing is uneven. The face has a fixed, sardonic, frightened expression; the upper body is rigid, the arms are bent and immobile, thighs and legs are stretched out rigidly ..." The description noted that this patient, a woman of twenty-one, died less than forty-eight hours after entering the hospital.

I also reread the description of the incredibly painful attacks, the contractions that arch the body from head to toe, choking the victim and then leaving him exhausted, covered with sweat and all the more frightened because he's fully aware that these paroxysms are serious and that their continual repetition must be dangerous for him.

Leafing through the book, I found the descriptions of sudden death from intrauterine injections of soapy water, of ether, of alcohol, potassium chloride, of bleach, of petroleum, from the embolisms, perforations, gangrene, abscesses, peritonitis, hemorrhages, liver and kidney infections, and the blood poisoning which can follow attempts at abortion. I'd noted down all of them for my thesis.

This evening, I found death on almost every page of that terrifying book: young women dying painful, horrible deaths, all described with impassive brutality in sentences deliberately stripped of emotion. But, faced with so many desperate, inoperable cases, the surgeon himself was obviously dismayed. And how could I avoid flinching as he must have flinched when, in spite of that dry, clinical style, he had to catalogue the incredible tools that were used. He mentioned hairpins, knitting needles, fountain pens, glass tubes, curtain rods, wooden sticks, wire, syringes, umbrella ribs, scissors, cherry tree branches, chicken thigh-bones, pincers, toothpicks, ears of wheat and children's forks. And this doesn't include the unhappy women who swallow poisonous mixtures or drugs to make the intrauterine devices more efficient.

I looked at the book's publication date: 1935; well before the miracle of antibiotics, artificial kidneys and the vast advances in medicine and surgery. Yet women who have had abortions still die, and according to the most recent statistics, Mariette's chances of being saved were only a little better than her chances of dying.

I felt too weak to get up but I leaned my chair against the library shelf to keep my eyes from those haunting pages. The window was closed and it was very hot in the little room. My mouth was dry. I felt I was chewing on a bitter herb made up of abortion and death.

Sunk over the notebook, I closed my eyes against the light. I felt drunk with exhaustion; sweating, but chilled. I was caught in a heavy fog. My brain seemed to be on the table next to the book with its descriptions of postabortive cases, its drawings, its color photographs, its statistics. In my head there was nothing but a nauseating dizziness. I wanted to cry; and I wanted not to go to bed and not to go to sleep as long as Mariette was in danger.

Saturday, 1 p.m.

Back in my room in the middle of the night, I finally fell asleep. I woke up around nine, stiff all over. My head was empty, and I felt sickeningly unhappy.

I got dressed quickly and ran over to the maternity ward.

Pascali had just arrived. He was dressed in his white coat, chatting with the supervisor in the corridor before going up to the operating room.

As soon as he saw me, he gave me a big friendly wave—an invitation to come closer. He obviously wanted to talk to me.

"Hey, Claude! You were telling me the other day that you'd like to strangle certain mothers-in-law because of the pleasure they get from frightening their daughters-in-law during pregnancy. Well! After what I tell you you'll be sorry you're not Congolese. I had dinner last night with a friend who's just back from the Upper Congo. It seems that there the old tradition of serving the mother of the bride as a roast for the wedding dinner hasn't entirely disappeared!"

But he could see by my look that, even to please him, I didn't feel at all like joking this morning. Suddenly he asked me kindly, "What's the matter? Trouble?"

I dragged him into the supervisor's office and explained the diagnosis I made during the night. He became serious at once.

"Wow!" he said, "Postabortion tetanus! Damn it! And only a five-day incubation period ... that may be bad. Let's go and see!"

Mariette was awake.

"Well, how's that wisdom tooth? Dr. Pascali and I are going to take a look at it," I announced gaily on the doorstep, as if a brief look could only be a good sign.

But at the same time I was scared to see that Mariette's face looked stiff and contracted. She hadn't had that look last night. There was a wrinkle of tiredness in her smile.

Chatting and joking with Mariette, Pascali began his careful examination.

The die was cast; I was no longer torn between the terror of truth and the frenzy of hope; so, in spite of myself I yielded to a doctor's curiosity and admired Pascali's dexterity, his gentleness, the precision of the gestures he made to avoid bringing on a spasm, and his way of uncovering and touching the patient without moving her.

Finished with his inspection, Pascali gave Mariette a big smile and stated, just as if the examination hadn't revealed anything out of the ordinary:

"Perfect! We'll talk to Mademoiselle Sauvage about the fastest way to get you well again."

We went back to the supervisor's office and without noticing that he had left me a hard chair, Pascali settled down in the easy chair. He looked worried.

"It's tetanus. The jaw muscles, the base of the tongue and the neck are already affected; the muscles of the face, back and abdomen are going to follow suit."

He scratched his cheek thoughtfully before explaining:

"Tetanus is a dirty business. I know it well! I was a medical student at the Claude-Bernard Hospital. That's where they have that great team of specialists. They've managed to reduce the fatality from eighty to forty per cent, but the modern tetanus treatment is really a bother. It has to be watched constantly."

In a few seconds he added, annoyed:

"Those girls are terrible. Worse than bitches in heat! They let anyone knock them up, and afterwards—the knitting needle, the soapy water or the probe.... Why in hell did *she* have to have an abortion?"

I didn't let him go on. I knew what he was going to say, or at least I had heard him talking about his theories before. According to him the female body is both an instrument of pleasure and capital to be exploited, and all pleasure, like all exploitation in a capitalist society involves a risk. For women that risk is the child. And it's just too bad for them! I didn't want him to talk in that odious way about Mariette, because I knew she had no low curiosity about pleasure and risk—Mariette, so forthright, who didn't play cynical games of chance, who had responded without calculation to the burst of her love. If there was anyone who was innocent, who had to be saved at any price, surely it was she!

So I cried, almost violently: "I'll take care of her case."

Pascali was astonished. He said, "It'll take ten days, fifteen days, maybe longer to get her out of this mess. Morizet will be back tomorrow night, and you told me that you planned to leave immediately after his return."

"There's no hurry. I'll stay as long as I'm needed."

"Fine. Let's get going, then," Pascali said.

Then he outlined the treatment to the supervising nurse: antibiotics, cortisone, tranquilizers to reduce the strength of the tetanus spasms, and also the different dosages of antitetanus serum which the pharmacy would have to prepare every day.

"Check pulse and blood pressure every hour," he ended. "It's essential to prevent heart failure. Remember this, supervisor."

"I'll take care of it," I said without leaving her time to answer.

Pascali agreed to this with a smile, then added:

"You'll also have to see to the arrangement of the room: shades permanently down and blue paint on the window to avoid light. If possible, no noise. It might cause an attack. O.K.?"

"Yes, Dr. Pascali," answered the supervisor.

"With this," he added for my benefit, "I think we'll have done the best we can for the moment. And hope we can avoid a tracheotomy. It's unlikely."

Pascali realized how upset I was. He added:

"Come on! Don't worry. If we all work together, we'll get her out of it."

His look and his voice were warm but he added, as an excuse to leave me alone:

"I've got to go to work now. A sensational cancer of the uterus that I'm stealing from my boss before he gets back. Enlarged total hysterectomy with removal of the ganglions. What a treat!"

He'd immediately taken up the rather bloodthirsty tone he uses when he talks about operations. He left. The supervisor was called into the ward. I was alone ... I sat motionless in my chair for a moment, to catch my breath. The familiar office with its everyday surroundings was very reassuring.

Then I went back to Mariette. At the door I met her glance. She watched me uneasily, and I felt a great need for action and a desperate desire for devotion to her rising within me.

As I came close to her bed, Mariette told me unhappily, "You see, mam'selle! Because of that tooth, the fever has gone up again. Am I going to have to stay here much longer now?"

She was speaking with some difficulty; one corner of her mouth was slightly pulled up.

No doubt it takes years of medical practice to develop complete impassivity. Mariette looked at me with gratitude and hope, with a kind of limitless trust. I wanted to lower my eyes and refuse that undeserved and crushing gift of faith. But I was supposed to act as if I hadn't even seen it. And I was even supposed to pretend that nothing was wrong! I needed time to be able to talk in an unworried voice with a natural air, so I took her wrist and pretended to take her pulse. But in spite of myself, my eyes examined the shape of her legs under the sheet. For the moment they were at rest, supple and alive. But soon I might see them rigidly contorted, like those of a criminal on the rack.

Letting go of her wrist, I finally answered:

"We must be sensible and put off your discharge for a few days; besides, I too have to delay my departure. None of our plans will be changed."

Mariette's smile took on the softness of the last few days and she cried with a heartrending rush of gratitude, "Oh, thank you for waiting for me, mam'selle!"

Just as I was about to finish my lie, the supervisor came into the room with the apparatus for taking the blood samples that Pascali had ordered.

Seeing the needle and the rubber tourniquet, Mariette turned pale and drew back from the apparatus.

"Ah, a patient who wants to get well without having tests," I said, smiling. "Come on! Be brave. A little prick of the needle—that doesn't take very long!"

Mariette extended her arm courageously. I put the tourniquet in place, found the vein, dabbed it with alcohol, and slipped in the needle. Frothy and red, the blood gushed into the test tube. I was happy to have to use my hands, to have something specific to do.

After the blood samples were taken, I stayed near her bed. On her way out, the supervisor had left the tranquilizers prescribed by Pascali on the night table. Mariette took them obediently, and then to quiet her I started to talk softly about our vacation, about *Nez de Cuir*, about the Ouche scenery, about walks we'd take together to explore the village and the countryside which I didn't know myself.

She listened to me, her hands neatly crossed on the sheet, like a good little girl listening to a story. She was smiling and kept interrupting me to ask naïve questions that showed she was combining in her imagination the promises I made her yesterday with a marvelous future just a few days away.

I knew that it would take her some time to fall asleep even with the help of the drugs. I wanted to stay with her and accompany her to the edge of the shadows. But the consultation nurse was worried because I was late and came to call me to my duties. I had to leave Mariette with a promise that I would come back very soon.

This was the morning devoted to problems of sterility. In the consultation room, next to the examination table, the recording drum of the insufflation apparatus loomed over the large nickeled box full of probes, specula and forceps. This machine helped me discover whether the

103

tubes were open. It was my main working tool this morning.

But today the sterility seemed to be more in my own head than in my patients' bellies. I quickly called in the first one and asked her the usual questions: "How old are you. How long have you been having sexual relations? How are your periods? . . ." I recorded the answers mechanically. I had the feeling that someone else was doing the writing, and that my mind was still in Mariette's room. The only thought that I managed to form was bitterly ironic: "I have to listen to these women who cannot have children and help them become mothers. I do this with the full approval of medical authority and of the law. But if they came in to tell me that they were pregnant and wanted to have an abortion, in spite of their distress and the dangers implicit in all abortions, I'd have to stand before them with my arms crossed, as if I were made of stone. And it's even more illogical that though Mariette wanted a child with all her heart, circumstances led her to acts which may prevent her from ever becoming pregnant a second time even if she survives the tetanus.

During this morning's consultation period, everything kept reminding me of Mariette. The first patient, a young matron of thirty-five, bright and pleasant, explained to me that her husband is a foreman and makes a good living; they have a comfortable small apartment, and a car. If they only had a child their happiness would be complete. So she came to ask me about her chances.

After her, an engaged couple of eighteen and twenty-two came in. They had read in a magazine that one out of five couples is sterile. Before they got married, they wanted to be sure they weren't. They're more fortunate than Mariette—they'll have lodgings where they can easily keep their baby.

The next patient was a Frenchwoman married to an Arab. I've been treating her over a period of several months. During her first visit, when she uncovered her pubis I saw that it had been plucked bare, and I thought that she'd recently had an abdominal operation. She explained that this was a Mohammedan custom she followed to please her husband. But, she added, her sterility—which for an Arab is a real sin—puts her in danger of being repudiated. Before I started a long and delicate series of treatments for the woman, I wanted to determine if the incapacity to produce children might not be the partner's fault. But she was terrified at the idea of her husband's fury—he would be enraged if he thought he was being accused of sterility because of impotence—and she begged me not to call him in; she was ready to undergo any treatment, no matter how painful. So I started to treat her, but so far without results.

This morning I'd given appointments to two husbands; the man is responsible for a third of all sterility cases. They came in. Neither was a Moslem, but confronted with doubts about their virility, they each immediately reacted with the same offended pride. In both cases, the husband's insufficiency was unquestionable. This further complicated my task; announcing to a man that he's the one who's "guilty" for the infertility of the couple means risking throwing him into profound depression and destroying his masculinity. But both of these husbands had come swaggering in so conceitedly, and each one was so sure of his reputation as a "strong" man; and then they were so nasty about accepting the evidence, that I was tempted to crush their vanity at a single stroke. One of them—as if his male dignity had been outraged—had a thousand excuses for not submitting to a simple sperm test. I had to apply real moral blackmail by insisting that his refusal would mean imposing a painful examintion—I even lied and said it was very dangerous—on his wife. During the whole negotiation, I kept thinking of Mariette, whose husband had left the entire responsibility and all the dangers of her abortion on her shoulders. Always the same male egotism! Just as I was about to lose my patience, the husband finally made up his mind. Happily for him and for me! I was so exasperated that I was ready to describe my diagnosis about his virility with real brutality in spite of the risk of causing castration fears: from the marital point of view he deserved it, but medically I didn't have the right to give him such a shock.

Then I had to listen to a young woman of twenty-five. She was pretty and very coy. After a certain amount of reticence, she admitted that she was afraid she couldn't make her "friend" marry her unless she got pregnant. I didn't push my psychological inquiry any further: her desire for motherhood was only a social pretext; it would be a kind of blackmail for her lover, who might well be trying to get away from her. Probably this young woman's sterility represents a subconscious refusal of a pregnancy that she simultaneously fears and desires. I'm sure that if

Lachaux had questioned her, this would have been his analytic explanation. Who can deny that this unspoken fear of pregnancy might provoke a nervous spasm or a glandular irregularity that would make conception impossible?

I made the young woman lie down on the examination table. I introduced a catheter connected to the insufflation machine by a rubber tube into her uterus. The examination technique is very simple and altogether painless: you inject carbon dioxide gas into the uterus under a certain degree of pressure; if it comes out through the tubes, you have proof that they are open and that no obstacle to conception exists. I started the machine. On the drum where the pressure registers, the needle indicated an obstinately ascending line: the carbon dioxide couldn't pass through the tubes.

I didn't like this young woman, who wanted a child only as a way to blackmail a man into marriage—no more than I liked the other women who explain: "It's my husband's family—they want an heir," as if they wanted to produce that son they ask me for not for themselves but for someone else.

But slowly, as I studied the curves recorded by the machine and completed my observations, my thoughts left Mariette. Professional interest caught me up once more. I felt the need to speak to my patients again—I know the value of talking to these women from experience. Some months ago I had a real triumph when a patient who had been sterile for three years became pregnant after only one conversation. Perhaps it was chance. But I'd rather think that she understood that I was ready to help her. She stopped thinking about herself as the victim of some unavoidable fate and her confidence in herself changed everything.

That success made me optimistic about curing sterility. Paradoxically it also taught me to be stubborn and patient. I don't leave it to others to carry out the examinations and treatments. It takes me a great deal of time to do it myself but it gives me the opportunity to talk to my patients as much as I should.

Though this was the last session of my internship at Gennevilliers, I didn't want to tell my regular patients. I don't know what I'll be doing in the fall, but I gave them appointments for late September anyway, and told them that the next two months they'll be lucky even without treatment.

And I was telling the truth: all specialists know that September is a fertile month, and agree that the effects of fresh air, sun and relaxation are very beneficial for the sterile couples who can afford a vacation.

And I didn't want it to look as if I was stopping treatment of any of the patients who put their faith in me because it might spoil their chances.

There's one patient especially that I'd have loved to pronounce cured this morning. Apparently she's sterile because of an infection caused by an abortion. I've been treating her for several months without results. How wonderful it would have been to hear the bubbling sounds of the carbon dioxide passing through the tubes on my last try; if the young woman could have told me with tears of joy in her eyes that she had a slight pain in the shoulder—a definite sign of victory! But this morning her injured belly was still silent. I closed her file optimistically. It seemed to me that classifying her as a definitive failure would have meant closing Mariette's file as well.

I'm sure that after I've been in practice for several years, I'll have to close some files when I've exhausted all the resources of science. It must be painful to do that, because a woman anxious to become a mother and a gynecologist worthy of the title don't accept defeat easily.

I went back to Mariette. She seemed to be sleeping. I put my hand lightly on her forehead. As if she'd been waiting for me to come back, she half opened her eyes and gave me a look of recognition. In spite of the drugs, she managed a grateful little smile. Then her lids fluttered a few times and closed again. For a few minutes she seemed to be struggling to wake up—but finally she succumbed peacefully.

A little later, I took her pulse and recorded it. It was my first official act of treatment and I did it almost religiously. Then I lifted her arm and tied on the armband of the blood pressure machine. She didn't wake up.

From now on I wouldn't have to worry about my lies, or about inventing stories that would only be contradicted by the facts later on. But I'm mainly relieved for Mariette's sake. Thanks to the sedatives, she'll never know that atrocious, unending rhythm: spasm after spasm and in between them the fearful anticipation of the next.

And I wouldn't have to be frightened by her locked jaws, or lips rimmed with whitish foam, or the sardonic grin of tetanus. I wouldn't have to see her hands tensed into claws, her forearms arched back, or her entire body tensed to the breaking point from neck to toes.

From now on Mariette's eyes will be closed, I won't have to see them as the only lucid and living part in a mask of convulsive grimaces. They won't stare out at me, begging and despairing.

8:30 p.m.

I've just finished eating dinner in the dining room, alone at the large table. Anna told me that Pascali was called on an emergency, and I swallowed a few mouthfuls without waiting for him. I wasn't hungry.

I spent the entire afternoon at Mariette's bedside. It wasn't like last night anymore. I didn't feel the bewilderment of the helpless onlooker, or even the sensation of the young soldier afraid of how he'll behave under fire. Now, thanks to Pascali, the chaos has been made into order and it can be subdivided into precise actions, and I feel passionately devoted to my task. I'll have to make no mistakes, neglect nothing, and fight. . . .

During the meals in the interns' dining room, you get fined if you talk about medicine. When I came to lunch, Pascali was sitting down at the table. He winked at me pleasantly—his way of asking, "How are things?" Right after the meal, he came with me to look at Mariette. He wanted to give me more precise instructions, and insert a catheter.

I watched him make an incision in the tender skin near the hollow of the elbow. He found a large vein and opened it with a delicate stroke of the scalpel. Then he inserted a thin tube, pushing it gently up the vein till it reached the armpit.

"With a catheter firmly in place," he explained to me, "we'll be able to inject the medicine more quickly."

Then he helped me set up an intravenous glucose drip and left me, saying he'd be back later that afternoon.

Now I was alone. The shade was completely closed, but at that hour of the day the sun was beating directly against the wall. Mariette lay on her bed surrounded by a blinding whiteness—the white of the sheets, the ceiling, and the shadowless walls.

She hadn't moved, even during Pascali's minor operation. The light streamed in through the window to light

108

up her face and put the familiar highlights on the curve of her lips. It was as if nothing had changed since the time when she'd still been able to smile at me.

But her sleep was no longer a childish romp among beautiful dreams. Mariette was sleeping in a drugged stupor. Her forehead was damp with sweat. Was she going to die in the flower of her youth because of a few bacteria on a dirty probe? Less than twenty-four hours ago I asked her, "Would you like to come to the country with me?" I felt as if I'd just spoken that sentence, but now it was lost irretrievably in the past. Now that Mariette was drifting further and further away in the deep waters of infection and fever, could I do anything but shout to her from the shore, "I don't want you to die!" Or even more childishly, "Let's go back to yesterday. Let's pick up our plans where we left off!" as if my own fate would be decided at that instant.

I stood by the bed, frozen into immobility by my sorrow. Then I shook myself. I had to do something to overcome my feeling of helplessness. I started to fix up her chart; to prepare the observation sheets and the graphs where I'd note the results of my examinations.

Next I wrote down the first figures for blood pressure and temperature (which I'd just taken). Both were satisfactory and the activity reassured me a little. Pascali said that you get the highest percentage of tetanus cures in postabortion cases, and I know he's right.

The ward orderly arrived in the middle of the afternoon, carrying a ladder and a pot of blue paint. He started to paint over the window.

When he'd finished and I was alone again, I started to feel vaguely afraid. The little room seemed different now. Under the bluish light reflected from the walls, it suddenly felt as if it had been invaded by night, by the unknown, by a thousand possible dangers. Suddenly the silence was heavier, thicker—almost funereal. But nearby, on the other side of the closed door, the thousands of noises of everyday activity continued as usual, in spite of the orders that had been given for silence and the constant reminders of the supervisor. They might be silly or stupid, but they were the noises of life—noises made by other patients: moving, gossiping, talking in the wards in spite of the heat. Only Mariette and I were living in this semidarkness, with its atmosphere of suffocating heaviness that increased our isolation.

It was almost 7 p.m. when Pascali returned. His first gesture was to switch on the overhead light. Then while he was looking at the figures marked on the charts, he asked me what I'd noticed during my watch. Then he examined Mariette.

Seen in bright light, her face seemed changed to me. It didn't look as peaceful as it had at the beginning of the afternoon. The lips, drawn slightly back at the sides, had assumed an expression of indifference, almost of disdain.

Very lightly, Pascali touched first the arms, then the abdomen and the thighs. Each time it was easy to see the muscles contract under his fingers. I looked at him uneasily. He thought a minute, then said, "It's all right for the moment. Our little sedative cocktail seems to be working. There are contractions, but as you can see, they're still feeble. Respiration is good. The diaphragm and the intercostal muscles are functioning well. What more can we hope for? But be careful—don't force the dosages. Otherwise there might be danger of shock."

He fell silent, looked again at Mariette, then added with some regret, "All the same, tomorrow morning we'll have to do a tracheotomy."

And seeing my sudden disquiet, he said, "Don't panic. In tetanus, a tracheotomy is just a precaution. After that, there's no worry of a breathing accident."

He switched off the light and we were back in the twilight. I felt as if I were under water.

"Soothing but not exactly cheerful, all that blue," he said. "Come out for some fresh air."

I refused.

"Oh, come on!" he insisted gently. "You've probably let yourself in for ten days of living like a bat in a cave. You don't think you can go that long without sleeping or eating?"

I wanted to be alone for a little while before making the effort of pulling myself together. I promised to join him for dinner. . . .

After a quick dinner—I ate alone beccause Pascali was operating—I've just taken a shower to get myself in shape. I've chosen some books so that I can try to get some work done while I'm on watch tonight. Anna filled a thermos bottle—the same one I used when I was cramming for exams—with very strong coffee, and I swallowed two amphetamine tablets. Now I'm all ready for this first night's watch with Mariette.

I stayed with Mariette until visiting hours so that her husband could talk to me. He arrived in the midst of the stampede of all the visiting relatives invading the wards. Startled by the darkness, he hesitated on the threshold for a moment. He probably thought that he had the wrong room, or maybe he was just afraid to come in. He's known since yesterday that his wife's condition is serious, but knowing isn't seeing.

After taking a few steps into the room, he suddenly noticed the rubber drain that pierced Mariette's throat resting on its white square of bandage. He moaned a little, as if he felt the pain in his own throat. "What's the matter, mam'selle? Is it very serious?"

His eyes were searching mine, compelling me to answer. They were full of terror, but he was eager to know. Mariette's husband was largely responsible for this disaster, and because of his original selfishness he deserves to share the burden of anxiety and guilt. I almost told him the bare truth without softening it at all. But my glance fell on Mariette. She looked so vulnerable in the shadow—with her mutilated throat she looked like the victim of a holocaust. She'd accepted everything from the beginning. She was still offering herself as the sole sacrifice for the happiness of the two of them, and if she hadn't been asleep under the influence of the drug, she would have lied out of tenderness. She'd have denied all the possible dangers; would have denied her anxiety and her suffering. She would have forced her face into a smile—and the tetanus would have turned her smile into a grimace of pain. I didn't have the courage to be severe with that man. He's so much like all men, but he's found a kind of dignity by being the object of such boundless love.

Just as Pascali had done for me, I started to explain to him that this tracheotomy was nothing serious, that it was merely a supplementary precaution. I invented explanations, I reassured him, and when I left him sitting at the foot of the bed, though his face was expressionless and dazed, hope hadn't completely left him.

Guessing that this second afternoon would be difficult after a night on watch, Lachaux came to spend a moment

111

with me. He too examined Mariette, and looked at the results of the first doses of the drugs. He seemed optimistic.

But after chatting softly with me for a few minutes, he excused himself. He couldn't stay any longer. He had to visit his family. He promised to come by again later in the evening.

So I was alone, facing a long afternoon that would drag on and on in that stuffy, humid semidarkness. The blue light only gave the room an imaginary freshness.

I had borrowed a comfortable armchair from the office. I installed it in one corner of the room and I put a little table next to it with a portable lamp that shines only on my papers. Before I got down to work, I took Mariette's blood pressure and pulse. I wiped the sweat off her forehead and cheeks and brushed away the whitish saliva that had dried at the edges of her mouth. I checked the vaporizer. Whistling softly, it keeps the opening of the drain moist. I also checked the drain.

Rouzeau, the ear, nose and throat intern, was called in this morning by Pascali. He came in at about nine with his instruments. He removed the pillow so he could see Mariette's neck more clearly. She was deeply asleep. He daubed the soft, downy skin with iodine, then took a scalpel and put the point of the blade on her throat. I turned my head slightly so I wouldn't have to see the incision in the skin, or the blood gushing from that tender flesh, or the instrument cutting the trachea.

Rouzeau is very skillful. Almost immediately I heard the whistling sound that indicated the opening of the trachea. When I looked again the tube was already in place and Rouzeau was cleaning up the blood from the wound.

A little later, Pascali arrived with a respirator and taught me how to use it. He showed me how to suction mucous material, which would interfere with the tube's functioning, from the opening.

"But," he cautioned, "don't try to do a deep tracheo-bronchial suction. It's difficult. Call me and I'll take care of it. You have to know how to do it and even if you're used to doing it, you can cause cardiac arrest."

After he left, I renewed the fluid in the atomizer regularly. In this ovenlike atmosphere, according to Pascali, you have to be sure that the bronchi are receiving constant humidification. In the course of the afternoon I also did three superficial suctions.

112

That was all that I could contribute to the tragic battle, the struggle between germs and healthy cells, the fight against death that my mind still refuses to accept—especially when I remember how young Mariette is.

And yet, maybe because of the wound in her throat, the drug-induced stupor she lay in looked more like death than the sweetness of sleep. (Yesterday afternoon, when he finished his work, the ward orderly looked at Mariette sleeping and said, "That was a beautiful kid!" as if she were already dead.)

I stayed by her bed for a long time. Those closed eyes, those features tinted blue by the light reflected from the walls, that forehead shining with sweat—what agony on a summer night.

Pascali came by at about five o'clock. He knocked softly on the door before he came in. "I was afraid that you might be asleep in your tent!" he whispered to me, laughing.

I was astonished to see how much pleasure those few friendly words and his laughter gave me—that showed me how exhausted I already was after one night and two days of watching over Mariette.

Pascali examined her and said that he was satisfied with the balance sheet: the same level of contractions, good cardiovascular state. Nonetheless, he thought it would be wise to undertake a deep bronchial suction before the night. He opened the apparatus, and delicately inserted a thin probe in the tube. Once more I admired his skill and the elegant precision of each of his movements.

"There!" he said, well satisfied, as he shut off the current.

It seemed to me that his voice didn't express vanity about the success of a delicate operation, but real contentment about a cure that was beginning well.

I was happy when he sat down in my easy chair to test it for comfort and even happier to hear him tell me about his day on duty.

Morizet, he explained to me, had arrived late that morning, half a day late and dead-tired because his car had broken down. Pascali had offered to take over his duties till tomorrow.

"Haven't even had time to shave yet!" he said, rubbing his hand over his black stubble.

Then he got up and said kindly:

"Can I take you away? You'll have just enough time to

drink something cold with old Lagriffoul while I look at his dressing! Come on. Your patient's doing very well. We should celebrate! . . ."

I said no because I didn't want to miss Lachaux's visit.

When Lachaux came half an hour later, I was still very happy. He sensed this and asked me:

"Good news?"

"Yes! Or rather a good discovery. I'm beginning to think that Pascali is better than I gave him credit for!"

Lachaux stared at me with his small pale eyes. Finally he said, "Psychoanalysis would teach you that this is true for everyone: In each of us there's a mixture of the best and the worst. One or the other comes to the surface depending on the situation."

"Until now I only saw the worst," I laughed.

"A better way of putting it is that you *wanted* to see the worst, because you had an immediate antipathy for Pascali. It was the same with me. When I first came here, he annoyed me because he was so confident that any woman who came his way would fall for him. His unwavering sense of superiority, and his certainty that medicine and internship give him royal rights over everyone, especially over patients, irritated me. I didn't appreciate his intelligence—and he's obviously very bright even though he's slightly vulgar—or his air of indifference in the face of the catastrophes and tragedies that he saw every day, or the very practical bent of his mind. Was that pretty close to your balance sheet?"

"Yes."

"Usually self-control means that you try to show yourself at your best. Well! For once self-control has functioned in the reverse—Pascali displays only his worst side. But his faults aren't what you might call organic: he can't resist an opportunity to be better for very long. Furthermore, I think that the saving grace of practicing medicine is that, except in pathological cases, it's impossible to stay bad forever. Disease is too pitiless to let you be without pity when it's your job to fight it. You were misled by the intern's snobbery that shows itself in irony, disrespect, a hypercritical spirit, indifference, the rudeness and a coldly practical tone. But these things can also manifest themselves in an honorable modesty, a certain romantic activism, and an excellent defense against overemphatic expressions of feeling. Important work can easily be made less frightening or even easier by irony, the way rudeness

114

can indicate great vitality trying to express itself by every possible means. Somewhere Proust mentions the cheerful, positive, indifferent, brusque look of the surgeon in a hurry. According to Proust, that's the unpleasant but sublime face of true goodness."

"Oh!" I said. "At least admit that internship dries some of them up and ruins them forever."

"You're right, and I'll admit it because that doesn't happen very often. But I can't complain about the others, because internship teaches them to be responsible and because it gives young men a true sense of reality that most of their contemporaries don't have. Four years in a hospital changes both the most selfish and the most optimistic view of things, and it really would be strange if being in constant contact with so much suffering didn't give rise to some sort of anxiety."

He took some time before adding:

"To sum it all up, my dear Claude, you took what's only a mask as Pascali's true face."

I felt happy, and full of indulgence. I said:

"Then it's lucky that he's been given the opportunity to take off his false face!"

Lachaux looked at me thoughtfully. "It's the same with all men. They all wear some sort of mask. But, except for some who really are unlucky, the time comes to take it off some day. And then, like in the parable of the Prodigal Son, everyone in the house rejoices. . . . Let's go eat! It's an occasion for killing several fatted calves."

Monday, 9 a.m.

This notebook tells me that Mariette came down with tetanus three days ago, on Friday. I've lost all sense of time in my dark solitude since then.

Every sixty minutes I check her pulse and blood pressure by instinct, without even looking at my watch. In between I take care of the many services that a patient asleep under heavy sedation needs; I feed her by a tube through her nose, I wipe the sweat off her forehead, and the dried saliva from her lips. I remove the mucous material at the end of the tube, check on the intravenous drip, and the vaporizer.

When I'm active I'm confident and almost happy. Pascali thinks there's progress and that Mariette is recovering.

In these three days a strange communication has been established between her and me, a deeper bond than the spontaneous rapport we felt the first evening and the feeling of friendship that followed. I'm fighting for her with all my strength, but in turn Mariette is silently fighting for me in her sleep. We'll save ourselves together, I from my guilt and she from the disease by a kind of mutual aid or communion. I know that if ever I weren't there, Pascali would be, as well as the supervisor, the nurses and Mme Sandrin during the night. But it seems to me that if I weren't with Mariette all the time, watching in the bluish semidarkness for the least sign of a change in her respiration or her pulse, or if I fell asleep—even for an instant— my poor little patient would be in danger.

Last night after dinner, Lachaux offered to keep watch in my place; I refused him and showed him the thermos that Anna had just filled with coffee for me. He scolded me:

"You're hardly eating, you're hardly sleeping, and now you're drugging yourself! ... Soon we'll have to start treating you!"

But I held out and was careful not to admit that I'd taken some amphetamine pills too.

When I returned to the hospital building, it was so hot in the room and it smelled so strongly of sweat and damp wool that I had to open the window and draw the curtains a bit. ... Not a breath of night air came in, not a breath of freshness. The air was stifling and heavy. It felt as if a storm was brewing. I was so depressed and lonely that I was sorry I hadn't asked Lachaux to stay with me for a little while.

Toward midnight, when I'd taken care of all the chores, I sat down in my easy chair. I felt so exhausted that I let my head fall back onto the chair. I ached all over—my head, my scalp, my neck and my shoulders all hurt. I was frightened at the thought that I might fall asleep, but I couldn't sit up again no matter how hard I tried. I felt as if I were paralyzed but the paralysis wasn't the sleep I feared and longed for—I was in a drugged stupor from the mixture of amphetamine and coffee. My brain conjured up an endless succession of fantasies and left me at the mercy of whispering nightmares, feelings of guilt, false hopes and unhealthy thoughts. Over and over again I heard echoing in my mind the question an old woman had asked me, her wrinkled hand gripping mine: "I'm not

116

going to die, am I?" The old woman was condemned to death—she had an inoperable cancer. But Mariette was young and healthy; her tetanus didn't seem to be critically dangerous. If she were well treated, she would be in the best of positions to recover. Then why was I thinking of her as if her light, regular breathing next to me was only one of those light night breezes which would be dissipated by the dawn?

Happily tonight it was Mme Sandrin herself rather than a replacement who was on night duty. She must have been worried because she hadn't heard me stir for a moment, so at about one a.m. she very softly opened the door a crack. The sound of the hinges creaking was enough to break the spell of my nightmare. And it was time to take the pulse and blood pressure again.

I had a little trouble getting to my feet. Mme Sandrin didn't say anything about it, but I guessed that her large face was turned toward me in the semidarkness as she talked softly to me. Her voice had that tone of sweetness and understanding that seems to say, when she bends over a patient, "Don't be afraid. I'm here!"

She pulled her hands out from under her apron to help me change the soiled draw-sheet. They were sturdy hands with short thick fingers, hands that can move an aching body as if it were the simplest thing in the world. As a night nurse without a diploma, Mme Sandrin hasn't learned her trade from books—she's been patiently acquiring a deep knowledge of suffering all alone every night for the last fifteen years.

When everything in the room had been put in order again, she offered to take care of Mariette if I wanted to rest for an hour or two on one of the beds in an empty room. She insisted with the direct kindness of people who know that material things like hunger, thirst and sleepiness can't be conquered, and that at some point you have to give in to them. When she saw that she couldn't persuade me, she left as quietly as she had come.

I was sure I'd fall asleep in the comfortable chair, so I sat down at my table. I opened my thesis notebook in the circle of light from my table lamp. Leafing through it, I found the notes I'd made about the law of 1920. I hadn't used them because of Lachaux's advice. He's always worried what the reactions of my examining board might be toward that controversial a subject.

But tonight all my courage has come back. "If I don't

117

write what I know to be true," I thought, "if I don't fight with whatever weapons I have to defend the millions of innocent victims of that dreadful law, then who will?"

I reread the text that Lachaux had censured.

It was all true. Every day for a year, ever since the morning I signed Mariette's premarital certificate, I've come up against this law—a law that draws no line between criminal abortion and birth-control information, as if abortions weren't condemned by every physician, while contraception is justly considered by most of the medical world as a kind of beneficial preventive medicine.

I put the papers back on the table. I felt more and more excited and nervous. I got up from my chair. I wanted to take a few steps around the room to unwind, but all of a sudden I noticed Mariette's face—it shone in the twilight, with all its features simplified, as if it had been reduced to its essence by the fever. Her face suddenly made me choke with rage—that came from rebellion and of pity—against the conspiracy of silence and the refusal to face up to social reality that had led Mariette to the hospital with a ravaged belly.

I turned back to the door. At one point, when I was drifting to sleep in the easy chair, I was almost ready to desert Mariette. But as I leaned against the door jamb, I felt as if I had answered the call to battle again.

But why this sudden return of anger? Probably because I've never watched such unjust suffering as closely as I've been watching it constantly for the past three days. It's even more tragic because the tetanus is always there, and its violence is only softened by the drugs. If the medication were suspended for a few hours, the paroxysms would begin to explode—the whole body would become rigidly arched, the teeth clenched, the chest blocked, and the rolling eyes in the hideously distorted face wouldn't express anything but total despair.

In short, what I was watching over was contained suffering; a potential for suffering held suspended on the point of boiling over. Under the apparent calm simmered all the troubles, all the innocent worries, all the painful tragedies; unmarried mothers, abandoned wives, couples estranged by the overwhelming burdens of pregnancy and motherhood, deformed children and stillborn children, children who were unwanted, mistreated and unloved—all the tragedies that could have been prevented by the simple advice to avoid them by using birth control.

I sat down again at my table and looked for the file card where I'd noted a gynecologist's confession:

"How could a physician help but feel more or less personally responsible, for not having the right, the courage or the wisdom to give a simple piece of advice to avert a pregnancy that he knew might end tragically?" He tried to decide where the responsibility lay, and he added: "Collective guilt in any case because of the fact that the law of 1920 was passed. . . ."

It's clear to all the doctors who favor birth control that the law, by equating criminal abortion with the dissemination of birth-control information, created an equivocal situation that caused a climate of mistrust and suspicion among members of the medical profession. I've noticed it in our hospital.

I was ashamed that I'd given in to Lachaux's advice. All at once, I decided to put back into my thesis everything that he'd asked me to delete! I don't even care if he proves that my rebellion is stupid tomorrow and that I'm very innocent to hope to change the text of the law by a little student paper.

I know that my rebellion doesn't seem very sensible. But at least it's worthwhile in one sense because it fills me with energy that will last until the miraculous day when life will be bearable for *all* women.

Tonight I'm full of frustrated, controlled rage, and I think that even if I'd been in front of the entire Board of the Faculty of Medicine I would have had enough courage to ask whether any doctor, faced with certain cases, with forty years' perspective, could endorse the cold, calculating decision made by a legislator who wanted to increase the population in 1920. In the light of what I've learned in medical school, I could never see the prescription of a contraceptive as an attack on life. I know that during the act of sexual intercourse enough spermatozoa are released to fertilize all women of child-bearing age in the world, and that of these four or five hundred million sperm only one survives. When such destruction and massive waste is permitted by Nature, why do they forbid me to prescribe a contraceptive capable of preventing marital discord, dangerous abortions, lasting sterility, a family disgrace or the birth of an unwanted child? In any case, what's the importance of one potential life, stopped by a diaphragm or a condom when it's weighed against all the disasters that could be avoided? Quite apart from its waste, Nature always gives rise to imperfect, painful, or even dangerous results, and then it's the doctor's duty to correct them. So why shouldn't I have the right to cure unhappy and excessive fertility the way I cure sterility? Yes, what doctor wouldn't feel continually torn, faced with the conflicting demands of legality and charity? And that must be the reason why so many physicians of every nationality have fought for voluntary motherhood for the last hundred years.

With growing exaltation, I worked until dawn to perfect my chapter on contraception and abortion. I stopped only to examine Mariette's condition. And each examination and every task gave me new strength, because each time it was like an illustration of the text I was writing.

Toward the end of the night, a light, refreshing breeze stole through the open window.

A little later, at dawn, the chirping of the birds and the rumble of the first morning buses told me that life was starting up again on the outside.

Mme Sandrin finished her last tour of duty and opened my door to say good-bye to me. She glanced at the room to see whether there was really nothing she could do for me. I asked her to close the window. She left again after saying she hoped I'd have a good day.

"And get some rest!" she added with a last reproachful look at my lamp and notebook.

Then the ward woke up. First came the parade through the corridors to the toilets, then the noise of washbasins and enema pans. Then the rumble of the carts carrying breakfast trays. Around my room, the whole hospital was beginning its daily activity again—like a large, self-sufficient beehive. For the others outside it was daytime now, full of noise, greetings, rested faces and bright summer dresses.

I wanted to get up but I couldn't. I fell back on my hard chair. My shoulders and insides ached, my head seemed ready to burst.

When the morning nurse came in, I had dragged myself painfully to the easy chair. The nurse advised me not to move and took care of Mariette. Then she left, closing the door. I sat motionless in my easy chair. I didn't have to worry about falling asleep any more—I was sick to my

120

stomach. My whole body ached, and the inside of my head felt as if it were being pierced by a thousand stings.

"This time, old girl, you're all in!" I kept repeating to myself. But I was still fighting; I couldn't let myself think ahead, and be tempted by the idea of leaving this room for a few hours . . . to lie down . . . to sleep. . . .

The nurse must have said something to Pascali as soon as he came on duty because he hadn't even finished putting on his white coat when he opened the door.

"Are we going to have to put *you* to sleep now?" he scolded.

Even more than yesterday, his presence comforted me so much that I knew I must be terribly exhausted. I started to tell him proudly that I was really in very good shape. He didn't let me finish.

"Everything O.K.? I'll examine your patient and if everything is going as well as it should, I'm going to send you to bed for the morning."

He went to the bed and examined the numbers and curves on the chart. Then, very lightly, he touched the abdomen, the thighs and the arms to check on the muscular contractions. He checked the tube, then concluded:

"It's going better and better. A little later I'll do a suction. Since I don't need you, I don't want to see you around until lunch. Now, beddy-bye."

He took my hand and dragged me out of the chair. I had to choke back a scream—my back hurt so much.

When I was on my feet, I pretended to put my papers in order so I could follow Pascali and the nurse out the door. I didn't want them to see me with my swollen eyes and drawn features.

Outside they had watered the flower beds. I could still smell the sweet, damp perfume rising from them. In the shade, it was still cool and for a few moments I felt faint. I stood and let the sweet fresh air wash over me—it touched my skin even through my white coat. "Soon," I thought, "it will be Mariette's turn to step out on this porch, dazzled and swaying a little as she takes her first steps as a convalescent."

In the residence I took a long, lukewarm bath to try to relax before I went to bed. I drew the shades in my room. At this hour of the morning, it's very quiet. Just in case, I put a bottle of sleeping pills on my night table, but it seems to me that putting all of this down in my notebook has already soothed my nerves. I've pushed away the bolster and the pillow that propped up my back while I was writing. Now, I'll stretch out on my tummy, my head between my folded arms, just as I used to when I was a little girl. I'd like to slip into an undrugged sleep, the deep, determined sleep of recovery and childhood, and to wake up only when everything's over: Mariette well again and ready to leave, me full of strength to fight my battle to the end.

PART TWO

The Land of Ouche

❧ I ❧

I spent the whole afternoon taking my usual nap. All around me the little garden lay overwhelmed by the heat and light of the sun. Ever since my uncle's death it's been going to seed; now weeds are encroaching on the cabbage beds and the brick walks.

But this hot, heavy summer that dries up the vegetable garden and makes the lawn brown just makes me feel lazy. The wasps hum insanely in the heavy air and the hollyhocks look exhausted. But the heat seems less oppressive and dry to me under the apple tree that I've appropriated for myself.

It stands at the end of the garden—a huge apple tree that must be very old. Its rough bark is coming off in brown peels and the branches—that the weight of the fruit has bent toward the lawn little by little over the years—form a vast leafy arch over me. To reach me, the sun has to flow through the leaves, broken and filtered into peaceful, indirect rays.

I've been in Mesnil-en-Ouche since the end of last week. Every morning I drag out an old folding chair that I discovered in the attic and set it under my tree. In this calm, subdued light, I drowse, limiting my horizon to the wall around the garden with its espalier overrun by nettles. Or else I look up and admire the complex architecture of the branches, the gnarled, powerful balance which pushes them away from the trunk though they're weighed down by apples ripening among the motionless leaves, and the clouds of buzzing insects.

125

I've just spent a week of purely vegetative—I almost wrote down vegetable—existence, so much so that I feel physically closer to my tree and the earth than to people. I've never left the garden; I've refused to show myself in this village where I'm a stranger. I've even declined to make the acquaintance of our closest neighbors. My mother insisted, but I wouldn't give in. I imagine she must have said I was exhausted after the internship when people asked about me.

In truth, what I'm living through is a truce, the truce that's held after the battle to bury the corpses. Medicine has its corpses, just like war.

Here under my apple tree I'm waiting for . . . not peace or forgetfulness, but only for a precarious equilibrium.

Mariette died a week ago.

It was Lachaux who came to tell me. It must have been twelve-thirty—three hours had gone by since Pascali sent me to bed. I was sleeping heavily, as if in a cataleptic trance. I didn't even hear Lachaux knocking on the door or coming in; he had to shake me to wake me up.

From the look on his face I could tell immediately that something very serious had happened. I asked at once, "It's Mariette?" He nodded slowly and I understood.

Dizzy and faint, I listened as he explained, "Her heart stopped just when Pascali was doing a bronchial suction."

But I wasn't listening any more. I was up, throwing on my coat and shoes. I ran into the ward like a madwoman.

The shade was pulled up, the window was open. The room was dazzlingly white again and strangely calm. Mariette seemed to be asleep on the bed in the midst of a jumble of emergency apparatus, syringes, and other instruments no longer of any use. But her sallow face, the slash in her throat for the drain, her thin, round shoulders, and her tragic and irrevocable stillness expressed the most terrible of all reproaches: "Why did you let me die?"

Suddenly chaos gripped me. In my stupor, I said to myself over and over again, with a feeling of utter helplessness, "I went to sleep. Mariette is dead. I've betrayed her. I broke our pact. Mariette is dead because of me . . ."

Lachaux, who had followed me in, said softly:

"As you know, this was an unforeseeable accident, exactly the sort of accident that no one can prevent. Nobody in this hospital has a lighter, surer hand than

Pascali. And at the moment of cardiac arrest he tried everything. Without losing his composure for a minute, he immediately started massaging the heart. He quickly asked for the resuscitator for artificial respiration; he called for Lourieu with his electrocardiograph. They only stopped when the indicator showed that there really wasn't the slightest cardiac contraction any longer."

I said nothing. Lachaux tried to get to me through my daze; he kept repeating over and over, as if he were trying to reason with one of his demented patients:

"I swear to you that no one could have done better than Pascali."

My silence discouraged him, and he finally stopped talking. Except for Mariette's motionless chest and the pile of instruments with their nickeled surfaces shining in the dazzling light, nothing seemed changed in the room. I could have believed that Mariette was still asleep. I closed my eyes the way I used to to hear her light breathing better in the bluish half-light and I listened for the soft whistle of the vaporizer. For three days it had kept Mariette company like a watchful presence. They had stopped the machine and taken the useless catheter from her vein. The silence in the room suddenly depressed me.

The supervisor came in with a nurse who started to reassemble the machines before beginning to clean the body. I took Mariette's hand. It was still flexible and warm. The supervisor came over to me and said, as if she understood my sorrow:

"She didn't suffer, Mam'selle Sauvage. Being under sedation like that, she didn't even know she was dying."

For the supervisor, this death was part of the daily pathos of the hospital and her sentence had the medically correct mixture of pity and indifference. In the same way, the nurse who was about to prepare the body before sending it to the morgue would be deft rather than reverent. In their eyes Mariette was free from everything: she'd escaped the pain of tetanus and the horror of being aware that she was suffering and dying. Pain couldn't reach her any more. For these two women, who were used to seeing people of all ages die hideous deaths, that was all this sudden, almost merciful ending meant. A few hours later, once her few personal effects were removed from the room and order was restored, it would be as if there had never been a twenty-year-old girl lying dead on this bed.

But there was nothing to comfort me in my bewilderment and helplessness.

Mariette was dead; and so was the little child that the abortionist had killed in her womb. For these two, there would be no more sun or smiles or rainbows. Their suffering had come to an end, but their joy and hope had too.

I leaned over Mariette as if I only now understood how sad it really was. Embracing her for the last time with the same rush of emotion as when her frightened eyes had searched for reassurance from me to fall asleep, I wanted to ask her to forgive me. But when I stooped down toward the bed, everything became confused—the world began to revolve around the inert throat and the black hole where the drain had been, where her last sigh must have come from. I felt as if nothing could hold me ... I was falling gently ... I was slipping into an endless fall ... I was going to join Mariette. It was like being put to sleep with a sleeping pill ... I was going to die.

I came to in one of the unoccupied rooms. I didn't object when Lachaux offered to take me to his ward to let me rest more quietly than I could have in the residence. In the trancelike stupor I lay in, I didn't care about anything, even the idea of falling asleep among the "nuts." I was yielding, I was giving up, I was refusing all burdens—even reason. After four days and nights when my only rest had been the moments when I lost consciousness, my body seemed useless and very heavy, and my brain was only an unbearable, diffuse pain. My thoughts seemed to walk in one spot without moving; I was caught in an endless nightmare haunted again and again by Mariette's face.

In the neuro-psychiatric ward, Lachaux moved me to one of the rooms used for rest cures. The light there is very soft, the walls are soundproof; the floor is lined with rubber. As soon as I was in the room, I reeled toward the bed. With a last effort I slid into it. In every part of my body I felt an immense need for relaxation, for letting go, for numbness; I wanted to fall asleep immediately. Lachaux left me alone for a few minutes. The silence was almost absolute. My pulse was racing and I knew that without a drug I wouldn't be able to fall asleep except at the point of collapse.

When Lachaux came back a little later, I gratefully accepted the barbiturates he offered me. Any drug would be better than the nervous exhaustion of insomnia or the thought that had come to me as soon as I lay down: "I'm in a hospital bed, just like Mariette. . . . Now it's my turn to fall ill. And among the insane . . ."

It's difficult for me to say exactly what the days I spent in this room were like. For three days I lost all track of the passage of time; I lived through long periods of drugged sleep—without fantasies or dreams—interrupted only by short periods of wakefulness when they made me eat.

Then on the morning of the fourth day, Lachaux told me that he thought I was sufficiently recovered. On his advice I stayed in the room one more day. He brought me his phonograph and my favorite records.

I listened to them to make him happy and pretended to be interested in them as long as he was there but as soon as I was alone again, I turned off the machine. I still didn't quite feel myself. I had the feeling of emptiness, of isolation, of drying up, and at the same time, a kind of strange detachment, beyond resignation or sadness.

The worst was over. With short, shaky steps I rejoined the tribe of healthy people who eat, drink, and live at peace, with no feelings of self-reproach. It wasn't hard to discover the source of my uneasiness: sooner or later I was sure that the day would come when I would forget Mariette's death. Would this forgetting be my cure?

A letter from my mother reminded me of my promise to spend a few days in Mesnil—that short vacation in Normandy that Mariette had looked forward to so happily. Mother was worried because she hadn't heard from me for ten days, and she complained that she waited for me in vain every evening when the bus from Evreux arrived.

"In my opinion, it's still a little early to let you loose in the country," Lachaux said hesitantly.

Since I insisted, he finally relented and gave me a detailed set of orders—his "prescription" for my cure.

On the morning of my departure I went back to my room in the residence. I was in the middle of packing my suitcases when there was a knock at my door. It was Alberte Apple, my old classmate.

Arlette had tried to call me, and had learned from Anna that I wasn't well. Since she was very busy with her magazine, she had sent Alberte to get news.

I still felt too tired to talk for long and I welcomed my visitor without enthusiasm. I really had nothing to say to her, and I certainly didn't want to ask her about the details of her life as a teacher at the Jules-Ferry Lycée, or about Arlette's activities. I knew that she would talk forever.

Alberte Apple had always been the aggressive, devouring sort of friend—she was so possessive and demanding that she lacked all tact or understanding. You couldn't help feeling sorry for her, but at the same time you felt like running away from her as fast as possible.

I hadn't seen her in over two years. She was still ugly, and she still stuttered. She had the same fat cheeks, the same oily skin, the same bewildered, near-sighted stare from behind her thick glasses. . . . She still massaged her nose thoughtfully with the back of her hand when some idea preoccupied her and she hadn't lost the habit of repeating sentences that she thought were important.

Falling all over me, she cried: "You don't look at all well! You don't look at all well!"

Then she began to take stock of my room.

Someone walked down the corridor whistling; a door slammed shut, another opened a little and you could hear a current of excitement in the masculine voices and laughter.

"Ah! You're so lucky!" Alberte murmured.

Her exclamation was so completely unexpected and so revealing that instead of just smiling or keeping still, I asked her teasingly, "What makes you say that?"

She explained sadly: "I live in a tiny hotel room, six flights up. I'm all alone."

"Do you think that I have a party every night?"

"At least you've got friends. . . . All those interns . . . I know that one of the interns is in love with you. Arlette even told me his name."

I knew that in spite of myself I looked flattered as well as amused.

"Pascali?"

"No. It ends in o."

"Lachaux?"

"That's it. Arlette thought he was very nice. She says that he's a physician with a future. Do you like him?"

"Lachaux is a very good friend—but that's all," I said. "You can tell Arlette that she was imagining things."

But Alberte didn't want to give up so quickly. Now she wanted to discover some secret sorrow.

"Don't you get along well? Arlette said that you have

130

great long discussions and that you always end up in agreement."

I had to be honest, so I admitted, "That's true. We think the same way about most things."

"Ah! You see!" Alberte cried triumphantly. And she added, again in that low, confidential tone, "Why don't you marry him?"

I was irritated by her incredible single-mindedness.

"Why? I have an independent life. I get along fine by myself and soon I'll be practicing an exciting profession. Why should I need a husband?"

"So that you won't realize you're all alone in the world some day."

She looked as if she were going to burst into tears. She repeated with fright, almost with terror:

"Realize you're all alone . . ."

Poor Alberte! She was so pitiful and it was so difficult to think of her—with her chubby cheeks, heaving bosom, fat thighs, and big hips—in love. But her desire to become a woman like all the others, to have a husband and children and not to get old alone suddenly reminded me of the night when—sitting across from Pascali's redheaded girl friend—I became aware of the fact that loneliness and ugliness are the same kind of disgrace.

It wasn't the first time that someone had almost tempted me to disrupt my discipline as a free woman and destroy my uneasy balance, and it wasn't the first time that a female voice had pleaded for surrender, for giving up and sinking into a man's arms, since only men can give a little happiness to a woman.

If it had been another day, I would have argued the way I did to try to convince Arlette, and explained what trickery love is, and that a marriage of "convenience" is even worse in a man's world.

But so soon after Mariette's death and my own recovery, I felt numb. I didn't have the energy. There was too much of a sense of awful fatalism in her death but there was also too much indifference, hypocrisy, injustice, and male egotism. That was preoccupying me much more than the things that Alberte Apple, still an old maid, would think about sadly before she went to sleep. . . . Alberte and I no longer spoke the same language. We would never agree. Life is a difficult proposition for every woman. I'd been unable to do anything for Mariette. If I wanted to help or to save other women, first I had to recover my health. Alberte's problem could wait; I'd take care of her some other time.

I pushed her firmly toward the door, explaining that I was leaving early in the afternoon and that I still hadn't finished packing.

I'm feeling better, and I think it's because I've been following Lachaux's orders to the letter: a pain killer in decreasing amounts and a sedative in case of insomnia or anxiety, a varied diet, no intellectual work and not too much reading. . . .

When he gave me my prescription, Lachaux commented on it point by point in a tone of friendly goodwill. I couldn't see the least underlying sign of feeling in his words or in his look. I couldn't help saying to myself that Arlette really had been imagining things that weren't there—unless it had been Alberte, with her obsession about men.

Lachaux made me swear to stick to his orders as well as I could. I've kept my word. I haven't misused my little supply of drugs: I take the smallest amount I need to get to sleep. I always used to say that I was allergic to nature, but I've made the apple tree the center of my life these days. I'd leave my notebook and index cards for the thesis in my room, and take along only a detective story to read under the tree, and I wouldn't even manage to finish that. During the first days my mind still felt too foggy to concentrate even on light reading and I limited myself to the monotonous but soothing exercise of watching the balance of the leaves against the sky or the zigzagging flight of a bumblebee in the light.

Any other time I would have screamed in anguish or died of boredom after three days of such laziness. But I'm still exhausted—I feel a weariness that's made up of mental indifference and complete physical inertia. Every evening I refuse to go and get the milk with my mother because the eight or nine hundred yards through the pasture to the farmhouse seems like a trip to the end of the world.

On the other hand, Lachaux would have been pleased to watch my appetite slowly come back. When I arrived, I was terribly thin . . . "A shadow of herself," my mother cried as she kissed me. For the last five days, she's been tempting me with fat chickens, fresh cream brought back from the farm, tender vegetables, raspberries and strawberries gathered from the garden. And my stomach has begun to feel more receptive. When I sit under my apple tree in a bathing suit, mother doesn't even have to pinch me to say confidently, "You're beginning to fill out, my poor child. You needed it!" And in the evening when I undress I realize that I'm getting a tan.

One day when I was teasing Lachaux about the slowness of psychiatric cures, he answered: "Nothing is gained by going too fast. You have to let time heal things slowly."

I'm beginning to think he's right.

The experience that I'm going through is, I believe, called *accidia*, or "dryness" in the *Imitation of Christ*. It's the most terrible of divine punishments. I shouldn't protest, I must serve my sentence in silence. I must bear the detachment as I've borne the paroxysm of grief, even if I know that after a while, when I've saved other patients, I'll end up by forgetting Mariette's death. My present aridity may only be the foreboding of this forgetfulness. But I look forward to that forgetfulness only with vague despair. . . .

Tuesday

This afternoon even the low-hanging branches of my tree and the tightly enclosed garden don't make me feel like a prisoner—I don't have the least desire to escape. But, following Lachaux's prescription, I've decided to get some exercise. I've got a hoe and when it gets a little cooler, I'll start weeding one of the paths. Right now the sun is beating down harshly, the garden seems to pant under its slanting blaze, and I have no desire to leave the shade.

Mother wanted me to take my nap indoors with all the shades pulled down because of the heat, but I insisted on sleeping under my apple tree as usual. The air here is nearly as unbreathable as out in the sun, but there's a feeling of being in the open air, a feeling of relief that I don't get indoors. At least that's what I said to mother. Knowing how stubborn I am, she gave up questioning my whims long ago; so she didn't insist.

The shade of my apple tree is the only place where I have a chance of getting some peace and quiet. It's my one shelter from gossip and small talk. During the course of an average day, I get three or four visits from mother.

133

I cut them all short with a sigh and a remark about the heat—if I didn't, mother would station herself next to my folding chair. In Mesnil, mother plays Lady Bountiful. Her props are her wool and knitting needles—she knits for the priest's "good works," as she explained to me the first day. But even the most pious knitting has never prevented useless conversations. On the contrary . . .

She made her last appearance half an hour ago, just when I was going to take up my notebook again. I immediately hid it under the pillow—if her curiosity had been aroused, mother would have spent all her time watching me to find out what I'm writing.

I'm almost ashamed to write this down because I know that in her own way my mother loves me. For instance, a little while ago she thought that I might be thirsty, so she came out to offer me a jug of cider that she'd been chilling for me in the well.

Ever since she came to Mesnil, she's taken up wearing "country" clothes, the kind that ladies' magazines recommend for a weekend in the country; but that sort of clothes is rarely made to be worn by rather substantial women of well beyond fifty. She has on a linen print dress today. Its pattern of large flowers manages to make her look enormous. Also, she has a rather peculiar straw sunhat perched coquettishly on her head to protect her from the sun.

"How do you think I look?" she asked me.

I looked at her heavy figure before I answered. Her breasts are those of an old woman, her face looks swollen, and her skin looks blotchy in the heat. All that's left of the delicate face she had when I was little are her beautiful eyes. She was famous throughout the entire family for those eyes, and it's probably because of them that my father married her. Those beautiful eyes are just about the only thing I have in common with her, but even they bear the marks of time—they're less clear now and they're crisscrossed with tiny red veins.

I almost said, "You look like a village butcher's wife all dressed up in her Sunday best. You're getting fat. You're letting yourself go."

She was so accustomed to my old insolence that she probably wouldn't even have replied. But there was no reason to make the misunderstanding there's always been between us any worse. I answered, smiling:

"You look like Princess Margaret trying to look like a country girl!"

Mother left happily; off to polish the furniture or maybe to fix the rice for the rice pudding that she's decided to have for dessert tomorrow.

I can build up a reserve of patience alone under my tree. And I need it. I arrived in Mesnil feeling just as a good daughter should. And when I walked into the house for the first time and found its unfamiliar rooms furnished with some of the old furniture we'd had when I was a little girl, I almost fell into my mother's arms, I wanted to cry, to forget my restraint, to tell her everything and be comforted.

My unhealthy look immediately frightened her, but she could never have understood the conflict in my beliefs and morality that caused it. She sat me down at the table and served me all my favorite things to eat. I was too tired even to taste them. I had to listen to all the local gossip, to be told that the pharmacist is old, married, and uninteresting, that the only doctor in Mesnil is thirty-three and still a bachelor (meaningful look, that our nearest neighbors are Parisians retired from business: "Very nice people. They have lots of money," she said, sitting with her hands crossed over her stomach, her eyes half closed, her expression half admiring and half envious.

She kept on talking until I felt light-headed from her words and begged to be excused, saying that I was exhausted.

She led me to my room. Again I was almost overwhelmed with affection—mother had used all her ingenuity to reconstruct my room in Louviers. Here the room has sloping eaves and the furniture is arranged a bit differently, but I was welcomed by my narrow couch, my small bookshelf, my work table and the lamp I had studied by for so many exams. Mother had even hung my four favorite prints on the wall: a Van Gogh, a Derain, a Monet and a Utrillo. When I was growing up, I'd stripped my room of all sentimentality: the dolls, toys, knickknacks and all the pictures that had hung on the walls during my childhood. I wanted it neat, empty, almost monastic and different, in any case, from the rest of the house. I thought of the fake mahogany and the imitation provincial furniture, the bad reproductions of paintings, the

135

cotton velvet, and the machine-made lace doilies as the accessories of a false, narrow, mean life that I hated.

"How lucky!" I thought. "I'll have this corner so that I won't feel like a visitor. I'll be able to be secure and at peace here—I'll really feel at home."

In my gratefulness, I fell into mother's arms with a tenderness I thought I'd forgotten years ago.

The next day mother woke me at about nine. She brought me buttered toast and steaming hot chocolate—the things that were saved for holiday breakfasts in the past. I thought her attention and kindness were very sweet.

While I started to eat, not hungry at all but childishly happy, she sat on the edge of the bed. She wanted to tell me the reasons that had made her decide to leave Louviers and come to Mesnil. She had gone over her finances. The cost of living was rising—and the small pension my father had left wouldn't get any larger. This meant that she wouldn't be able to keep the house she was renting. For a while she'd thought of working: but what could she do? She only knew how to keep house. She'd also thought of taking in boarders. But either solution would have made her feel humiliated; they would mean a fall in status. She would no longer be a middle-class woman who didn't have to work. Furthermore, at fifty-five, just when her daughter is about to get a prestigious M.D. degree, could the mother of a young woman doctor start working in someone else's house or open a boarding house for factory foremen or white-collar workers without humiliating her daughter? That would have been a real disgrace.

Her brother's small inheritance came in the nick of time to save her from an embarrassing situation. She chose to exile herself in the countryside rather than to face the sympathy and pity she knew she would get from her friends and even the shopkeepers in Louviers! In Mesnil, what with her pension, free lodging, and the lower cost of living, plus the vegetables she gets from the garden, she manages to balance her budget and above all, she's still a "lady."

A little later, I made a tour of the house. It isn't very large; the walls are timbered and bricks fill the gaps between wooden beams that are blackened with age; the timber is bent a little under the weight of flat, old-fashioned tiles, but the general effect of age is charming.

When I discovered the courtyard behind the house, I

realized that I had a chance to get away from the gossip and women's talk. The yard has no interest for mother because it's surrounded by walls and it faces back toward the countryside. She confessed to me at once that she gets bored there and only spends time there when she has to weed and water the garden. She'd rather stay in the kitchen, where the window opens onto the street. I always find her there, on the lookout behind her curtains.

It's cooler now. I'll be able to use the hoe. Cleaning up the paths can't be the most urgent task in this garden, since it's almost on the point of returning to its natural state, but it's something I can do by myself. And if I offered to help mother with her household chores, I'd lose my blessed silence.

Wednesday

At ten o'clock, as always, mother came to say good night to me in my room. I was stretched out on my bed, pretending to read. She went to the window, looked vaguely at the darkness outside, and sighed, "What a summer!" Then she kissed me and left to go to bed.

Soon I could hear her occasional snores through the wal. Once I was sure she wouldn't take me by surprise, I took my notebook out of the drawer where I hide it. Now I'm writing, sharing the narrow circle of light from my lamp with the moths that dance in its radiance.

The warm night breezes are drifting in through the wide open window. They waft in the sweet smells that have slowly been distilled by the alchemy of growing things during the heat of the day.

Lachaux's orders are proving more and more effective. Yesterday, after hoeing for an hour, my hands were blistered and my back ached. But then for the first time since my arrival, I slipped into a deep, relaxing sleep.

Today at the end of the afternoon, I felt full of energy though I was slightly sore from the exercise. When mother came through the garden at dusk, carrying her milk pail, I suddenly wanted a change. I wanted to be somewhere else, to be seeing something new and different. It wasn't easy to get permission to go to the farm alone. "The gates! You won't know how to open and close the gates!" mother protested. "If you don't close them right and a cow gets loose, it will be a disaster!"

But I refused to listen to her objections and she finally

137

got tired of fighting and gave me the aluminum pail and the key that opens the little door in the wall at the end of the garden. She stayed at the beginning of the path that runs between the hedges, shouting after me:

"After the second gate, you turn to the left, and then you go straight ahead."

The light was beginning to fade. It slanted through the hedges and along the edge of the embankment. As I walked, I had to watch carefully for the ruts of dried mud—every step I took might have resulted in a sprained ankle. But very quickly the path came out from between the hedges into a wide pasture. I opened and then carefully closed the first gate behind me and stopped to catch my breath.

In front of me—under the twilight that still lingered in the west before deepening into the blue of night—there was a wide plain bordered in the distance by the line of forest, a high dark barrier that loomed over the grassland and the hedges.

One star appeared, than another. I was afraid to be caught in the dark and walked steadily on through the meadow. After I passed through the second gate and turned to the left, I finally saw the lights of the farm.

In the courtyard a dog, chained to his doghouse, started to bark. A man appeared in the doorway. He must have recognized my milk container because he said to the people inside: "It's for Madame Sauvage."

As if this was enough of a welcome, he stumped inside. I followed him into the kitchen. It smelled of earth and animals. But the traditional cast-iron stove had been replaced by a white enamel butane gas range that stood between a large grandfather clock and the customary sideboard for dishes. High on top of a shelf was a radio.

There were three people in the room: a middle-aged man—the one I'd just seen on the doorstep—was sitting at the table in the middle of the room, writing in his account book under a bare electric bulb; a plump housewife in a linen smock was rolling out pastry dough at the other end of the table; and a young girl of about twelve or thirteen with a face as round and fresh as an apple was reading quietly on a low chair.

All three looked up at me when I came in. The man stared at me indifferently, the woman put on an amiable smile, and the little girl watched me with curiosity.

138

On the threshold, I announced: "I'm Madame Sauvage's daughter."

"Ah! You're the girl who's studying to be a lady doctor!" the woman said.

Now the man seemed interested. I'd put on a sweater and blue jeans over my bathing suit and pulled on some old sandals. Maybe he was amazed that a "lady doctor" was dressed so simply. The farmer's wife left her pastry and went over to the stone sink near the dish cupboard to wash her flour-covered hands under the water faucet. Then she took my pail and went out.

It was hot in the kitchen. The man stared at me without saying a word. I didn't want to talk either, and I moved closer to the door and looked out into the courtyard so I wouldn't have to break the silence.

The woman had turned on the electric light in the milk house. I saw her moving some metal containers that stood against a whitewashed wall. She came back with my pail. When I'd paid her, she went to the cupboard to get me my change. As she passed by the table, she exclaimed angrily, "Oh! That Maria!"

While she was getting the milk, the little girl had taken the rolling pin and had started to work on the invitingly soft dough.

"You want a good smack?" the mother said. "I told you not to touch that dough! It won't rise, with you in your state ... If that isn't awful—spoiling four pounds of my good flour and the yeast and all. And it's all her fault—I told her not to touch it. . . ."

The girl stood near the table, already tall and well-shaped in her checkered schoolgirl apron. She opened her mouth to protest, but when she saw her mother's hand raised menacingly, she thought it safer to keep still.

The tirade was so violent, and so uncalled-for that I had to say something. "Look, ma'am! Your dough is still in beautiful shape. Maria hasn't had time to spoil it."

"That's not it, mam'selle. You can be sure that I taught this little fool to make pastry. But today . . ."

The woman stopped as if she had caught herself on the verge of saying something obscene. Then she said, "She's having her first period. . . ."

"And why should that be any trouble?" I asked.

The mother looked at me, dumfounded.

"Well, it's because I put yeast in it. The pastry won't rise because the little girl's blood . . ."

139

At that point, the father got up and left the table. On his way to the door he said over his shoulder to his wife:

"Tell Maria not to go to the milk house or the storeroom. I don't want her to spoil everything! If she does, she'll be sorry."

Without looking at his daughter he left with the heavy confident tread of a man who doesn't want to be mixed up in these disgusting female matters.

Ah! As a "lady doctor" I must have seemed very stupid not to have understood immediately. Of course! I'd just stumbled on the superstitious belief that menstruation is impure—especially the first menstruation—and that all sorts of disturbing things happen because of it. Flowers wilt, cream turns sour, mayonnaise separates—everything ferments, spoils or rots under the influence of the rotten blood. Now I understood the man's disgust and the mother's irritation. In this rural district superstition is tenacious despite the signs of civilization—the butane gas range, the radio and the running water. I'd come across the same belief in Gennevilliers.

I was going to say, with a smile, that the influence of menses on fermentation has never been scientifically proven. I was even going to point out that menstrual blood is normal blood—not blood that has somehow been poisoned or altered. I turned to the girl to reassure her. She was under the glare of the electric lamp, sitting in full light. I saw the signs of the onset of puberty: purplish shadows under her eyes, a fever pimple in the corner of her mouth. Then I noticed that the corners of her mouth were drooping and that tears were wetting her eyes. Her cheeks had suddenly changed color under her healthy tan and her gaze also seemed pale. It expressed a new shame, distress at being soiled—a very personal defeat. The girl's troubled look seemed to make her mother even more annoyed.

"Oh! She doesn't have to go spoiling the pastries to give me trouble. Last night . . ."

She couldn't finish her sentence. The child threw herself forward, begging, "Don't say it, mother!"

She was crying with shame, but before I could say a word, her mother replied, as if proving that she was in authority:

"Why shouldn't I say it? You're disgusting; this morning the sheets and the bed were all dirty!"

She suddenly fell silent. Without really understanding what was happening, she saw with amazement that a strangely transformed daughter was standing in front of her, her face convulsed with hatred. Her face—so childish a moment ago—expressed such defiance, such womanly fury that it frightened her mother. She raised her hand as if to protect herself. But the girl's fury was so violent and so far beyond her age, that instead of stepping forward to attack her mother, Maria jumped back, evidently terrified by the explosiveness of her rebellion. She lowered her head, ran to the back of the kitchen, and fled.

"At that age, they act crazy: it's a good thing she went to bed," her mother said.

I left. It was dark, but a sickle moon lit my way and I had the lights of Mesnil blinking between the trees just ahead of me to guide me. I walked slower than I had on my way to the farm. In the soft, peaceful, clear night, I felt weighed down with pity and sorrow. I imagined Maria crouched in her little bed, choking with helpless rage.

I stopped at the second gate. On my way to the farm, I had stood and thought of Mariette as I watched the splendor of the sunset.

Mariette and Maria! At that moment their names and those two serious, innocent faces became confused in my mind. I thought of them both in the same halo of adolescence, facing the same obscure destiny.

Maria's first period and the missed periods that had driven Mariette to have an abortion were part of the same tragic misunderstanding and stupidity. Maria's father had the same horror of impure menstruation that a native of Borneo shows by his fear that the sight of his daughter's first menses will make him blind. Men have transmitted their disgust down from the most remote times. The farmer had been worried that his cider and his cheese might go bad so he'd been serious; otherwise he would have made coarse jokes to hide his uneasiness and his disgust. But the mother, as simple-minded and ignorant as she might be, still should have remembered her own childish dread.

But, not noticing her daughter's anxiety, Maria's mother was satisfied like most mothers with the silent thought: "You're thirteen years old. I had my period when I was your age and no one explained anything to me. I didn't die. Now you can do your best!"

And it was lucky that when she was irritated she hadn't threatened the girl with the prediction that she would have terrible cramps every month as a punishment for spoiling the pastry. Lachaux had once explained the painful cramps some of my patients suffered from: "Many women think of menstrual blood as coming from a wound. And a wound implies pain. So these women suffer every month—especially if their mothers, sisters, or grandmothers told them when they were little girls that pain is inevitable."

I'd felt guilty when I told Mariette about the rhythm method, and I had the same feeling tonight because I hadn't helped Maria or answered her look of appeal that had begged for my help and pity.

Will the time of equality between the sexes ever come? Will this world awake one morning to find that sexual inequality and that kind of superstition have disappeared? Will there ever be a world where young girls can live through puberty not as a humiliating defeat but as a "second birth"?

Thinking about it, I decided that I was right to have kept silent. This evening, anything I might have said would simply have made the mother more stubborn. As for Maria, she was too upset to listen to me. I would wait for a better time.

If I could do a little weeding there too ... uproot some harmful beliefs from that innocent young soul, if I could help her understand herself, it wouldn't be a waste of my time.

Thursday

I may have reached the saturation point as far as sleep is concerned. This afternoon my nap was short and I felt bad when I woke up; I had a headache and I felt heavy and bloated; my lunch seemed to be stuck halfway down my throat.

Out in the sun it was still too hot to take up the hoe again. I opened the detective story that I've been dragging around with me for four days. Until now, before I'd get to the end of a paragraph, I'd have already forgotten what the beginning was about, and I'd have to start over again. Today I read four chapters without stopping, an obvious sign that I'm getting better.

About five this afternoon mother came to bring me a letter. I recognized Lachaux's handwriting—and his name was written on the envelope next to the name of the hospital. Mother must have looked at it already because she announced as she handed me the letter:

"Look! One of your colleagues from Gennevilliers has written you. . . ."

I could tell by the way she looked at me that she was dying to find out more about it. I knew too, that each bachelor of a reasonable age who has a good job is a potential husband for me as far as she's concerned. Also, she's looking forward to playing the role of mother-in-law spending a long visit with her son-in-law (he would be well-off of course).

Watching her walk away, I thought of the strange psychology of mothers, and thinking about my mother brought me back to Maria's mother. She's been so unconcerned about preparing her child for her future as a woman. They always talk about the profound understanding of mothers for their daughters, about the traditions, the initiations, the beneficial rules that are passed from mother to daughter in heart-to-heart talks, about how the daughter's trust is awakened by the mother's wisdom and love!

How can mother fail to understand that her example would be enough to discourage me from marriage forever? How could she fail to recognize how confused her own ideas about marriage were all through my childhood? On the one hand, she was trying (and without much success) to shape me into playing the role of a slave, surrendering to the man in the sacred bonds of marriage. Marriage would definitely insure my security and happiness. So she tried to teach me to cook, to sew, to keep house; she dressed me in pretty clothes, she curled my straight hair, and she fought against my boyish ways. But on the other hand, I heard her complaints about her own married life and watched her make her husband's life miserable with endless emotional scenes. Then she showed that she could be mean, touchy and very prosaic. She only cared about taking care of the house and she would scream about a little scratch in the finish of one of her tables or about some cigarette ash on the parquet floor, and each time it was the whole male sex that was at fault. As far as she was concerned, all men—and especially my father—were incompetent and egotistical, besides being liars and thieves. So where was the easy life, the future without any unpleasant surprises and all the middle-class privileges, which according to her, were part of the normal marriage?

My parents had been married for five years when I was

143

born, so I know nothing about the first years of their marriage, except from mother's horrifying stories, and as she told it my father was always to blame for everything. Mother probably hoped that my birth would bring her husband, who was becoming less and less interested in home life, back to the bosom of the family. It's true that my father had an excellent excuse for spending hardly any time at home. He was a fabric salesman who represented several Lyons factories, so he was on the road most of the time. I was eight years old when their separation became final.

Because of the circumstances of his job, my father started to drink. He was killed in a car crash when I was twelve, leaving a very small pension. Mother settled down to morose resignation and matronly stoutness, slowly losing interest in complaining about her unsuccessful marriage, her wasted life and her misunderstood virtues.

From my childhood experience I retained a feeling of violent aggression against my father, doubled with scorn for my mother which is only beginning to fade with the passage of time.

Lachaux's letter, sitting unopened on the pillow beside me, took me back directly to my childhood. It's left a deep mark on me, but I didn't really understand its importance until Lachaux opened my eyes to it while discussing some of my patients.

Alone, I wouldn't have been able to reconstruct, from a distance of twenty-five years, the complexity of the relationship between a mother and her young daughter: the transports of bewildered, possessive love that threw us toward each other, the bursts of hostility that set us at odds almost instantly afterwards. For my part I hated her because she seemed a rival with whom I was contending for my father's love; and she hated me because she hoped unconsciously to be revenged for her unfulfilled femininity through me.

The most terrible trauma, which must have been what made me into a rebel, was the scorn that I was forced into feeling for my parents. I refused to see any resemblance to my mother in myself because I could see her satisfaction with a life that had narrowed to an endless round of domestic tasks and the continual sobs of a neglected wife or the vociferous demands of a shrew. I especially hated her for burdening me at home with a thousand chores that kept me from my school work. It was as if she wanted to prevent me from liberating myself by my studies from her state of female servitude.

As for my father, that was even worse. In other homes the father's authority was indisputable, prestigious, sovereign. My friends could look at their fathers with unbounded admiration. Mine, whom I had loved so much, seemed more incompetent and ridiculous every day.

Between my parents, I lived in an intolerant and exasperated silence, rarely broken. With an arrogant sense of outrage, I opposed my mother's tyranny; I scorned my father's flabbiness, and I trembled with impatient anticipation for the hours when I could get away.

My father had been dead some months when I had my first period. For me, as for young Maria, that event was a kind of test that my mother hadn't even bothered to prepare me for. First I felt disgusted by the blood. Then, when mother finally decided to explain to me that I now was a "big girl," I was terrified that something I'd done wrong had caused this humiliating thing. I thought that it was a punishment for my hostility to my mother that was making me definitely become *like her;* until then I'd refused to look like a girl and imitated the boys in their clothes, attitudes and games, secretly hoping for the miracle that would make a boy of me.

Every month, mother was overtaken by an inexplicable increase in domestic activity for some days—she would even climb on a footstool and carefully clean the crystal chandelier in the drawing room. Five or six days later, drying on the clothesline in the garden, would be those small white napkins which had so intrigued me when I looked at a pile of them in the closet next to the handkerchiefs. I only understood the meaning of this cleaning mania—which, incidentally, always coincided with bad moods—when the little napkins were also drying in the wind for me. The idea of a "big clean-up" has always been associated in my mind with the pieces of linen that my mother showed to the eyes of all the neighbors.

I've just opened Lachaux's letter: it's written in the tone of an older brother affectionately worried about the recovery of a younger sister. News from the residence: Pascali has been on vacation for three days and Morizet, who is losing his St. Tropez tan, can easily take care of everything in the half-empty wards—even my gynecological consultations.

Lachaux tells me he has a new patient. Arlette phoned

him to ask if he'd take charge of an "unhappy soul"—one of her friends. This unhappy soul in need of special care is none other than Alberte Apple.

He says it's not a difficult case from the diagnostic point of view but he doesn't foresee a therapeutically efficient solution except the injection of male hormones. And Alberte Apple doesn't seem likely to be contented with that.

Lachaux ends his letter by hoping that I'll keep him up to date about the results of the treatment he's prescribed.

I'll write him tomorrow that it's been a complete success and that I hope he'll be just as lucky in treating Alberte Apple with hormones!

Arlette—who's been married for a long time—and Alberte, who's beginning to run after men like a bitch in heat! I'm the only one of our school trio who won't give in. And yet, thinking back on our conversations, all three of us agreed that love was a vile and repulsive thing. The idea of motherhood horrified us. Since then, asking my patients questions or just listening to them has given me a much better idea of what was happening to us then. We were afraid of masculine domination, and especially terrified of being deflowered. The empty hollow in our bodies made us feel humiliated and vulnerable, and we frightenedly refused the idea of a destiny that couldn't be fulfilled unless we accepted mutilation or penetration.

Arlette was the first to become a traitor to our agreement. Now Alberte is going over to the enemy. As far as she's concerned it's not freedom but loneliness that makes a life without men miserable. She's ready to accept any marriage, any affair—anything seems better to her than a life alone, even if she has to give up her freedom.

I'll be the last one to go. I love my profession. It will be my husband.

10 p.m.

Mother has been in bed for a long time, and I hear her snoring on the other side of the wall. I'm ready for writing.

Toward the end of the afternoon, I picked up the hoe again. In three days I've already completely weeded the paths around the beds of cabbage, early peas, pumpkins, and rhubarb. Tomorrow I'll attack the thorns that are choking the raspberry bushes.

This evening mother didn't object to letting me go for the milk. At the farm the woman was alone in the kitchen. She explained to me that her husband was busy with a cow ready to calf. Before she went to fill my pail, she said with some embarrassment:

"If it wouldn't bother you, mam'selle, since you're a doctor, could you please take a look at Maria? She's complaining of cramps and she's running a fever."

She opened the door to a kind of bedroom-dormitory where the huge wooden bed of the parents filled up one whole corner. Two very young children were asleep in a small iron bed and Maria was sleeping in the third, slightly larger bed.

As she went in, the mother turned on the electric light that hung from a string in the middle of the room. Its light was dimmed by the dirt on the bulb.

"Tell the lady-doctor where you hurt," she told the child.

I touched her forehead. It was only slightly warm. Lifting the sheet back, and lifting up her nightgown and undoing her sanitary napkin, I felt her abdomen. The abdominal wall was supple. I told the mother:

"Nothing serious. A little aspirin and tomorrow she'll be all right."

But I didn't want to lose this chance to speak to the girl alone for a few minutes. I said, "I'll stay and talk a little while you get the milk. It'll take her mind off her cramps."

When she saw me walk in, Maria looked upset. Despite the fact that her mother had left, her eyes kept an undefinable expression of distress and refusal, and her entire body stayed tightly bunched up in the depths of the bed. She was probably afraid I'd accuse her of pretending to be sick. She wasn't ill; she had only wanted a little peace and quiet. Lying in her little bed, she was trying to recapture the sweetness and innocence of her childhood which had protected her for so many years. She wanted to bury these new, shameful secrets in her pillow, and find consolation for a life that had suddenly become serious, where there wasn't any more time for her to play.

Then, slowly, reassuringly, I started to talk. I tried to say something to comfort her, to tell her in simple words that menstruation isn't ugly or dirty, but a normal, necessary event that she didn't have to be ashamed or afraid of; that it was a sign that she was no longer a little girl, that soon, instead of playing with her doll, she could be a real mother.

As I talked I was thinking how useless my words were. I couldn't believe that it would only take a few minutes and a few words to transform this young girl's future, to open the eyes of a stupid father and an ignorant mother to the psychological needs of their child, to alleviate the daily drudgery of the farm wife and make her husband more attentive, more respectful and more loving, or to create the miracle of a world where men and women would finally be equal.

I think that only the missionary who has to abandon his lone convert to the heathen can understand my awful feeling of helplessness when I heard her mother step into the kitchen, and come in with my pail of milk. I gave the child a comforting pat on the cheek, and in an attempt to make her less frightened about having other painful periods, added:

"Today you hurt a little because it was the first time. But later, since this isn't a disease or a wound, you won't have any more pain."

Behind my back, the mother said nastily, "Did you hear what the lady doctor said? You're not sick. You don't have to stay in bed and tomorrow morning you'll help me do the laundry, since you got your sheets dirty. . . ."

Maria, despite my sorrow at seeing you start groping toward your hard fate, my friendship can't help you in any way. But I feel profoundly responsible and at one with you as you embark on the touching adventure of womanhood, which by chance you have started before my eyes.

I would have been so happy to help you, I would have tried so hard to free you! I hope that I'll free others. But I couldn't save Mariette, and I can't free you because you're still too young.

Friday

Today I planned to cut the thorns around the raspberry bushes. I dozed off in the shade while waiting for it to get cooler.

About three in the afternoon mother came out of the house. I watched her hurry to my side, smiling and flushed with excitement. She was obviously coming to deliver good news. As soon as she reached me, she announced:

148

"Someone's here to see you! From your hospital. He's in the living room."

Why did I immediately think of Pascali, who might have made a little detour on the Paris-Cabourg road to stop by and see me? Excitedly, I asked:

"Did he tell you his name?"

"No. He's very blond, almost white-haired."

"Oh! That's my friend Lachaux," I said.

My lack of enthusiasm must have showed my disappointment. But I was immediately ashamed of my small betrayal of our friendship.

"I'll go get him," I announced, jumping up.

"Not dressed like that?" mother exclaimed.

She was right; I couldn't receive Lachaux in a bathing suit. Despite the intimacy that came from living in close quarters at the residence, we'd never gone into each other's rooms in pajamas during the year.

I picked up my faded, ancient blue jeans—the same ones I had worn to go to the farm.

"Can't you dress up a little more than that?" mother said. "What will he think?"

"It's not worth it. Lachaux and I saw each other every day in hospital coats. He'd be surprised if I made an effort to be elegant for him."

Before I left the shade of the apple tree, I pulled my blue jeans on over my bathing suit. Mother didn't say anything but she looked on with disapproval while I completed my outfit with an old sweater. Lachaux couldn't accuse me of having become a slave to fashion during my vacation. . . .

As I walked through the garden, I thought about mother's description of my visitor. Caution and especially the desire not to criticize a potential suitor had kept her from saying: "A rather ugly young man, with freckles and a big nose." In a sudden joyous burst of friendship I smiled at the idea of seeing that comic face again, and finding again in those pale eyes that lively, precise intelligence which made Lachaux so comfortable to be with in spite of his lazy look.

He was waiting in the semidarkness of the living room with its drawn shutters, sitting on one of the hideous easy chairs of red and brown velvet.

"Let's not stay here," I said, taking his hand and pulling him up. "Come out under my tree. We'll be much more

149

comfortable than here in this depressing Victorian atmosphere."

Outside, in the full sunlight, Lachaux, with his unhealthy city pallor, suddenly looked like a white mouse that had come out of its hole a little too quickly. He blinked his eyes several times, then exclaimed, as if he had just now really seen me for the first time, "Oh, you've gotten a tan. You look well again. That's wonderful!"

He smiled a friendly smile.

"One part of my visit is already unnecessary. I was worried by your silence. I thought you might still be sick, and that your recovery mightn't be going well ... but here you are in good shape! I'm reassured."

"And the other reason for your visit?"

Then Lachaux, who always looks at me without embarrassment, turned his head away before answering, as if the question bothered him. Finally he said:

"I wanted some fresh air. You can't breathe in Gennevilliers. This morning they must have unloaded oil in the harbor; you could imagine being in the hold full of oil fumes. By noon the idea of eating in the dining room made me sick. I asked Tabarly to make the second rounds for me, got into the car and drove off."

He smiled his slightly crooked smile. "When I was a child, I dreamed about running away every night but it never went further than that. At twenty-eight, it's time for me to catch up. And thus, my dear Sleeping Beauty, I came to you!"

"O my Prince Charming, I was waiting for you."

We both laughed, but his face seemed somewhat tense. Was it the sun in his eyes? His upper lip was turned up, showing his teeth, and for a moment he really looked like a white rabbit.

When we got to the apple tree, he sighed with pleasure at the shade: "Ah! This feels good."

He sat down in the folding chair that mother uses when she sits down near me and began studiously following the flight of the insects around the branches. But almost immediately he apologized for his silence.

"I'm slightly dazed by the trip and the heat!"

His behavior seemed odd. His eyes were still avoiding mine. For a minute I thought he was regretting having made his visit. But the immobility of his face was quite different from the sleepy air that he takes on when he's indifferent or bored.

150

Slumped in his chair, he kept staring obstinately at the leaves.

To keep the silence from dragging on forever, I began to tell him about my days in the country, and since he kept letting me rattle on, finally I ran out of things to say, so I asked him for news about Alberte Apple. As he had done in his letter, he mustered an exasperated sigh about her obstinacy. She keeps asking him to do a "psychoanalysis." To tease him, I smilingly reproached him for a lack of professional ethics and a sense of devotion to his "unhappy heart"—since it was obvious that a solid "transfer" of the frustrated patient to her devoted analyst would be even better for my awkward friend than hormone injections.

But instead of smiling, he answered seriously, "She doesn't need analysis. Her case is simple. You know what she's hoping for?"

"She told me when she came to visit me the morning I was leaving Gennevilliers. She wants to be loved, not to get old alone, to have children of her own instead of spending her life looking after other people's children."

Till then I had felt that Lachaux was looking for an opportunity in the conversation to tell me something important. It was this sentence about Alberte that made him decide to speak. Suddenly he fixed me with a tense, almost painful look; he squeezed his lips together, as if he were hesitating before pronouncing momentous and irrevocable words; then in a low voice, almost stuttering, he finally managed to get out:

"Well! Claude, I really came because I was so unhappy and because I wanted to tell you that I love you."

He stammered almost uncontrollably at the words "I love you," then he stopped suddenly as if it terrified him to hear these three words on his own lips.

His light-colored eyes looked at me so bewilderedly that his intelligent face looked slightly ridiculous.

As for me, I was so astonished by his admission that for the moment I didn't know what to say. Lachaux in love with me! Despite Alberte's assertion, until now not one gesture, not a single word had led me to believe that he thought of me as anything except a good friend!

His eyes were fixed intensely on mine to watch for a reaction and when I opened my mouth, he raised his hand to stop me.

"No, don't say anything yet. Let me explain first. Otherwise I'd never have enough courage to tell you everything."

Now that the secret was out, he seemed to have regained his confidence. But the face that I knew so well took on a strange haunted look and when he started to speak again I heard his voice tremble passionately for the first time since we had known each other.

"You remember that patient of Flournoy's I described to you. Again and again, he saw an abyss in front of him and he had an irresistible desire to throw himself into it. The idea haunted him day and night, and turned his dreams into nightmares. Flournoy calmed him down by making him promise never to go to the mountains. Some years later, this patient, who considered himself completely cured, was brave enough to do some mountain climbing. He got killed falling over a precipice. It's the same way with me and love. I know that I'm ugly . . ."

I made an affectionate gesture. But Lachaux's eyes kept watching me timidly, and he didn't even leave me time to protest.

"Yes, I know that I'm ugly, and even worse than ugly, I'm laughable—remember Pascali's guest at that last party? That's why I've always mistrusted women. They can only upset and complicate the life of a man like me. I'm too occupied with my work. Love would only have hindered me, annoyed me, upset my timetable. So I eliminated it from my life and I ended up not thinking about it any more. And I thought that if you didn't think about love, you wouldn't fall in love just the way you don't see passersby in the street if you don't look out the window. And just when I finally thought I was safe (like Flournoy's patient), I met you. For a year I was close to you every day. You gave me your friendship. For a man like me that was incredible. It was only one step from friendship to love and I took it without even being aware of it."

As Lachaux talked, I gradually thought back on a conversation I had with him shortly before my departure. We were talking about a patient hospitalized after a suicide attempt. It was his third try. Each time seven or eight years went by between attempts, and each attempt was caused by a disappointment in love. The fact that seemed extraordinary to me was that all the women this man loved had a common trait: they squinted.

Then Lachaux had told me that Descartes—the famous man of reason—also had an eccentric passion for women who squinted. In relation to this curious case, we had discussed the phenomenon of love at great length. I had talked about the time when the state of love seemed to me to be a chronic or acute poisoning of the system, caused by the excretions from the sexual glands. And Lachaux had outlined for me a curious hypothesis developed by Swoboda. According to this hypothesis, adult life operates on a seven-year cycle: every seventh year is a year of extraordinary sexual and intellectual fruitfulness, a kind of renewal of puberty that can be accounted for by the periodic heightening of glandular activity. Without defining it exactly as a pathological state, Lachaux concluded that the state of ecstasy or emotional inebriation—that still undefined phenomenon commonly called *love*—manifests itself in the one afflicted by a heightening of esteem of the object of his passion, a blindness toward the loved one's faults and a refusal to listen to all the counsels of prudence.

Today this same Lachaux confessed his love for me. His voice had changed; it was husky and low; his face was suffused with blushes under his pale scholar's skin. Listening to him I felt both amused and intimidated. I kept still as he had asked me to. But maybe out of loyalty to him I should have stopped him at once. I felt that by letting him continue I was betraying his confidence. It was as if I were listening to a child innocent enough to tell me about some prank that I'd have to punish him for.

Lachaux took a long time to explain that, after so many months of intimacy, it was my departure that had suddenly revealed to him the fact that he loved me. He had made desperate efforts to reject the idea of this love. He had repeated a thousand times to himself that he could only be my coworker, only useful to me because he could explain cases of psychosomatic gynecology or understand delicate problems of female psychology. But these attempts to be reasonable were all in vain! Ever since I'd left Gennevilliers, he kept imagining me curled up in one of the chairs in his room, discussing and defending my ideas step by step as we'd done for whole evenings. When he sat down at his work table, he couldn't get interested in his work, he couldn't even open his books. He sat for hours with his chin on his hands, his pen idle, letting his mind wander.

Without me, his life seemed as empty as his room. Each day in the hospital was only a repetition of the last. He kept saying to himself, "She'll never love me," and then immediately afterwards would come the thought, "Why not?" Feeling that this uncertainty would leave him hopelessly in the grip of his obsession, he'd decided to come and ask me the question.

As Lachaux talked, his expression gradually became more and more poignant. It was as if he had received a mortal wound and, by describing his pain in detail, he was finding his own means of salvation.

When Lachaux finally fell silent, he seemed truly exhausted. His lips seemed parched from the heat. After his last word had been spoken, there was a singularly pointed and oppressive silence under the apple tree. The only sound was the buzzing of a wasp.

Now it was my turn to speak. A painful moment. Several times, Lachaux had told me of his long hesitation—he hadn't wanted to come to me because of his fear of hearing. "I don't love you." But I saw eagerness akin to hope on his pale face. How could I tell him the obvious truth that friendship isn't love? And how could I discourage him for good without hurting him too much, especially without shattering his masculine pride? I had to explain my feeling of closeness to him, an attachment that's deep and sincere. There was also my gratitude—without his friendship my life as an intern would have been awful. But why, I thought, does he want something more than friendship? And why does it have to be just when my meeting with little Maria has lifted me out of my torpor and given me the desire to revenge Mariette's death and to throw myself into battle again?

The silence dragged on. . . . I was beginning to panic about finding some way to express myself when mother came out of the house and went to the well. She had put on her flowered linen dress in Lachaux's honor but she couldn't resist keeping herself busy around the house as usual. The overwhelming vision of the matron that I'd decided never to become suddenly gave me a thought. "I must," I thought, "tell Lachaux that I don't want to get married without directly refusing his love. It may seem ridiculous to talk about a young man of twenty-eight in terms of candor and purity, especially one who's had so much experience with people because of medicine. But Lachaux still is candid and pure—the eternal boy scout, Pascali says—and he wouldn't dare to offer me love outside of marriage."

154

I looked at my friend. His eyes stared avidly and questioningly at me as if telling me that it was up to me to break the silence. For a minute I was ashamed to discourage him by taking advantage of his goodness and his honesty. But how could I act differently? You don't marry a man—or give up a career—out of simple friendship.

I sat up a bit straighter, I squared my shoulders; I let my face express all the pain I felt—then I took a deep breath and began:

"You know, Lachaux, that I care for you very deeply. But you also know that I've decided to become a doctor and you know what I want to do after I get my diploma. If I were religious and told you that I couldn't marry you because I wanted to become a nun, I'm sure you wouldn't try to thwart my vocation. I have another kind of vocation which made me choose medicine as my calling. It's just as demanding, and I can no more escape from it than if I had pronounced my monastic vows."

My thoughts took shape as I spoke. I felt stronger, more able to alleviate the hurt of my friend's disappointment quickly. Lachaux was still silent, so I continued. "I'm very grateful to you for offering me a life for two. I'll never forget it. But I can't accept it. My duty is to stay free, not to get tied down."

Lachaux objected timidly in a low voice: "To join one's lives is not to abdicate one's individuality. I think I can make you happy without suffocating you. . . ."

"I know you're loyal and incapable of trying to enslave me. It's reason, not pride in my liberty that makes me refuse your offer of marriage. To do what I want to do, I had to make the choice once and for all."

Lachaux looked at me with such tenderness that I was sure he was thinking more of me than of himself when he asked: "You're sure that you'll never regret this?"

"No. What I've decided to erase from my life seems to me to have lost its reality."

"I don't think that a woman can be happy alone in the world as it is today. You've seen how afraid your friend Alberte Apple is when she's faced with a solitary future!"

Never before had I felt so strongly that I had to be cruel. Lachaux was hanging on to hope the way a survivor of a shipwreck clings to the side of a lifeboat that's already overloaded. To avoid being capsized and drowning with him, I had to push him pitilessly back into the sea.

At least I would be sincere in telling him that marriage is a trap for women! I answered:

"Forgive me if I tell you what a young Communist activist I treated in Gennevilliers once told me. When I advised her to get married so she'd have a more secure life, she told me, 'I expect more from the revolution than from a husband!' I must help bring about the revolution that will establish true equality between men and women, because in my life, in my home, and all around me, I've seen the way that a few years of married life destroys most women."

While he listened to me, two wrinkles of infinite sadness and bitterness gradually pulled the corners of his mouth farther and farther down. Now he knew that the battle was lost. But since I gave him the opportunity, he fought bravely to the very end.

"I think that when you're in love, you sacrifice your liberty joyfully. I'll do everything you ask me to and I'll never ask you to sacrifice anything—especially not your career. You'll be free."

"No! I'm afraid you'll *never* understand, Lachaux!" I immediately regretted saying it that way. It sounded full of affectionate pity and rather scornful. I began again with more spirit. "No! I'll never be really free. You're about to take the competitive exams to get a post at a psychiatric hospital. When you've passed, you'll have to accept the position they offer you and you'll have to live at some godforsaken hospital in the depths of the country for four or five years before you're asked to come to Paris or some big town. If I were married to you I'd feel that I didn't have the right to interfere with your career. But what would I have to do during those four or five years at some asylum in the country except nursing our babies and changing their diapers? And I don't feel that motherhood is my calling! When I work to plan other people's families, my life will be so full and rewarding that I won't feel the need to fill it with my own kids. Or would you rather imagine it this way: there we'll be, forty years later, an old medical couple, a little ridiculous, the last two specimens of a scientific and idealistic bohemia, with our old hopes as our only children, hopes which have slowly faded into hideous abortions of our ideals?"

Lachaux smiled in answer to my thrust. But I didn't recognize his usual smile—this one seemed so feeble.

I seemed to see a flicker of desire in Lachaux's look

156

when I had mentioned motherhood, and suddenly I could see myself in his arms, trembling with loathing at his touch.

Did he suspect where my thoughts might be taking me or did the revulsion show in my face? He added, as if it were his last chance to change my mind: "Do you know how Stekel interprets the meaning of the story of Sleeping Beauty? According to him, it represents the liberation of a woman, tied to her childhood and her family, by a man who can free her from her infantile inhibitions and permit her to triumph over her past. . . ."

He suddenly fell silent. Mother was approaching, carrying glasses and a stone jug on a tray. Because the garden was sunny and hot, she had put on her straw hat. With the double smile of a mother and an attentive hostess, she announced:

"I thought Dr. Lachaux might be thirsty, so I'm bringing you some cider I cooled in the well."

Lachaux tried politely to get up and give her his chair. Mother wouldn't let him.

"No, no! I'm not staying, I have work to do. I'll let you go on with your conversation."

But this statement was only for form's sake. She stayed on to ask questions about my year as an intern (after all, here was someone who had worked with me, and I had really told her very little about my life), such as—wasn't I working too hard? I had looked so thin when I arrived in Mesnil. . . .

Lachaux bore this interrogation with a tense, mechanical politeness. It was obvious that he was making an enormous effort not to think about something else, but mother was blinded by her curiosity and didn't seem to notice it. I knew what agony he was going through but I couldn't think of a way to free him. Finally he looked wearily at his watch and said, "I must go. They're expecting me back at the hospital this evening."

"Oh! And I was hoping that you'd eat dinner with us!" mother exclaimed.

She was sincerely disappointed, especially because she would be missing a fine opportunity to ask all her questions. Then, trying to be tactful, she finally left us alone.

We said nothing for a long time. It wasn't an easy conversation to start up again. His face now showed hopeless suffering and discouragement, but he didn't have the air of total collapse that comes with completely unexpected despair. Lachaux was already prepared to hear my refusal when he came; probably he had predicted subconsciously that he wouldn't be able to convince me, but he was still hoping. Then, while I was forcing myself to use skillful arguments to discourage him without making myself feel too guilty, our dialogue had become a way for him to make an honorable retreat.

He got up. The light filtering through the leaves made his face look green. He smiled sadly at me.

"I told you everything, I'm leaving—that's the sensible thing to do. Otherwise it might become like one of those horrible railroad station farewells when the train is slowly pulling away and you don't have anything more to say to each other, so you look at each other, silent and embarrassed."

But he couldn't help adding sadly, "I was really so convinced that I was made for you! Being a psychiatrist, one thinks one is psychologically objective, but, psychiatrist or not, one doesn't really know anything about other people or about oneself."

I too wanted to be generous.

"What you thought you saw in me was only a passing illusion, an error of judgment. You'll be the first to smile about it in a little while. Remember what you told to me one evening about the overvaluing of the love object? You've put me on a pedestal. Soon I'd have disappointed you and I'd have felt unhappy to know that I was so much inferior to the idea you had of me."

Lachaux didn't protest; just shook his head slowly. He closed his eyes for a minute and I thought he was going to burst into tears—this man who had always been so reasonable and self-controlled. Then he looked at me again, his glance so full of love as he raised his eyes to meet mine that I had to blink back the tears.

As he left the shelter of the apple tree Lachaux recovered his usual self-deprecating humor and said, smiling:

"I've so often repeated to my patients that you must know how to silence your impossible desires! But because I couldn't suggest something better my psychotherapeutic advice didn't go any further. Here's my chance to develop a method. . . ."

Then he left—my ironic Prince Charming with his sandy-colored skin and his pale, pale eyes. I came back to stretch out under my tree. There are no traces of his visit except a jug and two glasses, where the flies are finishing off what's left of the greenish colored cider. I feel sad, listless, empty-headed; as discouraged and unhappy as during the first days after I arrived. It's no help to contemplate my leafy vault—I can't recover the feeling of relief its shade gave me yesterday. In the hot, clear evening that's falling, I can't seem to reconquer my peace.

Perhaps it's because I don't know how to deceive myself that I can't find the serenity I'm seeking. A few minutes ago I could only think of the impossibility of marrying Lachaux, and that thought forced me to defend myself without pity. Now that he's gone without the few words that would have made him happy, I'm touched by the overwhelming gift of his love; I'm moved by the false appearance of coldness which he gives to others, when a few moments ago he was trembling with passion and tenderness.

Now I can think back a little—I can see again my first visit to the neuro-psychiatric ward and watch Lachaux questioning the little boy he had installed in his easy chair while he himself sat on a little footstool to give the child more confidence. I remembered the hours I spent with him working on my thesis—before then my evenings had been slow and dull but near the man whose friendship I trusted, whose mind was so clear and precise, I started to feel secure and happy in my work. I remembered all the things we talked about in the difficult field of sexology—thanks to his tact, nothing was ever equivocal or embarrassing. Lachaux's actions had always been so sure and calm.

Now I'm alone again, without someone to talk to, without any recourse. Is it my fate never to be able to give myself to those who love me?

Often, to mask the deep friendship I felt for Lachaux, I'd humorously call myself his "disciple." Today, by rejecting him, I'm betraying a part of myself. And thinking back on his fairness, his patience, his perseverance and his integrity—I think it's the best part of me.

I know I'll miss Lachaux's friendship. Just as the noon heat keeps the walls and the tiles of my room warm even late at night, this friendship will keep me warm for a long time. But I don't have a place by my side to offer Lachaux for the rest of my life; the future I've planned doesn't have room for him. I could do nothing but refuse him though I feel cruel and at the same time afflicted with inertia in spite of my sorrow.

Poor Lachaux. He'll suffer in silence. At least I didn't hurt his male pride. When he thinks of me later on, he'll be able to tell himself that I sacrificed him (and with some difficulty) on the altar of duty and reason, and that my refusal was noble, because it was heroic self-denial. . . .

Besides, I'm beginning to understand what gave him the courage to make his declaration. First there were the conversations with Alberte. Because of her obsession with men he must have become convinced that I was silently in love with him, just the way he was in love with me. Then, in a more complicated way, there was what I told him after Arlette's visit about our discussions of marriage when we were in school.

After I came across the famous book by Léon Blum, Arlette and I agreed that it was unthinkable to swear solemnly to sleep with only one man all your life unless you'd gone through a long apprenticeship with him, and unless you had some real reason to believe that you could honestly keep your oath. We'd also been disgusted when we read somewhere else that marriage without love is possible if you're content with a "marriage of convenience." I told Lachaux that this was the time when, under my influence, Arlette pretended to reject masculine domination. We both refused to go dancing to avoid being led by our partners; we both rebelled at the idea of being reproductive machines devoted only to propagating the species, of having our freedom taken by a man, of submitting instead of commanding.

Lachaux is, of course, well-informed about juvenile psychology and sexuality. He immediately deduced from my account that Arlette's refusal, her revulsion and her shame were only the resolution of the last difficulties of puberty, the end of a difficult period when reactions to men are composed of fear and attraction, loathing and desire at the same time. She had quickly managed to free herself once she was away from the cloistered life of the boarding school, in the more worldly environment at the University of Algiers.

As for me, he probably thought because of his own experience, that my acceptance of myself as a woman had been retarded by the ascetic life of a scholar, but that, though dormant, my capacity for love would awaken with encouragement.

That thought could have come to him on the evening during Mariette's tetanus attack when I talked to him so warmly about Pascali, not realizing that I was hurting him.

With the help of Alberte Apple and Arlette, he must have concluded that I had finally resolved my conflicts and that he could shyly try his luck.

Poor Lachaux. I can't imagine his mouth on my mouth, or his skin against my skin. But I couldn't tell him that I can't bear the thought of touching him, just as Pascali wouldn't want to touch a plain girl like me!

It's true that some evenings in Gennevilliers I hated to be alone, but I only longed to have someone near me because I was tired. Today I'm rested, I've regained my strength and I have enough confidence in myself to save my liberty by discouraging my only admirer.

The evening is coming. "The patient's room is the physician's kingdom" says an Arab proverb. My kingdom will be tiny for some time yet.

I'll get the milk pail and go comfort Maria!

Saturday

Today has been the hottest day since I've come to Mesnil, and I was really looking forward to my nap under my apple tree.

Mother woke me up at four o'clock. Leaning over me, she gave me a touchingly sweet smile, her face red from the flaming heat in the garden. She waited until I was wide awake to tell me:

"Guess who's come to talk to you?" She spoke in the same mysterious voice that she announced "surprises" in when I was a little girl.

Thinking about Lachaux, I almost said, "Surely Prince Charming," but mother seemed so happy with her little game that I didn't want to spoil her pleasure.

"How could I guess? I don't know anyone here."

She looked at me as if she could hardly contain her pride, and hesitated—as if the news were so important that she had to be cautious about breaking it to me.

"It's the doctor!" she finally announced solemnly.

"Again! This is ridiculous. And besides, which doctor?"

"There's only one doctor in Mesnils, Dr. Ferrières. He wanted to see you immediately."

"He wanted to see me? Did you throw him out?"

When a subject is as important to her as this, mother is impervious to irony. She protested:

161

"Of course not! I told him that you were resting. He went off on an urgent call. He'll come by again in a minute."

And, afraid that the subtlety of her plans might be beyond me, she added:

"You'll have just enough time to get dressed!"

"Oh! I only need three minutes to pull on my blue jeans and a T-shirt."

Mother cried, "You're going to appear dressed like that in front of someone you've never met?"

"Why not? I'm on vacation."

"Can't you please me a little, Claude? Try to make yourself look a little nicer. Dr. Ferrières isn't from out of town like your friend who came yesterday. What is he going to think?"

"It's your doctor who wants to see me! I don't want anything from him. It couldn't matter less what he thinks about my clothes!"

I couldn't resist asking:

"What *does* he want?"

"The impression I got was that he needed you for a difficult case. Everybody knows that you've just spent a year's internship in a hospital near Paris."

There was something so forlorn and so pitiful in the way mother was watching me, that I didn't really want to be stubborn. After all, now that I was feeling better, the days were endless. I was waking up as early as I did in Gennevilliers and the delights of infinite leisure were going sour. I couldn't just sit and watch the apples ripening, weed the paths and fetch milk at the farm forever.

"Why not," I thought, "agree to meet this Dr. Ferrières, at least to find out what he wants?"

He was probably going to ask me to replace him for a few days and that would be an excellent way to get away from the boredom of being alone with my thoughts. To make a good diagnosis you need a free mind; you have to remember cases and not individual patients. Replacing someone for a few days would be the best way to forget Mariette and little Maria for a while.

"O.K.!" I said. "I'll put on a dress."

Mother was astounded that she had won so quickly. She glanced at me as if to assure herself that we were indeed accomplices from now on, then her face brightened.

She followed me up to my room.

"Which dress are you going to wear?"

I smiled because I'd just had a silly thought: why not take Arlette's advice and put on one of the two dresses given to me by the grateful seamstress from Gennevilliers to meet the Hippocrates of Mesnil?

The dresses had been in a suitcase ever since I'd arrived. When I took them out they were all wrinkled.

"Which one do you want to wear?" mother asked.

I pointed to one at random. She snatched it up and disappeared, saying: "I'm going to iron it."

So my idea got me at least a quarter of an hour of peace and quiet.

I felt hot. Mother had installed a shower in the small closet on the landing, so I gave my body to the refreshing streams of water. In the middle of my shower, I suddenly thought about my thesis: I couldn't spend my time working on it if I accepted the summer replacement job. "Never mind!" I decided. "After all, I'm on vacation."

I was still dripping when mother came back with the dress delicately draped over her arm.

With the speed and efficiency of a nurse she dried me, rubbed me down and got me into my dress; then she stepped back and cried in an astonished tone that would ordinarily have irritated me intensely, "Oh! You look charming in that pale green!"

She repeated, "You look charming! ... Really! ..."

I looked at myself in the mirror. Ten days of sun and open air have given my skin a healthy golden color; and my hair has lost its boyish severity because it hasn't been cut for over two months. My neck, shoulders and arms have filled out and now that my cheeks aren't so hollow and pale, my eyes no longer make me look as if I had T.B. Besides, yesterday Lachaux said that I looked well.

Suddenly mother was worried.

"What shoes are you going to wear? You need high heels for this full skirt."

"I never wear them. I don't have any."

Mother disappeared again. I heard her opening a closet on the landing and shuffling cardboard boxes. She came back triumphantly.

"I found this pair. They're too small for me but they should fit you."

The doorbell rang. Mother rushed down the stairs taking off her apron, and then I heard her say:

"Come in, doctor. Claude's expecting you. She'll be right down."

I slipped the shoes on and I was surprised to feel myself walking down the stairs not with my usual heavy tread but with the graceful gait that goes with thin dresses and high heels. "I hope I won't trip on the doorstep," I thought. I laughed. I felt as if I were truly on vacation.

The living room shutters had been opened in honor of the occasion, and mother was chatting in her most social voice. When I came in, Dr. Ferrières, who had been sitting in one of the Victorian chairs, stood up.

"Here's my daughter," mother said proudly. Then she excused herself with a tactful smile that was slightly too obvious. "Since you're going to talk medicine, I'll leave you."

Dr. Ferrières looks a little older than the thirty-three years mother had mentioned. He's of average height and well built, and has a healthy, country complexion. His hair is light brown. The first impression you get from his face is that he's a thoughtful man, of moderate beliefs, a man of definite intelligence. His chin, mouth and nose are a bit too large, indicating a strong will, maybe even stubbornness. His wide forehead and his direct way of looking at you are very confidence-inspiring. Mother and I had both been right about the reason for his visit: after apologizing for his intrusion, Dr. Ferrières asked me if I could replace him for ten days in August. He had to be at summer camp for army reserves and his usual replacement had just told him that he wouldn't be free.

Then he added that he had another, much more urgent and critical reason to ask for my help. This was what mother had told me about.

"For the last five days my cousin Jacques Ferrières has been staying wth me," he explained. "He's the son of my father's brother, who served as a doctor with the army and was killed in 1945 in Alsace. His mother died when he was born. I'm a year older than he is. My father was his guardian, and after his father died, we were brought up together. Jacques is like a brother to me. We roomed together in school at Bernay, we passed our entrance exams in Caen, then we went to Paris to medical school. Unfortunately, Jacques came down with T.B. during his third year. He had to spend two years in a sanatorium, and when he recovered he refused to go on with his studies. I must say that he was an undisciplined and indifferent student, and each time it was only his intelligence that saved him at the last minute. Until he was in boarding school with me, he was insufferable. He was thrown out everywhere, as if he always had to defy the system. But there were reasons: my uncle had brought him up rather severely, and only made him more stubborn. My father's affectionate influence seemed to have made him better behaved—he passed his baccalaureate, his entrance exams and his first two medical exams without any trouble. But even though he attended the hospital and the medical school regularly, he spent his evenings in Saint-German-des-Près with a crowd of avant-garde writers and artists. He used to laugh at me when I told him to lead a less chaotic life. He was used to improvising his life from day to day, to making it a perpetual game of chance, and he systematically ignored all caution."

Dr. Ferrières fell silent for a few seconds as if it was particularly painful to recall that period.

As soon as he had begun to talk, enunciating each word slowly and deliberately, I could see that the doctor of Mesnil didn't belong to the breed of people who talk quickly and easily. His mind is weighty rather than brilliant. But though this slowness and calmness are rather irritating to begin with, they soon make his conversation reassuring. Even the pauses that come when he's groping for ideas and the words to describe them create a sensation of peace rather than embarrassment in the long run. He went on in the same measured tone.

"Jacques was so sure that he was invulnerable that the lesion on his lung came as a rude shock to him. When he was condemned to inactivity for two years, he thought his life was finished. When he got out of the sanatorium, he said that he wouldn't finish his medical studies; that he wanted to see the world. My father and I insisted, but he had made up his mind. A friend suggested journalism and the possibility of fame as an international correspondent. He was enthusiastic. Five years later, having got no further abroad than Italy, England and Spain, he gave up that career. Since he wanted so badly to go to the Far East, my father finally found him a job as director of the South Vietnamese agency of a large Franco-American pharmaceutical firm. Then he would have the opportunity he longed for to travel in India and Malaysia. Two months ago, he came back for his first home leave in France. He was in pitiful physical shape. As you can imagine I'm rather used to alcohol poisoning in Mesnil and with Jacques the diagnosis was obvious. Besides, he admitted frankly that he'd started to smoke opium. Fortunately he had stayed on moderate doses; he's never smoked more than about ten pipes a day.

"I immediately took him to one of my old colleagues in Paris who specializes in withdrawal cures. Jacques agreed to enter a clinic. The withdrawal was relatively quick. After three weeks, my cousin stopped suffering and gained back some weight. And though he was still suffering from insomnia and latent anxiety, he started demanding permission to leave. My colleague phoned me to warn me about the consequences of a premature release."

Again Dr. Ferrières stopped. He looked at me more urgently as if what he was going to tell me would concern me directly, then still speaking calmly, he explained:

"Jacques kept harassing me with letters. He claimed that his imprisonment was intolerable and useless. He asked me to take him back to Mesnil so that he could finish his convalescence under my supervision. Just as he had once been consumed with the desire to leave for faraway places, now his letters were full of the exile's frenzied longing for his own home. I went to get him five days ago. My colleague told me that I was being unwise. But Jacques was so happy that I didn't hesitate. Besides he seemed to be in quite good physical shape. He had 'gained' a little as the farmers say here. He was even calm. I've followed the orders my colleague gave me to the letter. I continued to give him laxatives to decongest the liver and hasten the elimination of the opium. But in the last forty-eight hours, things haven't been going so well. He's complaining of sweating, migraines, chills, dizziness, and cramps again. He refuses to eat, to shave, or to wash. He has nervous tics and intestinal troubles. He says he can't sleep. I'm all the more upset because my colleague warned me about the risk of a relapse, and at the same time explained to me that it would take a long time before the metabolism achieved a new point of equilibrium. I'm afraid that if he's left to himself, Jacques might do something stupid. For instance, he might take advantage of the time when I make my house calls to dash over to Evreux with a forged prescription for opium and then the cure would have to be started all over again."

Dr. Ferrières hesitated again, then said:

"So, if you could spend a few hours a day with him, it would let me go to see my patients without worrying so much."

The natural, undemanding way he kept looking at me made me feel immediately drawn to him. It was almost the same impression I'd felt when I first met Lachaux. So I volunteered to start right away without even thinking that I might be undertaking a tedious and difficult task.

In the hall I called to mother to tell her that I'd be going away. She came to accompany us to the door after the doctor had apologized for dragging me off in such a hurry.

His car was parked at the edge of the sidewalk and as he was opening the door for me, I saw the curtain in our kitchen window move. Other curtains were lifted as we started off. The rumors would soon be flying.

Probably Dr. Ferrières thought that I already knew Mesnil. In any case, he was so preoccupied with his cousin's condition that he didn't stop talking the whole trip about what a disaster a relapse would be, so close to the end of a withdrawal cure.

As I listened to him, I was watching the little town pass by. I was rather astonished—on the road to the farm I had recognized the Ouche landscape that La Varende described so lovingly, but the main street of Mesnil was a sorry exercise in banality. Except for the ancient church, squat and austere, topped by a square sandstone steeple, and a very few houses with brick walls and old rust-colored tile roofs, the rest denied its Norman heritage and was like any ordinary rural village which was trying its best to look like a little town open to progress. As we drove along, I saw poor or pretentiously ugly brick façades, and roofs covered with machine-made tiles in an ugly red that had no warmth or shine. There was only one picturesque note: there were geraniums in most of the windows and balconies. At the far end of a wide rectangular square that's lined with chestnut trees (which must serve as a fair ground) was a town hall in the official style of the 1880's. At its side was a market building with small cast-iron columns and a zinc roof. There was an iron scaffolding for training the firemen, and a small column; a monument to those who had died in the war, topped with a crowing Gallic cock. For such a small town, the main street seemed endless.

I remarked out loud, "Well! Mesnil really goes on forever."

The doctor turned his head and looked at me, astonished. "Don't you know the countryside?"

"I came on the evening bus, when it was dark. Since then I haven't left my garden."

"Well, well! When I drive you home, I'll give you a tour of the town; but tour may be the wrong word since Mesnil is shaped like a caterpillar. There's only one street and, as you can see, we live at opposite ends. Anyway, here we are."

The doctor parked his car in front of a house which was set back some distance from the street.

As I got out of the car I looked up and saw a beautiful two-story house, built of golden stone that blended into pink brick, in the purest seventeenth-century style.

Noticing my admiration, the doctor said, "Forty years ago, when my father bought this house, it was painted white. He had the façade stripped to expose the brick and stone. He's the one, as you'll see, who filled the house with old objects and antique furniture. He was always very interested in Norman folklore."

He pushed open a beautiful oak door and ushered me into a foyer that was entirely paved in old white and blue stones, set in a diamond pattern. After the strong sun outside, the light was soft and gentle. Through the many little panes of a tall French window, you could see the lawn and beds of dahlias. The air smelled of furniture polish and the warm scent of the past. I had the feeling that I was entering a hospitable house that would soon become familiar, that I would find in it an unknown, almost unreal sweetness and peace.

As I stepped forward, I found myself in the middle of a semicircle of wooden saints. They stood on old Renaissance chests lined against the walls, and they looked like sleepy, kindly guardians of the hall.

The doctor smiled when he saw me looking curiously at them.

"My father thought it would be wise to have his most redoubtable competitors in his home. These statues are the principal healing saints of Normandy. Here's St. Lo, who restores hearing to the deaf and sight to the blind; St. Ortaire, who cures hunchbacks, bowlegs, and curvature of the spine; St. John the Strong, who heals children with weak legs; St. Firmin, who specializes in epilepsy; St. Laurent, whose death on a grill makes him the supreme protection against the fire of shingles; St. Mammaire, whose name dedicates him to heal abscessed breasts, as St. Vitus cures the dance that bears his name. Here's that fat clumsy fellow St. Gratien, who protects animals against all diseases and also keeps children from having nightmares: you can recognize him by the cow lying at his feet and the little child he holds by the hand. And this one with the foolish look is St. Vantrille, as infallible in cases of colic as his neighbor St. Benoit is for the diseases of the bladder."

I admired the strong colors of the tunics, the church vestments and the coats, the fair Norman beards, the gilding of the miters and halos. Each of the rustic saints had a pleasant, helpful face, with eyes too blue and lips too red. They already looked like friends to me and I was ready to attribute all the powers they claimed to them.

Passing from saint to saint we came to the bottom of an impressive oak staircase.

"Let me show you the way," the doctor said.

The first floor landing was half taken up by a huge, tall wardrobe. Its front was carved with two doves cooing at each other in a garland of roses and carnations, a tangle of undulating ribbons, shepherds hooks and garden rakes. There were several doors on either side of the wardrobe.

"Here's my cousin's room," the doctor said, pointing to the room on the left.

He knocked. He was answered by an indistinct grumble. He opened the door and stood to one side to let me go in.

The shutters were half closed because of the sun, and the whole room was in semidarkness. I saw my patient on a couch in the corner. His elegant navy blue silk pajamas made a dark blotch on the disordered sheets.

"Jacques, here's Mam'selle Sauvage. She's a doctor who's kind enough to agree to replace me during my military service. Until then, I'm going to let her get acquainted with my patients."

Dr. Ferrières had spoken in his most soothing voice. The sprawled shape sat up against the pillow. As he turned toward me with an irritating air of indifference, I could get a better look at his face. His skin was dull, a strand of dark hair lay across his forehead, several days' growth of beard surrounded a sad, hard, mouth and made his hollow cheeks look blue. Deep black eyes stared mockingly at me. His whole face—which bore the marks of the drug—had something cynical and desperate about it, but it was proud too. "If Dr. Ferrières is a bit like Lachaux,"

I thought, "he looks like Pascali, but he's stranger and more beautiful."

The patient took his time to look me over, and finally said in a deliberately offensive tone, "Ah! here's the big-hearted replacement, the white-coated magician who's going to bring me my emetics and laxatives! And why no enemas? Or why not get me a baby carriage when I can go out, or one of those nice little wheelchairs? Make yourself comfortable; fulfill your irresistible calling for nursing; satisfy your womanly desire to care for masculine deficiencies—your perverse need for handling chamber pots, basins, spittoons, dirty sheets, just as long as they're for men! I've been getting used to it for a month and a half. Sister Opportune at the hospital was ugly and much older than you are, but you can't be better than she was at draining my bile or pumping my feces."

He didn't once take his eyes off me as he talked. I was determined not to answer him. He was just a drug addict at the peak of a manic phase, but under his insolent gaze I suddenly felt ill at ease. I turned my head away, and for no real reason I rearranged a few strands of hair on my neck just to keep calm.

Did he see my embarrassment? His voice was even more ironic:

"If you're really that anxious to make some pocket money off me you can sit down, sleep, read or knit, but just be sure to keep quiet!"

He probably would have continued in this vein for some time, trying to hurt me so that he would feel better but the doctor, excusing himself with a glance, interrupted him calmly.

"Since you agree, let's start right away! I have three or four routine house calls to make before dinner, and Mademoiselle Sauvage will be able to keep quiet until I get back."

He pushed an easy chair near the window for me, gave me a pile of magazines and newspapers, then left. I heard his car start up.

As soon as Dr. Ferrières was out of the room, his cousin let loose an irritating snigger, sighed rudely and half turned his back to me to go to sleep. I almost told him, "You really don't have to worry that you might offend *me*! I've already met bastards like you and they've given me calluses on all my weak spots!"

But instead of showing this drug addict how much I

despised him, I chose to sit in my chair with the unconcerned dignity of a nurse. Basically I was almost happy
because his sleep—real or pretended—would give me
some respite in this hot, gloomy room. I hadn't taken
charge of a very docile patient! If life can leave deep
marks etched on people's faces, I would have guessed that
his had been a rather tormented existence even without
the doctor's account.

I sank back into the chair, and tried to relax every
muscle one by one. I felt uneasy. I was irritated with the
drug addict and with myself. What a difficult mission I'd
accepted! But I was stupid enough to do it. Too bad. I
absolutely had to recover my serenity and relearn the
patience I had had with Mariette.

In a few minutes I felt relaxed again and could look
around without being so irritated.

The perpetual need for change, the irresistible desire to
see faraway places that the doctor had described as the
dominant trait of his cousin's character, was confirmed by
the disorder in his room. Everything gave the impression
that this was only a temporary camping place, that these
were provisional quarters: half-unpacked suitcases lay
haphazardly on the floor, clothes were scattered just about
everywhere; a small white transistor radio was turned
upside down at the foot of a chair. But the feeling that
Jacques Ferrières had given to his room long ago as a
student still asserted itself in this disorder. The choice and
arrangement of each piece of furniture, the low couch, the
two comfortable chairs, the tiny table-desk, the bar built
into an old secretary, the profusion of ashtrays, the record
player—it all made you think of a bachelor apartment
instead of the room of a serious student.

My patient had stirred once or twice and mumbled a
bit. Now his face was half turned toward me, and I heard
his even breathing in the silence. Was he asleep or was he
only pretending? It was my job not to be fooled, and even
to be suspicious if necessary. I got up quietly and went
over to the couch.

Jacques Ferrières didn't move. Between his half-open
lips, his breathing kept its even rhythm. His beautiful
mouth, almost childish in relaxation, had no resemblance
to the mouth that had insulted me a moment earlier. Only
the hollow cheeks and the circles under his eyes revealed
the agonies of the withdrawal cure.

My patient sighed as if he were dreaming about something painful; then, without waking up, he stretched out his legs as if unconsciously searching for a cooler part of the sheet. And, twisting his shoulders so his pajamas half opened to reveal a tanned and muscular chest, he turned to the wall again.

I stood leaning over him and watching his peaceful sleep for another long moment. There was such harmony in the response of his half-naked body, in the relaxation of his face with its smooth, perfectly shaped forehead! I despised his face for being so beautiful. But maybe, for Jacques Ferrières as for Pascali, the misfortune lay precisely in his knowledge that he was beautiful.

I sat down in my chair again, and tried to think of nothing until the doctor returned.

It was close to eight o'clock when I heard the car stop outside the door. My patient was still asleep. Without making a noise, I left his room and went downstairs. The doctor had gone into his office to leave his instrument case. I told him about my eventless watch in a few words and asked him when I should come tomorrow. He thanked me, and said, "Tomorrow morning at nine if that's convenient for you."

He offered to drive me home. I refused. I wanted to walk a little, but instead of taking the main street, I followed a roundabout path that made a detour around Mesnil and went behind the houses to our garden.

As soon as I got home, mother sat me down at the table. She was longing to ask me about my patient. Perhaps she'd listened to what the doctor told me when we were in the living room or taken advantage of my absence to find out from the local gossip. When I mentioned an attack of malaria, she said:

"Well! I thought it was something worse."

Since I didn't comment on this, she added in a secretive tone, "Everybody says that the doctor's cousin is a drug addict . . . but the doctor is such a nice young man."

I pretended to be tired so I could get some peace and quiet by myself. But I was hardly lying. I felt upset and feverish and when I got to my room, before I turned on the light, I leaned against the window to try to cool my forehead.

The night hung heavy; the garden below was lost in shadow. For a long time I stood and breathed the smell of new-mown hay and grass, listening to the thousand noises that came in from the night—the rustling of the leaves as an occasional breeze passed through the trees, the cry of a night bird, the bark of a faraway dog, the monotonous croaking of the frogs. . . .

I wasn't sleepy. I felt that I could have stayed like this until dawn. When I was fifteen, on summer nights like this, I used to look out at the night from my bed. With the light out, I watched the innumerable stars or followed the path of the silvery puddle made by the moon as it moved across the floor. It seemed to me that I was waiting for something sweet but tumultuous, something that choked me, something so enormous that it swelled my heart and made me weep. But I couldn't have said what it was, and I asked myself if it was only the warm night that was flooding my veins with the fever that consumed me.

Finally I turned on the light. Tonight, as in the past, the moths immediately hurled themselves against the lampshade in a crazy dance. I lay on my narrow student's couch as I used to long ago, and now, as then, ideas and plans kept swirling endlessly around in my mind.

What would I do after Mesnil? When I left the hospital I had only had rather vague plans. I looked no further ahead than November and the defense of my thesis. Instead of taking over some physician's private practice—a job difficult for a woman to find—I thought that after two or three weeks' rest in mother's house, the wisest thing would be to go back to Gennevilliers and take the place of someone like Pascali who wanted to take a longer vacation. But I've had to give up that thought ever since Lachaux came to tell me that he loved me and left with my refusal. For him as for me, the close quarters of the interns' residence would soon become intolerable. I've promised him that I'll write to him often, but I don't want to stumble over my unhappy lover with every step I take. I must admit it upsets me to think of not going back to my old patients and I'm irritated at Lachaux for forcing me to make this sacrifice.

In any event, the promise I made to Dr. Ferrières will keep me in Mesnil for three weeks. Maybe I should be sorry that I accepted so quickly. Dr. Ferrières is friendly and easy to be with—a bit like Lachaux before he fell in love. As for his too-beautiful cousin, he exasperates me even more than the gorgeous Pascali at his worst moments.

At the bedside of this addict in his sumptuous pajamas,

173

I feel like a sister of charity who has been sent to a private sanatorium for millionaires by mistake. I've got better things to do in life than watching over seductive young men who are addicted to opium, and I hope that during the time I replace Dr. Ferrières, his patients will make up for his cousin's unpleasantness.

I'm sure that little Maria waited for me tonight when it was time to get the milk and that she was disappointed to see mother arrive in my place. I'm sorry that hurting her feelings was the price of taking care of a man like him, even if he's ill and not really responsible for his actions. Tomorrow I'll try to keep calm, no matter how hard I have to work at it. But I'd like him to know that if I chose to fight him, he'd find it hard to match my pride and insolence. . . .

Usually on the evenings when I'm irritated, as soon as I open this notebook and begin to set down the events of the day, I feel my nervousness slowly evaporating, as if I were freeing myself by my writing. What's the matter with me tonight? . . . I can't get rid of my absurd uneasiness.

Can I have already lost my precarious balance because of Lachaux's visit and because two young men intruded into my solitude today? But my rest cure under the apple tree can't have made me lose the habit of patience, even if sleep refuses to come.

At the end of this hot, heavy day, I feel damp and ill at ease, as if I were beginning to run a fever. It can't just be the heat. But what can I be waiting for that makes my thighs and my belly feel so heavy, that makes my chest and even the tips of my breasts feel so tense?

The breezes and the moths that come in through the wide-open window to attack the light remind me of my fifteenth year, of that time of uncertainty, of troubled thoughts and mad hopes.

But at twenty-five, the time of a schoolgirl's vague languorous longings is over. At twenty-five, you have to know where you're going: you should only stop for a reason and go on without looking back. And you should never get unduly irritated at the sarcasm of a casual, too-beautiful young man.

In three weeks, I'll be leaving and I'll be able to tell my drug addict what I think of him. In three months I'll have my diploma and then the important part of my life will begin.

Lachaux accuses me of having a suppressed desire to be an arsonist. He's right. Thinking of Mariette and Maria, I want to run out and light a fire like the great bonfires that were lit during the plagues of old.

And this time, I swear, no man will dare snatch the first burning torch from my hand.

❧ II ❧

Jacques

I seem to be slipping into the habit of keeping this diary the way old people or prisoners in solitary confinement start talking to themselves. . . .

Today I reopened the notebook because I *want* to talk to myself . . . I almost died of laziness and quiet and boredom during my first week of vacation at Mesnil-en-Ouche. For the last five days, if anything it's been worse.

Mother's so vain that she drives me mad. She's the one who got me into this. I can just imagine her talking to the shopkeepers in Mesnil: "My daughter was such a brilliant medical student . . . and she's had so much experience with patients . . . you know that she practiced in Paris?" forgetting to make it clear that I was only a modest "resident trainee" and that the Gennevilliers Hospital is one of the smallest in the suburbs of Paris. If she hadn't kept boasting about me, Dr. Vincent Ferrières, the only doctor in Mesnil-en-Ouche, would never have known I was there, slowly recovering my health under the apple tree in the garden.

The prospect of watching over a drug addict in this godforsaken town in the middle of the Norman countryside does seem a welcome diversion from my dull days. Ever since I got back a certain sense of stability, I've been bored just sitting around. Dr. Ferrières' proposition came at just the right time—it would give me something to do. So I had agreed to act as a nurse for his cousin.

Because of my promise, I'm spending three hours every morning and a couple more every afternoon at Jacques Ferrières bedside while the doctor makes his house calls.

Jacques Ferrières was nasty the first time we met. I guess he had a right to be, because he was sick, and maybe he just didn't like my looks, but in spite of all my efforts our relationship hasn't improved during the past five days.

Every morning I find my patient, an ill-kempt, sloppily shaved lump, lying on his rumpled sheets. His greeting is still just as deliberately rude as it was that first afternoon, but I pretend not to notice it.

When I walk in, I ask him: "Did you have a good night?"

And Jacques Ferrières gives me some sort of ironic answer with the same short mocking laugh that always irritates me.

"A perfect night! I'm sure Vincent gives me a tablespoonful of chloral hydrate every night because I sleep too well. . . ."

And then he raised his hand to let me know that he wants to be left in peace, so I won't be tempted to go on talking. So I shut up. After that we only talk when it's necessary, when I have to make him take some medicine for instance. The little transistor radio plays soft jazz in the half-light—the curtains are drawn because my patient says the light makes his headaches worse. The room is too dark for me to read comfortably. The doctor talked to his cousin about that.

"Why should anyone else enjoy himself when my head aches and I'm bored?" he replied acidly.

Several times, in a deliberately nasty way, he's mentioned the perversity that attracts women to sick men so that they can humiliate the men by caring for them like babies, since they can't emasculate them any other way. He even alluded to a peculiar custom of Melanesian women in the Trobriand Islands: they violate any stranger who ventures into their village brutally, leaving him half dead, while the men of their tribe watch with amusement.

So I settle down in my easy chair and sit motionless, my empty hands folded in my lap. Sometimes he sleeps and sometimes he listens to the music on the transistor and smokes one cigarette after another. We live in an atmosphere of cigarette smoke. On the second day I said:

"You shouldn't smoke so much. It's stupid when you're sick."

He struck a match—for a second his whole face was illuminated by the golden light—and he took a deep drag just to irritate me. Then he answered:

"In that case, you're even *more* stupid to be taking care of me."

Sometimes I feel his glance lingering on me, sliding over my breasts and legs. I think he makes his stare very obvious just to make me feel uncomfortable. I like it better when he sits peevishly with his eyes closed, his face stubborn and his mouth hard, and daydreams, yawns and pretends to ignore me completely.

I have all the time in the world to think about Jacques' case to fill the endless, silent hours of watching.

I'd never had the chance to treat a drug addict in the hospital, so I don't understand why he behaves the way he does and I don't really understand the point of the treatment I'm supposed to be supervising.

I've tried to look into it but neither Dr. Ferrières nor his medical library provides much help. There aren't any drug addicts to take care of in a rural district. If I were in Gennevilliers, I'd go to see Lachaux, because drug problems are part of his neuro-psychiatric specialty. So why not write him I thought, and ask him for his advice?

I've hesitated for a while: I feel very guilty about Lachaux's proposal and my refusal. My rejected suitor was my only friend during my whole year as an intern. He always protected me from the off-color jokes of the duty room and kept me from making the mistakes that come from not having enough medical experience.

Poor Lachaux with his pale eyes and his nearly white hair had left without persuading me to marry him. But at least he understood that nothing—and no one—could keep me from my path. Even if the road is long, I won't stop until all women have achieved equality, including the right to freely chosen motherhood.

When Lachaux was getting back into his car, I'd promised to write to him. It had seemed to me that Jacques Ferrières' case was an excellent pretext to keep my word and to prove to Lachaux that I appreciated his advice and that I was still faithful to his friendship.

His answer came in yesterday's mail. He wrote in a light, friendly tone, as if nothing at all had happened under the apple tree. His letter contained all the information I wanted about the psychology and treatment of drug addicts. A slim book came with the letter: *Opium* by Jean Cocteau, the diary of his withdrawal cure.

Thanks to Lachaux's letter I now know that there are two types of drug addicts. First, there are people who take to drugs because of an irresistible predisposition, the instinctual attraction of a morbid temperament to the lure of destruction. These are hard to cure. But besides what might be called "constitutional" drug addicts, there are accidental drug addicts. They're usually weak-willed people who are in a state of anxiety because of sexual problems, or people who are curious about drugs or who fall under the influence of people around them who take drugs, or finally those who seek a temporary euphoria or simply forgetfulness in drugs.

Lachaux is very precise in his letter:

"These accidental, acquired toxic states which the poison creates are the answer of the organism toward this noxious influence. In theory withdrawal is easiest for opium smokers. But convalescence is a difficult time; it needs to be supervised for several weeks because the craving, and with it the risk of a relapse, keeps recurring."

I'd given Lachaux a brief description of Jacques' welcome: "That," he explained, "is also a frequent reaction on the part of this kind of addict. They go through phases of excitement and depression until, when they're completely purged of the poison, they find their balance again. This may take a long time and supervision has to be constant. Read Cocteau."

Lachaux, as conscientious as always, added a long postscript to his letter:

"I almost forgot to spice my dull psychiatric stew with a little psychoanalysis. In the present case, I think it might be useful. You should know that Forel, Meyer and some others consider that a sexual and emotional conflict is the cause of drug addiction. These addicts bear within them a lasting internal conflict that they can't resolve: they're unhappy, dissatisfied, and find a fictitious resolution of their conflict under the influence of the drug. They're nearly always 'losers' who have failed in one way or another, or who cannot adapt themselves to the demands of life in society.

"I hope, dear Claude, that you can find something in these words to help you understand your drug addict better. And I wish you the best of luck if, in your search for the reasons of his addiction, you have to follow his frustrations back step by step to the time when he was an unhappy baby, who had to suck his thumb to fall asleep quietly. Psychoanalysts think that difficulties associated with falling asleep often prepare the ground for drug addiction. In any case, let me know if the current case confirms or contradicts this hypothesis."

Over the last five days I've learned a lot about Jacques Ferrières. Even though I never asked her anything, mother's made close inquiries of the Mesnil shopkeepers. People around here consider him a good-for-nothing. They don't mind his stormy adolescence or his instability or his laziness, but what they can't forgive him is that he doesn't have a good "position" in the world—this being the worst failure of all as far as the realistic Normans are concerned.

As for Dr. Ferrières, his judgment is colored by indulgent affection. He talks about his cousin as if he were a big child who has all the vehemence and violence of youth but also all its spontaneity and freshness. In effect, he considers him capable more of candor than of cynicism, more of good intentions than of evil plans, more of disinterest than calculation, more of sincerity than of bohemianism or exhibitionism.

"When we were young," he said, "Jacques' daring impudence, his rebellions, his moodiness, his temper and his fits of anger used to terrify me. He was like a young savage; he was carried away by an almost animal violence. Then the crisis would pass; he'd smile sweetly again. He'd apologize for having hurt me, and hug me, and he'd be so full of remorse that sometimes he'd even cry—and I always forgave him. And, of course, wherever he went he brought chaos with him. He ignored conformity and caution, and he was always waiting for the chance to do something outrageous. You might have said that he loved to set fire to everything, like a pyromaniac who by some mischance has been left in possession of a box of matches."

The doctor sighed, and went on. "I'm one year older

than he is and I've always been much stronger. Jacques didn't care enough to go in seriously for soccer or other sports, except in spurts. So in school I was an older brother; I'd protect him when he got into a mess or a fight. Then I'd try to scold him for his laziness, his lack of discipline and his insolence. But all the time I talked to him he just smiled that impudent smile of his, and I would stop so I wouldn't have to argue about his idea of morality—which was all the harder for me to understand because it changed from one minute to the next. Basically, Jacques has always dazzled and frightened me at the same time. Next to him, I felt passionless and timid, and I finally told myself that if I'd been as attractive and brilliant as he, if I'd had his sensuality and his thirst for life, if I'd been able to do wrong without feeling guilty, I would probably have lived as dangerously as he did. When he decided to study medicine because I insisted on it, I hoped that he'd find it something to hang on to, something that would stabilize him. I might have succeeded if the touch of T.B. and the stay in the sanatorium hadn't interrupted his studies. But he wanted to leave as soon as he was cured. There must be some Viking or pirate blood in him that's awakened by the northwester, the salty sea wind that blows the spirit of adventure even into our land of Ouche. Or perhaps he inherited his need to be continually on the move from his mother. My uncle married her in Algiers; she was of Greek origin. She died when Jacques was born. I'll show you pictures of her. He looks like her. She was very beautiful."

And after a moment of silence, he added:

"Maybe even now it would only take very little to save Jacques. But I don't know what he needs."

I was about to say that this question went beyond my competence as a nurse, and that in any event Jacques Ferrières didn't seem to want any cooperation. But the doctor looked so worried that I thought it would be kinder to keep still.

Thursday, August 1

The "methods à la Molière" seem to be working. Since yesterday my patient has been improving a great deal with the help of purges. But I wanted to be absolutely sure before I recorded his improvement in my notebook.

The time for frosty silences and rudeness seems to be over.

Yesterday morning I was completely amazed not to find my patient in his usual mess. He'd shaved, and he greeted me with a smile. Seeing my astonishment, he said with a twinkle in his eye:

"Ah! Mam'selle Sauvage, the way you're looking at me revives me completely. . . ."

I must have looked bewildered. He explained:

"When you walked in you looked like a doctor who finds a patient who has recovered his will to live instead of a corpse. Look, I even shaved. And this afternoon, I'm going to ask you for my dressing gown and slippers so I can take a walk in the garden."

All morning, he rested happily, propped up on his pillow, chatting pleasantly.

At one point he asked for something to drink. The bottle of mineral water was warm so I went down to the kitchen to get another from the refrigerator.

Old Catherine, Dr. Ferrières' housekeeper, was fixing lunch. She's tiny, she's always dressed in black, and she's always just as neat as when she starts work in the morning. Mother told me that she's worked for the Ferrières for forty years. Her husband was killed in 1917. She never had any desire to get married again and she's always worn widow's black. Incidentally, that's the only thing she has in common with the other fat, red-faced women of her age I see gossiping on their doorsteps as I walk down the main street. Catherine is always working. She's quiet and efficient and she never has to be told what to do. Until now, we've barely exchanged ten sentences, but maybe she was only waiting until she could talk to me alone. As soon as she saw me walk into the kitchen, she left her cooking and came toward me with the decisiveness that quiet people show when they have something important to say.

"Mademoiselle Sauvage, just between the two of us, can I tell you a little about Monsieur Jacques? You can see that he's just come through a very bad time. You shouldn't mind if he isn't always as nice to you as he should be. He's even mean to me but I know that he loves me. And he knows that I love him too, as if he were my own. That's because I took care of him when he was just a baby. When his father brought him here on his first home leave, Monsieur Jacques was only a year old. He was awfully sickly. He came from Africa, and that's not a good place for a baby. But at that age they pick up again fast; two months later when his father took him away, you wouldn't have recognized him—he was so fat and rosy. Dr. Ferrières and his wife, Monsieur Vincent's parents, wanted to keep him with us but the major didn't want that. But it would have been better for everyone since his mother was dead. A man who lives by himself can't take proper care of a little child. Jacques had a sad childhood; they were always on the move and there were only strangers to take care of him, and then when he was older he went to boarding schools. We saw him only once a year, for two or three weeks during the summer. He said that he was happy here, that this was his real home. He wanted to stay but even when he was older, the major always refused."

"Why did he refuse?" I asked in surprise. "It would have been so much better!"

The old housekeeper looked at me, her blue eyes dark with emotion.

"Yes, it would have been much better. But the doctor could never get his brother to agree. I even overheard a discussion between them about Monsieur Jacques. The doctor said, 'Why are you so stubborn? Why do you insist on raising this child all by yourself? You're only making him completely unmanageable! Every time he comes back here, he's wilder than before.' And the major said: 'I'm not making him "unmanageable." He has a difficult temperament, he's not like Vincent. He has to be handled with firmness!' They talked a long time. And the doctor, who is a very quiet man, finally got very mad. I didn't hear the end of the quarrel but when I thought about what they'd said and added up the things that I remembered, I finally understood why the major didn't want to leave him with us."

Again Catherine stopped and stared at me: did she have the right to confide such a weighty family secret to a stranger? Then she went on, groping for the right words.

"The major married for love. Here they say it was a mismatch—his wife was a nightclub singer and he met her in Algiers where she was touring. He adored her. He lived only for her. It's true, she *was* very beautiful! When she smiled at you, you just melted. You'll see Monsieur Jacques' smile when he's better. It's just like his mother's. Maybe Monsieur Vincent told you that Monsieur Jacques' mother died a few days after his birth of childbirth complications? It was terrible for the major and we were afraid he would go mad with grief. . . ."

Catherine fell silent again, as if she recoiled from the enormity of what she was going to add. Then she said with a voice muffled by emotion:

"Well, mam'selle, I'm certain that the major could never love Monsieur Jacques. In his mind, the child was responsible for killing his mother! But you can have awful ideas like that in your head without even wanting to, and without even knowing they're there. I'm sure the major thought he loved his child and that when he was strict with him, or punished him, he was doing his duty. But—and it's terrible to say this, man'selle—he wasn't punishing him: without knowing it, he was getting revenge. . . ."

She looked at me as if to excuse herself for bothering me with such painful family stories.

"I'm only talking to you like this, mam'selle, so you'll understand Monsieur Jacques and forgive him when he's not as nice to you as he should be. It took me years to guess that, years of thinking about it, and nobody else understood; not the doctor, or the major, who was after all an honest, just man. But the harm was done. Monsieur Jacques' bottles were sterilized, and he had clean diapers because the major made sure of it, but he never got a kiss when he was in his cradle and no one sang him a lullaby to put him to sleep.

"I remember the day when the major caught Monsieur Jacques smoking his first cigarette in the attic with Monsieur Vincent. They were eight or nine years old. Monsieur Vincent got a scolding from his father, but it was terrible for Monsieur Jacques. The major almost predicted prison and the death penalty for him. Until he was fifteen years old, that's the way it always was and later, when he came to live here, it was too late. . . ."

The old housekeeper didn't have to know about psychoanalysis to guess that a child who's never known his mother will feel the lack his whole life. Drinking, smoking or taking drugs later on is only a way for the adult to compensate for what he didn't have when he was a baby.

I thanked Catherine for telling me all this, and assured her of my loyalty to the family, and went back to the room only to find Jacques asleep.

I bent over this sleeping Prince Charming. It looked

as if his checks were starting to fill out, as if youth was beginning to win out over the weariness that showed in his face. But I was looking deeper than at the tired face of a man in his thirties; I was looking for the face of a child hungry for affection and deprived of love.

I sat down in my chair again. Now I thought I could make out an air of indescribable sadness coming from him. The old housekeeper had discovered the truth by instinct. If he had had love and attention thirty years ago, today's drug addict would have been attuned to life forever; he wouldn't have denied reality to try to satisfy his desires; he wouldn't have been contented with the realm of imagination or dreams instead of action; the baby starved for tenderness wouldn't have become a rebel full of hatred, searching for the softness of his mother's breast in drugs.

So, I thought, Jacques Ferrières isn't as deeply cynical or as bad as he looks! The demon that makes him do so many senseless things doesn't come from some constitutional perversity but from the dissatisfaction and the anxiety of a childhood without love. If I can believe Lachaux's letter, he belongs to the category of drug addicts that can recover, with encouragement and sympathy.

I closed my eyes and I was astonished to realize that all at once I enjoyed sitting in the sultry semidarkness, watching over this young man's sleep as attentively as I would watch the sleep of a little child. Then I smiled as I remembered the various things that Jacques accused me of.

I resumed my watch at Jacques' bedside, while he slept with that somewhat feline immobility that doesn't bother me any more. I felt happy, dulled by security and bathed in quiet patience.

Watching for recovery, preparing for it to the best of my ability and leading it to its conclusion was all in the pattern of my profession; it was only the normal devotion of a physician to a patient. There was no need to analyze the strange feeling of well-being I felt; I was simply going through what I'd done for Mariette with Jacques Ferrières, but this time I was sure my patient would recover!

When I came back to start my watch again at about four o'clock, Dr. Ferrières had finished his consultations. He was waiting for me to get there before he set our patient up in the garden. He helped him down the stairs and across the hall. I followed, carrying the transistor radio and the newspapers.

Catherine had prepared a lounging chair, an easy chair and a low table under the arbor.

Jacques was somewhat short of breath, so he lay down immediately. Dr. Ferrières was in a hurry to make house calls so he left us alone almost at once.

The rest of the afternoon was spent in short cheerful conversations against the background of subdued music from the radio, followed by silences when Jacques would quietly watch the flight of a wasp drunk with the heat; he tried to take a look at the newspapers, but after three or four attempts he gave it up, exclaiming:

"Two months without news! It's too much all at once! I have the feeling that I'm falling off the moon."

Several times, when I was sure he wasn't watching, I took a look at him. Under the gentle light in the arbor he looked paler than he had in the half-dark of his room. His cheeks, which were beginning to show the day's growth of beard, were marked with deep wrinkles; small drops of sweat formed on his forehead. The time of the dizziness, cramps, and heavy salivation of the withdrawal seemed past, but my "cured" patient still needed to be treated with special attention and taken care of. As I'd read in Cocteau's little book, even though he wasn't physically in need of the drug, he would keep "floating" dangerously for some time.

Shortly before eight o'clock, since the doctor hadn't come home yet, I called Catherine and we each took one of his arms and helped Jacques back to his room, walking very slowly. He went back to bed at once. Catherine brought him his dinner tray, and he carefully ate some chicken, a few strawberries and drank a large glass of milk. But, close to eight-thirty, when I wanted to leave because it was gradually beginning to get dark, he called me back.

"Don't leave me alone before Vincent gets back. . . ."

During the afternoon, our glances had kept meeting, and Jacques would smile lightly at me each time. Now his face was tense, as if he'd gone back to the troubles of the past few days. But his eyes, looking into mine, showed worry rather than insolence. His cheeks suddenly became pale and the shadow of his day's beard made them look sallow.

Seeing me bend over him with worry, he tried to reassure me:

"It's nothing. . . . Just nerves . . . My nerves have been really shot for the last two months. I get upset each night at dusk."

He'd closed his eyes. Luckily I heard the doctor's steps on the stairs just then. On the landing, I explained the problem to him briefly. He went over to the couch, took his cousin's wrist and felt his pulse.

"A slight lack of balance in the nervous system," he said. "I'm going to increase the dosage of belladonna tonight, and by tomorrow it will be gone."

Just by coming into the room, he had lifted the grayness and let a calm healthy world into the house.

When I got outside, the main street was deserted and all the doors and windows were already closed. It seemed as if it was my turn to feel the oppressiveness of falling night and the great silence of the countryside in all my nerves. It was something sharper than the simple sadness of dusk, a sadness that suddenly wrenched my heart. . . .

Mother had begun to worry because I was so late. I explained to her that I'd been obliged to wait until Dr. Ferrières got home. She told me about what she'd done that afternoon, but I couldn't pay attention; I just nodded my head. My thoughts kept coming back to Jacques Ferrières as I'd seen him tonight—and that picture of him was so vivid that I could almost feel the softness of his skin under my fingers. I tried in vain to push away the thought—as if it were an animal obstinately rubbing itself against me.

Back in my room, I asked myself again, "What can I do for him?" If he ever wanted to accept my help, as he had tonight, I think I could really accomplish something. Instead of just sitting quietly in my armchair, I think I could help give him the strength to really recover, to have a definitive cure as a reward for his patience and perseverence.

But at the same time, I was deeply afraid of trying to help him: What if I were inadequate or awkward with him? Maybe my goodwill would work against him.

In order to forget my worry, I tried to read, but my thoughts kept coming back to what Catherine had told me, and then I'd go over each tiny detail of what Jacques had said, and review his smiles of the day. Would he accept my help? What if he became disagreeable, indifferent and full of disdain again? If only I could have told him how close his unhappy childhood made me feel to him. . . .

I threw down my book and turned out the light, but I felt so feverish and so uncomfortable that I thought I was going to have my period. I figured it out: except for the unlikely chance that it was four or five days early, it couldn't be that. I wasn't sick; I was only—for no reason at all—"floating" too.

Toward dawn, just before I woke up, I had this dream: I was sitting as usual in Jacques' room. He was stretched out on his couch in his most arrogant mocking way. Then he started to talk. I sat rigidly in my easy chair, gathering all my strength to confront an intelligence infinitely quicker than mine. But he didn't stop talking. His words came faster and faster, and after a while my attention became painful, as if I'd been forced to look fixedly at a blinding light. . . . I fell on my knees at the edge of the couch. I begged Jacques to forgive my stupidity, to forgive me for not understanding him. But he talked even faster and I crumpled to the floor. Finally he brutally ordered me to leave the room because, as he explained to me, he was irritated to see me so limited in intelligence and he didn't feel at all like forgiving me. . . .

The nightmare woke me. I was so affected by it that when I left to go to the doctor's house, I was really afraid of spending another day of silence with Jacques so—to give me something to do and to prove that I was capable of doing difficult intellectual work—I took along some notes and file cards for my dissertation.

Jacques' welcome reassured me. He seemed even more relaxed than the day before. He'd shaved and let Catherine straighten up his room.

As I came in, he smiled, saying: "I'm getting better and better."

And he added, in a way that would have sounded ridiculous if anyone else had said it, but that was funny because of his light touch:

"I'm so rejuvenated by your care that if you feel like taking me for a walk, you'll have to use a baby carriage instead of a wheelchair."

Then, without realizing how much this sentence touched me, he added:

188

"Thanks to you, I'm as happy as a well-fed baby today."

He laughed a happy boyish laugh but the double row of his teeth sparkled with masculinity.

The morning went by in easy conversation and I didn't have time to open my thesis file. And I wouldn't have felt like it, because Jacques showed that he could be a brilliant conversationalist.

I made him eat his lunch and was getting ready to leave when he said, "If you don't have anything important to do this afternoon, then be nice and don't wait till four o'clock to come back. I'm not tired enough to go to sleep, and if you're not here I'll be terribly bored. . . ."

So I sacrificed my nap for my "well-fed baby." I told mother, who insisted that I take a rest, that the doctor had asked me to come earlier and she left me in peace, thanks to my little white lie.

As soon as I came into his room, Jacques said:

"Thank you for coming back so quickly! You may think I'm silly, but I hate being alone. It's like some punishment. I'm sure it's a holdover from school. I was always made to go and stand in the corner, or they'd lock me up all alone in the study hall during recess to write out two hundred times: 'It is forbidden to talk in class.' I used to hear that phrase all too often, and maybe that's why I enjoy talking so much now."

Then he said, as if he'd suddenly discovered a very important thing:

"You're not wearing the dress you wore this morning!"

I felt myself blush. Was he going to think I was a flirt? I immediately explained:

"It got spotted when I was eating lunch."

"Ah well! All the better! You look even prettier in this one."

The doctor must have heard me come in because he came up to the room after accompanying a patient out the door. I was still speechless from the shock of receiving such an unexpected compliment when he walked in.

He only stayed a few minutes and he thanked me for coming so soon too. As soon as I was alone with Jacques again, I started talking about the first thing that came into my mind so there would be no more discussions of my dress, and especially not of my "prettiness." I was afraid Jacques was making fun of me.

The doctor's visiting hours stretched on toward four o'clock so we went down to the garden.

"Let's have recess without waiting for an okay from the inspector general," Jacques said.

He took hold of my arm and leaned on me to get down the stairs.

As soon as he was settled down under the arbor, he fell into a quiet, innocent sleep. I was sure now that he'd complimented me purely out of kindness and that he'd already forgotten it. Besides, when a patient is getting well, his nurse always looks pretty. . . .

A little before five, the noise of the doctor's steps on the gravel startled Jacques from his nap. He woke up, cheerful, smiling and calm.

The doctor apologized for not having come to help me.

"I had to see a lot of people today because they know that I'm going to be away for ten days. You'll have to forgive my fellow citizens for still being a little antifeminist. A 'lady doctor' is still a strange idea for them. Apart from some consultations from women, I don't think you'll have any work during my absence, and I'm a little less embarrassed for asking you to be my substitute."

His cousin immediately said with a smile:

"Good! I'm still in great need of Doctor Sauvage's services as my personal physician."

The doctor looked at his watch.

"Now I have to take a patient to the hospital in Bernay and on my way back I have several urgent house calls to make. So don't wait for me to come back the way you did yesterday. Even if I'm not home, leave around eight o'clock.

"No!" protested his cousin. "You can't just take her away from me. Why don't you ask her if she'd mind waiting for you instead?"

The doctor looked at me.

"With pleasure," I said cheerfully. "But I'd appreciate it if you'd stop by our house and let mother know."

It was after eight o'clock when the shadows began to thicken under the arbor and the green of the leaves started to get dim.

"Let's go back in," Jacques suddenly decided.

In the sky to the west, the clouds flushed pink at the approach of the sumptuous sunset. Without bothering to ask Catherine to help, Jacques took my arm again. Again he leaned on me, the sturdy nurse, and I escorted him, adjusting my pace to his, happy in my voluntary servitude.

As soon as he was settled on his couch again, he said:

"Thanks to you I won't get nervous tonight. Yesterday I must have seemed silly to you. Even when I'm in good health I've always hated the loneliness of a room at dusk. I absolutely have to get out, and mix with a crowd, and fill my mind with noise and movement and light. I think that I'd be capable of doing almost anything just so I wouldn't have to feel alone. It's terrible, the compulsion that drives me into the streets every night. . . ."

He stopped for a while, as if he were thinking about painful things that were hard to talk about.

"If only you knew, Claude—you'll permit me to call you Claude? And you call me Jacques, as if we were old friends from medical school. . . ."

Without giving me time to answer, he went on in a muffled voice that was so emotional that he seemed to be truly sincere:

"If you only knew how ugly my life has been, how many disgusting things I used to do, how many odious parts I used to play! I'm sure that's why I'm afraid of being alone: I'm afraid to find myself face to face with what I really am—I'm afraid of finding myself face to face with a bastard."

He looked at me intently, but almost gently.

"Maybe I'm wrong to talk to you about myself like this. Life has taught me how dangerous it is to show yourself as you really are . . . but it's really terrible never to be able to express what you feel, never to meet a person you can confide a secret to or confess to. The past is past and mine is ugly enough that I don't have any desire to recall it to life. But I'd like to explain myself to you. Why? I don't exactly know. Perhaps because, though I'm still in pain and flat on my back, I'm emerging from a crisis and because you've been kind enough to help me. There's surely something of that in it. Or because you're innocent, fresh, and honest—exactly the opposite of most women. There's something in that too. But it's mainly because you know how to keep still, and because you know how to stay sitting quietly with your hands empty and at rest— and that's the sign of mastery of self and of real stability. I've often watched you for the six days that you've sat in this easy chair, always quiet and attentive, while I was pretending to be asleep. I know what you're worth. You're a very rare kind of woman."

The window was wide open and the last, almost level light of the setting sun lit up Jacques' face. Never had he looked so proud to me as at that moment. It was as if this confession had liberated a great strength within him.

"You have no idea how good it is to be secure for once, to be friendly with a woman whom you can trust and who only wishes you well. I'm a man of pleasure, tied to women of pleasure, and I've never really loved any of them. I fall in love so I can feel the entire scale of pleasure and regrets that I'm capable of feeling but immediately afterwards I fall out of love because I've finished my game. And since I'm the only one who counts in the affair, that's my only way of continually reassuring myself of my power. No woman seemed worthy of my spoiling my life for, and I've pulled every possible cowardly trick in my struggle to keep my freedom. You can see what I mean: I'm hard with others and weak with myself. But unfortunately I like to please, I know how to caress with my claws sheathed and I can arouse sympathy. So it all gets sick very quickly! There must be something masochistic in most women. The more you explain to them honestly that you're not worthy of their love, the more obstinately they tell you that if you weren't worthy of it, they wouldn't love you. And finally they end up hating you. . . ."

Night was falling slowly. Shadows filled the room. The air became softer; Jacques' face gradually began to fade into the darkness. The moment he fell silent, I moved toward the lamp. He stopped me immediately.

"No, Claude!" he said harshly, "Don't turn on the light! I don't want you to be able to see me."

For a moment we were silent. Like an attentive psychoanalyst, I was determined not to say anything unless Jacques asked me a direct question which would show that he'd come to the end of his monologue. And how could I, who still had so much to learn about life, have said anything without seeming very innocent in contrast to this man, who could distill his many experiences into a few words so well? He was clearly not really talking to *me*— chance alone had made me the audience for the confidences he made in a dark hour of his life.

His voice went on in the shadow.

"I don't remember which great saint said that we are

predestined to damnation or salvation. You take a step, you bog down, you get out of it, you bog down a little further on, and each time you carry all your ingrown faults with you. You don't even know whether you'll be a normal human being or a monster if you follow your instincts, and you keep watching yourself live without being able to affect your fate. Free will is only a delusion. Sometimes a wise man goes mad but madmen like me never become wise. No; you don't shape your fate. You submit to it. . . ."

Jacques sighed.

"Yes, my life is ugly and I've done nothing to try to change it. But sometimes I become conscious of my failure, conscious of having deviated indefinitely from my aim and from true happiness. There must be some reserve of purity and innocence deep within all of us, because sometimes I'm convinced that I've been unfaithful to a great desire and I no longer know whether the man I've become is the result of my life's impurities or because I was unable to obey the tremendous urge I had when I was young."

He stopped as if his confession had suddenly overwhelmed him. This succession of confidences in the almost total darkness gave me a strange feeling—his mixture of honesty and cynicism had all the security of an old friendship and all the trust of complete freedom. I wanted to move closer to Jacques, to put my arm under his head and stroke his forehead compassionately and calm him like a child. I only bent forward a little, holding my hands firmly to keep myself from reaching out to him. And his voice went on sadly.

"Claude, it's awful to feel that it's too late, that you've missed some decisive turning point in your life . . . Oh! who will get me out of myself, out of this mess? Who would know how to persuade me that there's something on this earth that's more important than my selfish pleasures?"

This time I couldn't tell whether or not he was asking me a direct question that needed an answer. I didn't have time to hesitate. A car stopped in the street in front of the house.

"Here's Vincent!" Jacques said in his usual voice. "Turn on the light! Otherwise he'll think there's something wrong, or that we're playing hide and seek."

I turned on the light. Suddenly the night was pushed back out of the room. I went toward the great dark rectangle of the window. I wanted to give Jacques time to erase all the remorse and shame he felt for his unpunished sins from his face.

As the doctor walked into the room his cousin told him happily,

"Vincent, good news! Doctor Sauvage said it's all right if we call each other by our first names. What about your calling her Claude, too, and she can call you Vincent?"

"Of course," he said, somewhat surprised, "if it's all right with her."

"Sure it is. Now let's have dinner. Claude, do stay and eat with us."

I wasn't hungry. I couldn't wait to be alone. I declined the invitation by pretending to have a headache and left in spite of the protest of Catherine and the two cousins; but I did promise I'd accept their invitation for another evening.

Mother was waiting up for me. I quickly ate some cheese and fruit, then went to my room. I had to think about the day—today's events, I felt, were beginning to seem terribly important to me. It had all happened so fast! In two days, Jacques Ferrières had shown himself to be a perfect patient, cheerful and gentle—not at all like his unpleasant self of the first days. First I'd thought this new Jacques was brilliant, superficial, fickle, and able to be funny without being cynical or cruel. And just now, tonight, he'd shown that he could be profoundly attractive and human.

For two hours, he'd stripped himself of his self-display, his half-protective, half-mocking tone. He'd humbly admitted that he was perverse, sensual and unstable; he'd told me honestly about all the various aspects of his life; his long periods of cruel selfishness as well as his brief repentances. He unveiled his entire being in front of me. Why this confession? Why reveal these secrets to such an insignificant listener? Was it because he was going through a last period of discouragement? Or did he guess that I'm very innocent and was he just amusing himself by dazzling me? I could swear that he only wanted to unburden himself by talking about himself and that he was completely sincere.

Last hypothesis: by showing such a deep disgust with himself, he wanted to warn me about himself. . . . Jacques was afraid I'd fall in love with him! Now I was really

194

being ridiculous. If he thought that, he would never have called me by my first name, or have told me that I was pretty. And above all he'd never have been so careless as to tell me about the woman who could save him from himself, if he thought I was in any danger of falling in love with him. . . .

If I'm going to talk nonsense, I might as well go to bed and try to get some sleep! I smiled to myself as I took my dress off. Pretty! Pretty? Maybe the dress, but not me!

It was still very hot under the tiled mansard roof of my attic room, so I took a shower before I went to bed. While I was drying myself I couldn't resist looking at myself in the mirror. It was true! I didn't look at all like the pale thin girl who'd come to Mesnil twelve days ago, an older-looking, sad, gray girl. My reflection in the mirror was tanner, and less dried-out looking: my whole body seemed to have acquired more substance.

"Pretty?" I asked myself. "Let's be objective and allow for a certain amount of kindness. No! not pretty. As Pascali would say, just barely suitable for asking out on a date. . . ."

This was such a strange thought that as I was falling asleep, I surprised myself by smiling in the dark at the idea of my unfamiliar new body.

Sunday, August 4th

Today, because Jacques thought it would be a good idea, I took some time off and for the first time in a week I had the whole morning to myself. Mother brought me Sunday breakfast in bed—the usual hot chocolate and buttered toast. I'd slept well; I was hungry. And I was happy and ready to be nice. Mother saw that at once, and she took advantage of it by sitting down on the edge of the bed and complaining that she had an invisible daughter . . . but then she said that she was happy to make sacrifices for my sake. Then she cleverly insinuated the doctor into the conversation and began to tell me why he's still a bachelor.

Vincent became engaged to a young Parisian girl from an excellent family toward the end of his medical studies. He loved her very much. But once she realized that he couldn't be dissuaded from taking over his father's practice in Mesnil, and that she'd have to spend her life as the wife of a country doctor, she broke the engagement. Ever

195

since, Dr. Ferrières has been slightly distrustful of women. No one here has heard rumors about an engagement or even a serious attachment—except perhaps, some old gossips say, to a young widow in Evreux whom he supposedly goes to see from time to time. "Even if he's having an affair with her," mother said, "it couldn't be very serious. Besides, when a doctor is as busy and as involved with his profession as he is, a serious involvement could only complicate his life."

In short, mother thinks Dr. Ferrières is a reasonable bachelor who doesn't impose any excessive "privations" on himself.

I listened to her indulgent account and nodded my head in agreement to keep her from going on and on. This morning I didn't really care about Vincent. I was wholly occupied with a new aspect of Jacques that I'd just discovered.

I'd seen him stubborn and ill-tempered, then gradually getting better, relaxing and smiling, and finally opening up to me as if he wanted to know me not just as a nurse; so I thought I'd seen every facet of his character. But yesterday and the day before yesterday, instead of making small talk to pass the time, I had the surprise of having a very interesting and extraordinarily fruitful conversation with him. And when we talked about a subject I thought I'd mastered completely—birth control—I suddenly felt reduced to the silent role of a listener.

My discovery began the day before yesterday, Friday afternoon. Jacques was stretched out on his couch, leafing through a magazine. I didn't want to disturb his reading, since it seemed to interest him, so I opened the material for my thesis. I'd brought it over three days before and left it on an end table near my easy chair.

For a while I was absorbed in my work, and then Jacques interrupted me:

"May I ask what's causing that frown of concentration."

As soon as I told him the subject, he cried:

"Really! You're interested in contraception?"

He seemed delighted. He explained, "I know all about birth control—the pharmaceutical house I represented in Viet Nam has been following the experiments with the contraceptive pill for three years. So I had the opportunity to go to the Philippines several times to observe Gregory

196

Pincus, who worked mainly in Puerto Rico. Two years ago in New Dehli, I was at the International Congress of Family Planning, then I went to India five or six times to see family-planning teams at work. I'm really quite an authority on the subject. I could give you firsthand documentation on all that's being done in the Far East and even in the United States."

It had never occurred to me that Jacques might be so knowledgeable about contraception. At first I listened to him with surprise. Then, as he talked, I gradually remembered that he had refused to go on with his medical studies after two years in the T.B. sanatorium, that he'd tried for a while to make a career of journalism and that then he'd left for the Far East. The fact that he'd become addicted to opium there had made me completely forget his medico-pharmaceutical activities in Saigon.

Jacques was so involved in his subject that he didn't even notice my surprise. He leaned forward on his elbow as if he were about to spring up and help me with my thesis, and he was so enthusiastic that I smiled and said:

"Thank you for your kindness! But my ambitions are quite modest. I'm limiting myself to a discussion of what I was able to learn about the question during my last year at the hospital. In other words I'm presenting the position of the French physician faced with the problem of birth control in France."

Jacques looked at me with amusement.

"It's still a very good topic! And are you for or against? If I know you as well as I think I do, I'd bet you're in favor. . . ."

"Entirely!" I said, happy that he'd understood me so well. "It's a question of the whole world's future, a problem that goes far beyond me, but it's especially a question of the future of women, and as a woman and as a doctor, I feel directly concerned about it."

"Fine! I'm entirely in favor of it too. Despite my male egotism, I don't want to lower our dear companions to the rank of brood-mares if they don't feel like foaling every year. I'm for sexual freedom for others as well as for me. After all, let anyone sow his seed if he wants to! And since I don't run the risk of getting pregnant, I don't see why I should disapprove of something that doesn't concern me at all. On the other hand, since I have visited India and taken a look at Japan and China, I feel very concerned about what's going on there. You have to see

197

them—more than four hundred million Indians and several hundred million Chinese—starving to death like dogs, to understand that when they finally decide they've had enough of that and sit down unannounced at our table, it'll sure as hell make everyone else's servings a lot smaller! Even if they don't take strong measures, with an additional two billion people on the earth—and at the current rate, that'll happen very quickly—we'll all be reduced to eating our old clothes to feed ourselves."

I smiled, but Jacques went on very seriously.

"I swear to you that if you've seen it from close up, it's not funny at all. An eminent American scientist has seriously predicted that the end of the world will come on November 13, 2026, if women continue to give birth at the rate of their natural fertility. I'd be ninety-six years old in 2026. That gives me a very small chance to watch the cataclysm, but then you never know with the advances they're making in geriatrics! And when you see Calcutta or Bombay it's not at all reassuring. It would be easy to calculate: six billion people in 2000—the minimum predicted number—won't leave many square yards for anyone and since we have a reasonable chance of being around in forty years, you have to admit that having only a few square yards to pace around in won't be particularly funny! One might as well immediately reserve a little cage in the zoo! . . ."

I spent the rest of the afternoon listening to Jacques' often amusing tales of how hard it is to institute family planning in underdeveloped countries, and about how impatiently they're waiting for the "absolute weapon" of birth control that they've been promised—the contraceptive pills that are inexpensive, easy to use and completely safe.

"For example," Jacques said, "when they tried to introduce the rhythm method in India, they discovered that the tradition of abstaining from sexual intercourse for at least eight days after menstruation means that sexual relations are resumed at the most favorable time for conception. They also noticed that couples traditionally abstain during numerous ritual occasions and so they don't take kindly to being asked to abstain even more. But they encountered their most serious difficulties when they tried to give illiterate village women necklaces of varicolored beads on a copper string, for them to keep track of the sterile days of their menstrual cycle easily. Some of the women said they were bothered by the copper, others believed that the beads were magic and that they only had to move them around to be safe; and others, instead of counting off the beads one by one, counted them off all at once so they could get to the infertile period quickly; then they were amazed when they were pregnant a month later! And, to top it all off, some of the women ate the vaginal contraceptives that had been distributed to them just like candy!"

Jacques told me, to my surprise, that because of this failure and because bed is the only source of amusement the peasants have, the government decided to offer free medical care, repayment for lost working days and a bonus of thirty rupees to any Indian who volunteered to be surgically sterilized.

"It used to be," Jacques went on, "that flood, famines, polygamy, child marriage, and the prohibitions against widows remarrying were much more efficient than all the rewards for sterilization could ever be. And that's the tragedy. A woman doctor on one of the family planning teams said to me: 'Modern man is stupid. On the one hand, with penicillin, quinine and D.D.T., we do everything to keep people from dying, and then we have to find ways to prevent life.' And while the children die of malnutrition, sacred cows graze calmly wherever they please and fifty million sacred monkeys quietly devour food that could feed as many million children. 'Do not kill': India lives by that rule and now it's dying of it!"

For the last two days, I've been sitting in my chair, leaning forward with my skirts pulled down over my knees and my chin resting on my fists like a nice little girl listening to "Once upon a time...." But what Jacques tells me is much more fascinating than "Sleeping Beauty" was even when I was five.

"One morning in Calcutta, a little before dawn, I saw the cart that goes around to pick up the bodies of people who die during the night...."

That was how Jacques began, the day before yesterday, to tell the story of the liberation of women in a country where girls used to be married at the age of five, and where widows were forced to throw themselves on their husband's funeral pyres, a country where, for thousands of years, sterility has been considered the most terrible sin of all.

Yesterday afternoon we left India—with its sari-clad women, its sacred cows, its monkeys and its exotic odors—for Japan, the country of innovations that has very quickly become—because of the triumph of feminism—the country where birth control is a matter of choice.

So I learned about the origins of birth-control propaganda among Japanese women. It's a story that began about forty years ago. At that time, not far from Kobe, in a countryside famed for its beauty, one or two women a week would commit suicide by throwing themselves under a train. A kind-hearted Japanese woman had the bright idea of putting up a billboard by the side of the railroad track; the sign said: "Wait a minute," and went on to ask those who were about to commit suicide to come and confide their sorrows to her....

A few months later this generous woman met a kind young doctor and said: "Doctor Majima, you can't imagine how many women have come to see me after reading my billboard. And all of them say that they can't go on living because they're pregnant. My resources are limited and the Public Health service refuses to do anything. Can't you do something to help these unhappy girls?"

Dr. Kan Majima was then practicing in a very poor quarter of Kobe and every day he signed several death certificates for babies who had died in hovels because of unsanitary conditions. He had no special knowledge of gynecology but he decided to become a specialist in it, since it was essential to his new calling. He went to the United States and then to England. Once back in Japan, he opened its first birth-control information center in the middle of Tokyo in 1923. He was helped by everyone who saw the germs of a future war in Japan's expansionist, warlike policies, because he was trying to avoid disaster by damming the frightening increase of births. But the military clique succeeded in suppressing his propaganda and the declaration of war on the United States finally killed it. Dr. Majima was even arrested and imprisoned.

By 1947, the Japanese population increase had reached alarming proportions. American demographers, called in by General MacArthur, said that Dr. Majima had had the right idea. In 1947, the Japanese Diet threw overboard its old-fashioned religious ideas in the name of modern science and voted for a law which was the first of its kind in the world: a law of "eugenic national protection." Three experiments were immediately begun in three villages. They were under the control of the director of the Medical School in Tokyo. Seven years later, in these three experimental villages, seventy-five per cent of all households were practicing birth control, and ninety-four per cent of the families with four children were using it. Pregnancies had decreased by half. And as early as 1957, the government was able to announce that because of the law of eugenic protection, the number of births and of deaths were even throughout the country; every twenty-five seconds, a Japanese was born and one died. It was a complete victory for the lady from Kobe and Dr. Kan Majima. But this triumph had only been made a reality at the bloody price of legalizing abortions. Once the decline in births had begun, they had to try to replace abortion with birth control. The state immediately increased its birth-control propaganda, and from 1957 on the number of abortions has decreased.

"A triumph of female discipline," Jacques concluded. "And a triumph that's unique in the world, because now a third of all Japanese women are practicing birth control. It's a triumph of the patriotism of Japanese women too. All it took was explaining to them that not only the fate of their country depended on them, but perhaps the fate of the world as well. The idea of being able to be responsible for a new world order just because *they* produced children, especially when the old male feudalism had only managed to lose the war, was enough to flatter even the most charming and light-headed of Japanese women. That also proves, my dear Claude, that when you know how to go about it and can find their point of honor, you can get anything even from the most stubborn women!"

He smiled at me, gently teasing me about my militant feminism.

Yesterday evening when he said good-bye and invited me to come to lunch today, Jacques promised that he'd tell me about the experiment that's being performed in Puerto Rico. That was what I was thinking about this morning while mother was telling me about Dr. Ferrières' love life.

Since I had the morning to myself, I stayed in bed a while. Then I stood under the shower for a long time, happy to be washing my tanned skin and firm flesh. Then I did some exercises rather like a joyful African dance competely naked in front of the open window. . . .

It was almost one o'clock when I left the house. The people of Mesnil must have been sitting down to their Sunday dinners because the main street was almost deserted. The sun was beating straight down, without a shadow touching the houses, and I was walking gaily down the middle of the street. Suddenly I jumped when a bicycle bell tinkled a few paces behind my back. I turned to look and recognized the girl on the bicycle. She must have recognized me too because she put on the brakes. When she was level with me, she got off her old, muddy, squeaky bike. From a small cage on the luggage rack, a hen looked up at me with a round bright eye.

"So my little patient wants to run over me!" I cried. "Well, Maria, that's a nice way to behave!"

Maria looked at me anxiously, blushing with embarrassment at having startled me and ashamed of the bicycle, which was too big for her. She didn't know quite how to excuse herself. I smiled reassuringly. Her face relaxed immediately and she smiled at me in turn, revealing pretty teeth not yet ruined by Norman cider. I asked her:

"Do you come into town very often? You'll have to drop by, since I don't get the milk at your parents' farm any more."

"Oh, no, mam'selle, I almost never come in during vacation. Today I'm taking a chicken to the school teacher to thank her."

And, drawing herself up very proudly, she said:

"It's because I finished school."

I didn't want to be late for lunch at the doctor's house, so I started to walk again and Maria walked beside me pushing her bicycle, her hands high on the handlebars. Because of the heat, she'd pulled her hair out of her face with two combs above her temples, and they stretched the skin at the corners of her eyes.

"Here's the school," Maria announced.

The architect who built the hideous building of coarse stone and brick had at least had one charming idea: instead of the usual wall all around the schoolyard there was an iron gate. Everyone can see the yard planted with linden trees and chestnuts, and the tiny playground paved with rust-colored tiles as they pass by in the street. Two beds of rhododendrons and a small staircase with pots of geraniums at every step mark the living quarters of the school mistress; farther away on the same side is the broad bay window of the classroom.

As I stopped to say good-bye to Maria, the door at the top of the stairs opened. A young woman appeared. She appeared to be about twenty-two or twenty-three. She stood motionless on the threshold in the full noon light for a few seconds, as if she were blinded by the sun. She had black hair and a very dark, olive complexion. Surely the Mesnil school teacher can't be a Norman?

Then she turned to the gate and when she caught sight of Maria, her even, rather melancholy features lit up.

"That's our teacher," Maria said admiringly to me.

She leaned the bicycle against the iron gate and hastily untied the cage.

"Well, tell your teacher that she has a very nice little pupil and that I congratulate her on your success."

But Maria wasn't listening to me any more. As soon as she had untied the chicken, she threw me a quick: "Good-bye, ma'am." and ran toward the young woman. The teacher leaned down and hugged her affectionately, and then they went inside together.

"Now there's a teacher who knows how to make her students love her. She must care about her work," I thought, as I started on my way again. I smiled as I thought of how Maria had rushed up to her.

Ever since I've been taking care of Jacques, I leave it to mother to go get the milk every evening so I haven't had another opportunity to see the first little "patient" chance gave me in Mesnil.

This morning Maria no longer had the fever pimple at the corner of her lips; there were no circles under her eyes, and today I didn't see the shame and fear that had been in her eyes that first evening. She seemed to have recovered her childlike peace of mind. "In a few days," I thought, "I'll go by the farm and talk to her again."

When I got to the doctor's house, he'd just come in from his rounds and we sat down to lunch at once.

Jacques had insisted that he was strong enough to come down to the dining room. His cheeks were soft and fresh-looking, he had a twinkle in his eye and he apologized for having come downstairs in his dressing gown.

"A lazy convalescent, but one with a big appetite!" he said as he sat down, turning to Catherine, who was bringing in the first course. She thanked him with an almost maternal smile.

The doctor seemed tired from his morning's work. He

gulped down his food, with his elbows leaning heavily on the table as if the meal were also a time of rest for him. It was Jacques who started talking to break the silence.

The dining room looks out over the garden. It's a beautiful, rectangular room that Vincent's father decorated, as he did all the rest of the house, with antique Norman furniture. Opposite me stood a magnificent two-piece Louis XIV sideboard. Catherine's polishing has given it a smooth, deep glow. At my left a dresser held a collection of pewter pots and earthenware, and when Jacques noticed that I was curious about them, he described them to me, talking about each object's origin and use with a precision that proved he had a much deeper attachment for his adoptive region and house than I would have thought possible.

"The most beautiful antique pewter," he said, "is light grayish-white and has a clear ring when it's tapped, while the other is darker and has a dull ring because the artisans didn't respect the exact proportions for the alloy that had been imposed by the statutes of the guild any more."

To show me exactly what he meant, he went over to the dresser, brought back the most beautiful pieces, and surrounded my plate with pots, measuring cups, and bowls bearing the sought-after marks and initials: those made by François Hebert marked with the "lake of love surmounted with a crown," Patrice Sohier's with the "eagle with spread wings," Gaspard Marchand's with the "crowned hammer" or with the "ship," Charles Houssemainc's with the "name of Jesus."

Then he lovingly defended the quality of Norman pottery—judged by connoisseurs to be too rustic, coarse, and severe compared to the elegant Provençal pottery—and he showed me an earthenware fountain, in a magnificent maroon color that hung on the wall near the door. Its brass spigot emerged from a stylized shell adorned with little white lozenges.

"Isn't this fountain graceful?" he said triumphantly. "Most collectors aren't acquainted with this type of Norman pottery and, since it's dark red, they'd label it as coming from Avignon."

He was so enthusiastic that his face had taken on some color and the gestures he made as he described each object were like quick, delicate caresses. I was fascinated by this new side; once again I was lost in wonder at seeing a new personality so different from all the ones I'd seen

204

before. I watched Jacques without hearing a word he said. I couldn't follow him in his burst of enthusiasm. Was he talking to amuse himself or to amuse me? And if it wasn't all a game, how could he pass so easily from rudeness to humility or lyrical descriptions? I felt culturally inadequate before all the riches hidden in Jacques, and the natural, deep perceptiveness he revealed. He dominated me. Intelligence, feeling, instinct, joy in living—it was all beautifully blended in him. It was Vincent, leaning on the table like a casual day laborer, and me, with my completely bookish, intellectual brain, who were the barbarians.

My amazed admiration must have been obvious. Jacques stopped suddenly and said in the severe tones of a schoolmaster:

"Claude, you're not listening!"

I felt myself blush. He burst out laughing, then he shook his finger at me as if threatening me with a beating, and passed my sentence:

"This time, you will write out one hundred times 'The pottery of Nehon is reddish brown; that of Sauxemesnil is yellow.' And next time, I'll demand a pledge!"

We drank our coffee under the arbor. Vincent sat down in one of the lounge chairs. He put down his pipe-smoking equipment next to him, sighed, and looked at his watch:

"I hope for a change no one will bother me this afternoon."

He settled himself comfortably and seemed to be dozing. Jacques was quiet so he wouldn't disturb his cousin—after he gave me a wink to establish a friendly conspiracy between us—and he became absorbed in the movements of a ladybug that had landed on his newspaper.

You could hardly hear the faraway sounds of the village. Stretched out near Jacques, I closed my eyes with a feeling of infinite happiness. I was drunk with heat. I only asked that this moment of intimate silence last a little longer.

A little later Vincent was bothered by a fly. He stirred in his lounge chair and woke up. He took his pipe, filled and tamped it down carefully, lit it and, still half-asleep, started to puff quietly on it.

"Do you want to go to sleep, Claude, or do you want me to keep on playing Scheherazade?" Jacques asked me.

Turning to his cousin, he explained:

"For Claude's benefit, I'm doing a world-wide survey of birth control in a thousand and one afternoons. We've just arrived in Puerto Rico. Unless, of course, it bothers you?"

"If you're sure that it interests Claude . . ." the doctor grumbled.

And I said, to avoid a disagreement between the two cousins:

"It's part of my thesis. Jacques, do go on."

"Well, Puerto Rico is the scene of yet another revolution born of one woman's initiative. You've surely heard about the American, Margaret Sanger, the redheaded rebel. After a struggle that lasted sixty years and that was interrupted many times by prison and exile, she finally succeeded in imposing the acceptance of birth control not only on the United States but on the whole world. Two years ago, I saw her in Puerto Rico. She isn't a redhead any more. Now she's a tiny old lady but there's still plenty of willpower and sparkle in her pale gray eyes! . . . Before her time, it was known that oral contraceptives did exist; for example there was a sterilizing tea made from lichen— American Indians leaving on the war path gave it to their wives so there wouldn't be any unpleasant surprises to greet them when they returned—and the chemical substance extracted from peas was also a contraceptive. But all of them were risky, because they didn't always work. Margaret Sanger was convinced that it was possible to discover an efficient, harmless contraceptive pill. In 1950 she posed the problem to an American endocrinologist, Gregory Pincus. He thought that progesterone might be the key, since it was already known that it prevented ovulation during pregnancy. I won't go into the laboratory experiments that Pincus used to verify his hypothesis. You know that when Americans want to solve a problem, they do it in a big way!"

Jacques glanced in Vincent's direction. He was listening vaguely, apparently not very interested in the subject.

"After administering progesterone to thousands of female rabbits with excellent results," Jacques said, turning toward me, "they started testing it on volunteers among Dr. John Rock's patients in the hospital at Brookline. It still worked, but unfortunately rather large doses of progesterone were needed. Pincus and his team then manufactured and tested, one by one, one hundred and seventy-five new synthetic hormones. They finally stopped at the hundred and seventy-sixth: norethynodrel. In early 1956 the Puerto Rican experiment began. Puerto Rico is an island that's as poor as it is populous. As soon as women

206

heard about the experiment, they stampeded to volunteer. At the end of 1959, Pincus and Rock were able to announce that the efficacy of the new pills had been established with certainty. The 'absolute weapon' demanded by Margaret Sanger had been discovered."

Jacques stopped for a moment to emphasize the importance of this event. Then he said:

"Several different kinds of pills have already been introduced in the United States and in England. In France, you'll have to wait six months or a year. They have to get around that damn law of 1920!"

"Will these pills be sold in France as contraceptives?" asked Vincent, who seemed to be really awake at last.

Jacques smiled.

"Of course not! Luckily for Frenchwomen and for pharmacists, the pill also works against sterility. It will be authorized in cases of sterility—just as condoms are officially sold to prevent venereal disease and the rhythm calendars to calculate the most fertile periods. You must have realized that!"

The doctor seemed about to speak but before he went on to ask his question, he puffed on his pipe three or four times:

"Do you think your 'absolute weapon' has been completely perfected? No problems or accidents in your statistics? No problems of hormonal balance? No risk of cancer in cases of prolonged usage?"

"When I say 'absolute weapon,' I'm exaggerating. It's still just the beginning of a new technique: a V-1 rocket next to the earth-to-moon rocket. But the main thing was to seriously investigate the problem and to force nature to reveal the weak points in the mechanics of reproduction. It'll be perfected little by little. Naturally there are problems. Long-term troubles? It's still too early to say. In any event, women are cautioned not to use them for more than two years. Risks of cancer? I'll answer you in ten years but there's little chance. Endocrine imbalance? I saw some Puerto Rican patients with mustaches but the cynics say that the women there are naturally very hairy. Failures? They're very, very rare if the pill is taken regularly twenty days a month. It's a great beginning and Margaret Sanger—who knew the time when abortion was the primary method of contraception—can be pleased."

The doctor again puffed thoughtfully on his pipe. He finally said:

"It may hurt you to hear it, but I think your pills have a rather bitter taste to them, just like the disappointment that's come, over time, with the tranquilizers that were supposed to give all anxious and nervous people perfect chemically-induced serenity automatically. Read the medical reviews and you'll see that they're beginning to back off a little, quite a lot in fact, from complete approval."

I'd listened to Jacques in silence, almost trembling with happiness at this great step forward. "Don't use longer than two years," the label said. How much would my Gennevilliers patients give for two years of almost complete security? Certainly it wouldn't have taken more than that to avoid Mariette's fatal abortion. Vincent's unexpected reluctance astonished me. When the pill was ready to be prescribed by French physicians would he refuse its benefits to his clients? Would he be one of those doctors who, under the pretext of waiting for necessary improvements, would make his patients wait indefinitely? But these were the real tranquilizers for all the women haunted by the fear of pregnancy.

I looked at the doctor, stretched out on his lounge chair. I couldn't tell whether he was really awake. His face was slightly swollen with the heat, and he looked very placid. His masculine indifference inspired me to ask:

"So you don't have any birth-control problems here?"

"Some, to be sure, but less than in town. Furthermore, the Norman farmers have a reputation for being cautious and very attached to their possessions and, since they're afraid of being deceived, they prefer wives who aren't too well-informed. As far as the Norman women are concerned, they're just as suspicious as their husbands, and they might see the sign of the devil and dangerous magical properties in pills that are capable of such miracles."

Was he being ironic?

"Then you wouldn't welcome an efficient contraceptive that's easy to prescribe *and* has the approval of the law?"

The doctor tapped the bowl of his pipe against the table two or three times to empty it, then smiled understandingly at me.

"I suppose you're talking about the radio, television and press campaigns for a law to authorize the use of contraceptives? I know the plan. We're discussing it at present in the regional medical association because it requires the collaboration of the physicians."

He turned toward Jacques and explained:

"At the last election of the executive council, they asked me to be a candidate. I was elected deputy member of the association's council."

"I didn't know about the election. What a compliment! Bravo, dear counselor!" Jacques said, not showing whether he was serious or making fun of him.

But the political career of Dr. Vincent Ferrières was less important to me than the future of birth control in relation to the medical profession. I asked:

"Don't you think it would be progress if every doctor could prescribe and oversee contraception every time it seems necessary to him?"

Did the new counselor feel that my question touched the dignity of the regional council? He sat up to answer me. Then, with a sententious air that I'd never seen in him, he started to talk, groping a little for the right words.

"Today we're rediscovering the limitation of births. We're forgetting that the French were the first to practice it and had such success that for a hundred and fifty years the French birth rate has always been the lowest in Europe. We should, therefore, not be astonished that the present propaganda for birth control has been echoed even in the National Assembly. They've introduced new legislation to replace the 1920 law."

"I hope you agree that it must be replaced?" I asked sharply.

"My position, which incidentally is that of the medical association, is very clear. If the 1920 law is as indispensable to the country's vitality as its advocates maintain, then they should make it fair—which it certainly isn't right now. If it's useless to the country and harmful to marital relations, as its attackers maintain, they should drop it! But that's the lawmaker's business and not the physician's."

I must have looked surprised because he went on:

"In this proposed law, the question is really whether the physician should be turned into a counselor and director of contraception, or in other words, whether contraception should be put under medical control. But you know as well as I that strictly *medical* reasons for contraception are relatively rare.... Some heart or kidney diseases, certain blood diseases, serious tuberculosis.... Even being very liberal in the borderline cases, you'll only find a very small number of medically counterindicated pregnancies; but there are millions of women who don't want any children for strictly personal and nonmedical reasons. And this proposed law would also include advising these women to help them avoid becoming mothers. And there's where the council is no longer in agreement."

I was more and more amazed. Was he playing on words? Or did he mean that, for a doctor, the cases for prescribing contraception should be almost as rare as the cases for therapeutic abortions? I remembered the number of officially sanctioned abortions for mothers; 28 cases in four years in the Paris hospitals and, for the same period, 132 cases in the whole of France.

"But," I protested, "it isn't only a question of any old personal motivation! It's a question of valid medical and social reasons for preventing pregnancy!"

Vincent must have felt my astonishment because he explained in his most patient tone:

"That's where we enter the underbrush of casuistry, where we begin to get mixed up with all kinds of arbitrariness: with considerations of individual convenience, of momentary comfort, of the happiness of the family situation and Lord knows what else, escaping all criteria of medical judgment. So it would simply be the doctor's feelings about it that would give him his position on the necessity of advising or even imposing contraception. How far can an honest physician go in his liberality without precise criteria? They've talked about the new pills as 'free-love pills.' Would I prescribe them to a young girl of fourteen who came to tell me: 'Doctor, it's either the pill or an illegitimate child because I'm definitely not going to be a virgin much longer—I don't want to run the risk of being frustrated!' Would I prescribe a contraceptive to advocates of so-called motherhood by choice who basically want to chase a lover or get a husband without any danger? Would I take the place of parents or a husband or a priest for solving moral or religious problems? How far would I intrude into the area of decisions about having children that has been left to married couples so far? It would be easy in an extreme situation or in desperate cases—which, incidentally, are the ones that the partisans of birth control *always* bring up: the hovel where six people live crowded together, the drunken father, the mother exhausted by repeated pregnancies, etc. . . . But what should I say to the uncertain, hesitant couple who count on me to decide for them. Should I believe the word of a woman who claims in good faith that she doesn't want a child when, as often happens, she obviously desires it in the depths of her being? Should I give in to someone who claims a financial insecurity that I know is false? Should I give in to a couple's egotistical side, to their refusal to face the future? I hardly exaggerate what the practical application of such a law would be. . . . The council first wants to look at the problem as a whole so it can take on the responsibility that the legislators want to drag all the medical body into, only with full consciousness."

I was getting furious. I tried to put him on the defensive.

"To be a physician . . . doesn't that obligate you to be perpetually responsible?"

He replied with a shrug.

"Yes, responsible to myself and even to others. But in the present case, the responsibility they want to impose on us is very serious. Looking at this proposal more closely, you can see that the legislators are happy that they can make such an inexpensive present to their voters, and they'll pass this law mainly for the advantage of men who don't want to be responsible for their pleasures and for women of all ages who want to give themselves without any risk. And if, as one might assume, excesses come to light very rapidly, the lawmaker's secret thought will be that it is we, the physicians, who'll be in charge of moderating them. From time to time I get forms from the Social Security people—they're worried about their deficit and so they appeal to my civic sense not to be too generous about prescribing a ten-day rest period for a simple cold or else ask me to prescribe aspirin, which is cheap, when the patient needs cortisone or antibiotics, which are expensive. If this law passes and if the birth rate drops dramatically, every physician will get circulars asking him to limit his prescriptions for contraceptives."

Jacques had been watching my exasperation mount since the beginning of the discussion. He suddenly decided to come to my help:

"Aren't you exaggerating your responsibilities a little? If the law lets you be the judge of your prescriptions and if your patients leave with the prescription they were hoping for, who can complain?"

Vincent thought for a moment and finally said in the same pompous tone:

"Who can complain? All those who later see that in all

good faith I gave them bad advice that day; that I was the sorcerer's apprentice. The expression 'family planning' will only be really valid when the time comes when we can prevent all pregnancy with certainty and inversely, can insure that pregnancy will occur one month after the desire for a child with just as much certainty. Medically we're not yet at that point and the physician mustn't run the risk of helping women avoid all possibility of maternity for several years and then finding themselves definitely sterile. Or else he'll have to accept the reproaches of the families to whom he's given too much confidence in the virtues of family planning!"

Jacques looked as if he were beginning to get amused. He glanced at me to tell me to keep quiet, and said with his most innocent air:

"Listening to you, I get the impression that your medical association is all for promiscuous breeding."

"Certainly not! But the association's job is to prevent the medical profession from embarking willy-nilly on an undertaking that it shouldn't be involved in, and that's mainly a political way out for an embarrassed lawmaker. It's easier to pass a law authorizing physicians to prescribe contraceptives freely then it is to improve the social legislation, or to start construction on housing for young families, or to give them the responsibility of making their own decisions about regulating the size of their families."

Vincent stopped. He was flushed from talking so much, and he drew a handkerchief from his pocket and mopped his face. In the short silence that followed, Jacques let out a low whistle of sly admiration.

"Well," he said, "that council agrees with you! You claim to have difficulties expressing yourself, but you just served us a beautiful slice of eloquence!"

He started to laugh with a pleasantness that softened the irony of his compliment. I kept still. I couldn't have said one word, I was so furious.

There was a noise on the gravel path. We all turned to look. It was Catherine. She stopped at the entrance of the arbor and announced:

"Monsieur Vincent, you have to go to La Grimaudière right away. Two men had a fight."

Vincent stood up at once, picked up his smoking paraphernalia, excused himself and left the arbor.

As soon as he was gone, Jacques said in a tone of real pity:

212

"Poor Claude, what a session! You seem to have 'gotten quite a turn' as they say around here. You have good reason. Till now you only knew my cousin as the country doctor with all the incomparable qualities of a Balzac hero. And when I say this, you know I'm not making fun of him. But you've just discovered to your disillusionment that there's another Vincent who's inflexibly rigorous and convinced of his moral infallibility. He was like that at school. He'd catch me in a corner and lecture me about morality. Upright, self-contained, and utterly sure of himself, he'd give me strong doses of short, severe moral truths. We must have had some ancestors in the Ferrières family who were faithful to Puritanism—I'm told it was widespread in Normandy for a long time. My father had traces of it and so does Vincent. The disdain of comfort and the taste for strong and absolute answers to every question that my father had, could be explained by the fact that he was a military doctor submitting to professional discipline and administering to the health of the group rather than to the individual. But finding these same character traits in Vincent—the antithesis of the tolerant, pitying, humanistic philosophy of life that a daily medical practice tends to encourage—is really surprising."

I said: "I imagine that the influence of the medical association council, pontificating and legislating around its green baize-covered table, suits his hereditary Puritanism. As far as contraception is concerned, religious morality has influenced middle-class morality and even medical morality so much that it's still considered a sin to think of love as something apart from reproduction, or of pleasure in love as separate from the risk of having a child. In the middle of the twentieth century, when man has domesticated nature and knows how to control procreation, it's extraordinary to see that the members of the council still use a purely religious criticism of birth control—not a biological or medical one. But they legislate with supposedly 'scientific' arguments and they want to make women live in the constant terror of getting pregnant— with abortion as their only solution—just as in Biblical times."

I was so mad that I was sitting straight up in my lounge chair. If I'd been alone I would probably have cried. I held myself rigidly under control because I was afraid of looking ridiculous before Jacques. Our lounge chairs were close together. Jacques was sitting at the edge of his and he leaned a bit toward me as he said:

"Leave all those doctrinaires to their talk and their superstitions."

I was still so annoyed that I couldn't answer. He said, "Let's talk about something else?"

He put his hand gently on my arm, to persuade me to stop thinking about irritating things for a while. Until now Jacques had only touched me when he leaned on me for support to walk out into the garden. I was startled by the unexpected warmth of his hand on my skin. But I didn't want to pull my arm away. Was it because I was nervous today that I accepted his gesture when I've always resisted the least male touch?

I lifted my eyes to him. He was smiling and watching me attentively. His expression had nothing equivocal about it and suddenly all my annoyance left me. The joy that the touch of his hand gave to the little part of me that it covered, radiated all over my body. It was an absurd joy, a purely bodily joy that somehow wasn't at all sensual. I felt confident, protected and calm under his heavy, firm masculine hand, as if I'd suddenly happily discovered skin, nerves and muscles that I'd never known existed before.

I looked at Jacques' hand and at his face again. What triumphant vitality shone in his beautiful, dark eyes! I smiled too, and said happily, "Did you know you had a special healing touch? Your laying on of hands has just cured me!"

I leaned back into the lounge chair. I was afraid of prolonging the contact with him but since I didn't want to put a real end to the pleasure of our new intimacy I asked:

"Why, when you can work such miraculous cures, did you ever decide to study medicine?"

Jacques leaned back in his chair too, and answered:

"A longing for far horizons!"

He told me how when he was still a student, he used to dream of leaving school and running away. His father was dead then, and the affection of his uncle and Vincent and the family life that he loved in Mesnil was what kept him from leaving. Some years later, just after graduation from school, when he had to choose a profession, his uncle couldn't discover any profession that definitely attracted him, so he pushed him into medical studies. Jacques didn't feel comfortable doing any sort of work that would keep him in the same place for a long time. But he finally gave in to his uncle's insistence. After all, why not study medicine, since it could be a way for him to write and travel? Once his studies were finished he'd set out for faraway places—he didn't want to feel he'd missed the chance of seeing an unknown sky or a beautiful stranger. But when he came out of the T.B. sanatorium he refused to wait another three years. He left school, and accepted the first job that would make it possible for him to leave at once, for any foreign country at all.

This account confirmed what Vincent had told me, but with more detail and romanticism.

"During these past eight years there have been more squalls and tempests on my way than gentle trade winds," Jacques said with a nostalgic smile. "And I had to come back here to the docks several times to be repaired."

As he talked, his face took on the expression, smiling yet sad, of the adolescent who'd wanted to run away. At fourteen, he must have had the same eyes, sometimes soft, sometimes savage and hard, the same lips that could be both tender and bitter. It was these eyes and these lips that had made me want to take care of him and treat him like the odd mixture between child and man that he was, ever since the first time I saw him.

He leaned a little toward me and asked confidentially:

"Claude, why did *you* choose medicine?"

A wave of joy took my breath away. Jacques' question had suddenly filled my body with the same warmth as the touch of his hand on my arm. Before I answered, I wanted to be able to tell him that no man had ever leaned toward me with the same look, that I'd never felt the same freedom, the same trusting exchange of ideas with any other man. But I was afraid of provoking one of the amused, mocking looks he gives me whenever I say something very innocent.

So I answered, forcing myself to keep my voice cool.

"It wasn't an early choice for me either. It all goes back to my last year of school. . . ."

Then I started to tell him about my adolescence, my years in the lycée and my friendship with Arlette. And as I talked I realized that, except in this notebook, I'd never confided so much to anyone, that I'd never dared tell anyone about my ambitious plans. Looking back at my ambitions over the years, they seem as innocent as they were grandoise. I was even astonished to discover that so many important things had happened in my years as a schoolgirl—important things that Jacques forced me to rediscover by questioning me in a way that would have made me stubbornly silent if anyone else had been doing it. And as I told him everything about myself—I even talked about my work on my thesis and my plans for the future—I felt a deep joy and a great relief. It was as if all the difficult decisions that I'd been keeping entirely to myself for far too long had been stifling me.

We were still talking at eight o'clock. Then Catherine came by to tell us that Vincent had phoned from Bernay. He was still at the hospital, where surgery was being performed on one of the fighters who'd gotten two knife wounds in the stomach, and he told us not to wait for him before starting dinner.

"We'll eat in ten minutes," Jacques said.

Catherine went back to the kitchen. We stayed a little longer in the warm darkness. Jacques was quiet, as if he were digesting everything we'd learned about each other. I wished that this moment would never end, and that, from time to time, one of us might just ask quietly in the deepening darkness:

"Still there?"

"Yes, still here. . . ."

In the calm softness of the setting sun, what was there to ask about except the certainty of the other's presence and friendship?

Suddenly Jacques jumped up and put out his hand to help me up.

When we were face to face, he smiled that sad yet mocking smile of his and said:

"Now that you've told me so many things about yourself, my dear little French Margaret Sanger, I understand your reaction to Vincent's speech much better. "You're a real rebel just the way she was. Maybe I could have been one too and succeeded at something. . . . Now I'm nothing but selfish failure."

At ten o'clock Vincent joined us at last. We were in Jacques' room, sitting side by side at the card table. I was trying to put a jigsaw puzzle together. Jacques was leaning over my shoulder, watching and laughing delightedly every time I made a mistake. We were behaving just like children. We'd been giggling together for over an hour.

When Vincent came in, we both raised our eyes at the same time and saw that he was astonished to see us so happy together.

"What *are* you doing?" he asked with an almost comical surprise.

Jacques gave me an amused wink and explained:

"Claude can't play gin rummy, or chess, or even checkers. But luckily I found my old box with the puzzles from La Fontaine's *Fables* and she's sweating it out with the 'The Shoemaker and the Financier.' But that was a very easy one, don't you remember? . . ."

He threw his head back and let out a wonderfully free laugh as if by reopening the old box he'd brought all the old happiness waiting there since their childhood back to life.

I looked at Vincent again. He didn't look surprised anymore but under his healthy tan his face suddenly looked pale and dejected. He was breathing with difficulty and examined me tensely—you might almost have said that all at once I was a problem for him.

"Maybe," I thought, "he's embarrassed by the conversation we had this afternoon." If that was it, I'd been so happy afterwards that I was ready to forgive him. To put an end to the uncomfortable feeling in the room, I asked him in the friendliest possible tone: "Vincent, what have you been doing for so long in Grimaudière?"

He didn't answer at once, but instead lowered his head so he was looking only at the table, as if the unfinished puzzle suddenly preoccupied him more than his afternoon's work. Finally, he said, "Two brothers had a knife fight. Catherine must have told you that one of them needed an emergency operation: double intestinal perforation. The other only had a few cuts and he's at the Bernay police station now."

"Two brothers?"

"Oh, brotherhood doesn't matter in a drunken quarrel, especially when you're drunk on Calvados. Read de Maupassant again!"

His eyes were still lowered on the puzzle, and he answered even more shortly than he usually did, as if he were only talking out of politeness.

"Why were they fighting?" I asked, to try to get him out of his bad mood.

"They're both bachelors. They run a farm together. A little while ago they hired a new farm girl and she was the

217

reason for the fight. Before he was anesthetized, the man who'd been wounded explained to the police that the smell of the girl around the house had driven them insane."

"A classic case!" Jacques said. "The old olfactory instinct—well known to sexologists and breeders. With the smell of a woman in their nostrils, your two patients were no longer two brothers with a hired farm girl but two males, each wanting to appropriate the female who'd strayed into their territory! I can't remember which nineteenth-century sexologist recommended that wives should never admit a strange woman into their house because of the risks of tempting the husband. And Valensin, reporting on very recent research on unconscious olfactory perceptions, says they can affect our behavior in love without our knowing it, just the way the smell of a female animal in heat stimulates the male. He even thinks that a violent olfactory impression could explain what we call cases of love 'at first sight'! Remember Henry IV and Gabrielle d'Estrées?"

Vincent didn't answer. He was still staring at the puzzle. It looked almost as if he were pretending not to have heard Jacques' remark. When Catherine called him for dinner, he left the room without saying a word.

His sudden exit didn't appear to bother Jacques. He just said, "My dearly beloved cousin and very honorable council member is sulking. His second moral crisis today! When I brought up the physiology of love by referring to the olfactory affinity between a dog and a bitch in heat it must have bothered him. But what he sees every day on his visits to the farmers should be proof that comparative sexology is valid. I must admit I was sure I was going to shock him by talking like that, but I only did it to get a little revenge. At school when Vincent preached morals to me and made me angry, I retaliated the same way. He used to be very religious and inhibited then. So just to irritate him, I'd slip dirty postcards into his prayerbook. When he found them during mass, he'd get that same stiff expression you just saw."

Remembering his past tricks, Jacques laughed in his usual irresistible way and I joined in; it wasn't very nice but I was happy because his story had given me a deeper insight into the secrets he'd had as a boy.

It was getting late and since Vincent didn't come back, I went home.

It was the first time that I'd come home so late, and mother was already asleep. She probably didn't want to wait up for me because it might seem like a reproach for my being out late, but she'd left me a note on the table in the foyer: "The teacher came to see you at about seven. She wanted to talk to you but she didn't tell me what she wanted to see you about. I said she should come back early tomorrow afternoon. Good night."

As I walked up the stairs, I thought about the pretty woman I'd seen standing at the school door. Did she want to talk to me about Maria? That was probably it. If I could do something to help her, I'd be happy to. My happiness that evening gave me the treasures of sympathy and the desire to help all the rest of humanity.

When I got to my room I didn't turn on the light right away. The moonlight splashed the floor in a large silvery puddle. I went to lean on the windowsill. At the end of the garden, the old appletree glistened in the moonlit brightness, and I thought back to the time when I wanted to prolong the vague sadness of my recovery by hiding under the prison of its branches; about the time when I'd been so close to a nervous breakdown because of Mariette's death that I no longer had confidence in myself and thought my spirit was broken forever. And now, two weeks later, that same prisoner felt happy again, carried away by a joy that wasn't hidden, but total and triumphant. Can a person change so deeply in a few days? Can you start out in blue jeans, rigid and secretive, proud and distant toward others, and so quickly become a young elegant Parisian?

I should have been horrified at the change Jacques had brought to my peaceful Norman vacation. Everything in my past was going downhill because of him, but when I thought about the past few days, I couldn't blame myself. I even smiled. "Here," I thought, "is where the solitary bookworm finally discovers the unexpected sweetness of masculine companionship, the sweetness of abandoning herself to an unchanging lazy day-to-day intimacy. . . ."

At that moment, looking out on the garden bathed in moonlight, in the ever deeper, purer silence of the night, I felt at the height of fulfillment. It all seemed too marvelous—that Jacques was there for me in an unending exchange of looks, smiles, words, and gestures; that it was possible for me to admire him, approve of him, to come to grips with exciting problems thanks to his adventurous spirit; that there was something about him that made him different from other men—and it brought me such a feeling of trust and sureness that I didn't even think of asking myself seriously where this friendship would lead me or how long it would last!

Catherine had warned me: how can you help but forgive Jacques everything when sometimes he acts like an older brother, sometimes like an executioner, using wheedling and mockery, sincerity and self-display . . . how can you resist forgiving him when he laughs like a child?

I closed my eyes so I could recall his laughter better, and suddenly I was overtaken by such a violent desire to be near him that I leaned out into the night and looked to the east as if I could already see the first light of dawn against the line of the forest at the edge of the plain, announcing the morning that would soon reunite us again.

Monday, August 5th

I was happy last night but this Monday hasn't been a good day.

After lunch, I went back up to my room to wait for the schoolteacher to come. It was almost two o'clock when I heard the door bell ring and went down to meet her.

Mother had already ushered her into the drawing room and I found her there, sitting very stiffly on the edge of one of the big red Victorian chairs. When I came in, she stood up quickly. She's a little taller than I. A pleated white linen skirt made her waist look very small; a dark green blouse enhanced the dark skin of her arms, her neck and her face. A large ribbon, the same color as the blouse, pulled her black shoulder-length hair neatly back. She seemed a bit shy but her dark gray eyes looked at me frankly. Seen close up, her features seemed less regular than I had remembered from her brief appearance on the schoolhouse steps, but her face radiated internal strength and determination, and that gave her a kind of proud beauty. She certainly didn't resemble the fleshy blonde young women of the Ouche countryside. "Is she from Provence?" I wondered, but when she began to apologize for imposing on me her accent was pure Norman.

I asked her to sit down. She sat on the edge of the chair in the same uncomfortable position again. I wanted to encourage her to speak, so I said, smiling:

"I'm ready to listen."

For a moment, a shadow of discouragement veiled her clear gaze. She cleared her throat slightly, then began, "Mademoiselle Sauvage, my husband is doing his military service in Algeria. He came home on leave for two weeks at the beginning of the month of June. Now I'm two months pregnant, even though we were careful. . . ."

At Gennevilliers I'd gotten used to this kind of preamble. In their various ways all the different openings lead to the same goal: from the young woman who pretends to be asking about information on abortions "for a friend" to the one who mentions a hemmorrhage in the hope of getting a curettage, even if she doesn't openly suggest it. . . . "Isn't there some way, doctor, to get a little operation?"

So I asked her reassuringly, "When will your husband have finished his military service?"

I expected her to mention a date far in the future to arouse my pity, or at least to tell me something vague—a typically Norman thing to do. But the answer was as direct as the way she'd spoken since the beginning.

"He'll be demobilized in four months and he'll be returning to France in a few weeks."

"Well, well! Everything's fine! The father will be here before the baby," I exclaimed, taking advantage of the unexpected help the news had given me.

The young woman looked at me very seriously. She was silent—she doubtless understood my maneuver—and her lips were slightly compressed as if her discouragement was beginning to win out over her hope. Finally she said:

"I'm not upset about having a child, even though we didn't want one right now. Unfortunately, at the end of June, a few weeks before summer vacation, there was a slight epidemic of German measles at the school, and I caught it."

From then on I could see what might well be a catastrophe for both of us looming up before me. Nevertheless I tried to counter her harsh look with an optimistic tone.

"Oh, German measles is such a harmless disease! . . ."

Her dark gray eyes were reproachful.

"Not at the beginning of pregnancy, as you well know, Mademoiselle Sauvage. At the time I didn't think about it, especially because my period is often late and I didn't even think I was pregnant. But the day before yesterday I was leafing through an old magazine, and I came upon an article by a doctor that reminded me of what I'd already read about the danger of German measles during early pregnancy. This physician said that at the Academy of Medicine and at the Committee for the Protection of Children, they think that there's approximately a ninety-five per cent chance of malformations due to German measles in the first weeks of pregnancy. He cited cases of cataracts, deafness, heart disease, club feet, and even mental retardation. He mentioned the blindness of the little Dutch princesses that all the newspapers talked about."

She was so upset that she had to stop a few seconds to catch her breath, making a painful effort to finish that long sentence.

Until then she'd been talking with a tone of unbending courage, without any attempt to seek pity. But suddenly, she began again with a lost, almost desperate expression:

"You can figure it out . . . it wasn't even three weeks between my husband's leave and the beginning of vacation. Ever since I read the article, I haven't been able to stop thinking that my child will almost certainly be a monster."

She looked at me with an air of unbearable anxiety. In spite of myself, I lowered my eyes and turned half away. But I was ashamed of my evasion. I needed a little time to get control of myself, so I pretended to be absorbed in contemplating the carpet, as if I were trying to concentrate and figure out the exact dates and chances.

"According to some specialists, these statistics would be the result only in a particularly serious epidemic," I finally said. "In general, the chances are much smaller."

"Yes, I know, that was in the article too."

What comment could I make to this woman—who would probably be the winner of a hideous lottery? Where could I find more reassuring words?

As she talked to me, little by little she had huddled deeper into her chair. Under my look, she sat up straight again, and mastered the painful droop in the corners of her mouth. I watched her anxiously. It was like looking at an acrobat regaining his balance during a dangerous performance. Finally, with the same perfect dignity she had possessed from the beginning of her visit, she said simply:

"Mam'selle, I thought that you might consent to ask Dr. Ferrières to perform an abortion."

I recoiled from her tone of certainty.

"But that's absolutely impossible! The law forbids it."

Without raising her voice, she said, "I know. That was in the article too, but they also said that when the authorities were discussing German measles at the meeting about Protection for Children in 1957, the solution of abortion was forbidden but only by a very small majority. In four years some of the professors who were 'against' must have changed their opinion and come to understand that one can't ask a woman to carry a child, who will doubtless be deformed, for nine months. Mam'selle, just think—this could happen to you or to someone in your family! If your child had a fifty per cent chance of being deformed, would you let it be born?"

She continued to hold herself very rigidly, her expression tense, and her lips compressed, but she was unaware of how pathetically her face was trembling and of the unspoken appeal in her eyes.

I should have sent her away before she collapsed in despair, or else I myself should have fled. But pity forced me to say something, to discuss, to negotiate. . . .

"Why do you want me to talk to Dr. Ferrières?" I finally asked softly. "He has no reason to grant me what he'll have to refuse you."

The answer came like a gunshot, and it was much more effective than if she'd been humble or beseeching:

"Because I trust you. I've watched myself go mad for the last two days, and I didn't know what to do. I thought the doctor would refuse. But yesterday Maria told me how nice you were to her, how you took care of her when she had her first period, and how you found the right words to comfort her. Then it seemed to me that you are a woman and a doctor, so you could understand me, and you could find the right things to tell the doctor, words I couldn't find. . . ."

She looked at me compellingly.

She repeated: "I trust you."

By instinct she had pronounced the key word, the one that indissolubly binds the doctor to his patient, that forces him to act.

It was time to act. Her look was shaky again; she began to remind me of women giving birth who exhaust themselves by obstinately suffering for hours and who finally collapse because of their useless effort.

My visitor too was approaching the limit of her resistance. Her face looked pinched and near exhaustion.

"All right, I promise you I'll talk to the doctor," I said

in a voice which sounded strange to my ears, as if someone else were speaking.

The joy that illuminated her face, the way each part of
her body seemed to relax, and the gratitude that threw her
toward me with a vital force ... I recognized them
because I'd already met them the day I promised Mariette
that she could have a child again.

I guided my visitor gently toward the door and said,
"I'll talk to the doctor tonight or tomorrow afternoon, and
tomorrow night on my way home I'll stop at the school to
give you his answer."

As soon as I was alone again in the foyer I had to lean
against a piece of furniture. I felt totally empty, drained
of all my nervous energy.

I'd promised Jacques that I'd come early. It was time to
go. It was an effort to go to the kitchen and tell mother
good-bye.

I walked down the street feeling quite empty-headed.
My knees were weak, and my legs were shaky. Seeing
myself reflected in a shop window, I thought: "If Jacques
could see me now he'd tell me I look like a pregnant
woman who's had German measles." The thought that I'd
be able to ask him for advice in a few moments gave me
courage again.

When I got to the house, I glanced into the waiting
room. The door had been left open to encourage a breeze.
I saw a dozen patients, both men and women, passing the
time in quiet conversation. The office hours would probably last quite a while. I had time.

I went into the kitchen. Before I faced the doctor, I
wanted to ask Catherine about the teacher, since I knew
almost nothing about her.

Catherine isn't like the cliché of the classical housekeeper to a doctor or priest, who is always ready to explode at
the thought of the secrets confided to her employer. I was
sure to get accurate details and an unbiased opinion from
her.

As soon as she saw me come in, she left the dishes and
came over to me, wiping her hands on her apron. She
thinks that Jacques is feeling better because I'm taking
care of him, so she showers me with attentions to show
her unspoken gratitude. I didn't even have to invent an
excuse that would explain my curiosity about the schoolteacher. As soon as I asked my question, which she'd

never think was nosy because it came from me, she started to tell me what I wanted to know.

"The teacher? That's Simone Vallin, Rose Blanchot's daughter. Around here we call her mother 'Blanchotte,' and when she was smaller we used to call Simone 'Blanchotte' too. Now that she's a teacher, we wouldn't dare use that nickname any more. A year ago she married a young man from Evreux who was also studying to be a teacher. Now he's doing his military service."

I was astonished. She hadn't seemed at all like a country girl, much less a Norman. I couldn't help asking:

"What do her parents do?"

"Her mother lives with her now. She used to work on the Quatremare farm. It's not far from Mesnil. And her father was an Italian farm worker who hired himself out for a season at Quatremare. As soon as the summer was over he went back to his country. He was a handsome man. Simone was born the following spring."

We both started at a hiss of steam from the top of the stove; a pot had boiled over. Catherine ran to take it off the fire. She came back at once, eager to go on with her story since I was so interested in it.

"Simone was a pretty little girl. Blanchotte was very proud of her and worked hard to bring her up right. She wanted her to be just as well dressed as all the other children to make her forget that she didn't have a father. You know how nasty children can be to each other without even knowing what they're doing. Her playmates' favorite way of making fun of her was to call her the 'hedge chick.'"

Catherine smiled, not with the rather scornful compassion an honest, upright woman has for a bastard, but in apology for a Norman expression that I might not understand.

"A 'hedge chick' is what they call an illegitimate child around here—because it's like a chick that a hen brings unexpectedly back to the farm, after disappearing and laying and hatching her eggs in a hedge. I think it was that sort of offhanded insult that made Simone so proud and ambitious. She needed to succeed more than the other children. They all had fathers. She worked very hard, and since she was intelligent, she was first in her class at everything: in catechism and in all her other classes all the way up to graduation. The teacher encouraged her. She was accepted at a teacher's college, and she graduated a year ago with her license. She came to Mesnil to wait for her husband to finish his military service. She's so ambitious that people were surprised that she accepted such an unimportant job."

Till now, Catherine had been talking quite quickly, keeping up with the flow of her memories. She fell silent for a few seconds as if what she was going to say to me needed some thought, and then went on more slowly.

"I think she wanted to come back to Mesnil to get revenge. She wanted to hear herself called 'Teacher' and 'Madame Vallin' in the schoolyard where she'd been pushed around and called 'hedge chick' and 'Blanchotte,' and she also wanted to have her mother live with her and to make everyone treat her with respect. At first, maybe from jealousy, people didn't like her. They said she was a bit distant and a little above herself, but the children took to her right away. They love her and more have finished school this year than ever before."

Now I knew enough about the teacher. I thanked Catherine and on my way upstairs, I went over the different details that made up a sympathetic and coherent picture of Simone Vallin.

The fatherless childhood and the jealous teasing of her playmates—how well that explained the loneliness and savage pride I sensed in her. How strange she must have seemed to these northern farmers with their heavy bodies and slow movements—this Mediterranean girl with her graceful stride and her beautiful head held high. The narrow little country world, so smug, so self-satisfied, so limited, so petty, must have been irritated by her tenacity, her ambition and her desire to escape it. She deserved to be helped.

My thoughts must have shown in my face, because as soon as I walked through the door, Jacques, who was lying on his couch, said, "Are you going through a Puritan crisis too? Just look at your expression in the mirror!"

I was so involved in the teacher's problem that I forgot that it was a professional secret. I told Jacques all about the visitor I'd just had and the commitment I'd made.

My story made Jacques laugh.

"Oh, Claude," he finally said, "forgive me for laughing at such a sad story! But I doubt if I could even recognize your little teacher and stranger's troubles are always quite bearable. As they say, distance makes corpses easier to take. But you must admit that your story is pretty funny! Yesterday you have a discussion with Vincent about birth control and force him into taking a categorically orthodox position; and now today, you want to ask him to perform a completely illegal abortion just to make you happy. Go easy when you ask him. Otherwise you might give our dear deputy councilor a stroke!"

He lay back and laughed.

"Jacques, be serious," I begged him. "Think of what this poor girl is going through. What she's hoping for is a therapeutic abortion. That's possible, after all, in exceptional cases. But how can we convince Vincent? You know him better than I do. Tell me what to do!"

Jacques stopped laughing and thought for a minute, staring at the ceiling.

"Barring a miracle, I don't see how you can persuade him. And you certainly can't talk to him while I'm around; he'll think I pushed you into this just to annoy him."

Then he added, as if the idea had just occurred to him, "Remember Dr. Majima and the philanthropic lady in Kobe who installed billboards for desperate pregnant women along the railroad line? There's nothing in the story that says she wasn't charming and that Dr. Majima wasn't susceptible to feminine charm. You're charming. Try to make the story really touching. After all, Vincent the Puritan is still a young man with a heart. . . ."

I'd left the door ajar so I could keep an eye on the foyer. The deep Norman voices in the waiting room faded little by little. When I finally heard the last pair of heavy shoes scraping the tiles, I went down and posted myself at the bottom of the stairs. Finally the door of the consulting room opened and Vincent came out, escorting an enormous farmer with a huge moustache. The farmer seemed to be having some trouble putting his black leather wallet back into his smock pocket. Vincent looked surprised to see me and when the man finally got himself organized and left, he came toward me with a puzzled look. I smiled reassuringly.

"I'd like a little consultation too, doctor."

His face lit up. He ushered me into the office and closed the door behind me.

The large room was humid and hot. The air was thick; you could almost describe the long succession of patients who had undressed one by one during the afternoon, by the traces of smells each one had left behind.

"There were a lot of people today," I remarked.

"Yes, quite a few. Luckily that takes care of a lot of examinations—now you won't have to do them while I'm away."

His smile was friendly but his eyes were still watchful. He was trying to guess the reason behind my unexpected visit.

I couldn't start talking immediately. I wanted to get my thoughts in order, so I pretended to be interested in what would soon be my office.

Vincent had hardly changed the office his father had left him. Like the dining room, it looks out on the garden and even in the full sun of midafternoon the shade of a large chestnut tree veils and calms the light.

Against each wall stand old wardrobes with grillwork doors—now they're used as bookshelves. A heavy country table with its top carved out of the heart of an elm trunk has become the desk. It has the warm patina of long use. For the patients there are two heavy cane-seated chairs that have resisted the weight of generations of farmers' haunches. Facing the patients, I'll sit on the comfortable tapestry seat of a Louis XIII armchair. With the patience of the true collector, Dr. Ferrières senior assembled rare objects round himself—antique grandfather clocks, various knickknacks, and old chandeliers, chests and andirons—as companions for his working hours. In the peaceful light, the textures of oak, elm, iron, copper and pewter blended in harmonious unity.

Vincent himself pointed out one innovation he had made: out of a small spare room adjacent to the office he had made a room for examination and treatment; its walls were painted in shining white enamel. From my chair I could see a large assortment of surgical instruments gleaming in the cabinets. "Surely," I thought, "he has everything here he'd need to free Simone Vallin from her agony. . . ."

That idea gave me the courage to begin pleading my case.

I told the first part of my tale—the easiest one—in one single breath. I described my meeting with Maria, stopping in front of the school building, the appearance of the teacher, her visit yesterday when I wasn't there, and mother's note that I found when I came home last night. I

228

forced myself to keep my voice cool and detached, as if I were leading up to a completely natural question.

Vincent had gone behind his desk. He sat down in his Louis XIII chair again. He slumped against its high back as he listened to my story. He seemed tired. How could he not be after four hours of consultations in that enervating humidity? But he made an effort to give me his undivided attention and at the beginning he was even smiling cordially. But as my tale progressed, I saw that his expression was gradually becoming more and more surprised.

When I got to the epidemic of German measles, he added some details:

"That's right. Six cases at school, and Simone Vallin had it too. It was just at the beginning of vacation. The children stayed home and it stopped."

"Did you know that she was already pregnant?"

Vincent frowned.

"Pregnant! No, she didn't tell me anything about it."

I thought I could detect some emotion in his voice.

"That's right. In June she didn't even know it herself. She only thought her period was late."

I added, emphasizing the date:

"Her husband was home on leave during the first two weeks of June."

Vincent's face was hardening. I countered his look and said very slowly, giving each number the utmost significance and seriousness:

"She's now two months pregnant and she had German measles during the third week of her pregnancy."

I finished very quickly—because I knew that if I stopped now I wouldn't have the courage to start again.

"She hopes you'll perform a therapeutic abortion and I promised her that I'd ask you."

Vincent took a deep breath. Without taking his eyes off me, he leaned slowly toward the desk and put his elbows heavily on the elm tabletop. His face showed decision, stubbornness, and pain. It was the expression of a man who knows that he is morally obliged to choose the most difficult of several possible solutions. His voice was hollow when he finally spoke and he had trouble finding the words to express himself.

"I think, Claude, that you wanted to spare me from having to go through a painful encounter by coming to me and speaking for Simone Vallin. She wasn't lying about having German measles—she's altogether honest. I know

229

her very well, and I know she's incapable of lying. I sincerely sympathize with her. She's going through a terrible ordeal. But you couldn't have let her think that I would perform an abortion. You know as well as I do that therapeutic abortions are forbidden in cases like hers."

"She knew that and I pointed it out to her again."

Vincent paused for a few seconds, then said, "Then the question is settled. But if you'd find it hard to tell her that unfortunately I can't do anything for her, I'll talk to her."

I thought he was going to stand up to show that there was nothing more to be said. For a minute I was panic-stricken: here in the quietness—and the privacy—of the office, was my last chance to talk, to argue, and to try to persuade him; once we were on the other side of the door, I could say nothing more, especially in front of Jacques—or Vincent might think it was all some kind of plot and would never give in.

But he didn't get up. It was as if he considered it a point of honor not to evade the consequences of his decision. He lowered his eyes and was concentrating on putting his papers in order. Was he hiding his emotions or only obeying that obsession for order that made him mechanically put each thing back in its proper place even when he was in Jacques' room? Maybe his refusal came from an innate horror of disorder and confusion that forced him into the rigidness Jacques hated so; perhaps it came from a kind of experimental severity that was his way of disposing of anxiety, doubts, complex situations and shades of meaning—in that case any argument of mine would be in vain. . . . Or did I see in front of me the delegate of the medical association, not sitting in a simple Louis XIII chair, but perched high above me on a massive pedestal, a terrifying pyramid of juridical codes, principles and laws; and, from this eminence, watching serenely over individual tragedies and passing severe judgments on the most painful questions? My only chance was to immediately hit on the argument that would touch Vincent's honest generosity—I know he has it—that vast reservoir of kindness that made him decide to be a country doctor and devote his life to alcoholic clods who, both in medical terms and in terms of their value as human beings, are often a total waste. A doctor as completely devoted to his profession as Vincent Ferrières can seem to be a conformist—no doubt because of a throwback to the old Norman trait of caution—but he can't be afraid for himself, or unjust, or cowardly. But what approach to choose before it was too late? The feeling of urgency terrified me; suddenly I thought of the argument Simone Vallin, that paragon of honesty, had used.

Vincent was sure I wouldn't give up so easily, so he kept quietly and methodically cleaning off the top of his desk. When I began again he lifted his eyes and faced me seriously.

"Simone Vallin knows that abortion because of German measles is forbidden. But she also knows that the idea of permitting it was discussed at the meeting of the Committee for the Protection of Children in 1957. Out of the twenty-nine members present, thirteen physicians of unquestionable scientific ability and moral dignity voted in favor of therapeutic abortion. If only two votes had been different in 1957, it would have been yes. And if the vote were taking place today perhaps the physicians defeated by two votes in 1957 would win. Then everything would be different for her. How can she help being disgusted by that idea? She knows that the physician's duty is to counteract the harmful effects of nature's mistakes as best he can; she knows that he's the only one who has the courage to help people in the face of everything, sometimes even in the face of the law. And she knows you well. No doubt she thought that you would have voted 'yes,' that you would agree to help her and prevent such a frightful injustice from being committed against her and her child."

Vincent had stopped rummaging among his papers and was watching me with undivided attention. He had one fist cupped within the other and had raised them to his chin as if he wanted to gather up all his strength. His face showed the patient gravity I'd noticed every time he argued with Jacques or me.

"It's a serious problem," he said slowly. "A serious problem—one that should only be discussed very cautiously in the newspapers and magazines, because there's a real danger that it might cause unnecessary worry among mothers and families. They've overdramatized the issue and published a lot of exaggerations in popular magazines, even about the frequency of malformations."

"I pointed out these exaggerations to her."

"There is a fifty per cent risk in the first four weeks; less than fifteen per cent in the two following months; and then the risk becomes zero. Those are the statistics. But all of the malformations that these statistics take into account aren't serious; Talleyrand's and Byron's club feet, for example, didn't keep them from having rather successful careers, and there are other malformations that are even less serious and less of an obstacle to leading a very normal life. And certain more serious cardiac or ocular abnormalities have become easily operable. But the problem isn't one of quantity anyway. Above all it's a question of principle!"

I wanted to mimic Jacques: "When you lean hard on principles they give way," but Vincent doesn't appreciate that kind of humor. I only remarked ironically:

"Oh yes. The famous absolute respect for life, the super-sacred unconditional principle. It has no flaws; it's faultless. But it does have loopholes—it lets young boys be killed in wars, it lets criminals condemned to death be executed on the gallows, and it lets political enemies be eliminated. And for the physician, the dogma becomes, if I may say so, even more absolute; it gets transformed into a true fetish, however much it's corrupted in practice by the occasional compromises and hypocrisies. Respect for life: that sounds very nice, and I believed in it at the very beginning of my studies. To be the one who preserves life—what a noble task! As long as the most miserable breath remains, put everything to work to keep it. . . . What could be more noble or beautiful? Respect for life, certainly! But two years ago in a hospital I saw a premature baby die of the cold because there was no incubator. In our day a child died of the cold just as it might have in the Middle Ages, and the director of the hospital wasn't dragged before a court and the Minister of Health didn't resign immediately! Certainly one should respect life. But how should we judge a society that's intent upon defending the dubious existence of a four-week-old embryo and does almost nothing to really protect children once they're born! How much a deformed fetus cares about being born doesn't matter to the moralists and the legislators in parliament. But you—you're going to deliver Simone Vallin seven months from now and you run the risk of having to put a child who's deaf, blind, or mentally or physically crippled into her arms. . . ."

"You speak about the fetus 'caring.' I know the argument: if therapeutic abortions are permitted in the interest of the mother when her life is in danger, they should also be permitted in the interest of the fetus when it's threatened by serious malformations. But Claude, how can you call this act of idiocy 'therapeutic' when it consists of killing an invalid to prevent him from being an invalid? It's really nothing else but euthanasia performed—and with good reason—without the consent of the person who's involved. If you reject respect for life as being a reason that's too vague or too hypocritical, at least you can't refuse the embryo the right to live, the natural right of every human being."

"Yes!" I cried passionately. "I do refuse it because that's also the Catholic argument for refusing the most legitimate therapeutic abortions, even if the mother has to die because of it."

"I'm not speaking in the name of religious morality but in the name of biological morality that's accepted by as many unbelievers as believers."

"If your biological morality doesn't differentiate between destroying a few-weeks-old embryo, a formless lump of flesh, a tiny bean with mouse paws, and destroying a seven-months-old fetus which could almost live outside the mother; and if this biological morality doesn't differentiate between killing a fetus and real infanticide, that means it's as inhuman as religious morality, and I reject it."

From Vincent's look I could see that I'd touched him to the quick. He shook his head as if denying an unjust accusation.

"Yesterday you were pleading for the right of women to motherhood by choice. Today I'm the one who's protecting the liberty of a small defenseless creature and you're reproaching me for it! What right do you have to give the death penalty to a human being who hasn't even committed a crime? What would you think of a code of justice that would condemn fifty to eighty-five per cent of all innocent people to death? Those are the real chances this embryo has to be born perfectly normal; and if that embryo is normal, would you be asking for legal authorization to assassinate him in his 'interest'? What principle of law could permit you to commit this 'crime against persons unknown,' that might deprive a Pasteur or a Fleming of life?"

I shouted, "That's insane! You're treating me like a criminal. But you know very well that I'm not asking for the abortion; it's Simone Vallin, the mother. And you also know that she's not driven by selfishness. I think that only she, with all the perceptiveness of her maternal love, can measure—certainly better than you or I can—the risk that she can take for the flesh of her flesh. If you refuse to consider the abortion as being in the interest of the embryo, do you also refuse to consider the mother's interest and her anxiety? Surely you're not going to deny that this terrible anxiety is legitimate and one hundred per cent real? The doctor should be able to ask the parents, 'Your child has a fifty per cent chance to arrive in this world deformed. Do you want him to be born, or not?' And once they've been sufficiently well-informed of all the possibilities, the parents should have the right to a free, conscious choice. Besides, you favor exactly this freely made parental decision for family planning."

Vincent looked worried.

"Do you realize what you're suggesting? Giving parents the right of choosing between life or death for the embryo—even in circumstances as dramatic as these—is like going back more than two thousand years, to the terrible right of choosing life or death that the Roman *pater familias* had over his children. And it's worse than the Spartans: at least they drowned only deformed children in the Eurotas River. I wonder whether any legislator would dare include your ideas in a civilized legal code—systematic euthanasia of embryos on the sole pretext that they *might* be born badly formed."

"But the parents?" I exclaimed. "The anxiety of a pregnant woman in the face of such horrible uncertainty?"

Vincent thought a moment.

"Do you think one has the right to kill just to calm even the most dreadful anxiety? Have you considered the guilt a mother might feel all her life thinking that the child *might* have been normal? Furthermore, if you made exceptions in cases of maternal anguish, that would be the first step toward therapeutic abortions for mental reasons. The law in France prohibits them, but they're the reason for ninety per cent of all abortions in the countries where there are abortions just for the sake of pleasing people. In France, it would open the door to similar abuses. And even if one stopped at German measles, how would the physician be able to tell, after two months, whether the woman was sincere like Simone Vallin or just wanted to get rid of the child? That doesn't even take into account the errors that are made in good faith. You can see where your negative eugenics could lead—to all the excesses that horrified civilized people when they were advocated and carried out by the Nazis."

It was getting late: Vincent had looked discreetly at his watch two times already, and his tone had suddenly become so formal that the discussion couldn't last much longer. What could I say? What could I do to shake my dedicated, conscientious, narrow-minded opponent in the few minutes I had left? Like Goethe, he had made his choice for once and for all: he'd take injustice rather than disorder.

I was furious and humiliated that I'd let this obstinate man with his limited ideas dominate me continually, that I hadn't been able to make him grant the validity of even one of my reasons. At that moment, I hated even his calmness; maybe the secret of his success at keeping it rested in his shoulders with their powerful tense muscles. Uncertainty gave rise to a kind of panic in me and the panic to a cold fury toward Vincent, towards the medical board, toward all those who give themselves the right to dispose of the happiness and freedom of others in the name of principle. And what had happened to the man in this debate? I'd seen the doctor, but where was the man? As if the vocation of being a man weren't more important and far older than that of being a physician! As if Dr. Vincent Ferrières, respecting the code of medical ethics and obeying the law by refusing to give Simone an abortion and spare the embryo and its mother a long chain of disasters, wasn't going to be avoiding his real human responsibilities by choosing the easiest solution! "Men are always very brave about enduring women's unhappiness." If I said that to Vincent, he'd answer: "Of course. You're pleading for your sex," forgetting that all men, even physicians, legislators and moralists have behaved selfishly forever.

I looked around me at the peaceful cozy decor of the office—the old furniture, the knickknacks, the files, the papers, the books—and I wanted to shout: "I understand! In the calm of your office, hiding behind your ethical code, without a mother's anxiety before your eyes, without brothers and sisters, without the pressures of a family, of constantly being around other people without losing your temper, the problem remains theoretical and easy to resolve: of course it's no! But in front of Simone Vallin, in front of the reality of a woman's hopeful, terrified, begging face would it really not be a problem any more,

235

would you have no doubts, would your answer still be no?"

My insane frenzy must have shown on my face because Vincent started talking again as if he wanted to calm me down at any price. He spoke in a tone of affectionate compassion that would have touched me deeply in other circumstances.

"You're tired, Claude," he said softly, "and it's my fault. I interrupted your vacation too soon. Ever since you agreed to take care of Jacques, you haven't had any rest. This visit from Simone Vallin has shaken you. Psychologists know that abstract reasoning has less power over a person whose feelings have been upset by a concrete event. But think over what I've just said. As terrible, tragic and poignant as individual cases are, you cannot compromise if you have respect for life. My reasons for refusal may seem invalid to you, and above all, horribly unjust in the face of Simone Vallin's tragedy. Yet one must accept, one must bow."

"Bow?" I exclaimed. "One must bow before the disaster, and forget the victim?"

"It's not a question of bowing before a disaster, but of having faith in the progress of medicine. A therapeutic abortion, if it were authorized for German measles, would only be a defeat, a solution too barbarous and too simplistic as well."

I faced Vincent squarely:

"Today, for Simone Vallin, there *is* no other solution and it's barbarous to refuse to give it to her."

But Vincent wouldn't give up.

"Just think. If you perform an abortion once, out of compassion, you'll have to do it again every time you come across another pitiful case just to be true to yourself. How often would you do this murderous thing? And where would it lead you?"

"Killing an embryo isn't the same as killing a child. And in a case like this, who would call destroying an embryo only an inch or two long murder?"

Vincent repeated patiently, "It would be murder because from the first day of its life, the embryo is a human being, a man in miniature."

"Wrong!" I said rudely. "I learned in medical school that at the beginning the embryo is organized in a very different way from a human being."

Vincent shrugged his shoulders. Then he stared at me as

236

if he wanted to summon all his strength to convince me that he was about to say something very important.

"I don't care about embryological subtleties. What I know to be true is that there's such continuity, and such gradual evolution from the egg's first stage of development when it's still only a tiny ball of cells, all along the way to the completely formed child at birth, that it's impossible to find one decisive moment that separates nonhuman from human. A new individual is born at the instant of conception. From that point on, whether you attribute an immortal soul to it, or no supernatural destiny at all, you must consider that being as a human being and respect it as such even when it consists of only one cell. There's no other position a doctor can take. A doctor is free to be for or against various methods of contraception, according to his personal convictions. But in no case, except when pregnancy might be fatal for the mother, can he consider abortion as anything but murder."

He looked at his watch and got up. My time was up. I had lost. And my anxiety was so obvious that Vincent said in a tone of friendly concern:

"You really seem tired, Claude. Go home and rest! I'm not leaving till tomorrow night. I've kept a large part of the afternoon free, and I'll have plenty of time to give you your instructions."

I didn't move. I felt paralyzed by despair at my failure, as if I were caught in the meshes of a heavy net of conventions, misunderstandings, store-bought morals, and rigid laws, and were being irresistibly dragged where I refused to go.

In almost the same tone of pity a doctor uses with a very sick patient, Vincent asked:

"Do you want me to stop by the school tonight on the way home from my house calls?"

I shook my head.

"No! If I must forget that I'm a woman and be only a doctor, at least I'll do my job well. I'll go and see her tomorrow night."

I spoke in such a low tired voice that Vincent started to come around his desk, probably to make some friendly gesture. But my expression stopped him at once, and we stood for a few moments, silent and unmoving, like two strangers brought together only by chance.

❧ III ❧

The Well

Tuesday, August 6, 10 p.m.

Vincent left right after dinner to get to Camp Mourmelon by tomorrow morning.

As soon as he left, I asked Jacques to excuse me, saying only: "Simone Vallin is expecting me."

He looked intrigued as he watched me leave, but he didn't ask any questions. All day long, neither he nor Vincent had made any reference to the teacher. In the office, when Vincent was telling me about the patients I'd have to take care of after he left, our looks met several times, and we both quickly looked away. I was sure our thoughts were the same. He was sitting in his Louis XIII chair again and I'd taken one of the cane chairs; you might have thought yesterday's discussion hadn't stopped, but with a tacit understanding, we didn't come back to it. There was no reason to—I understood perfectly well that Vincent's "no" was final.

When I came out of the house, it was dark. The street was deserted and I met no one on the way to the school.

I stopped at the gate. In the bright moonlight the geometric pattern of shadow in the playground, cast on the smooth sand by the chestnuts and linden trees, seemed very light and the courtyard took on the mysterious freshness of childhood.

238

I hesitated a moment before I turned the iron handle, and asked myself one last time, "Am I a coward?" This thought had obsessed me all day long. I kept asking myself: "This evening, when I find myself face to face with Simone Vallin, what will I tell her?" I could take the classical, moralizing tone, and recite all the arguments that Vincent used yesterday: "One doesn't have the right to destroy a life. . . ." Or I could begin some vague treatment, and tell her it was very new. The treatment wouldn't be of any use but it would leave her the illusion that her child would be born normal right up to the time of its delivery. That's more or less the same trick Pascali uses to get rid of patients who beg him for a shot to restore menstruation: "You promise them everything they want," he explained to me, "but you prescribe progesterone injections for them . . . they never cause abortions—quite the contrary. By the time they realize it, you have peace because it's too late for them to argue, and there's no risk of being hauled in by the police." In the present case, this procedure would be less dishonest: only a fifty per cent lie, since the child has one out of two chances of being born normal. Or else I could comfort the unhappy young woman by minimizing the gravity of the possible malformations. But could I do this when I knew about a mother in Gennevilliers who'd been deceived by a doctor with just that kind of optimistic language, and who was faced with the awful news that her child had been born blind?

"Am I a coward?" I asked myself again as I turned the handle and listened to the creak of the iron gate on its hinges. I concluded: "No, I'm not a coward but I'm caught in a network of such ancient medical traditions that even if some of them seem horribly anachronistic in a world thirsting for liberty and progress, I find it hard to free myself of them in one blow at the age of twenty-five. . . ."

My heart pounded as I crossed the yard and walked up the steps. On the ground floor, a beam of light escaped through the shutters to my right. She must have been watching for me—no sooner had I knocked than the corridor lit up and she opened the door.

I was feeling more and more ill at ease. In a few minutes I was going to have to uphold words and ideas that were deeply at variance with an essential part of myself.

An Oriental lantern of blue, yellow, green and red

glass, that her husband must have brought back from Algeria, lit the corridor dimly. Only when we got to the dining room could I see her in full light. Even if I hadn't known her, I would have been able to see the marks of sleeplessness and worry in her face.

After a few words of welcome, she fell silent, waiting calmly for me to begin, but her eyes were searching my face hopefully and fearfully. I could tell that she wanted to know the answer at once, and though I was upset too, I tried to counter her look with a neutral expression.

I didn't tell her that Vincent had refused right away. I began by recalling the code of medical ethics, the fact that Dr. Ferrières was a member of the medical association, and the formal prohibition of the law, and then, with my eyes lowered in embarrassment, I reminded her that not all fetal malformations are serious, which makes the percentage of real risks much lower.

Simone Vallin was silent, sitting very straight at the other side of the table. Facing her, I was ashamed to hear myself talk like a guilty person trying unsuccessfully to justify himself. Couldn't she understand? She was silent. I lifted my head. Her face expressed a poignant mixture of amazement, determination and defiance. I could no longer hold back the admission:

"The doctor told me," I finally said tonelessly, "that despite the sympathy and admiration he has for you, what you ask of him is completely impossible."

Her face remained immobile for a few seconds, frozen in a kind of impossible calm. It reminded me of the dizzying instability of an acrobat on the high wire with only the void lying in wait for him—then suddenly with a silent, despairing collapse of her whole being, her face seemed to shrink, to fall apart, to lose the marks of age and individuality. For yet another moment she tried to control herself. She lifted a hand distractedly to her face but the intense effort she was imposing on herself to look calm made her gesture jerky and mechanical. In spite of herself, the corners of her mouth trembled, her nostrils narrowed, her eyelids trembled, and tears glimmered in her eyes. Suddenly she fell against the table, pale and breathless, her face the mask of a dying person.

I got up and went over to her. I put my hands on her sob-wracked shoulders. Since I couldn't bear the burden of her pain, I wished I could at least find the words to comfort her. But what use are words in the face of such

240

despair? While she was begging me to do something, I could only offer her pity.

Gradually her sobs subsided. She finally lifted her head, and raised a swollen, bloated, unrecognizable face. She kept crying softly. Her wide eyes, pale with anxiety, stared at me with intolerable fixity. Could she see me through the tears I watched rolling over her pale cheeks? Suddenly she begged in a low, pitiful voice:

"Please don't forsake me! You're a doctor! You know how to do it—get rid of this child . . . it can't be born. A little while ago you lied to me. I know it'll be deformed. . . . You can't let it be born!"

She continued to beg, pitiful, obstinate and forsaken, as if I were her last recourse.

In the face of my silence—I protected myself with it like a weak shield—she redoubled her entreaties:

"Please don't refuse me. You don't have the right to refuse me. . . ."

Her voice became humbler and humbler, beseeching like her tearful eyes in her ravaged face. Her hands pressed my arms.

I finally found the strength to try to comfort her. I wanted to gain time with meaningless words and soothing phrases that wouldn't throw her into despair again: "Don't cry." I said, "be reasonable. . . . We'll take another look at the situation when the doctor comes back. . . ." But her voice was hoarse with panic, her eyes were riveted searchingly on mine and her hands, damp with sweat, clung to my arm. Her begging had closed her ears; she didn't even seem to be able to hear me. How could I make her understand that I was in close sympathy with her tragedy without causing her more pain; how could I tell her that I resented it cruelly in my womans' heart and with all my reason, that I wished I could share her misery, but that I was completely powerless before the laws made by the stupidity and the selfishness of men!

The voice continued stubbornly and despairingly. It changed pitch and she shrieked:

"Please mam'selle . . . Help me get rid of it. . . . Oh, please help me."

Was I afraid of yielding to that immolated, tormented face? Did I want to cut off all retreat? I finally said:

"You must understand. . . . I can't. . . . I swear to you that I can't. . . . It's too serious. For a doctor it's forbidden . . . absolutely forbidden. . . ."

241

Suddenly she pulled herself up, her chest heaving, her whole body in a state of such sharp tension that she moaned with pain. Summoning her last remaining strength, she stared at me fixedly for a few seconds, her eyebrows drawn together, her forehead tense, her mouth compressed into a hard line. Her eyes, still misty from the tears, shone with defiance, rebellion and fury. Then all in one breath, she shouted at me:

"You refuse. It's not fair. I'm only asking for justice. If I had money, I'd find someone who'd do it right away. I could even go abroad. You know that better than I! It's not a question of morality, it's all a question of money."

I was silent, hoping this crisis would be the end, would let her gradually relax into resignation, but she added in a frenzy of hatred:

"So that's your justice! Disasters always happen to the same people. You know how to manage things; if something went wrong, it wouldn't matter—the doctor would find some way for *you!*"

What did "for *you*" mean? I didn't understand. I looked stupidly at her. Her eyes were defiant, and she filled in the details with a sneer.

"The people around here are talking . . ."

This time I understood. I felt myself blushing. In Gennevilliers, the young women patients used to sigh as Pascali passed by, "At least with a doctor it's clean and quiet, and if something goes wrong it can be fixed," and this afternoon at the end of his briefing me, Vincent said: "I think it would be better if you slept at your mother's house. It's not far from here, and if there's a night call, Catherine can come to wake you"; and then he added a little awkwardly, "In such a small town, it's the wisest thing to do."

Simone Vallin looked at me, only waiting until I reacted to insult me again. Why answer her? Even if she was wrong about the doctor and me, I knew that this afternoon I'd felt vaguely disturbed at the idea of living alone with Jacques for ten days. Yet since I'm so militant about sexual freedom for women, how can it matter to me if the village gossips are spying on me and I'm the subject of their rumors?

She continued to watch me, poised for another insult. My silence obviously puzzled her. She must have taken it for disdain because in a sudden transport of rage she took three steps backwards, swayed against the wall, and clawed at the wallpaper. She started to scream.

"You tell me to wait and be resigned? Wait and see? No, I can't wait. . . . I'll get an abortion. Never mind how, somehow I'll get one."

There was such destructive fury and suicidal frenzy in her eyes that I shouted in turn.

"You can't do that!"

But she went on relentlessly.

"I *will* do it. And so you'll know I mean it, I'll tell you why!"

She looked at me for a few seconds as if her life itself depended on the secret that my refusal was making her divulge. Then, she screamed:

"My husband has a young brother in an asylum near Evreux. We often went to visit him. He's twelve years old. He's microcephalous . . . does that word mean anything to you? He has a bird's head, his ears are bigger than his skull, he has narrow-lidded eyes that never focus on anything for more than a second, and from time to time he opens his drooling bear-like mouth . . . and suddenly, for no reason, out comes a hideous scream. You know that German measles can cause microcephaly, and you want my child to live . . . incurable, imperfectible, in a herd of those small beings that I see at every visit, planted in a room with a floor of metal grating and a pit underneath for their excretions? . . ."

She paused, then shouted hoarsely:

"I will have an abortion! I have the right!"

In a flash I saw before my eyes the whole arsenal of crude abortion methods: rue, wolfsbane, shaggy wormwood—they were only a few among many others just as inefficient but even more dangerous. I imagined the village angel-maker, some enormous matron with dirty fingers, plunging a long needle and gropingly piercing the soft translucent little skeleton that already has a beating heart. I imagined Simone Vallin infected, losing blood, her face pale, her pupils dilated and turning blue, I imagined her dead. . . . Just when I could see the coffin leaving the schoolhouse with little Maria in tears among the cortège of children, she stepped toward me and with tragic bravado that chilled me to the marrow of my bones, she asked:

"Haven't you ever seen women die after an abortion?"

As I heard those words I knew with dreadful certainty

that I was trapped. I moved toward the door but she was ahead of me and grasped the knob in her hand. The room's four walls seemed to crush my chest. I looked crazily around me at the dining room—it was very new, with a few pieces of shoddy "furniture for young marrieds." She knew she'd gotten to me and she repeated with a sneer:

"You never saw them die?"

Then she watched in amazement as I ran up to her and shouted imperiously: "Shut up!"

For a few seconds we faced each other, both breathless. Could she guess that I wasn't seeing her face then but Mariette's?

I should have explained my "shut up," but it was dangerous to speak. I would have been gradually letting go of my tight control over myself if I confided to her that I had the same inexplicable sympathy for her as for Mariette, that I didn't want a second death on my conscience. I might only say something innocent but it could lead me to the terrible phrase that would implicate my whole life.

I was afraid; dizziness was overwhelming me. A few more minutes and I'd be tempted to make her a promise. It was better to leave right away. But she resolutely barred the door. I had to say at least the few words that would let me escape!

"I must think about it," I murmured painfully. "I'm not promising you anything. I'll be back. . . ."

Her swollen face suddenly flushed with joy, with gratitude and the illumination of hope. She seized my hand as it reached toward the doorknob.

I released her grip, ran through the little corridor and only stopped when I got to the street.

There I stood motionless for a few seconds, getting hold of myself. Leaning against the ironwork gate, I kept asking myself: "What have I said!"

Friday, August 9

For three days I haven't stopped coming and going, examining patients, using the stethoscope, giving shots, writing prescriptions.

The fact that I'm a stranger here—a fault that usually keeps the peasants from trusting you for many years— hasn't won out among Dr. Ferrières' patients over the desire to get a close look at that hitherto unknown phenomenon in Mesnil: a woman doctor at work. But Norman logic—which always gives rise to cautiousness—came into play in the end and all at once I was rumored to have a specialty: because of my sex, it seemed natural for me to be particularly expert at "women's diseases" and "children."

Day before yesterday—very early, because the country doctor's timetable is based on the farmer's timetable—I started my apprenticeship in rural practice.

The first patient who saw me drive into the farmyard and get out of the doctor's little car couldn't help staring at me. He looked me up and down with the same unnerving gaze he uses to estimate the weight of a calf on the hoof. I seemed to surprise him or even disappoint him, but he surprised me no less by leading me into a room where an imposing matron lay in bed. "Search her!" he said, which meant, I discovered after he explained, that I was supposed to examine his wife. In the village, the new doctor was rather more tactfully evaluated—I was looked over the way one delicately examines a cantaloupe at the fruit vendor's. . . .

I must admit that without my year's training at Gennevilliers, I would have been really confused. Even more than in the hospital, everything here is so different from medical school and the textbooks, that it doesn't seem like the same medicine. Without laboratory tests and X-rays, I have to rely on what I can learn from the pulse, tongue, abdomen and urine, like the practitioners of a hundred years ago. With the help of all these impressions and guesses, I can never be entirely sure I'm right.

But every time I walk into a farmhouse or a house in the village, I feel very happy that I'm in touch with patients again. Sitting at the edge of the bed, I question them patiently, while I relearn the art of gently, deftly feeling a painful stomach; I listen attentively while I tap a feverish chest. The other members of the family stand in a quiet circle around me and the patient politely turns his head away to cough. Then, in the solemn silence, the oracle speaks.

Basically this proves to me that there's no difference between my patients in the Ouche country and in Gennevilliers; a patient likes to feel important everywhere; he'd

245

even like to think that the doctor is only preoccupied with him.

Like Gennevilliers, the procedure for encouraging a patient's trust and confidence is simple: listen, take your time and never seem hurried.

I quickly gave in to the customs of the countryside—I accept the ritual coffee that's served at the end of all visits, but when the pitcher of hard liquor makes the rounds, I have the privilege, being a woman, of taking my coffee straight. Thank God! Otherwise they'd have to carry me home dead drunk at the end of the day.

Nonetheless, at the beginning I did make some mistakes. In cases that weren't serious, I thought it was a good idea to prescribe simply a fresh compress or a diet, because I thought they'd be grateful to me for avoiding expensive prescriptions that weren't really necessary. (Mother had warned me about the proverbial greed of the people of Mesnil and the surrounding countryside.) But I discovered very quickly that I was wrong and that they expected not just words from me but a little action. Medical action is a sign of science and power, and the woman doctor has to wave those two reassuring flags even more openly than her male counterpart. The key word as far as farmers are concerned—and many city people too—is "shots." I learned this because of the number of patients who told me they'd been cured by shots without ever having found out what kind of shots they had—they probably attributed a magic value to them that was totally independent of the medicine that was injected. Just performing the act was beneficial in itself, like a sorcerer's spells and incantations. But then I realized that shots weren't always psychologically effective, because besides the people who are "all for shots" or who "believe in shots," I discovered some patients who "don't want them no matter what."

Since Vincent had warned me not to attack a peasant's medical prejudices when they're more or less harmless, I gave in to them. In the same way, I stopped trying to reform their strange ideas about the cause of diseases; they thought of it in terms like "obstructed winds," "turned blood," and "nerves stronger than blood."

Three days of experience in rural practice as a pediatrician isn't enough for me to draw any final, firm conclusions. But if I had to submit a report on child-rearing in the Norman countryside of Ouche, I would note right away that though there are many beautiful, well-formed, healthy babies here, I found babies who had rickets, or were overstuffed with cow's milk, or were buried in their cribs in the darkest corners of ill-ventilated, poorly lit rooms. Some were given fly-covered nipples on old soda bottles to serve as baby bottles. Children with rickets in the middle of the country, in the sun, in the fresh air? ... I thought I had made some mistake. But how could I doubt my diagnosis when there were the pale bloated faces, the rachitic rosary, the deformations of the chest and the big bellies as evidence?

Sometimes they asked me to treat their childrens' "anemia" or "weakness" with "tonics," and one man even asked me what I would recommend as a good tonic for healing his hernia. The people in Mesnil also thought that intestinal worms were a common disease—next to tonics, the cures for children they ask me for most often are worm medicines. A child only has to scratch his nose once and the people around him say "he isn't well"; they say he's got worms and the doctor is called in to make them go away. And I had to be very insistent to be allowed to treat eczema (called "saint's disease" around here) or impetigo (the local name is "milk rash"), because the parents thought these things were good for the health of their children! In the past three days I've begun to understand the remark Vincent made one evening when he came home from his rounds very irritated—a remark that seemed very bitter to me then: "Exercised with honesty, rural medicine satisfies only the physician, if it even satisfies him."

What can the country doctor—both pediatrician and gynecologist—do when he's faced with the way rural life is organized? Taking care of the house, the children, the smaller farm animals, and doing a good part of the work in the fields, are all women's responsibilities and the work has to be done in conditions that are mostly still quite primitive. Once she's a mother, how can a woman nurse when her child's hungry if she can't stop working on whatever else she has to do? So I no longer wonder at the children's disgestive problems they call me about. Milk left to the flies for hours and poorly measured formulas in dirty bottles are enough to explain the serious diarrhea that the frightened parents ask me for "shots" to cure. Then they leave the child to suck on an old nipple fitted over a cork or else on a piece of candy wrapped in a bit of cloth—to keep their children from "getting a hernia from crying."

Since I was instantly promoted to being an expert gynecologist by local gossip, I would examine women at home—or see them during my office hours—who said they had a "disease in the stomach." Their female servitude wears them down and makes their lives miserable, even more than it does my patients in Gennevilliers. Even when they're pregnant these women don't get any rest—they only go to bed when the first signs of labor appear. They are on their feet for the churching all too soon because work is pressing. At forty, these large healthy-looking women reveal, on the examination table, collapsed abdomens, calcium deficiencies, stretch marks, varicose veins, inflammations of the uterus and prolapsed uteruses; and without exception they say they want to go through menopause soon, because it will finally free them from the danger of a "poisonous" husband. I didn't understand the expression "poisonous," so one of them explained: "Oh yes! A husband who makes too many babies. Mine has given me seven children already."

I haven't yet had to draw on my knowledge of psychosomatic gynecology for any of these women, worn out by one pregnancy after another. And I haven't seen any of the nervous types with little lesions and large imaginations that Lachaux and I kept sending back and forth to each other in Gennevilliers. There are no "imaginary invalids" here! These women are so overburdened with work that they don't have time for introspection. . . .

Often, when I'm making my house calls in the little town, I meet farmers coming from the tax collector, the grain merchant, the wheelwright, or the lawyer. They stop for a while at the café and then they go home rather drunk. All the while their wives are waiting for them on the farm, taking care of the washing, the chicken coop, the stable, the children. . . . In the country, the man is king all his life, but the trap closes on the young farm girl as soon as she gets married. Her fate has led her to an existence that goes endlessly on and on, never changing, always harsh and gray. While the man goes to town, visits the country fairs and keeps his contacts with the world, the woman is dedicated to motherhood and the cares of the home. Too bad that for humans it's not the male who sits on the nests and brings food to the little ones the way sparrows or pigeons do—that would force him to stay home too.

When I told Pascali that I intended to replace a doctor during the vacation, he kindly warned me:

"Get your driver's license! That's the only diploma that'll be useful to you."

Once I got this precious document, I could drive the little car that Vincent left me along with a list of the roads where his patients would wait for me. They watch for the car and wave me down as if I were a bus driver.

I like this string of hamlets and of spots that have special place-names but aren't even hamlets, of farms and hills which I'll soon know by heart, like the stations of a familiar train route. But I like the unexpected calls even better. They take me across the huge, melancholy plains surrounded by the distant forests, looking for some lost roof in a hollow at the level of the meadows and the hedges.

I've been awakened at dawn by an urgent call and I've tasted the smell of early morning in the country, the ineffable savor of the air in a new-washed world, rejuvenated, refreshed, and still damp from the dew, with the first cry of the nightingale piercing into the blue, as if drawn from the meadows by the new light.

I know the noons too, weighed down with the humid heat of growing things; the fields, drunk with the light, lie motionless, seemingly ready to catch fire under the enormous burning sun—yesterday it was terribly hot, and as I jolted down a particularly bumpy lane through the meadows on my way back from my morning tour, the whole white-hot sky seemed to turn dizzily around me without the relief of a single cloud, without the least veil of mist.

And I love the drive home in the clear golden evenings, enveloped by the silence of dusk and its stifling sweetness. As I pass through the hamlets with their low houses and their pastures, the road seems to belong to me alone and it leads me back to Mesnil with the faithfulness of a waterway.

My days start early and end very late, though the clientele I have, as a substitute, is barely a third of the patients Vincent was seeing just before he left.

Since I'm an inexperienced driver, I don't dare go fast on these tiny, unfamiliar roads. And I often have difficulty finding the isolated farm houses I've been called to, and end up following a bumpy dirt road that leads me across the fields to the cesspool—luckily it's summer and the ruts are as hard as cement! I also have a problem each time I question a patient because I often stumble over an expression in the local dialect. Thanks to Catherine I know that a "runt" is a little child. But what could a "close-ass" be, or a "surprise"? I had to learn that a close-ass is the last child born to a family and that a surprise is a child born to a couple who hasn't had one in years—they also say charmingly a "delight." While I'm on the subject of these runts, close-asses and surprises—I always have to be on guard during my questioning, because of a strange family vanity that delights in exaggerating past diseases, transforming the least chidren's colic into green diarrhea or simple bronchitis into bronchial pneumonia. I take my time about it, and I try to pin down the slippery truth as well as I can.

A psychoanalyst watching me would say that I'm more or less subconsciously making myself go even slower than can be accounted for by the fact that beginners always have to feel their way slowly for a while. I'd have to admit that he'd be right. Since my visit to Simone Vallin I've been living in a permanent state of hesitation, of tension, of refusing to make a decision. If I let office hours last a little longer than necessary, if I drive unnecessary miles by not sensibly grouping the visits on my rounds, if I try to be totally absorbed in my medical work, it's mostly because I want to get away from my own problems.

I know all too well that I'll have to make a decision—and without waiting too much longer—since I promised Simone Vallin that I'd come to see her again. But every morning I give myself a little more time, another period of grace.

Since Mesnil is strung out along one main street, I have to pass the schoolhouse several times a day. Each time I do I feel ashamed and sad thinking about her standing behind her curtain and looking at my comings and goings, watching and hoping; she probably hasn't stopped hoping for a single instant these past three days.

I didn't promise her anything; I didn't even set a time for giving her my answer; but I know that in my haste to get away from her I'd spoken very imprudently. The ambiguous words I said so I could escape were a kind of acquiescence, after my initial refusal, or at least, couldn't Simone Vallin interpret it that way? Despite her outburst of rage, she must have felt she'd succeeded in her efforts to shake me; she guessed that my refusal was less firm in my own mind than when I came. And the way she'd seized my hand . . .

I was glad she hadn't seen me run into my room a few minutes later, upset and trembling!

Since then I keep turning Vincent's arguments over and over in my mind: aren't the moralists and doctors who speak of the "interest" of the fetus in "benefiting" from the abortion giving sentimental rather than truly scientific advice? If I agreed to help the teacher wouldn't I be giving myself an arbitrary right over life and death? As if to support Vincent's arguments, I remembered what I'd learned from my teachers in the hospital and the efforts I'd seen to save the lives of people who were total losses to society—a veritable night-and-day all-out mobilization of forces for a bum, for example.

"Respect for life," Vincent said. I answered: "Fetishism." But blind obedience to a rule can be necessary, even if the rule seems absurd, unjust and inhuman.

One morning one of my teachers made the following remark to us in front of a little hydrocephalic: "Be careful! It's so tempting to do away with him! Remember the Nazi doctors. And once you get started, you go downhill very quickly. Under the pretext of protecting the human race, on the principle of eugenics, you start by sterilizing alcoholics and the insane—to get rid of physical and moral 'failures'—and in the end you're legally exterminating your enemies. Who doesn't know someone he'd like to see disappear? And, above all, who can claim he's not a 'failure' by *somone's* standards?"

"It's so tempting!" Yes, the reason I was so fascinated by the idea of performing that abortion was, I discovered, largely because of my purely physical need to escape from my nightmare. The idea of repairing the most horrible injustice with one simple act was fascinating. But wasn't I still too young and too easily influenced to make such a decision? And what if Simone Vallin's threat was simply blackmail?

But as soon as I remembered her tormented face and her defiance, I couldn't believe that she'd been lying to me, that she wouldn't, by whatever means, carry her decision through to its logical conclusion. Of this I was sure: whatever the risks, she would have an abortion!

"So it's a refusal to help a person in danger," I said to

251

myself, but Vincent's voice seemed to whisper the common sense argument: "If someone deliberately throws himself into the water and if I don't help him because of the risk of drowning myself, am I responsible for his suicide?" I had my own life to lead, my own freedom to think of—the thing she wanted me to do, which seemed easy enough to me, could get me involved in real difficulties—if there was a slip it could get me into prison or wreck my career.

"The embryo has one chance out of two of being deformed," I said to myself. "Do I have the right to let him run that terrible risk, to let him ever be born?" But logic immediately forced me to take the opposite side: "If I'm sure that a man who is drowning under my eyes has one chance out of two of becoming a murderer and being executed, should I stop to ask whether or not I should drag him out of the water?"

But what value did logic have in the midst of so much illogic and so many contradictions? How many times had I heard in the hospital at the bedside of a patient who'd had cancer and died after terrible suffering, that it was good that his ordeal was over! They knew he was incurable, but nonetheless they'd used all the resources of medicine as if to delay the hour of his deliverance! If I said no to Simone Vallin couldn't I call myself a coward, tied to a narrow, cautious, conventional medical ethic? Wasn't I admitting that I was incapable of those magnificent indiscretions that are the true signs of a great soul?

"Don't be affected by the specific case—be guided by principle," said Vincent. But if you're a physician can you ignore the personal, family or social difficulties that are the "human" context of each patient, and are as much a part of him as his illness or injury, without being unjust? Wouldn't it take more courage, in Simone Vallin's case, to agree to her demand than to refuse it? If therapeutic abortions are permitted for pregnant women suffering from certain circulatory, kidney or respiratory diseases, why refuse them for a moral reason? Does the body have a greater right to consideration than the soul? Should only physical suffering be considered? Isn't there a mental agony that's as horrible as the risk of physical death?

"So, what shall I do?" I asked myself as I drove along the back roads of the land of Ouche. What should I do to become the free woman that I want to be—obey the selfish unjust law made by men, or the law of my heart?

Should I hesitate between my "duty as a doctor" and my "duty as a woman"? I want to spare Simone Vallin seven months of useless anguish or the dangers of an illegal abortion. In that case, doesn't real love of your neighbor and true charity come from disobeying the written law?

I didn't for a minute consider confiding in mother. Jacques would have been my only help, but I couldn't ask him. Why? I couldn't have said. Maybe because this ordeal was decisive for my career. This problem was making me face my duties toward another woman, and nothing could make me avoid a decision which in the last analysis must come from me alone.

For the last three days, I've seen very little of Jacques. He accuses me of deserting him.

"You're running away from me," he says, laughing. "You're escaping from me like Galatea running to hide herself in the willows."

Then he says with an air of comic submission, "I wait for you in vain. I'm Hercules at loose ends because the charming Omphale has gone away for a walk and left me alone with the spinning wheel."

It's true—I come by very early in the morning, before Jacques gets up, to ask Catherine to give me the list of patients who've called and asked me to visit them. At noon, I manage to get to lunch late so I don't have to spend as much time at the table. When visiting hours are over, I come to sit under the arbor for a few minutes, while Jacques, the model convalescent, reads or sleeps innocently. I glance at my watch and escape almost immediately on the pretext of having to make visits which give me an excuse to disappear until evening. I don't linger after dinner, being careful to leave one or two patients to see before I go quietly to bed at my mother's house, as Vincent asked me to.

Tonight I really did have two calls to make. First, I wanted to take another look at a baby who had bothered me a little. Even though I'd made it clear that my recommendations were important, I found him half-suffocated under blankets and a quilt—that's the peasant treatment for a "chill." ... Then I went to examine a newborn baby who had been vomiting for two days; the family had thought they should cut out all liquid feedings to cure it.

My itinerary took me by the girls' school twice and I

253

couldn't help looking at it; a light was shining through the shutters on the ground floor. Was I expected?

It was close to eleven when I came home. Mother was asleep and I went directly to my room.

I was tired and feverish, and I knew why: it's the third day of my period. I didn't have the heart to lean on the windowsill and look out over the sleeping garden and the night. How can I believe, tonight, that the world is in perfect harmony, and my body a promise of joy? How can I think that I'm free just because all day I drove the car along endlessly unfolding roads? The lighted windows of the schoolhouse reminded me just a few minutes ago of how exploited my sex is, and my present discomfort is another reminder of the constant treason of the female body.

I wasn't sleepy so I sat down in front of my little table. I opened my black notebook ... I felt crippled and discouraged. The silence and solitude of the night depresses me. Why did I leave Jacques so early and why didn't I go back to him after I'd finished my two calls? Why did I deprive myself of these moments, why did I avoid their sweetness?

Tonight Jacques asked me again to stay a little longer; he insisted with his now-usual kindness. He took an interest in what I'd been doing during the day, and I almost accepted because I was so happy to hear his voice become more attentive and gentler just for me. To be frank, I'm happy to find his playfulness, his kindness and his slightly protective smile to greet me when I get back from my tiring round of calls.

What is the feeling that always pushes me away from staying alone with him? It's certainly not fear of gossip; I feel independent enough not to mind public opinion. Is it the unconscious and gratuitous desire to be unhappy? Lachaux taught me that in every manifestation of masochism there's a large dose of the desire to punish yourself. If I try hard to understand myself, I'm forced to admit that I'm ashamed about my attitude toward Simone Vallin and that I'm trying to compensate for the scornful opinion that she rightly has of me. It doesn't matter that she's wrong in thinking that I'm Dr. Ferrières' mistress—and I'm sure the whole village thinks that too, since they can't imagine, in their peasant greed, that I could have difficulty deciding between the two cousins. It would be beyond their wildest dreams to think that I'd let such a good match get away! What Simone Vallin wanted to do by throwing Dr. Ferrières' name in my face was to get at the happy, secure woman inside me who she thinks doesn't care about her unhappiness. She doesn't know me well enough to understand how much I'm suffering because of her. How could I feel free and relaxed around Jacques as long as she's spending days of horrible waiting because of me? I must decide, I must say yes or no.

All day long today I've kept asking myself if my indecision isn't due to cowardliness. When I think about it, I think I've been suffering for the past three days the way almost all women do during their period.

If only I could leave my lack of resolution and my doubts under the shower the way I'm going to wash off all traces of my period from my body. . . .

Sunday, August 11, 3 a.m.

This time I've made up my mind; no matter what happens, I'll have no regrets. If I were a fatalist, I would believe that destiny had made the decision for me.

Yesterday, at about five o'clock, at the end of a very busy office hour—in Mesnil Saturday is market day and all the people from the surrounding countryside come to town—I went into the garden as usual before starting on my rounds.

When I got near the arbor I was surprised to hear Jacques' laughter blending with feminine voices that sounded familiar. The first face I saw through the leaves was Alberte Apple's, red and sweaty. I couldn't see the speaker facing her; but it could only be Jacques—who else would Alberte look at like a bulldog drooling greedily in front of a tidbit, or like an ogress watching a fat baby—a look of such obvious lust that it was disgusting and obscene?

Arlette was sitting next to her on a cane chair, dressed in an elegant mauve silk dress, gracefully holding a glass of orangeade and laughing and looking flattered at one of Jacques' jokes.

None of them heard me arrive. As I walked toward them I could see Jacques without his noticing it. As usual, he was stretched out on his lounge chair, in a thin silk dressing gown and pajamas. His legs were crossed, and he was indolently balancing a soft leather slipper on his toes.

255

This sounds just like the everyday Jacques, but since I know him well, I could see a deep change in him: his eyes were sparkling with pleasure, his voice had taken on a deeper, richer timbre; his body, despite his lounging posture, didn't give an impression of relaxation, but of alertness, of readiness to attack. Never even in our best moments of friendly intimacy had I seen him shining with such intense joy. I was so surprised at the sight that I accidentally bumped against an empty watering can lying on the path. All three looked up. My interruption dissipated the vague, gossamer sensuality between Arlette and Jacques; it didn't happen quite fast enough, though, to keep me from suffering a painful shock.

Arlette was the first to rise. She came up to me quickly and hugged me affectionately; she was clean, freshsmelling and perfumed. Alberte, her large thighs stuffed into a pair of tight linen slacks, got up clumsily to give me a sweaty hug in her turn.

I had to hide my emotions, pretend to be surprised and look delighted, then listen to the reasons for their unexpected visit with the appearance of lively interest:

"Gilbert and the children and I," Arlette explained, "are vacationing in Acquigny, where my father retired two years ago. Gilbert wanted to go on a trout fishing expedition to the Risle—it's about twenty-five miles from here. I took a look at the map, and thought it would be a good idea to pick up Alberte—I knew she was in Evreux. Father and Gilbert are absorbed in their rods and flies, so we took the car and skipped over to Mesnil to see you and to get together like in the old days."

It seems that once they got here, after trying to find me at my mother's, they happened on Jacques. He was crossing the hall to go out to the garden just as Catherine opened the door for them, and he spirited them off under the arbor so they could wait more comfortably until I finished my office hours.

"Alberte and I thought you were still feeling the way you were when your friend Lachaux came to see you," Arlette said. "We thought we'd be waking up Sleeping Beauty, lying under her apple tree. But your mother said you're all involved in medical activity and Monsieur Ferrières says that you're working too hard. We've been here nearly two hours. We were beginning to wonder if we might not have to leave without even saying hello. We have to start back very soon. Otherwise my father and Gilbert will get worried."

"Then promise you'll come back soon!" Jacques exclaimed with comical exaggeration. "A school friendship is a beautiful thing but visiting the sick is one of the works of true charity. I'm a neglected convalescent. You noticed it yourselves; Claude has become an invisible woman. Have pity on me!"

"What a shame that Mesnil is so far away—I'd like to come keep you company!" exclaimed Alberte with such charitable ardor that her fat cheeks flushed.

"A shame, indeed!" Jacques answered. He thanked her with a smile that made the poor girl blush even more, while he threw a look of shared amusement at Arlette.

Sitting across from Arlette and Jacques, I watched their every expression. Jacques started animatedly to tell them funny stories about my activities as a nurse and Arlette didn't once take her eyes off his mouth. She kept looking at his lips with a mixture of provocative flirtatiousness and modest submission. As he talked, Jacques confidently, carelessly caressed her body with his eyes through the thin material of her dress. His gaze lingered just under the shoulders at the line where her skin emerged from her bra, followed the supple line of her hips down to her thighs and her calves, and then climbed with calm effrontery back toward her face; and Arlette let him do it, apparently happy at feeling desired instead of being annoyed at being thought easy.

I've never had such pains in my chest in my life. When Jacques invited me to testify to his good manners as a patient (according to him they merited frequent charitable visits), I had to breathe deeply to unblock my lungs, and command my tense face to take on an interested friendly expression before I could answer.

Once they got to the arbor, Jacques must have arranged it so that Arlette was seated close to him in my usual place. Probably from the very beginning his eyes were constantly telling her "I like you. What will happen between us?" In this peaceful corner of the garden, in the same spot where I'd spent so many close happy hours with him, it was awful to be suddenly rejected and excluded, to suffer this painful feeling of dispossession, of nothingness, of desertion. Jacques was suddenly far away from me and happy without me. I was excluded from his happiness. . . .

Straining myself to keep calm, I listened without hearing. My ears were ringing but my eyes never left Jacques, as if I were watching for some evidence that would prove he was really treacherous. Little by little, as he talked more animatedly, the gestures he made with his hands seemed to become more enveloping and more coaxing; at one point he half sat up in his lounge chair to persuade Arlette to come back to Mesnil very soon, and he put his hand on her arm with a gesture of long-standing familiarity—the same boyish, friendly gesture he'd made to me after our discussion about family planning. But his hand lingered delightedly on Arlette's soft skin, that skin that I had touched in the past—the warm skin of a sensual, earthy creature, a woman of the flesh. And Arlette didn't pull her arm away, didn't refuse the prolonged possessive caress.

This was so unexpected and so cruel that it paralyzed me for a few lightning seconds and made me choke.

Happily Arlette and Alberte were much too occupied by watching Jacques and laughing, slavelike, at something funny he said, to notice me. All three left me to my delirious imaginings long enough for me to get hold of myself.

Arlette finally looked at her watch: "We've got to go."

She got up. Alberte and Jacques followed suit and I had to stand up too, my throat dry, my legs shaky, my heart beating with heavy, dull thuds.

Jacques said good-bye in the foyer. At five-thirty in the afternoon he would have looked out of place in a silk dressing gown on the steps or the sidewalk.

I'd seen too much and I was suffering too much. At the moment of leave-taking, I looked away so I wouldn't have to see anything more, neither the prolonged pressure of fingers, nor the exchange of looks, nor Jacques' triumphant air, nor Arlette's shining eyes. But I did hear the promises of phoning and fixing a date for another visit very soon.

Once Jacques had gone back to his room, saying a last smiling good-bye to my friends from the landing, I wished I too could have disappeared to hide my suffering. I was done in.

But I still had to see Arlette and Alberte out to the car.

At the car, they kissed me good-bye. At the last minute they probably realized that they'd come to see me and had hardly talked to me at all.

Arlette said slightly condescendingly:

"The country agrees with you! I've never seen you looking so good." She looked at my dress. "Or so elegant. Why were you so stubborn in Gennevilliers? Now you see how, with just a little effort! ..."

Alberte improved on this in her heavy-handed way.

"That's true! You do look better than in Paris."

Then, lowering her eyes, she said meaningfully, "Your mother told us that the local doctor is a very nice young man, and single." She exclaimed, with more enthusiasm and feeling than a professional matchmaker would have shown, "Do marry him!"

"Alberte's right," Arlette repeated affectionately. "Marry him! We'll all come to the wedding."

With that encouragement, they fell silent and since I didn't answer, we looked at each other in somewhat embarrassed silence for a few moments.

Alberte's round, shortsighted eyes glittered enviously. She seemed to be saying: "Ah! You're lucky! You've found a husband!" As for Arlette, I could read her thoughts easily: "You're hesitating ... but you'll get there like all the rest. ... A man's arms, protection, security, a beautiful house—that's well worth the sacrifice of your independence. ..."

I wanted to scream at them to go away. Their involuntary cruelty was unbearable. My throat was dry and constricted. I was at the point of collapse. I pushed my two friends into their car. Arlette started the motor. They turned around to shout, "See you soon!" Alberte's plump hand kept waving out the window for a minute after they left.

As soon as the car was out of sight, I got into the doctor's little car. I left town and drove aimlessly straight ahead, automatically handling the car in a daze. My brain was empty; I couldn't even put two thoughts together. I felt completely confused, totally dazed, and overwhelmed by the deepest despair and sorrow. The car had been standing in the sun all afternoon and it was terribly hot inside. Sweat was running down my forehead and my cheeks, half blinding me; but it seemed to me that despite the sun, I was moving forward into a black world thick with ashes and soot.

I don't know how long I drove like that. I found myself on a narrow unfamiliar road, looking dazedly around as if

I had just awakened from a nightmare. The place was deserted. The pale loam of the plains, cracked by the heat under the thin cover of stubble, stretched out endlessly on all sides. What instinct had made me avoid the bushes or the forest and stop in the midst of this solemn immensity, this silence beaten down by the sun, whose desolation was so exactly attuned to my unhappiness?

The light was so cruel and harsh in this wilderness that I lowered my eyes. For a long time, I listened to the pulse in my temples, stupidly looking at the reddish grass on the bank near the car. The air was becoming stifling again in the motionless car. I drove on.

When I left Mesnil I moved in a kind of cataleptic rigidity, with each nerve and muscle tense—it was horribly painful but in spite of myself it kept me from collapsing. The tension became so intolerable that all at once I felt I'd reached the limit of my resistance: if I didn't stop immediately, something was going to explode inside my chest or my head. I looked around me. I saw a huge tree, standing alone in the middle of a meadow, not very far from the road. It gave the only shade nearby. I barely had the strength to drive up to it, open the door, and let myself slide down to the ground. And with my face on the grass, I renounced all human dignity and accepted all shame; I wept with great suffocating, despairing sobs. In my pride I'd thought I didn't know how to cry any more, but now I abandoned myself, hiccuping and runny-nosed, to my sorrow. I cried for a long time. When I finally lifted my head again, my eyes were burning and my whole body hurt; I felt mauled and broken as if I'd had a bad fall, but the tears gave me relief. I was beginning to come to life again. But I was unable to take the wheel yet and I thought: "I'll visit the patients on my afternoon's list this evening or tomorrow morning."

The sun was still quite high in the sky. I had a little time to rest before dinner. I stretched out on my back and lifted my eyes toward the tree that sheltered me. I almost burst into tears again when I recognized a russet trunk, knotty branches and ripening fruit among the dense leaves, just like the fruit of the apple tree whose shade had so often been my refuge in the garden. In Normandy an apple tree is a commonplace thing, but finding one at a moment like this was such irony! Why did I ever leave the security of the garden to go to help Jacques? Why had I

260

made my own suffering? Why had I played with fire? I'd asked myself so many times, coming home from my sessions as his nurse, "What's the matter with me?" as if I myself had caught something, and was feeling a little ill! The next morning I'd forget about it in the happiness of going back to be near him again. Naïvely I believed that I was experiencing a friendship, and I let myself be caught in my own deception!

I closed my eyes, trying to understand why, when all was still simple and could still be undone, I hadn't recognized that the astonishing joy my body felt just because Jacques was near might be dangerous. As if a girl who is clear-headed and honest with herself couldn't tell the difference between involuntary uneasiness and the deliberate acquiescence involved in searching it out! Why wasn't I afraid when our intimacy grew, when I let myself be taken in by the seductiveness of that thin face, those hard lips, those too-soft eyes? Why didn't I run away as soon as I was tempted to touch his cheek when he was sleeping? And somehow I believed that our friendship would always be light and sweetly innocent. . . . An intonation, a look, a simple gesture between Jacques and Arlette proved to me in one single instant that this loving friendship . . . But why should I be afraid of the word? It wasn't a loving friendship . . . love had swept my old self away. What's left of the independent strong girl I wanted to be? What's happened to my disdain for a devouring, unreasoning, ravaging love, that has kept me happy in my loneliness so long?

"Jealous! You're just plain jealous!" I said to myself out loud. It seemed to me that I'd lost everything—my will power, my dignity, my conscience. Jealous! Oh! I must be very jealous to have suffered so much under the arbor, to have wept, screamed, and clawed at the grass because of a face observed on the sly, because of one single glimpse of Jacques' hand resting on the same spot where I'd felt my flesh burn so deliciously a few days ago. Arlette and Jacques! How could I forget now that I'd surprised them in their freedom with each other, and without me, before their desire! Once again the familiar disease of loneliness had take hold of me—I was feverish and exasperated—and it was even more terrible now that I'd tasted the happiness of being part of a twosome.

I felt such emptiness, such dispossession, that I almost

started to cry again, holding my head between my arms like a child.

I was ashamed of my weakness. With a painful effort I managed to pull myself off the ground and sit up. My head felt empty. I had to lean against the apple tree to stand up. I could feel its cracked bark between my fingers and its big roots under my feet. I was so exhausted that I had to lean on the tree trunk to catch my breath.

How late was it? I looked at the sun, now low on the horizon at the edge of the grasslands and for a moment the apple tree seemed like an axis that the meadows and forests and sky were wheeling dizzyingly around. Then the world righted itself and fell into place again. My ears stopped buzzing and an incredible silence filled me, like the silence of the countryside in the peaceful light of sunset. I had to leave. I felt the rugged bark one last time. "This evening and tomorrow," I thought, "I'll go back to the apple tree in the garden. I'll try to listen to its lessons and its wisdom. Will I recover there that feeling of lightness in my body and the peace of mind it's already given me—a serenity above sadness and desire? Will it give me the concentrated stubborn strength to make me overcome my new emptiness? Will it help me find the slow maturity that, over and above my error of today, will bring me back to my truly solitary struggle?"

I got back into the car. Before starting up, I looked at myself in the rear-view mirror: I saw sticky strands of hair, swollen eyelids, red eyes. When I got back, I'd have to comb my hair and make up some excuse, like a grain of sand or dust in my eyes that would explain the state of my eyes to Jacques. I smiled bitterly, thinking that above all I'd have to keep my dignity where he was concerned and get used to being impersonal again, and pleasantly indifferent, like an old friend. I'd need all my courage. Until Vincent got back I'd use the same old recipes to get rid of jealousy without falling into romanticism: pride and work! After that, I'd see.

I went back. I'd put down the top of the car and when I started to drive the wind felt cool and refreshing.

Jacques was waiting for me to come back before he started dinner. First I combed my hair and bathed my eyes but I still needed the help of dim light, so I told Catherine not to turn on the dining room chandelier right away.

Jacques didn't seem to notice anything.

"Lots of work this afternoon?" he asked casually as we started to eat.

I listened to myself lie. To fill up my late afternoon, I invented three visits and described them in full detail. I would have said anything to delay the moment when Jacques—I was sure he would—started talking about Arlette. So I kept talking—there was no other way to keep my suffering at a distance in the dining room where I once was so trustful and happy!

I looked around me at the old sideboards, at the pottery and the pewter gleaming in the last rays of the sun. It was as if I'd imprudently walked into a den of thieves, and suddenly discovered the danger, and now I was pretending to be calm to get closer to the door without arousing their distrust. But the danger tonight was inside me.

I felt tired and wished I didn't have to keep talking. But I had to, so I'd have the courage to be silent about the essential thing; so I wouldn't descend into the sordid hell of complaints, insults, recriminations and tears. I had to talk so I wouldn't force Jacques to say: "What are you complaining about? I didn't hide anything from you. I frankly admitted to you what kind of man I am." Yes, I had to talk now so I wouldn't be tempted to confess: "I saw you when you were unhappy, suspicious and lonely. I thought that I could save you by loving you." I was afraid of hearing Jacques' ironic laugh, hailing me as an idiot, a second Alberte Apple who thought she could tie him down!

I'd gotten to the tale of my third imaginary visit of the afternoon. I was using a case I'd looked at the day before yesterday so I didn't have to make up everything: a ten-year-old girl, suffering from what seemed to me was a tubercular peritonitis. I was amazed that they hadn't called Dr. Ferrières in earlier. The parents finally admitted that their daughter had been treated by a faith healer for three years, with herb poultices, signs of the cross and prayers.

Jacques interrupted me:

"Typical! My uncle and Vincent have often said that even nowadays the peasants of Upper or Lower Normandy will call in a faith healer at the same time as a doctor, if they don't call in the faith healer first."

The phone rang.

"Well, here we go! At this time of day it's probably an emergency," Jacques said commiseratingly.

We heard Catherine come out of the kitchen—I leave the task of taking telephone messages to her; only she can penetrate the usual hysteria of the caller and discover exactly how serious each call is and how urgent.

She appeared in the doorway almost instantly.

"It's an accident around Grandhoux, mam'selle. . . . A workman half-buried by a well cave-in. His legs are caught and they can't get him out. He's in so much pain that he needs a shot right away while they wait for help. They called Dr. Mahieu from La Ferté but he isn't there."

As soon as I heard the first words she spoke I thought, without even considering how cruel I was being toward the buried man, how lucky I was to have an excuse to get away.

I got up.

"Tell them I'll be there right away."

Jacques looked at me, hesitated for a few seconds, then said:

"I know Grandhoux. I used to go hunting around there. It's way the hell out. A lost hamlet at the end of impossible roads. You'll never get there in the dark. Go get your case. I'll get dressed and come with you."

I didn't even have time to say yes or no to him. He'd already left the dining room and was dashing up the stairs to his room.

My heart beat harder. I felt depressed again. I went to pick up the emergency kit in the consultation room.

Vincent had shown me the kit before he left. It was more than a simple black bag—it was really a leather suitcase that contained, as he explained to me, all that I'd need to treat an injured person if I were called out unexpectedly.

I deposited the suitcase in the corridor. Jacques must have heard me.

"I'll be down in a second!" he shouted.

I leaned against the newel post. It was near to dusk, and the big foyer was beginning to get dark. The air was warm, and I breathed the clean smell of furniture polish. Ranged along the walls on their old oaken chests, the statues of the healing saints were still mounting their peaceful guard over the house. The evening light caught on the bright colors of their costumes, on the blond beards, on the gold of their halos. When I walked into this old home for the first time, I'd instantly fallen in love with this warm breath from the past and the peace it diffused.

Only sixteen days had passed since my first visit and I'd been living alone with Jacques in that big silent house for the last four. "Wasn't it a dream?" I murmured. I didn't dare answer because if I spoke, time—which seemed to have stopped for a moment—would begin again and these sixteen days would fall forever into the past.

After I leaned on the banister for a while, the beating of my heart calmed down and I could breathe more easily. I looked closely at the familiar row of wooden saints. It seemed to me that I was leaving them at the end of a fantastic adventure and that they would stay here as witnesses to what had taken place between Jacques and me. Thanks to them, even if I disappeared into a world without desires, without memories and without joy, these sixteen miraculous days wouldn't die entirely.

Jacques' footsteps coming down the stairs shook the banister against my back. Now I had to stop dreaming, keep a clear head and play my role without mistakes.

Jacques had exchanged his dressing gown and pajamas for a pair of light colored slacks and a sports jacket. His shirt was open at the collar and he was almost running. He caught me with one hand as he ran past me, snatched up the suitcase with the other and dragged me by the arm to the door.

The little Peugeot was parked a few yards away by the sidewalk but Jacques dragged me toward the left where the garage stood.

"The car's here," I protested, thinking he'd made a mistake.

"Let's take my car. We'll get there faster. It must be working—Vincent was still using it five days ago."

He opened the garage door. Since the Peugeot spent its days and nights in front of the house, I'd never gone inside. I saw the sleek red body of a small sports convertible in the back.

Jacques took a rag and quickly cleaned off the windshield and the seats.

"You'll see in a minute—it can really go! And with the top down, it'll be even better!" he said as he slammed the door after making me get in and sit down.

He turned the ignition key, and pulled the starter. The motor began to purr. He tapped the accelerator very quickly two or three times in succession, releasing and immediately throttling a deafening crescendo. He leaned forward, listened attentively, and looked at me radiantly.

"Listen to that! Perfect! We can go!"

With two quick movements he was out of the garage. As soon as he was in the street, he started to accelerate. As we passed the last houses of Mesnil, he turned on the headlights, then, with his hands firmly on the wheel, he put his foot down.

In ten seconds, the warm evening air became a cool breeze against my cheek; it cut my breath as if my nostrils had been stopped up; it whistled against my ears, mixed in with the lament of the motor on its one unvarying high note. The road, still straight for a while, made way on each side for two dark walls that rose endlessly up out of the night and the hood disemboweled the air with a roar like a hurricane.

Jacques was crouched in his seat, silent and alert, entirely given over to his joy. The diffuse light from the dashboard vaguely lit up his face. I wished I could keep from looking at him but he still had some irresistible power over me. Despite myself, I examined him stealthily. Had I ever seen him so beautiful? His masculine profile was straining toward the road; his look was shining and young; his lips were half open, drinking in the wind.

It was strange to be rushing into the night to an "emergency," driven at eighty miles an hour by the man I thought I'd lost forever! Suddenly a thought took me by surprise. "This new attentiveness of his ... The way he's putting himself spontaneously at my disposal ... Maybe nothing *is* lost."

Until then I'd been sitting tensely and leaning forward in my seat. Suddenly I felt peaceful and relaxed; I let myself sink back against the seat and let go completely.

I threw another swift glance at Jacques. Had he noticed how upset I'd been? Like a child on vacation who's just found his favorite toy, he seemed more and more carried away by the tumult of the drive. Entirely given over to the joy of finding his strength again after three months of imprisonment, his eyes were fixed on the road. He only cared about the wonderful rediscovery of speed, freedom and his health. I watched him as eagerly as I had this afternoon—with all my soul. He turned his head toward me and shouted through the noise: "Wonderful!" For a second I saw his white teeth gleam as he smiled at me, and the next second he turned back to the road.

I was alone again, and hurt. I felt discarded and excluded, the way I'd felt under the arbor. I couldn't hold onto my illusions any longer. Jacques wasn't talking to me, or smiling at me, but at his new-found freedom and his own happiness. He was happy without me this evening too. . . .

I closed my eyes, so I wouldn't see the face that hurt me any more. It's useless to ask people for what they can't give you. Jacques would never be aware of anything but his endless need of independence, his free, impatient way of going through life.

I was in mortal danger. I wanted to stop, to get away. I threw my head back into the backwash of the windshield to try to clear my mind in the wind.

Jacques put his foot down hard on the brake and the car pulled up sharply. The tires squealed as we went around a very tight curve. The air was suddenly hot and heavy again. I opened my eyes. We'd just left the main highway for a secondary road. We drove more slowly for a few hundred yards. It was impossible to go fast on this narrow road, zigzagging between the edges of the meadows which stretched out on either side under the bright moonlight.

Now that he no longer had to focus all his attention on the driving, now that the delirium of speed was gone, Jacques seemed to remember my existence. He began to talk to me again. The motor was purring softly. He didn't have to raise his voice any more.

"Another two miles. We've got to keep our eyes out for a small hill on the right, in about five hundred yards, and then take the second road on the left a little further on."

He kept up his monologue. I was still. I never wanted to open my eyes again, never to see the white fences lit up by the headlights at each corner, or the pastures lit up by the moon, where heavy sleeping shapes slowly lifted their muzzles as we passed by.

"We're almost there," announced Jacques. He seemed very much at ease in this network of narrow roads.

"Thank God," I thought. "At least my mind and my hands will have something to do."

Jacques drove on very slowly.

"We must be here. On the phone they told Catherine that the well is in the meadow, about eight hundred yards from the hamlet of Grandhoux, not very far from the road. Keep watching to your right!"

I half sat up in my seat. Jacques had dimmed the lights to help me see better, and the car was moving at a walking pace.

At first I didn't see anything in spite of the brightness of the moon on the meadow, then in the direction that Jacques pointed out I thought I saw some lights above the fences in the middle of a field and a circle of moving shapes.

"That must be it!" Jacques said. "Now let's find the entrance to the pasture."

He put on the headlights and the feathery moths began to dance in their beams again.

A small dirt road led off from the right side of the road.

"Here we are," Jacques said and without hesitation he drove the car between two barbed wire fences.

In the pastures on each side of the road, horses raised themselves ponderously to their feet and stretched out their muzzles curiously at us.

A bumpy path led us to a meadow. The headlights glanced off a few apple trees in neat rows, some enormous heaps of earth and a small hut with a tarpaulin for a roof. Next to the hut people were gathered near the curb of the well. It was very low, almost at ground level, and the point of a little iron crane that looked almost like a gallows leaned out over it.

Jacques stopped a few yards away from the well. He shut off the ignition and turned off the headlights. The only thing left to give us light were four or five storm lanterns that had been placed on the ground.

When we pulled up, everyone turned toward our car and our unfamiliar faces, but because of the usual peasant cautiousness, no one made a gesture of welcome. Jacques was quicker than I and jumped out of the convertible first, announcing:

"Dr. Sauvage, substituting for Dr. Ferrières."

Then a man came forward—a peasant with a big red face and a moustache. He politely lifted his cap to Jacques.

"I'm the mayor of Grandhoux. It's certainly nice of you, doctor, to come so quickly even though we're so far from Mesnil."

Then, after a moment's hesitation, he explained to Jacques as he led him toward the well:

"Doctor, it's a really bad accident. One of the well-digger's assistants is trapped down there; he's caught under the concrete reinforcing ring. His boss is trying to get him out. But it'll take some time and the poor man is in pain. Just listen to him!"

A small engine was running noisily at the foot of the crane under the hut's awning.

"Stop the motor!" the mayor ordered.

The winch motor puffed on two or three times more. It hadn't completely stopped when a shriek of agony came up from the well, the scream of someone being tortured or torn limb from limb—a monstrous sound with nothing human left in it. I'd never heard a scream in the hospital that expressed so much suffering; and the shriek redoubled every time the muffled sound of a hammer blow rose from the hole.

The mayor watched Jacques in silence. He seemed embarrassed. Continuing to ignore me, he finally said:

"Doctor, maybe someone should go down to help the man."

"Sure," Jacques answered, coolly.

"Ah! Thank you, doctor!"

But after this burst of gratitude, the mayor added quickly, to relieve himself of all the responsibility:

"Only, be sure to be careful going down. The well is already nearly twenty-five yards deep."

Pushing aside some farmers who were gaping at us, he took another three steps toward the little well curb—it was hardly ten inches high. Jacques followed him and I followed Jacques.

This time we were near the edge of the hole. Jacques and I leaned over a narrow circular chimney whose smooth gray cement sides seemed to sink endlessly into the earth. At the very bottom, lit from one side by a large miner's lamp, you could clearly make out a man. He was naked above the waist, and he was hitting an enormous broken cement ring that lay on the ground, with a sledgehammer. At each movement the rescuer made in front of the light his shadow jumped, revealing the injured man whose lower body was caught under the cement. And at each blow, as if the sledgehammer were hitting his stomach, the poor man struggled desperately like an animal caught in a trap, lifted his head, tried to move his body and clawed the soil with his hands, shrieking fearfully, then fell back, his throat rattling, while the head well-

269

digger stepped back and gathered his strength, despite the screams, for another blow with his sledgehammer.

I closed my eyes and listened horrified, twice, three times, to the muffled sound and the heart-rending screams.

Jacques took me firmly by the arm as if he were afraid I'd get dizzy. I looked at him and said:

"It's horrible! We'll have to go down at once!"

He drew me back gently.

"Let's go find the emergency kit!"

The farmers stepped back to let us pass. Jacques came back to the car with me, took his flashlight from the glove compartment, and then opened the suitcase on the seat for a quick inventory.

Vincent is careful and methodical. Everything was in perfect order: syringes, alcohol, phials, instrument box, tourniquets, bandages.

"Perfect!" Jacques cried as he focused the flashlight on the bottom of the case. "There's even a small bottle of oxygen."

He opened the stopper lightly. The gas started to whistle.

"And to top it all off, it's full!" he said delightedly, like a child discovering a new toy.

Then, serious again, "If you agree, I'll give him an injection of morphine and digitalis."

I thought I'd misunderstood.

"What do you mean? I'm going to go down!"

I heard Jacques' laugh in the shadow.

"That's right ... going down on that swing, showing your legs like a Fragonard shepherdess. ... Be reasonable! Well-brought-up young ladies, even with a doctor's diploma, don't go down wells in linen dresses."

To really convince me, he added:

"If Vincent were here, he'd tell you I'm right. ..."

I was more and more amazed.

"When we got here you announced: 'Dr. Sauvage, substituting for Dr. Ferrières.' I'm the substitute!"

He laughed again.

"The trouble is that no one seemed to believe it. The mayor kept calling *me* doctor, on the strength of my prepossessing appearance. How would I feel if you took my license away from me in front of all these peasants? So, be nice and let's compromise. To be nice to me, you let me go down with the little suitcase and after I've come

270

up again, you can file a complaint against me for usurpation of identity and illegal practice of medicine."

He started to laugh again.

"Just think of Vincent's expression! Let me at least have that pleasure."

"But what if something serious happens down there?"

Jacques became serious again.

"Serious for whom? For the wounded man? In the circumstances that he's in now, a simple nurse could do as much for him as a professor of medicine. I've studied medicine for three years, and I've had experience in first aid in the jungles of Viet Nam and Malaysia. Let me go. The man's in pain. Come on!"

He closed the suitcase again. He picked it up with one hand and pulled me toward the well with the other.

On the way, he said, "Don't worry. When I was a kid, I used to go down with old Jerome, the well-digger in Mesnil. It's fun and there's really no danger."

They'd started up the winch motor again. The mayor came up to us.

"The other assistant well-digger will explain the procedure to you, doctor."

"It's not necessary," Jacques answered off-handedly, "I know how to do it."

At the end of the cable hanging under the crane boom, a small plank of wood was hooked on like a swing.

The mayor called over the assistant well-digger, who was adjusting the mechanism. He came quickly out of the hut. He was young and built like a bull. He had blue eyes and a thick mop of red hair. He installed Jacques on the plank, put the suitcase across his knees and carefully attached its handle to the cable hook.

Jacques had left his jacket in the car. Now, in his immaculate light colored slacks with the big black suitcase on his lap, he swung round slightly over the hole. On the narrow wooden board, he had the calm air of a jockey sitting on his saddle at the weighing-in before a race.

I looked at my feet, at the level of the well curbing, at the narrow cement tube where he would be turning around and around and swaying dangerously from one side to the other. Had he been telling the truth when he said that he was experienced in such descents? I wanted to call him back. But I didn't dare to in front of the farmers, who were looking at me curiously. I only said: "Be careful!"

Just then, the assistant put the winch in motion. My

271

words were lost in the creaking of the pulley and the cog wheel.

He disappeared slowly into the well, first his feet, then his legs, and then the rest of his body, as if swallowed up by dark waters. When his head was level with the well curb, he looked up and smiled at me in a slightly mocking good-bye. His happy smile seemed to banish the darkness for a second, and the possibility of falling and all the unforeseeable dangers lurking at the bottom of the well. Then I couldn't see anything any more but the thin cable unwinding, vibrating slightly, into the depths.

I closed my eyes again. I felt as if the board and its passenger were plummeting with the speed of a stone. I didn't have the courage to look again until the winch stopped; then I forced myself to lean over the cement rim. When he let go of my arm, Jacques took all my resources of energy with him.

The chief well-digger had stopped hammering. He steadied the board and helped Jacques stand up near the injured man in the narrow space left in the shaft. The cement-lined shaft seemed to act like an acoustic tube; the screams and moans of the injured man seemed to come from only a few yards below the surface. Despite the distance, I could see as clearly as if I had focused on him with binoculars, his features were convulsed by pain, and his mouth was wide open in that interminable shriek. The earth must have kept falling. Except for his head, which was in continual movement, the rest of him was covered with soil. Jacques' movements were clearly visible, because the well-digger, backed up against the wall of the excavation carved out by the cave-in, held his lamp high to help Jacques see what he was doing.

Jacques opened his suitcase and prepared the phials and syringe. For a moment his back obscured the injured man. He must have freed one of his arms to give him the shot. His movements were calm and precise, as if he were in a neat white hospital room instead of in that soft, brown, crumbling rock, working with torn, bloody flesh and broken bones.

Less than a minute after the intravenous morphine injection, the screams lost some of their piercing horror; they became hoarse cries, then quickly subsided into an endless, monotonous lamenting moan rising from the well, mixed with the smell of freshly moved earth and the moldy odor of a cellar.

The man no longer moved.

The well-digger had put his lamp on the floor as soon as the injection was given. His head and shoulders were again in the circle of light. Standing next to the concrete ring, he picked up his heavy sledgehammer and started working again like an untiring machine.

Except for his hands, Jacques was now out of sight. He seemed to be huddled against the earthen wall to take up less space. You could see his hands holding the oxygen mask over the victim's face.

I got dizzy listening to the hideously monotonous moan and the well-digger's grunts coming up with surrealistic regularity, followed each time by the vibration of the cement. The moldy odor of the earth, the thought of Jacques at the very bottom of the endless seamless cement tube, and the hypnotic sight of his hands made the well seem to revolve slowly, then faster and faster around those hands cupped over the unmoving face. My legs were shaky. I just had enough strength to pull back. Just in time. The assistant must have been watching me. He rushed up to me:

"You mustn't stay here, ma'am. It's dangerous when you're not used to it. The curb is too low." He added; "This could go on for a long while yet. Come and sit down in the hut. . . ."

He gave me a tool chest for a seat, in the middle of a pile of tools and gas cans. I would have preferred to lie down on the grass, but a small crowd—some fifteen people at least—were watching me curiously, so I thought it would be better to sit on the chest. The man arranged a neatly folded sack on it to make it a little more comfortable.

The motor turned slowly in the hut, keeping up its peaceful chug-chug; the noises from the well were muffled.

As soon as I sat down I felt a little better, but I stayed a while, dazed and incapable of thinking clearly. After the succession of events that I'd gone through without a moment's pause since early afternoon, I was surprised to find myself alone. Even Jacques had left me in peace for a moment. The descent had gone well, the shot had been given and the man seemed to be in less pain, so in my turn I had the right to catch my breath. For Jacques, spoiled and self-indulgent, the descent had been only a game, just a little more dangerous than his usual games, and so a bit more exciting. If I'd refused to let him take my place, he probably would have thrown a childish tantrum, like a child who doesn't get an electric train the second he asks for it. He'd also made it clear to me that my refusal would have been an insult to his dignity as a man in front of these people. I thought fondly: "How well I know him now, my impulsive Jacques, who can't be persuaded or reasoned with. He's barely free of the opium, and he's ready to throw himself wholeheartedly into the first available adventure!"

The hut—a few boards covered with a tarpaulin to protect the winch motor—looked out on the well from a distance of about six feet.

In front of me the silhouettes, lit from below as if by footlights, were outlined against the starry sky. From my vantage point I felt like a spectator at a shadow play.

I was so tired that at first I didn't pay any attention to the buzz of conversations. But finally I began to listen to the comments provoked by the accident.

News travels quickly in the country; from the village and from the nearby farms, came the neighbors—entire families, big tall men with their strong, healthy wives and young blond children who clung in fright to their mothers' skirts when they got close to the well. They lowered their voices as they arrived as if they were talking in church. They stood motionless over the hole, fascinated. What were they thinking? Were they sympathetic or simply curious, or cruelly happy? I wondered if the sight of this unhappy man half-buried eighty feet under the ground made them suddenly conscious of how lucky they were in the security of their own outdoor work. Or were they thinking about the high wages well-drillers are paid, and thinking that at those prices, a well-digger ought to take on the risks of an accident?

They kept coming—the new arrivals pressing close to the edge and pushing the first comers back, so that they too could look a little and not miss this choice event that broke the monotony of country life.

After making sure I was all right, the young workman again took up his position near the edge of the well; I could see him, about three feet away, his back bent, ready to put the winch into action at the first signal from his boss.

Then the mayor came back. This time, he was accompanied by a big policeman he called "chief" with the familiarity permitted among official personages. They both started to question the workman. The "chief" was obviously opening the official inquiry.

I could hear the workman's explanation. At a depth of about twenty yards, he and his partner had found the usual flinty clay of the countryside. He pointed to enormous heaps of yellowish debris lying near the hole in the moonlight. Since a mixture of clay and flint crumbles very easily and caves in at the slightest trace of dampness, the two workers had carefully cemented this dangerous layer, digging in about three feet, putting in a circular mold and casting the cement in it, then digging again for another yard and beginning the molding and cement casting again. At the end of another twenty yards, the ground had changed; the clay was there mixed with calcium carbonate.

The young well-digger pointed to a smaller heap of dark brown, almost black soil, sprinkled with dark oddly shaped pebbles.

"That's it, the soil you get before you hit chalk."

Then he fell silent, obviously embarrassed.

"And then?" the police sergeant asked firmly.

"Well, then, my partner he said that we would dig without cement for five or six yards to get to the chalk and then we could cement the whole height all at once. That would have saved time, to get the bonus."

"Then what?" the policeman insisted.

The poor boy seemed more and more unhappy.

"I asked my pal: 'Are you sure that it won't cave in?' And he said: 'The soil over the chalk might cave in when it's humid. But there's no danger of it in such dry weather!' I'm the youngest one in the team, sir. I don't have much experience. I didn't dare say anything because of the bonus, but I know very well that the soil just above the chalk is likely to cave in."

The police sergeant wrinkled his brow suspiciously.

"Are you sure your partner decided by himself or was it the boss who told you to keep going?"

The young man protested:

"Oh, no! It's not the boss. My buddy even said: 'Let's hurry up with the cementing! Otherwise we'll get bawled out. And then it's good-bye to the bonus.'"

He seemed about to raise his hand and swear that he was telling the truth ...

"How did the accident happen?" the policeman asked more mildly.

"I was here at the winch, hauling out a load. I heard a big noise at the bottom. I looked. The last cement ring had fallen, I saw it on its side and then he started to scream. I couldn't do anything by myself. The winch is the only way to get down and I couldn't go down on it because there was no one to work it. So I jumped on my bike. I knew that there was a telephone in the Verville castle where the boss was working. I called him from the Grandhoux café. He was here in fifteen minutes. He took a sledgehammer and I let him down right away. You know, it's not easy to break a cement ring with a sledgehammer to get someone out from under it. I wanted to relieve him, but he wouldn't let me. He's already been hammering for forty-five minutes."

The policeman might have thought that the young worker would answer more frankly when he was overcome by emotion, because he went on with his interrogation.

"I see. You were digging in ground likely to cave in without reinforcing it with cement. But cement, once it's poured holds well; it's solid. So why did the last ring get loose?"

The worker seemed to be more at ease back on a technical point.

"Cement isn't solid to start with, sir. It takes about ten days for it to set. There must have been a little water leakage in the well; the soil above the chalk got crumbly and started to cave in. And the ring fell because it wasn't held up by anything any more. . . . A cement ring like that weighs nearly half a ton. . . ."

He nodded toward the bottom of the well and concluded very seriously, "You have to have guts to go down after a cave-in like that. Since the last cement ring has fallen, it means that the cement hasn't taken well and the next one may fall in too. And a new cave-in would crush or suffocate whoever's down there."

The policeman nodded in acknowledgment and walked away with the mayor.

Then it was quiet. I sat on the tool chest, unable to move. Now I was scared as well as dazed. At the bottom of the well, the tragedy playing out had suddenly touched me; part of my life was in danger along with the life of one of the three men exposed to the risk of death.

Then the buzz of loud voices started up again, along with the sound of the motor, the muffled vibrations of the cement under the sledgehammer and the thin wail of the injured man.

I was dripping with sweat, exhausted and beaten; I thought I was going to be sick. I tried to control myself in the midst of the disaster by clutching the rough fabric of the sack.

The new arrivals, curious about the unknown silhouette in the hut, whispered among themselves until someone who knew explained that I'd come with the doctor who was down with the injured man. I leaned against the wooden wall and closed my eyes. Since I couldn't be alone with my suffering, I didn't want to have to watch the revolting peasant indifference to somebody else's suffering. I wanted to scream at them, these healthy spectators, so smug about being alive and as impassive as their oxen.

I tried to block out the sight of their faces by thinking of Jacques, bravely smiling in acceptance of his male responsibility—before disappearing into the darkness in my stead. The thought was like the blow of a whip. No! I wouldn't wait to see what happened, collapsed in the hut. Even if I could be no more than an impotent shadow at the edge of the well, at least I'd be on my feet, watching over the three men who were confronting masses of earth that might make their grave at any moment.

I got up and walked the few steps that separated me from the hole. I leaned over and looked down the long smooth line of cement rings. In spite of myself I couldn't keep my eyes off the last gray cylinder, the one that might fall like lightning before the end of the rescue. I tried to make out Jacques next to the well-digger, who was still hammering away, but I could still only see his hands in the circle of light; they were motionlessly cupped over the oxygen mask. The rest of his body was invisible. Did he know that he was in danger; that the thousands of tons of earth might cave in? Was he watching for a ton of fresh cement to fall?

I remembered the well-digger's explanation about the danger of water infiltrating into the cement. I could sense the thick dampness oozing from the well. I could almost feel the soil sliding lightly, like flour, down the walls into the excavation where Jacques was sheltered. I could taste the earth. Suddenly I felt dizzy and afraid again. Again my knees buckled and my head sagged forward as if I were already starting to faint. Just then two hands grabbed me by the shoulders and pulled me back. It was a young woman, hesitantly smiling at me in apology for her gesture. I didn't think I'd ever seen those shining eyes before. She had a lovely sleek helmet of black hair.

"Don't stand up, ma'am. If you want to watch without getting dizzy, then kneel down."

As she spoke, she pushed down on my shoulders. I was too surprised to object to looking so awkward in front of the unsympathetic audience. I yielded to her pressure. She must have guessed my embarrassment—she instantly kneeled down next to me to encourage me.

I felt better as soon as my knees touched the ground. I smiled thankfully at my neighbor. Then somewhat ashamed, I murmured:

"Am I bothering you?"

"No, ma'am, absolutely not," she protested. "I finished everything I had to do. I telephoned for the ambulance from Evreux. Now we just have to wait." She added, to explain why she'd called the doctor from Mesnil, which was such a distance away, "I even finally managed to reach Dr. Mahieu from La Ferté. He's on his way. As soon as he gets here, he can go down to replace your gentleman."

She probably thought I was wondering why she had been doing so much. She pointed toward the bottom of the well, smiling sadly:

"*My* husband is the boss of the digging."

For a minute I hadn't understood what she meant when she said "your gentleman," referring to Jacques. It was the comparison with "*my* husband" that made it clear. She said "your gentleman" out of respect the way she would have said "your lady" to Jacques if she'd been talking about me. She thought I was married to Jacques. . . .

I was overjoyed. She thought of us as two wives, waiting side by side at the end of the wharf for the ship that's been lost in the storm at night to come home. Now I understood the security I'd felt as soon as I'd knelt down; it didn't come from feeling the solid ground under me, but from seeing that someone else was feeling the same anxiety I did, from the watch we were keeping together over the two who were at the mercy of mounds of slipping earth that could bury them at any moment. I must have unconsciously understood the sisterhood of our waiting and worry when she pushed my shoulders down to make me kneel.

I looked at her dark head, leaning slightly forward to see the bottom of the well better. She was forcing herself to look calm but I could tell she wasn't because her whole face was tense.

She'd been wearing her housedress when news of the accident had reached her, she must have rushed out like a madwoman without taking the time to put on another dress. In her housewifely clothes, she seemed to have brought some of the sweetness of her home with her, the simple tasks of her day, the prattling of her children sitting under the lamplight in the evening. ... What her light linen smock proclaimed was that it wasn't only the rescue of one human life that was at stake, but her family's happiness too.

I looked down so I wouldn't seem to be staring at her, then I looked at the bottom of the well. Her husband was still hammering, all covered with muddy sweat. At one point, he stopped to catch his breath. He was panting. I couldn't see his face but it was easy to imagine it—the face of a blond giant, very gentle and a bit childlike. He didn't even lift his head to look up at his wife. At that point his first duty was to drag his buried assistant up toward the light. Only the rescue mattered. The man started pounding ferociously at the cement ring again.

I wanted to show the young woman how close I felt to her without worrying her more. I said: "Your husband is very brave!"

She lifted her eyes and smiled gratefully, murmuring: "Oh! yes, I'm very lucky. ..."

Suddenly she said, pulling herself up and holding her head high: "He's got a wonderful job."

She was happy that she could confide in someone.

"I had trouble getting used to it at first. I told him: 'It's too dangerous, become a bricklayer—it shows you don't love me if you keep doing this sort of work!' He would laugh and answer: 'You know I love you.' He'd kiss me but he'd go off anyway. He's good and he does everything to make me happy. Just by putting my hand on his wrist, I can get everything I want, except making him leave his job."

For a moment I imagined them together: he, a typical Norman, huge, blond and strong, leaving for his dangerous work with a calm determined look; she, dark and delicate, letting him go off without a whimper because she didn't want to go against his wishes.

"Now I'm used to it. I've learned to wait. I smile when he leaves and I smile when he comes back. Now that we have the children, I just say: 'Take care.' Then he hugs me and laughs again. Men are like that!" she said resignedly, "Even when they love you, they never know what pain they cause you!"

She fell silent and I wanted to tell her as we waited together, "You don't realize how much this last sentence unites us, what a bond it makes between us! And it's not only because we're waiting together. It goes much further—you've made me discover more about myself than I could in ten years of self-analysis. Kneeling beside you, I've suddenly discovered that you can't talk about love—it just *is*! And, tonight, the blows of your husband's sledgehammer aren't cracking just the hard cement; they're destroying the false image of Jacques I built out of my jealousy, too. Tonight I've discovered that when he was trapped by his own game and began to realize that it could be dangerous, his instinct was courageous and he was brave enough to go down. Is every human being so stifled by misunderstandings, mistakes and pretenses? The heroism Jacques is showing now has made me discover proof of the qualities I'd guessed he had but which hadn't been proved by his past actions. Vincent was right: Jacques is better than he looks. It took this moment of truth to reveal him to me as he really is underneath all of his superficiality and his laziness. . . ."

I looked down at the bottom of the well, at the edge of the last cement ring, at those two elegant hands that were soiled by the earth, and I wanted to shout:

"Oh, Jacques, what inner light is suddenly shining from you? What new man has arisen in you? Whoever you may be, I don't care. This simple woman has revealed the evidence of love to me: *I accept you as you are because I love you.* Just the way her husband obeys some sort of attraction that pulls him to the depths of the earth, you're one of those people irresistibly drawn by the call of adventure and desire. Now I know that you have to let these men go with a smile—hot-blooded men who are always ready to face the unknown or the abyss—you have to let them go with a smile and then smile again when they come back."

I felt such a wave of joy rise in me that I drew myself

up unconsciously. I looked at the full moon surrounded by clusters of stars; I breathed the smell of hay that was wafted in from the four corners of the plains by a light, warm breeze. Everything in the clear, peaceful sky, in the perfume-laden breath of night air, contradicted the catastrophe. Soon the rescue would be over. How good it would be then to take a few steps on the soft grass, to relax, to walk slowly through the meadows leaning on Jacques' arm, on solid ground. . . .

Suddenly a plaintive hoot drifted down from a nearby tree. It came twice more. At the second hoot, silence fell among the bystanders and when it came the third time, someone exclaimed in a low voice behind me, "The wood owl hooting . . . Not a good sign . . ."

To my surprise the young woman threw herself against my shoulder in fright, saying hoarsely, "That's right, ma'am. That's the spirit of a dead person coming to fetch the dead!"

The hooting started up again, lugubrious, insistent and sinister. Again, she started. My hand was resting on the rim of the well—she seized it and held it tightly. I was amazed by the old superstitiousness that had suddenly come to the surface and was making her tremble with terror. I tried to reason with her. It was useless. . . . In spite of her common sense and everything she'd been taught in school, my words couldn't penetrate the ancient peasant horror of magic influences and evil spells. For her, it was a certainty: death was on the prowl; it was very near; the owl was really a bodiless phantom, ready to descend into the subterranean shadow to take possession of the souls of the dead. And I was overcome by the absurd contagion of the old, illogical instinct. I shuddered too. I was vulnerable and ready to yield to panic—like the day I was walking toward a farm and watched with horror as a snake slipped away almost under my feet.

My hands were tense on the thin curb. My eyes, indeed my whole body strained toward the bottom of the well as I began a new, exhausting wait by the side of the terrified girl. A kind of stiffness petrified my wrists, my calves, my back, glued my knees to the earth, even locked my jaws; the only way I could tell that my body existed was from the strange twinges I felt in my arms, my chest and my shoulders. Time alone existed, creeping by, and the sand that kept sliding down the wall against Jacques' back seemed to transform the excavation into an enormous hourglass. In ordinary life a few minutes passing by or a little sand crumbling doesn't matter. But this evening each second carried away a chance of life. Death was stalking hidden in the depths; maybe he'd already been announced by the imperceptible crumbling of the sand. ... A muffled crackling, and dizzying masses of cement and brown earth would cave in, crushing, burying the three men and—the young well-digger had put it well—all three would die at the bottom of that hole that no help could reach in time.

As he left to join the crowd, the police officer had asked the worker: "How long is your boss going to be down there?" and he'd answered: "Oh! a good half hour." Had ten minutes passed since then, or twenty-five, or more? In my state of nervous anxiety I couldn't tell. My eyes searched for the young worker; leaning over the well with his hands on his knees, his eyes never left his boss. I didn't dare ask him. But, insanely, I wanted the time that was still left to pass in a single instant.

Cars, motorcycles and bicycles kept coming and going around the well. Feverish and weary, I paid no attention to the new arrivals. But then a voice announced: "Here's the ambulance," and at once there was a surge of curiosity among the bystanders.

The heavy vehicle was moving forward through the meadows. It looked pure white in the moonlight and it was topped with a lighted red cross. Its headlights slowly swung from rut to rut. It stopped a few yards away from the well. Two men in white coats stepped out of it and asked, as soon as they reached the edge of the hole, "Is this going to take much longer?"

"You got here at just the right time! It's almost over. In five minutes we'll be lifting them out," the young worker said victoriously.

"Then let's get the stretcher ready," one of the ambulance men said calmly.

The crowd moved toward the ambulance and the young woman, the worker and myself were alone at the edge of the well.

"Five minutes" the young worker had said. Five minutes made three hundred seconds . . . the final stage of the wait seemed so long to me that I closed my eyes and began to count slowly. I gave myself to a thousand so I wouldn't be disappointed.

The young workman's prediction was right. I had just

282

come to number 483 when the blows of the sledgehammer stopped. An impressive, solemn, incredible silence fell. But without even catching his breath, the head well-digger shouted: "Hey, Pierrot, get the cable ready!"

The worker leaped toward the hut and started the winch. I opened my eyes but didn't have the courage to turn my head to the young woman and smile at her. Wasn't it too early for rejoicing? I had the feeling that coming up would be difficult. Maybe it was then that fate would play its last trick.

I looked at the bottom of the well with a new upsurge of worry. Jacques and the well-digger were both bent against a huge piece of cement, cautiously pivoting it around to get the injured man out from under it. Little by little, the lower half of his body came into view. It seemed to be nothing but a shapeless heap of dirt.

Immediately the boss knelt down beside his companion, took him very gently under the armpits and lifted him, then got up again, holding the awkwardly disjointed body up against him.

Jacques helped him, as, still holding the injured man tightly in his arms, the boss sat him down on his lap after settling himself on the plank, which was balanced at the end of the cable. Following his directions, Jacques took a rope and tied both men firmly to each other under the armpits, and then he tied them to the hook of the cable to avoid all risk of them falling in the course of the ascent. The injured man, still under the influence of the morphine, was moaning softly. His head was slumped down on his chest, so that he looked like a corpse.

"Okay, Pierrot," the boss shouted.

The assistant started up the motor and the winch began inch by inch to hoist its double load.

I watched these various preparations in a daze. Why didn't Jacques come up first—he was a voluntary rescuer and the well-digger was just doing his job.

The young woman must have guessed I would be disappointed. As the winch was started up, she turned to me and said apologetically, "It's difficult and very dangerous when two of them come up at once in such a narrow well. You have to be used to it."

All the curious bystanders had come back near the rim of the well. They were watching the injured man and his rescuer slowly rise the way, as at the seaside, one watches a net slowly being drawn in, a net that may break before reaching the shore.

Near me I felt the young woman go tense with impatience, hope and redoubled fear.

For my neighbor, for the onlookers, the drama was coming to an end; only a few more turns of the winch and the victim, tied to his rescuer, was going to rise out of the darkness and danger at the end of the cable. But for me, Jacques was still at the bottom of the well and the slow turning of the winch threw me once more into anxious waiting.

Leaning over the hole, I listened intently for every noise. A shoe scraped against the wall every few seconds, and I thought of the stories about avalanches that are sometimes released by the mere cough of a mountaineer, and felt that my heart had stopped each time it happened. Couldn't a series of tiny shocks loosen the already precarious hold of the last cement reinforcing ring near the bottom? At the least noise, I imagined Jacques, with his head raised to watch the two men ascending, suddenly seeing—with horror, and without the least chance of escape—the second cement ring come caving in on him.

"They're almost here," the workman shouted, slowing down the speed of the winch.

The police sergeant, with the help of another policeman, had begun to push back the docile crowd. My neighbor got up. I followed and we went to stand near the hut. Only the two ambulance men in their white smocks and the stretcher remained in the light of the storm lamps.

The noise of an approaching car smothered the sound of the winch motor.

"Here's Dr. Mahieu!" one of the curious bystanders announced.

"He's sure come at just the right time!" a second voice exclaimed just as the two heads appeared at the level of the rim, first that of the well-digger, who was smiling under his mask of sweat and dust, then the other, his head dangling and looking very pale, like the victim of a crucifixion.

The crowd had fallen silent, ill at ease before the sight of the two men tightly bound to one another, rising like two ghosts covered with the same funereal dust. But already the young assistant had swiveled the boom of his crane and brought it over solid ground. The ambulance

284

men untied the rope quickly, and gently took the injured man from the well-digger's knees and deposited him, moaning and inert, on the stretcher—which was instantly surrounded by the crowd.

"You're interfering with the doctor! Step back a little!" shouted the policemen.

Despite their efforts, the crowd was suddenly so thick that I could barely see the back of the physician in his gray jacket as he bent over the injured man.

As soon as her husband was free of his pitiful burden, the young woman ran to him and he took her tenderly in his arms. They were exactly the couple I'd imagined: he, very tall, very strong; she, small and slight. She was completely, blissfully happy. She leaned against his warm broad chest for a few moments with her eyes closed, savoring her return to peacefulness, to the joys of her life. And the blond giant caressed her shoulders with his strong, earth-covered hands as if he was amazed to rediscover after his terrible ordeal all the sweetness love had given him. Then she lifted her head and said:

"See how silly I am. I'm crying. I'm sorry. I don't know what's happening to me today." Then she asked him: "Was it very bad?"

He laughed before he answered her—the joyful laugh of a young man, with his white teeth gleaming. Her question seemed to release the same burst of physical strength in him that had kept him from thinking of the great danger he was in down at the bottom of the well.

"It sure took a long time," he said. "My back was beginning to ache."

He laughed again.

"There wasn't much room with the three of us at the bottom as well as the cement ring. Even when the doctor stayed so close to the side, I wasn't very comfortable. . . ."

I hadn't left the shadow of the hut. There was nothing for me to do. Dr. Mahieu had arrived and was taking care of the injured man. All I could do now was to wait alone. When the young woman ran to her husband, I almost ran to the well and got to my knees again to talk to Jacques. But I restrained myself: once he was back up, I was afraid he would be annoyed at me for making him look ridiculous in public by worrying too much and transforming the end of the dramatic rescue into a farce.

But when her husband mentioned Jacques, his wife turned toward me and exclaimed:

"The doctor's still down at the bottom! Shouldn't you send the plank back down? That's his wife. . . ."

He looked at me, greeted me awkwardly and rushed to the winch. The plank went down at the end of the cable.

I went back to the well but I didn't kneel. This time I would be strong.

I saw Jacques take hold of the plank and try to sit down, holding Vincent's suitcase in his hand since there was no rope to fasten it.

Leaning over the well beside me, the boss shouted to him:

"Leave the suitcase behind! My assistant will go down and get it. . . ."

Why did he say that? Was Jacques, encumbered by the suitcase, in danger of being crushed as he passed the lower ring, or of falling as he came up?

I wanted to shout to him: "Hurry! Oh! for pity's sake, hurry!" Bits of soil kept falling, making a series of little "splats"—muffled, but audible. Maybe it was only a question of seconds before the final cave-in. Never had I felt such a feverish desire to make time go faster.

The boss must have thought Jacques hadn't heard him, because he repeated in a louder voice:

"Leave your suitcase, doctor!"

Jacques put the suitcase down, then installed himself on the board, balancing himself as calmly as if he were preparing for a game of see-saw.

Finally, lifting his head, he said, "I'm ready."

The winch began to turn and in the thrill of joy I felt, the noise seemed unreal for three or four seconds. No, it wasn't possible. Something was going to happen, an accident, a delay, a disaster! But Jacques got beyond the dangerous ring without difficulty and began his ascent, leaving below him, as each second passed, a little more of the subterranean night. He was bobbing in the void and the tips of his shoes scraped against the wall too, but the noise didn't bother me any more. It could all cave in now—it could crash to the bottom, loose its chains in a total cataclysm. What did it matter to me? I wasn't afraid for Jacques any more. With every yard he came closer, my joy became more intense, my delivery from fear more certain.

But when he finally emerged from the well, dirty from head to toe and smiling under his ruffled hair, I stood stock-still for a few seconds as if struck dumb. He leaped

286

lightly off the plank in front of me and I, nailed to one spot by my overwhelming happiness, incapable of talking, suffocating with joy, couldn't stop looking at his face. I'd looked at it so often before tonight and yet I'd known it so little.

"See how easy it was? You really didn't have to worry!" Jacque said, teasing me affectionately.

Here indeed was yesterday's Jacques smiling at me, the Jacques I knew before Arlette intruded. I was so happy. The irresistible force that threw the young woman toward her husband threw me toward Jacques, in the same miraculous kinship, in the same feminine acceptance of love. I pressed myself up against him and when he put his hand around my waist, enfolding me in his arms, the rest of the world ceased to exist. I couldn't feel anything but the warmth of his beloved skin against my skin, his muscular, masculine body pressed close to my body.

It was a sensation unknown to me, and its violence was frightening yet marvelous—perhaps the feeling of being born fully grown or of being resurrected would have this same, indescribable force. My heart racing, my temples pounding, too upset to say a word, I surrendered myself wholly, without reserve, as if I'd been waiting for this moment from the first day of my life.

The well-digger and his wife had discreetly drawn nearer to the ambulance to leave us alone, but as soon as the ambulance started up, bearing the injured man and Dr. Mahieu toward Evreux, the bystanders began to wander back toward the well, as if something might still happen there.

Jacques still held me close to him but I wasn't embarrassed to be seen that way. It was the expression of love between two people, and I wished the whole world could see me in the arms of the one I had chosen among all men.

"Let's get out of here quickly or we'll be caught," he whispered.

Taking advantage of the darkness and the commotion, he pulled me to the car. I would have liked to say good-bye to the well-digger and his wife, but he was right: if we'd stayed any longer, it would have been impossible to refuse the mayor's invitation; we'd have had to go back to Grandhoux with him and join in an endless celebration of the brave rescuers and the happy ending. "Since the kit is still at the bottom," I thought, "I'll go and pick it up tomorrow in La Ferté at the well-digger's house. It will be easier for me to thank his wife in the quiet of her house than in this hubbub. Tomorrow I'll tell her how close tonight has made us." But above all, though I didn't dare admit it frankly to myself, I was eager to be alone with Jacques. When he took my hand I followed him obediently.

He gunned the motor and drove away like the wind. At the roar of the motor, the farmers close by jumped in terror and leaped quickly out of our way.

"We're free!" Jacques said after a hundred yards of frightening jolting across the fields.

He slowed down and smiled at me several times, as we bumped along over the ruts of a little dirt road. I no longer tried to avoid his eyes as I had on the way out. On the contrary, I didn't take mine off his face. I was sure I was beginning a new life near him, taking an unbelievable revenge on bad luck, waking up from a terrible nightmare.

Had the same young woman gone through all of these ordeals in such a short time? Now, sitting quietly on the red leather seat, I stayed still and let myself be carried off like a consenting victim. I thought: "Which of the two Jacques, each so unlike the other, is the real one, the one who was caressing Arlette's arm this afternoon or the one who just went down to the bottom of the well in my place?" I concluded that the question didn't make sense any more. The man who was carrying me away into the blue, damp night was the one I'd been awaiting for sixteen days. I lifted my eyes to him. The full moon riding high in the sky fully showed his profile and nothing kept me from contemplating it freely any more, from watching him with tenderness and confidence, love and pride. His usually carefree face was flushed with vigor and shining with energy. It was like the birth of another man; and looking at him, I felt a second self awaken in me.

Jacques was driving slowly to spare me the jolts as much as possible. Around us, the night breezes brought a strong smell of grass and earth. I was happy, I felt good. I leaned against the back of the seat and inhaled the air greedily. It bore the warmth of living things. Never had I felt such youth or such hope within me. Happiness was here, in the form of my companion. I let myself lean against him in a warm torpor. After these exhausting hours, I marveled at this miracle: no longer did I despise

... I wanted to praise, to approve, to wholly admire, and to keep this exalting reality, this certitude of happiness close to me. I didn't regret anything that had happened this afternoon—even the suffering of jealousy had been necessary, because no love should exist without jealousy or faithfulness. Coming out of the shadow of my long ordeal, I could submit to servitude obediently, with my eyes open, and discover in it the paradoxical joy of feeling free.

The night was so light that you could see the countryside as clearly as in broad daylight. I just looked at Jacques, and he answered me with a smile, then made a funny face. Coming so soon after the dramatic moments we'd just lived through, his return to childishness enchanted me—weren't we two children surprised by happiness? I looked joyfully around me as if to make the whole world a witness of our happiness. We still hadn't left the side roads. In the middle of the meadows, I thought I recognized the solitary outline of the large apple tree I'd found refuge under just this afternoon. Had I come this far? I was curious to see.

"Let's go over there to that apple tree!" I said.

Without Jacques' boyish smile I probably wouldn't have dared make the suggestion—it even surprised me myself.

He looked at me, astonished. I repeated my wish, touching his arm. Immediately Jacques obeyed. I didn't take my hand away as the car bumped along the cart track. Under the silk of his shirt sleeve, I felt his muscles move with every jump of the steering wheel. It seemed to me that I was performing a magic rite of exorcism. I was going to take Jacques away from Arlette on the very same spot where I had suffered and wept because of her.

Jacques brought the car to a halt when its hood was inches away from the trunk under the low, spreading branches and I saw that I'd been wrong. It wasn't the same tree.

By contrast with the brightness of the night, the shadow under the leaves seemed almost black; the air floating there had a lukewarm softness, alive and almost sensual. My eyes adjusted to the darkness very fast. I was still holding Jacques' arm. I could see my hand, tan against the white silk of his sleeve. I couldn't withdraw it now or raise my eyes. I felt Jacques looking at me. Could he guess what I was feeling?

Gently, to free his arm, he took my wrist in his left

289

hand, and kept it there. Then he put his right arm around my shoulders. In the shadow, I leaned back and welcomed his mouth, closing my eyes. When he lifted his face, it was I who demanded it again, as if I would die without his kisses.

When we released each other, I was dumfounded and breathless, tied to life only by his rapid breathing that sounded just like mine in the darkness. We were still. Around us, the countryside and the silent night seemed to forget us in our happiness.

Jacques spoke first:

"Why have you been running away from me for four days, silly Omphale?"

His voice was soft and caressing. Like an animal who has discovered his nest and feels safe and secure, I snuggled up to Jacques. Now I could answer. Love was no longer a degrading fantasy; after this imperious beginning, it became the easiest and the simplest thing of all. I had let my lips go soft under his kiss and now I could let them admit my passion without false shame. I said:

"I was afraid of you, afraid of loving you. And in the legend it's Hercules who wins in the end because he is a man."

"Do I look so threatening?"

"You did, the first time I saw you. And yet, even that evening I wanted to see you again."

His voice in the shadow murmured:

"I wanted it too."

Again we fell silent. I felt an overpowering weight of happiness within me close to this unknown body whose presence already seemed so secure and familiar near mine. But suddenly, thinking of the four painful days when I'd been avoiding Jacques, I remembered the teacher. In all truthfulness, it was shame about my indecisiveness rather than fear of love that had made me take to the road. It was to punish myself for my cowardice that I'd fled the intimate talks in the all too obliging solitude of the house. And first my overwhelming jealousy and then my overwhelming happiness had made me forget the young woman completely! One moment of tumult in my heart and I selfishly blotted out the rest of the world!

I pressed closer to Jacques. How good it was to be able to search for a body in total confidence, and lift my eyes toward a motionless face above mine, and feel dominated! Now I could confide everything to Jacques:

"Jacques, I've had problems for the last four days."

His voice scolded me but his arm around my shoulders pulled me closer.

"What problems? Why didn't you tell me? It would have helped."

"It's Simone Vallin. She's threatening to get an abortion. She's afraid her baby will be born an idiot. A young brother of her husband's is shut up in an asylum. I don't know what to do. . . ."

"Of course Vincent has refused?"

"Absolutely. He acted as if I were an anarchist, a rebel and a dangerous fanatic."

He said sarcastically: "He's certainly no anarchist."

Then after a moment's reflection:

"Let's leave the dear boy the way he is! It's a little late to change him; but you, Claude, you can go into action for the two of you, since you're his substitute."

"I have no medical reason."

His voice became firm.

"Yes you do. Vincent was born with a timid bourgeois soul. But you belong to another race. You can commit yourself deeply when you have to, and you can throw caution to the winds."

Only yesterday, I would have smiled to hear such words coming from his lips. But today, they took on a decisive force, coming from a man who had just risked his life for a stranger without being under any obligation.

"Oh, Jacques," I murmured, pressing my forehead into his strong shoulder, "I'm not sure. . . . I don't dare. You're strong—tell me what to do!"

"Obey your intuition."

"It tells me to help Simone Vallin. But then I hear all of Vincent's arguments."

"Don't worry about them! For a decent human being, there's no other criterion than what one believes. Deep down inside, everyone knows what's good or evil. Conformity only leads to acts that have no value."

"It's hard to decide, the first time. An illegal abortion is so serious! I'm so afraid."

"Throw yourself into the water! There's no better way to learn how to swim. Or else make a bet with yourself."

Had he made a bet with himself when he went down into the well? But before I had time to ask him, Jacques went on.

"Everything is all right as long as it's been clearly

thought out. Unhappily, clarity is the rarest thing in the world. That's why rules, codes, morality, and definitions of good and evil have been made—they're for the use of the majority of people like Vincent. It takes exceptional individuals to do exceptional things. You're one of them."

He fell silent, then in a muffled voice:

"What I'm saying to you, I wouldn't even try to explain to your friend Arlette. She's the kind of girl who wants marriage and freedom, protection and independence, a husband and a lover all at the same time. As the English proverb says: women are terrible; they want to have their cake and eat it too."

I lifted my head to take these words in fully. They fell on me like a healing dew in the darkness. So Jacques was putting Arlette in her place—a pretty girl, flirtatious, insignificant, empty. Since he talked about her like this at such a moment, it proved he didn't admire her at all: she was simply one of those women that you meet and flatter casually in passing, the way you pat a beautiful animal.

How clear everything suddenly became, how simple and easy it all was again. There wasn't a problem any more. I would perform the abortion. In two days—the time it would take to prepare the young woman—I would be free, free to come and go without shame and free to love. When I was beginning to share the happiness of all women, how could I abandon her to her unhappiness? This would be my revenge for Mariette's death and my victory over Arlette's betrayal. This therapeutic abortion and my love—I guessed it now—were linked.

I said with determination:

"Tomorrow morning, I'll go and see Simone Vallin!"

I sought Jacques' lips to seal my decision with a kiss.

A slight evening breeze had come up. For a long time, we listened to the vague rustling of the leaves above us. The air was getting cooler. I shivered.

"Let's go back," Jacques said.

He took his jacket, which he'd thrown in the back of the car, and put it on my shoulders. It was warm and light; it had Jacques' smell, his smell of lavender and tobacco. I pulled it closer around me as if it were part of him. The motor was purring softly. Jacques was backing up slowly to get out from under our dome of leaves. We found ourselves in the middle of meadows bathed in the moonlight to the far horizon. Now I no longer feared the light. All had become light within me. I looked at the old apple tree behind me and thought: "Some day, I'll come back to this place and I'll be able to say that my new life began there."

Behind the visor, there was a little mirror. I looked at my face the way I had when I left the apple tree this afternoon and I smiled when I discovered, not a face swollen by tears but slightly sleepy features and lips bruised by kisses.

Jacques drove slowly back over the little cart track, then took the narrow winding country lane to get back to the main road. I felt like asking him to step on the gas and really let the car go, heading away from Mesnil so our trip would never end. I said nothing. I simply put my hand on his leg, as if making sure that our closeness was real, and we drove quietly all the way back to Mesnil.

As we passed in front of the doctor's house, we saluted the little car that was waiting by the sidewalk like a faithful dog.

Jacques drove on to mother's house. He stopped in front of the door and leaned toward me for a quick kiss, then got quickly out of the car, came round to open my door, and helped me out.

As soon as I'd found my keys and opened the door, he jumped back in his seat and started off, shouting with a big, happy smile:

"I'll see you this morning!"

Mother had left me a note on the hall table: "If you're hungry, there's food in the kitchen. It's starting to get cold again at night, so I put the cotton quilt on your bed."

I took off my shoes so I wouldn't make any noise going upstairs. It would be useless to wake up my mother—always so worried about what I eat and so alert to the dangers of catching a cold—if all her motherly intuition hasn't shown her in her sleep that I've just been brought back by the man I love, who is *not* the very serious Dr. Ferrières.

Despite my weariness, I'm not sleepy. It seems to me that I'm still kneeling in front of the rim of the well, that I'm still in Jacques' arms under the apple tree. . . . How can it be that a meeting at the edge of a well and a conversation in a car can decide an entire life like this?

I feel that I've gained years of experience in the last few hours. For days I've been searching for myself and hesitating. The trial came—my "moment of truth" like

Jacques'—and in the end, two things became clear to me—my duty as a doctor and my surrender to love.

Learning to understand love isn't the same thing as analyzing it in psychology texts, or explaining it in terms of hormones and glands. It's suddenly understanding that the exhausting wait is over and that it isn't a question of chance but of destiny fulfilled. It's understanding that from the moment the miracle occurs all the rest of your life falls into place: love is here, not just necessary for life but the substance of life itself. Now I know that, outside of love, all the rest is only mockery or deception. Pity the poor people who wait for love all their lives and die without ever finding it! Tonight, in the fullness of my happiness, I feel ready to pity Alberte. . . .

"Jacques!" . . . Just whispering this name makes my heart pound in my temples. I don't have to ask myself questions or wait any longer. Jacques belongs to me, he is inside of me, he is both himself and myself. His hand, touching mine ten days ago under the arbor, wrought this miracle, but much earlier—ever since that first afternoon when our eyes were challenging each other, I knew that he was concealing a painful secret. Each hour I watched over him as he recovered, each hour that I thought of him back in my room, brought new confirmation of this suffering hidden under his harshness.

Today I saw this nonchalant cynic, cured of the drug, stand up like a man. He broke away from all the warnings of logic and yielded to a manly temptation, to the dangerous pleasure of being a hero.

Since tonight, I've forgiven him all his past: before me, he didn't exist, and it was me that he was groping for through all those other women; before he met me was the time for failures, for confusion, for deceits; it was the time of a life wasted, of a bad life, and a life of unavowed sorrow that turned into a cynical smile and bravado, like a child who has done something bad. But in childhood, rebellion and anger always find their pardon in the sweetness of family life. Jacques was a young orphan; he never knew indulgence. Life was a pitiless stepmother for this child who'd had a hard childhood. I will protect him as Catherine did long ago when she made the rebellious little boy's punishments less harsh; I will help him fulfill himself.

Tonight when he went down the well in my place, he was playing a game like a child, but he showed enough loyalty to risk his life. Under my eyes, he suddenly awoke to responsibility and courage. I will keep him from sinking into indifference and evil again.

In the course of this night, I've come to understand many things: with the young woman near the well, I discovered that a marvelous union existed beyond her and me in the truth of love, and this union, which binds me to all women from now on, forces me to help Simone Vallin.

Going down to help the injured man, Jacques set me an example. Without an act of devotion as freely done and courageous as his I wouldn't be worthy of my happiness.

Tuesday, August 13, 6 a.m.

If someone had asked me eighteen days ago, "Until now, have you ever been really happy?" I would have replied instantly, without needing time to think: "No."

But ever since the day before yesterday, I can say: "Yes." A full, radiant "yes," without any doubts. But can happiness—that simple, enormous thing—be described? Let's try, in the glow of this night which is already turning into day.

I was up and out by eight o'clock Sunday morning. Most of the people of Mesnil, indifferent to the bell that rang for early mass, were still asleep, and almost all the shops were closed.

The sun was already bright but the air was still slightly cool. Everything seemed neat and clean, refreshed and rejuvenated. After the fever of my night, I walked cheerfully through the purity of the morning. "This is the way," I thought, "that I'll remember Mesnil later on. With its streets empty, and its windows decked out with geraniums."

I was walking with firm confident steps. Probably when one is immeasurably happy one should savor one's happiness at home. Otherwise, outside, your happiness may distract you, and make you seem uncaring or snobbish. That almost happened to me with Mme Vasse. She has a grocery store at the center of town where all the important people in Mesnil do their shopping—mother has chosen it for that reason.

Mme Vasse was sweeping the sidewalk in front of her shop. I'd probably have passed without even seeing her if I hadn't been warned by a whiff of that smell of coffee and soap that is the trademark of all country stores coming from the wide-open door. Fortunately I greeted her in time. It would have been awful if I hadn't. Mme Vasse was my first patient—in mother's opinion she was the one who "launched" me among the town's shopkeepers. She insisted on having my opinion about her fibroids. I concluded, like Dr. Ferrières, that an operation was necessary, and since I hadn't told her anything new, I refused to charge her anything. If I hadn't said hello to Mme Vasse, I would have given the impression that my free consultation had been charity—an insult she would never have forgiven me. The awful result: mother would have been obliged to change tradesmen and patronize some grocery shop for "the less important."

I walked happily as far as the schoolhouse. I'd only had a little sleep, but the freshness of the morning made me feel young and confident. My love seemed to have forged a new soul for me in one night. All my troubles were over—now was the time of serenity and certainty. And indeed, why even think about it?

"I promised. A promise is a promise," Mariette had said to explain why she hadn't been able to avoid her abortion. And I have given my word to Jacques. As I thought about it, I took a deep breath. I felt as if I had to obey him. All I had to do was to follow Jacques' advice and I'd be performing my first act as a free woman and showing myself worthy of the title that for six years I've been tenaciously preparing myself for.

I turned the handle of the iron gate without hesitation, went up the steps, and knocked at the door.

Simone Vallin came to open it for me. She seemed to be busy cleaning house; she was wearing rubber gloves and holding a rag in her hands. Was she trying to keep herself calm by doing routine chores? In the full light, the change in her features was so startling and the bitterness in the corners of her mouth so marked—along with that frightened look in her eyes as she watched me intensely—that as soon as I stepped over the threshold, I said, to free us both from suspense:

"I'm going to help you."

For a few seconds she looked at me in amazement as if she couldn't quite understand. She'd hoped too long. She leaned against the wall. Her lips trembled. She was deathly pale and I thought she was going to faint. I moved to hold her up. But with the same self-control that had impressed me so much during my first visit, she pulled herself together. Her face flushed slightly. She looked ravaged by fatigue and sleeplessness, and by the torment of imagining the birth of a deformed child. Then she smiled with deep joy as if she'd never stopped hoping deep within herself. That smile was all the reward I wanted.

I couldn't stay longer. I had to make up for the time I'd lost yesterday afternoon. I spent the morning going from patient to patient, so completely, overwhelmingly happy that I had to watch myself all the time so I'd remember to speak calmly to my patients, and not smile at them smugly when they told me all the details of some grim history of their illness. I had to reread my prescriptions three times for fear that a slip of my pen would send some poor creature who only had a slight cold straight to the cemetery. Incidentally, I pulled only one boner: I asked a patient absentmindedly: "Did your mother ever have any children?"

He looked so amazed that I realized at once that I'd made a mistake. To rescue myself, I added immediately: "Since your birth, of course. . . ."

Aside from this small incident, everything went quickly, and very well, as if my patients were determined not to make any difficulties for me that morning.

I'd promised Simone Vallin that I'd insert the first catheter at the end of the morning. By noon I was at her house. While she lay down on her bed I explained to her about this small preliminary "operation" she had to have. To reassure her, I showed her the catheter, the one that I was going to put into position, in its sterile tube. During the quick, but painful insertion, she remained motionless as I'd asked her to. She didn't cry out at all. Her face only flinched slightly two or three times. Then I helped her stretch out on the bed to rest.

"Tonight and again tomorrow morning," I said when I left, "I'll replace this catheter with two others, and tomorrow night I'll be able to operate."

Her mother accompanied me to the door. I looked at "Blanchotte" with curiosity—could I depend on her if something went wrong? She may have been pretty once. Now, at fifty-five, she's already an old woman, but her gray-blue eyes—her daughter has exactly those eyes—were reassuringly steady. On the doorstep she thanked me with simple dignity.

Since mother complained every morning that she never

saw me any more, I'd promised her the day before yesterday to spend this Sunday with her, except in case of an emergency.

I could easily have made up a pretext to cancel this at the last moment and join Jacques but I decided against it. I'd been so overflowing with happiness since last night that I thought it would be selfish not to give mother a little pleasure. But when I think back, it seems to me that by not allowing myself to have lunch with Jacques, what I really wanted was to discipline myself. Since I'd associated Simone Vallin's abortion so closely with my love for Jacques in my mind, I wouldn't have the right to be fully and freely happy with Jacques until she was definitely free....

I suppose that for those who've never known the happiness that I'm feeling right now, it would seem like fabulous, unimaginable, and even frightening good luck. And by sacrificing the few hours I could have spent with Jacques, I was probably trying to exorcise bad luck and remove its threat from my love forever.

All during lunch, mother kept telling me how satisfied the townspeople were with my medical skill. She kept making allusions to how much the region would benefit if I stayed on as Dr. Ferrières' assistant, especially if the association became closer. ... Mother didn't actually pronounce the word "marriage" but I could guess by the way she puffed up with pride that she already saw herself as the mother and mother-in-law of doctors.

"Why are you smiling?" she asked me.

I didn't dare tell her that I was amazed by her 'motherly intuition'—the way I'd been last night when I walked up the stairs. I changed the subject and asked for news about the grocer's wife so I wouldn't have to answer her.

Right after lunch, I took my folding chair and went to rest under the apple tree for a few moments.

As soon as I lay down under the friendly branches, I closed my eyes and the old relaxation came back. The shade was warm and welcoming; I felt that I was waiting for Jacques here. Soon he would be at my side, as he was last night. ... Finally I fell asleep in a marvelous state of expectation, lulled by the warmth and my tiredness.

When I woke up at five, I reproached mother for letting me take such a long nap.

"You're so tired these days!" she told me, "and you

seemed to be having such a nice dream! I came to look at you two or three times, and you were always smiling."

I blushed.

After I took a shower to wake up completely, I was tempted to go and see Jacques. But I pushed the thought away, telling myself that it would be a small act of cowardice: I still had a few house calls to make before dinner. I told mother I'd be home at about eight and went to finish my rounds.

I was back in Mesnil at half-past seven, and went by the school. Mme Blanchot opened the door for me. My patient hadn't been in too much pain, and the tranquilizers I'd left for her had been enough to calm her. I changed the catheter and then chatted for a moment with Simone. She too had been feverishly happy since the morning. She confessed to me that in the course of the afternoon, she'd dozed off and had a nightmare: I'd just come to visit her again and I explained that I was leaving for Paris, and had to desert her. She woke up in a panic but the pain in her lower abdomen reassured her.

So at the very moment when I was asleep and smiling at love, Simone Vallin had been in the middle of a nightmare. I was happy that I hadn't gone to see Jacques.

Grandhoux is some ways away, and reports about what had happened at the well mustn't have reached Mesnil yet: mother didn't talk about it either at lunch or at dinner.

After dinner, mother settled into her easy chair with her hands crossed on her lap and her eyes half closed. Under the pretext of telling me something about my patients, she wanted to tell me all the scandalous gossip of Mesnil, the tales of adulteries, miscarriages, venereal disease, and local debauchery—debauchery that, incidentally, seems to be kept within reasonable limits by the stinginess and cautiousness of the peasants. Intimidated by my silence, she finally stopped at:

"You look funny, dear. You must still be tired. Go lie down."

Would she have understood why I kept silent? After these days of being near Jacques I felt as if I was coming home from a wonderful trip. I felt completely out of place in my own house with my mother. Yet this evening I would have loved to talk about my love to a sympathetic listener. I was ashamed of my weakness; she would never understand.

299

I kissed mother good night and went upstairs to go to bed. As always, when I returned to my attic room, the heat that had built up during the day forced me to go to the window. The moon was already high, and was beginning to shine down into the garden. An honest smell of recently watered soil rose from the vegetable garden. But from farther away, from the immense silent plains, the first night breezes were bringing me the perfumes garnered from acres of stubble, of new-mown grass and meadows—a heady odor almost as sensual as a kiss. Near the well in Grandhoux and under the apple tree last night, I'd breathed in the same smell, and the memory was so strong and so definite that it was enough to call up my desire to be near Jacques again, in his arms with his lips on mine. I closed my eyes and, breathing hard, I stood for a long moment confronting the night. Then I forced myself to come back and sit down at my table. I didn't want to open my black notebook again; it was still too early.

I took a sheet of paper and began to write a long friendly letter to Lachaux. When I'd finished it, I reread it and realized that almost all I wrote about was Jacques' cure, as if all my thoughts could lead only to him. ... I tore it up. I didn't want to hurt Lachaux, and his love would make him perceptive enough to read my feelings between the lines.

I started the next day by visiting Simone Vallin. The second catheter had done its job too, and when I withdrew it, I was able to insert the third one very easily. Simone didn't complain at all. We fixed on the hour of nine p.m. for the operation and I promised to come back and see her during the day.

A list of calls awaited me at Dr. Ferrières' house. When Catherine gave it to me, I asked her how Jacques was; he'd exhausted himself by puttering with the motor of his car all Sunday afternoon, and he was still asleep.

I spent the morning driving around Mesnil and the countryside. There was a kind of sensual delight in not hurrying, in making my work last, in not going back to Jacques too quickly. I remembered the formula Lachaux had used to describe unconscious masochistic tendencies: "Pleasure from pain." My "pleasure" today was more complex. Now that it wasn't entirely self-punishment any more, my chaste, self-imposed wait, without looks, without kisses, without blushes, without touching, without mutual temptation, was a marvelous preamble to the flowering of my happiness.

At one p.m. I arrived at the doctor's house for lunch. I was tired, sweaty and more affected than I wanted to be at the idea of seeing Jacques again. There was a message for me on the telephone pad: "Dear Claude, One of the parts in my car needs to be replaced. I'm going to get it in Evreux. It's half-past ten. Don't wait for me to eat lunch and please don't think that I'm sulking because you've stood me up for a whole day. See you this evening. Jacques."

While she served the hors d'oeuvre, Catherine began to tell me something about the visits I had to make this afternoon. I didn't listen to her. I was wondering anxiously, "Does Jacques really need this part? Did he take just any pretext to go on a jaunt? Or has he disappeared out of a feeling of chivalry so he wouldn't be tempted to abuse the power he has over me? Then I was suddenly panic-stricken. If Jacques was really angry at me because he'd wanted to be with me, he might not understand the reasons that were making me keep away from him until tonight. What if he'd gone off to see Arlette . . . ?

I must have looked so disturbed that I frightened Catherine.

"You're working too hard, mam'selle. Just being a doctor is hard enough for a woman. And on top of that to have to do all that driving! Monsieur Jacques just said a little while ago before he left: 'It's too bad that Mademoiselle Claude hasn't taken me on as her chauffeur. It would make it easier for her!' "

I was amused at the thought of Jacques offering to be my chauffeur. Suddenly I felt better. Only another half day of patience. Oh, Jacques—tomorrow, you'll drive me wherever you wish, forever. . . .

I ate quickly. When I came in I'd noticed that the waiting room was beginning to fill up already.

Until five o'clock I had the usual parade of enormous, corseted perspiring matrons, and mothers bringing in their children to see me.

One patient kept me much longer than the others—a young girl of eighteen, blonde and rosy-faced. She had what seemed to be an acute generalized eczema. She explained to me that she went to a village fair Sunday

301

afternoon, and to her great despair she came down that evening with this terrible disfiguring rash. She added that every time she went to a village fair she had a similar accident. "Psychosomatic trouble?" I asked myself. This would be my first case of it. I questioned her thoroughly but I learned nothing except how sad her rashes made her because she couldn't enjoy the feast days of the village patron saint. Questioning her further, I learned that she also broke out in a rash whenever she put Mercurochrome on her cuts. But what relationship could there be between cuts and the country fairs? Suddenly I remembered: there's mercury at fairs too—in the smoke from the guns that are fired at the shooting galleries.

I wrote out a prescription and added my advice to give up country fairs and medications based on mercury. As I carefully filled out her medical chart for Vincent's sake, I felt delighted. My perceptive diagnosis would prove my competence to him.

The last person I saw was a fat stupid-looking girl of seventeen. She'd barely sat down when she announced that she hadn't had her period for three months and wanted to make it come. In earlier consultations I'd already seen two young women who told me that they weren't having their periods; one said it was because she'd done the laundry with cold water, the other said that she'd gone into a pond barefoot to rescue a drowning chicken. Both had asked me for something that would make them menstruate again. I hadn't fallen for their stories and I'd put them off gently but firmly. They didn't insist. But this patient didn't seem to want to understand. "They told me you'd get rid of it for me!" she kept repeating stubbornly even when I was ushering her out the door. Were they making fun of this simple-minded girl by sending her to me . . . or did they want to test me?

I glanced at her chart as I filed it. She was called Alexandra Jumel. Her first name made me smile. It was so ridiculously pompous for the poor farm girl.

The file cabinet was full of other Jumels, each one equipped with a medical chart that had been carefully kept up to date by Vincent: aside from that of Jumel, Léon, agricultural laborer and Jumel, Marcelle, house-wife, I discovered charts for nine Jumel children, Alexandra being the eldest.

The eleven file cards, placed side by side, gave me a lamentable picture of the family. I only had to glance through Vincent's short notes to know that at the age of forty the father is so soaked in red wine and calvados that he's already had three episodes of delirium tremens. The mother, still young—only thirty-six—but ruined by being pregnant almost continually, has become an enormous slut and complains ceaselessly of having a "pain in the belly." For the children, the balance sheet is equally catastrophic. One twelve-year-old boy committed to the psychiatric hospital in Navarre near Evreux for sexual perversion, a little girl of nine afflicted with bed-wetting and an epileptic boy of eight; while the others have to content themselves with the ordinary childhood diseases. As for Alexandra Jumel, at the age of seventeen she's already had three miscarriages, and she had to be admitted as an emergency in the Bernay hospital for two of them in a row. The eleven charts represented an impressive number of house calls, consultations, examinations and hospital stays at state expense. I thought of the degenerate American family that's used as an example by all the proponents of eugenics because in nine generations it cost the state two million five hundred dollars.

In my practice here I'd already had several occasions to form an opinion about these peasant families. I found that what some of my hospital patients had told me about working-class families was true for them. In the countryside in Ouche, as at Gennevilliers, I discovered that the largest families are always found among the poorest people. I've already been called in by families of agricultural laborers—the lowest class among the rural working class—and found seven or eight people (often more) cramped into two or three rooms of a tumble-down hovel swarming with runny-nosed, badly cared for children who would hide under the kitchen table when I walked in and watch me stupidly. Each time I was struck by the falseness of all the sacred myths people maintain about the large family: "They were happy because they had so many children." "Happy families"—where the father turns all the money into alcohol; where the mother, burdened by her pregnancies, founders in degradation; where the daughters, left to themselves, sleep around in barns or behind hedges as soon as they reach puberty; where because there's nothing else to do, the parents keep producing more children when they're drunk, filling the orphan asylums and state homes with new inmates.

Before I put the eleven Jumel charts back into the file, I

looked again on the chart of the poor girl who'd be condemned to "abortive" tea by my refusal, and then to the hands of some village "angel-maker." My conscience and my medical education make me refuse to give her an abortion. But as soon as I've delivered Simone Vallin, it will be my duty to begin an active campaign for birth control, despite Vincent's hostile attitude. For him, the child that Alexandra Jumel harvested in the corner of some thicket is the well-merited penalty for illicit carnal pleasure: "All she had to do was abstain. . . ." But behind this Puritanical severity lies the old bourgeois traditionalism, the unconscious desire to keep woman in her age-old role of servant of the species: for this, procreation must be hazardous, animal, almost irresponsible.

I was sorry that I hadn't discussed this with Vincent before he left, even if I knew he'd disagree. He would certainly have objected that my attempts at family planning would be absolutely useless for just those families that need them most, the feeble-minded peasants whose parents are drunkards and who have swarms of ill-kept children. No doubt he'd have shrugged his shoulders if I'd remarked that between the well-behaved Malthus-oriented bourgeois in Mesnil and the prolific drunkards like the Jumels, there's a vast number of couples who could benefit from sex education, and could no doubt intelligently plan their families. I would have really irritated him by adding that I think a physician is being unjust and cowardly to refuse an abortion to a woman if he hasn't taught her a few simple precautions which would have meant she wouldn't need one.

Just as I was thinking that, Catherine brought me the long list of calls. If I wanted to finish in time, I had to leave quickly. I thought it would be best to take with me all the instruments I might need so I wouldn't have to come back and risk meeting Jacques. I took them from the instrument cupboard of the little examination room. Because of the chance of a respiratory accident I took both the Mayo cannula and the portable oxygen flask. I also carefully checked the contents of my emergency kit.

I wanted to be absolutely sure I wasn't forgetting something important, so I went over all the things I'd have to do, as I used to in my room in Gennevilliers, with my books open on the table. Then I was afraid of looking ridiculous in front of the nurses and interns. But today I have no witnesses. Was that why I felt constrained and ill at ease instead of feeling the usual excitement of anticipation? I walked away from the cabinet, went back to the office and sat down. I was shaking a little; my heart was beating faster: "This isn't one of the routine events of daily pratice. This is something forbidden and illegal. When I've performed this abortion, I'll have put myself outside the law!"

I sat for a long time with my elbows on the desk and my chin on my hands, looking down at the blotter, at the prescription blanks imprinted with the name of Dr. Vincent Ferrières, at all the things that didn't belong to me any more than did the surgical instruments and the catheters I'd been inserting for two days. I was worried: since I was performing an illegal abortion, wouldn't it be more honest to get the necessary materials by my own means, and to do it only after Vincent's return? Since I wouldn't be his replacement then, my action wouldn't involve his responsibility. Otherwise, this abortion would become a breach of his trust, a kind of treason. But, on the other hand, should I fail to keep my promise at the last minute because of scruples arising from medical loyalty? I thought: "Would I have drawn back if I had resolved to throw a grenade at German soldiers during the occupation? I would have known that I wasn't the only one who ran the risk of being shot and that I would also attract retribution on innocents. Today, I'm the terrorist who may be pursued and Vincent is the hostage. ... So much the worse for me and for him! Only one thing matters: that the thing I'm about to do is necessary."

Besides, it was already too late to begin my inner debate again. Any thought of caution could only be a trap. After days of hesitation and anxiety, I'd decided that this was a just act, and I'd accepted all the risks in advance because I wanted to be true to myself. I wasn't just acting at the mercy of chance. From Mariette to Simone Vallin, all my actions held together: a long chain of events had led me to choose Vincent's best curette from among his instruments, even if I had to use it against the order he typifies, whose commands I reject. I made my decision under that apple tree, near Jacques.

Was it my turn to want to have my cake and eat it too, like the proverb Jacques had quoted? I smiled.

I got up and went back to the cabinet. It was impossible to turn back. The idea that Jacques might call me a coward and put me at Arlette's level was suddenly unbearable to me. He had told me under the apple tree: "You belong to another race. You can commit yourself deeply when you have to, and you can throw caution to the winds. ..." All I had to do was repeat this sentence over and over to myself until the hour of the abortion and I wouldn't feel at odds with myself any more.

The instruments, bottles, syringes and oxygen container were all carefully arranged in the emergency kit. This was the case I'd already taken to Grandhoux and I only had to add a few more things to it. Very early the day after the accident, someone had brought it to Mesnil, with a letter from the well-digger's wife. She wrote that she and her husband were very grateful. Since then I hadn't had time to go as far as La Ferté, where they lived, but by telephoning the hospital in Evreux, I learned that the injured man had had a leg amputated and seemed to be out of danger.

I put my case in the little car. My heart was calm again, and my internal agitation had calmed down too.

I went to the kitchen to tell Catherine that I probably wouldn't have time to come home for dinner, and I asked her to give Jacques a prescripton blank on which I'd written: "This evening at nine o'clock I'll finish the job. Think of me and wish me good luck."

I made my house calls without hurrying uselessly and without impatience. I got back to Mesnil when night was falling. Aside from the three cafés around the city hall, all the shops were closed. The main street was deserted and black. I cautiously stopped the little car at some distance from the school. I took my instrument case. It was so heavy that it made me lean to one side as I walked to the school.

As I crossed the courtyard, I saw a light shining through the curtain, as it did the evening I'd refused Simone. I was expected. A few more steps and I'd be in the room. At this decisive moment, I felt more deeply calm and clear-headed than at any other time in my life. I knocked on the door. Her mother opened it. She took the instrument case and showed me to her daughter's room.

I sat down for a few moments on the edge of the bed and questioned Simone. She described the pain she'd felt in the course of the afternoon. She spoke without self-pity and without appearing to want any pity from me.

"Fine," I said. "Dilation must be complete now."

I got up and began to unwrap my surgical material.

Mme Blanchot watched everything I did, ready to help me if I needed her. I asked her for a little low table and I covered it with a sterile bandage. I opened my instrument and bandage boxes, opened the bottle of antiseptic, prepared a syringe which I filled with a vial of Pentothal. I placed the Mayo cannula and the oxygen bottle within reach. Everything was ready.

I took the syringe and asked Simone, with a smile: "Shall we begin?"

She raised her arm toward me, looking at me with a clear trusting gaze. Then she closed her eyes. Under her light nightgown, I saw her heart beating rapidly.

I placed the tourniquet above the elbow, pushed the needle into the vein, took off the tourniquet and began to inject the liquid very slowly. I'd done exactly the same thing so many times to put a patient to sleep in the hospital! I seemed to hear the anesthetist's voice advising me at the beginning of my apprenticeship: "Push very slowly. Watch for the slightest indication of a halt in respiration. Stop the injection at once and give the patient a little oxygen. And wait until breathing resumes before completing the injection. You'll make no mistakes with this technique."

Never have I followed those directions so scrupulously. I'd warned Simone: anesthetizing with Pentothal, without trained help and without facilities to handle a respiratory accident, would be the most dangerous moment. She'd accepted the risk without hesitation. As I made the intravenous injection, I felt I'd split into two people—it was as if I were standing next to myself, watching myself with superhuman attention. She fell asleep at once.

Until then, the mother had stayed in the corner of the room, watching quietly and attentively. I asked her to come closer and help me. We placed the body across the bed, brought the basin to the outer edge of the mattress, and I explained to my amateur assistant exactly how she should keep the thighs bent back close to the abdomen. I inserted the speculum and withdrew the last catheter. I was ready to begin.

Before taking the curette, I glanced around me for a moment, not from last minute hesitation, but because I wanted to imprint the setting of these decisive moments firmly on my mind: the pale green wallpaper, the low couch with its coffee table piled with books, the wardrobe with a mirror on its door, and the knotty walnut dressing table, the lighting fixture hanging from the ceiling with its three chrome arms. Like a drowning man, I recorded all these details in a flash, taking in the bright red slippers left on the floor, the dahlias in a vase on the table in front of the window, the light-colored dressing gown thrown over a green velvet chair, and the two round, smooth knees under my eyes, the two tan hands lying next to the body on the sheet, and the shining circle of the speculum between the thighs.

I pulled on my gloves and picked up the curette. The impression of being two people had gone. Now I was acutely conscious that my whole body was poised and ready for the most precise, delicate activity. And then I thought: "*I* am doing this! My adolescence is over. I'm holding the power of my whole life in my hands."

As soon as I plunged in the curette, I was sure of the perfect economy of my gestures, of perfect precision. All my senses were alert, and I accomplished everything that I had to do without hurrying but without losing a second. At the same time, I watched the patient's breathing with utmost care, so I could use the cannula and give her oxygen at the smallest sign of anything going wrong.

In this mood of clear, controlled exaltation, my fingers seemed to extend to the very tip of the steel of the curette. It would be impossible to make more careful, gentle movements to keep the living flesh from being too wounded.

As soon as I was sure that nothing was left of the embryo, I put the instrument back on the table. The couch was low, and I had had to kneel on the floor. I leaned back and met Mme Blanchot's eyes. Half sitting on the bed, leaning over her daughter's chest to keep her legs in place, she hadn't been able to see anything of the operation. She was pale, and her eyes were questioning me anxiously, but she hadn't for a moment left the position I'd told her to stay in, and she'd been so steady and quiet that I'd completely forgotten her.

I realized how worried she must be, and I immediately told her, with a smile:

"Everything went well. It's all finished."

"Oh! thank you, mam'selle."

Her voice trembled with gratitude. But she was waiting for my command, and didn't budge. I looked at my watch. I'd taken a quarter of an hour; the usual time for a curettage. Soon she would regain consciousness.

I cleaned off the blood, pulled out the speculum, and applied a cotton pad. When I told Mme Blanchot that she could let go of her daughter's legs, I covered the bloody remains that had fallen in the kidney-shaped enamel bowl with a bandage so she wouldn't have to see it. This was all that remained of the embryo.

I stood up, as did Simone's mother. We arranged Simone comfortably. She let out a small moan, and half opened her eyes. Leaning over her, I murmured softly several times, "It's all over."

Her eyes closed again but she sketched a slight grateful smile to make me understand that she'd heard. She tried to talk to me but was only able to mumble a few words that I couldn't make out. Her lips were pitifully drawn in pain. She fell asleep again, and her features kept their expression of painful repose. Her mother and I, standing face to face, looked at each other for a moment in silence. We understood each other without needing words.

After I turned on the bedside lamp and turned off the overhead light I told Mme Blanchot that I was going to stay with her daughter for an hour. To reassure her, I added: "A simple precaution. It's the recommended procedure after a delivery or a curettage."

"Then I'll bring you something to eat, mam'selle."

She disappeared. I began to put the instruments back into the case, keeping only the Mayo cannula and the oxygen near at hand in case anything went wrong. I pushed an easy chair near the bed, so I could watch her face more comfortably. She continued to doze peacefully.

Her mother came back a little later. She had put a pot of brewed coffee—not that weak instant stuff but real coffee with a comforting smell—on a tray, with country ham, bread, butter and some pears. She left the tray within easy reach on the low table, and went off again.

I let myself lean back in the chair. Only then did I realize that the physical well-being I thought I felt during the operation was only an illusion: all my muscles hurt, my heart was beating rapidly and pounding in my temples, and my head ached. I was sore, bruised, and nauseated too; I'd also just finished going through a difficult operation and I too was painfully coming back to life again.

I drank the coffee and nibbled at the ham. Then I felt better. I closed my eyes. I had to let this hour by Simone glide away; it was the last dead time. Now, every minute that passed became a new little victory, another tiny step toward liberty!

"Free! Soon I'll be free!" I murmured and in the silent room the word seemed to have immense reverberations. Yes! Free soon to begin anew, to run risks, to utilize my medical knowledge for just and gratuitous actions! For six years, I'd been the little student who kept quiet; thinking and preparing herself. Tonight I'd just thrown my first bomb against one of those reassuring façades that hide social iniquities and cowardice.

Simone Vallin moaned and said a few meaningless words. I opened my eyes again, and pulled myself up anxiously, but she wasn't completely awake and she soon became silent again. As I leaned back again in my easy chair, I saw a small trace of blood on the floor near the bed. I scraped at it with the toe of my shoe. Now I had to dispose of the remains of the fetus, wrapped up in a cloth, clean a few bloody instruments, and the terrible task would be completely done.

Was that why I felt so light, and so free? Now my heart was beating less quickly, my head ached less and if my thoughts were still floating, I was no longer in that awful stupor of just waking up, like the torpor that still engulfed Simone. It was as if a mysterious transformation had occurred upon the completion of the abortion; I felt ineffably detached from the past, and completely at peace.

My watch said it was ten o'clock. Only twenty more minutes of watching over my patient. Already the curettage was in the past; I was beyond it. What mattered now was the woman I was in the process of becoming, since I had won the right by my action—the woman who was going to go back to Jacques.

Simone took a deep breath. It alarmed me, but then her breathing became peaceful again. I closed my eyes and again the surroundings disappeared.

I had refused love for so long. . . . I had wanted to live free from all love for so long! But was it my fault—a difficult childhood with a weak father and a mother whom I despised for her female servitude? I'd sworn never to resemble my mother! Was my perpetual revolt against my condition as a little girl really my fault?

Yet tonight this same girl is preparing herself to repudiate what she's always judged to be indisputable; this same girl feels an eager, indescribable joy in the love that filled her with contempt till now. Two days ago I discovered my true native land, my climate, my haven. For two days, the past has had no value. My love has eradicated all the rest; he has come, he who has broken through the circle of my solitary delirium by taking me in his arms. Here he is, gentle and caressing, ready to hold me close to him. Twice tonight, I will have begun at the beginning again. ...

Simone's mother knocked lightly on the door and came in, excusing herself:

"Mam'selle, it's been longer than an hour. You must be tired. If you think she's all right, maybe I could take your place."

Simone was breathing quietly and her pulse was regular. When I checked the bandage, she half woke up; and recognizing me, smiled.

"Go to sleep," I told her softly. "Everything is going fine. I'm entrusting you to your mother until tomorrow morning."

She hadn't hemorrhaged. I pulled the sheet gently up almost to her mouth, which was now relaxed in happy exhaustion.

Five minutes later, I was out in the street. I didn't want Mme Blanchot to leave her daughter to help me so I carried the instrument kit to the car by myself.

Now I was free, completely free! Never had the night air seemed so light, so pure. I wished I could take a walk for a while; the freshness of the night air after the stifling room was making my head turn. But the case was heavy; I deposited it in the car with relief, and with a few turns of the wheel, I was in front of the Ferrières house.

When he left Mesnil, Vincent had given the house key to me. I was using it for the first time and though the moonlight was bright, I had to grope to find the lock and open the door. I went in carefully, and took off my shoes so I wouldn't wake Catherine.

The tall French door that faced the entryway was still open. It let in milky light that bathed the whole foyer; beyond, the garden deepened mysteriously into the dimensions of the night. I happily breathed in the soothing, familiar smell. Under my bare feet, the blue and white slate lozenges seemed to be made of a soft fresh substance; the old chests along the walls took on a deeper luster, and the row of healing saints, so like children's toys, continued to stand guard. They all stood in a half circle, just the way they had that afternoon when I walked into the house for the first time. I was wearing a summer dress and my first high heels that day, but I would have laughed with disbelief if one of those miracle-makers had told me I'd be in love—not without some defensiveness and hesitations—in so short a time. Would I have believed that he and his colleagues would witness my defeat two weeks later in the same foyer, and that two short days afterward my life would take a new turn?

I'd put the case down near a chest to shut the door behind me. As I leaned down to pick it up, I met the kindly face of Saint Gratian; according to Vincent he was in special charge of children's nightmares. I smiled at him. I murmured happily, "Good saint, keep ghosts and nightmares far away from my love!" As I deposited the case in Vincent's office, I was still smiling indulgently at the thought of how unnecessary my prayer had been—I'd been filled with elation ever since I left the schoolhouse. My certainty of happiness became deeper every minute. From now on, even without Saint Gratian's help, neither doubt nor sadness could touch me. . . .

Once I'd put back all the instruments, I came back to the foyer. I was still barefoot. Since the tiles were cold, I ran lightly over to the first step of the oaken staircase. "Only a few more steps separate me from Jacques!" I thought. I lifted my eyes toward the staircase that curved upward into the darkness of the upper floors. The silence, which until now had seemed so welcoming, suddenly became oppressive.

I felt my heart beating harder and harder. My knees were shaky. I had to lean against the heavy banister. "What's wrong with me?" I thought. "The man I love is near. Nothing is keeping me from him now. If I go up to the landing and push open the door, I can say: 'Jacques, it's me! I did what you said I should do.' He'll tell me how brave I was. He'll take me in his arms, and ask me: 'Are you happy?' And I'll answer by embracing him with all the joy of my love, a love that goes beyond the passionate desire of the senses. It wasn't only desire that pushed me to Jacques. Even if he is handsome, even if I wanted, almost from the first day, to touch his skin and breathe in his breath still warm from his lips, even if I was overcome

312

with happiness by his kiss, it's the revelation that he's a far better person than he looks; it's esteem, confidence and admiration that have brought me to love him. I wanted to conquer him. At the same time, I wanted to deserve his love by doing something that was worthy of his heroism in Grandhoux—and purify it of everything that could have made it vile. I've taken risks, both as a woman and as a doctor. Tonight is a double victory. And I, who've been living in distraught anticipation of this moment for two days, am now trembling as if suddenly love were frightening me!"

I stood motionless against the banister, my eyes lifted toward the dark hole of the staircase. I felt strange, anxious but terribly happy. Was it Jacques' being so near that was upsetting me just when I was realizing that I'm not quite as free of my past self as I thought I was?

For a moment I forgot where I was. I was fifteen again, back in the darkness of the school dormitory, dreaming of my future as a woman and feeling vague hopes, anticipations and fears that made me wistful to the point of tears. And I'd had one nightmare over and over again: a man whose face I couldn't see would come over to my bed and lie on me and emprison me with his limbs. I couldn't recognize him but I knew he was going to hurt me, tear me and soil me. I'd wake up suddenly, panting from fear and shame. And then I'd lean over to Arlette's bed and take her hand to calm my fears.

Have I changed so little that tonight I'm afraid of that very real man, the man I love? What connection could there be between Jacques and the hideous specter who haunted my nights when I was fifteen?

A clock chimed once and echoed through the house. It brought me back to reality. I opened my eyes and murmured: "Come quickly, Jacques! Come quickly!" I was shaking. I couldn't move. I was paralyzed. I felt nailed to the first step. I wished that Jacques could be there without my knowing it, so that I could surrender myself with my eyes closed, lose myself in him and let myself be carried away.

Suddenly I was ashamed of being so scared. I wasn't going to spend the whole night like this. "Losing yourself in love" isn't waiting like a sleeper who only dares offer herself in a dream!

I looked up. If I called, Jacques would come out of

his room and come down to join me. But could I shout his name like a child who's afraid of the dark? I had to go up. Should I knock at his door? I probably only asked myself that to put off what I had to do while I thought about it. But suddenly, another thought went through my mind. "Suppose no one answers? What if Jacques isn't home?" In a flash, I imagined him not there at all, but gone in pursuit of Arlette. For a few seconds time stood still; everything seemed to whirl around me and I gripped the banister with the dizzy feeling that I was going to faint, emptied of all my blood.

Then I was so horrified that I ran up the stairs without thinking. When I got to the last turn before the landing, I saw a ray of light at the level of the floor which was just at the level of my eyes. I gasped, "He's here! He's here!" and, choking with joy, I leaped up the last few steps. I crossed the landing in two strides and opened the door. Jacques was lying on his couch, reading. He looked up as I slammed the door and sat up, smiling.

I ran to him like a madwoman. I stumbled against the bed. He took me in his arms and I could only murmur, "Jacques, my love, I've come to you!" Then came the boundless, delirious moan. . . .

Friday, August 16th, 3 a.m.

I haven't written in this notebook since Tuesday when I had the courage to leave Jacques' arm and come back to sleep at home so that mother wouldn't worry.

That was the last cautious thing I did. Since then, I haven't wanted to lose one single hour of my endless, blissful happiness or of my love, because each second of it fills my body with sensual delight and my soul with blessedness.

How I've changed in three days! I don't recognize myself. My body has only just discovered its true vocation. I tremble with joy. I've forgotten all the theories and resolutions I ever had. I've yielded to the temptation that had been preparing to defeat me for twenty days. I fell at his knees and trembled with the womanly pleasure of giving and obeying, with the exalting pleasure of humiliating myself willingly in pleasure.

My "male protest" is over! My adolescence—when the idea of male penetration and domination terrified me and when I felt that woman is always defeated in the act of love—is over and done with. I don't even try to deceive myself by persuading myself that I've tamed Jacques. I've let myself be conquered. I've accepted the submersion of myself in the act of love, I've even consented to make myself passively docile. I've accepted my destiny as a woman which is, according to the sex manuals that I refused to believe, the attainment of full physical and psychic pleasure—by being possessed by the man I love and finding satisfaction in my yielding. Why should I be ashamed of this gift? I've discovered that it comes not only from the body but also from the soul.

Only now, when I'm alone in my room, near my narrow student's couch for the first time in two nights, can I really judge how absolute the negation of my past has been.

Tuesday afternoon I came to see mother before I started out on my house calls. I'd lied very little to her until now, but I explained that I was expecting urgent calls from several patients and from women about to have babies. It would be silly to make Catherine run all the way over here in the middle of the night to call me, and it would be much more practical for me to sleep at the doctor's house. Since it was a question of professional duty, mother made no comment and when I told her I was in a hurry, she even helped me to put my underwear and toiletries in a little suitcase.

Jacques had asked me to tell her this lie, and I obeyed him without hesitation—which shows how completely my love has erased everything else in half a day. Nothing but Jacques had any value or importance to me any more, and if he hadn't suggested it to me, I'd probably have slept out every night anyway as if no one in Mesnil, not even my mother, would be worried or surprised. I wouldn't even be in my room right now if Jacques hadn't decided last night that I should spend the last part of the night at home so Vincent wouldn't have the shock of finding us sleeping together when he got home today.

Yesterday at dinner time Vincent telephoned from the base at Mourmelon. He told us he was starting back, but that he intended to start out very late and drive quietly during the night, to avoid the August 15th vacation traffic jams. He expected to get to Mesnil at about five or six in the morning.

I listened to his news without emotion. There was no reason for me to be bothered by the fact that he was coming back and my substitution was ending. On the contrary, now I wouldn't have to worry about office hours and house calls any more, so I'd have the whole day to spend with Jacques. We were both free and we certainly had the right to love each other. I saw no reason why Vincent should object. So it didn't matter if he found out about us as soon as he returned.

That's what I told Jacques as soon as I hung up, but Jacques, who'd been listening on the extension and making funny faces as Vincent talked on in his pompous way, entirely disagreed.

"I know what he's like, that cold fish," he said. "He may not go to church, but as far as he's concerned, all love outside of marriage is just fornication, that awful sin of the flesh. If he finds us sleeping together when he gets back tomorrow morning, or even if he only discovers without being warned somehow that we've been in adjacent rooms for three nights, he'll look at you reproachfully, the virtuous citizen looking at a lost woman. And he'll give me his dramatic scene of Puritanical indignation. I've gone through it before. It would be rather painful! Let's spare him the shock and let him find out little by little. Tonight I'll set the alarm for three a.m. so you can go back and be sleeping at your mother's when he gets back. Tomorrow, at lunch, we'll have time to broach the subject cautiously and tactfully. . . ."

We went to bed around ten . . . I almost wrote "chastely," because sleeping with Jacques has become such a natural thing by now.

It must have been because I was so happy that I woke up before the alarm rang. I lay very still. Jacques was next to me sleeping in that deep exhaustion that follows the act of love. I felt him close to me and warm against my skin. I stayed very still so I wouldn't wake him up. I felt wonderful snuggled up against his strong shoulder. With my eyes open in the dark, I wondered if it was really my body that was brimming over with such primitive, sensual pleasure.

Jacques' body hid the window from me, but it was wide open to the starry sky, and the night reached me with all the smells from the garden and the clear silence that stretched over the plains, interrupted from time to time by a dog barking far away. This evening, everything was harmony, softness and fulfillment.

I stayed still, enjoying to the hilt my last minutes of waiting, this moment of reprieve close to Jacques. In a few minutes the alarm would make me get up, and my body would start suffering from loneliness and his absence, almost as if half of myself had been torn away. I had become like other women. From now on I couldn't live without a man, but that didn't make me sad any more. Since I went to Jacques after the abortion, I've wanted everything that's happened to me. I haven't been able to be calculating, clever or cautious for even a moment. I haven't once regretted my irremediable surrender, no more than I tried to escape, that first night, from the force that invaded me and tore me, growing irresistibly within me, making me moan with pain before it made me happy. His eyes shone so happily that I stifled my cry and gave myself in silence to prove to Jacques that his domination was complete.

Today I'm no longer afraid of him. And it doesn't hurt any more. ... I get dizzy every time I'm separated from him for a few minutes and remember the profound pleasure his body now gives to mine.

The alarm must be about to ring. I lifted myself carefully on my elbow to look at the little luminous clock on the night table. It was twenty minutes to three. I only had fifteen minutes to get up without waking Jacques. After it rang it would be too late.

I'd read in Cocteau's little book that the return of potency is the best sign of a complete cure for the drug addict. But I've been afraid for the past three days that Jacques, still in the process of recovering, might exhaust his newly recovered strength. And I was afraid of my own weakness too. If he started to wake up and drowsily put his hand on me, all my resolutions would melt and I would surrender myself immediately. It was high time for me to get up!

Jacques' moist skin was glued to mine and he grumbled when I tried to detach myself from him. Again I lay still, waiting until his breathing became regular again. The night was light. A milky moonlight bathed the room and I looked ecstatically at his beautiful sleeping face. I wanted to lean over him and say: "I'm yours ... I didn't exist until you kissed me ... because of you I've just been born. ..."

I held my breath for another minute or so and vaguely wondered why you suddenly love someone. Why only that person and no one else? Why this incomprehensible difference between the man you love and all other men? Is it just because of circumstances, or does it come from deep, secret currents of attraction that you can't escape? Is it simple hormonal chemistry or else, as the old myth of Androgynes says, the other half of yourself miraculously found again?

Jacques' breathing was regular again. I moved slowly and cautiously. I reached the edge of the bed, got up and walked to the night table without making a noise. It was five to three. I groped for the alarm button and quietly pushed it in.

Ten minutes later, like a burglar, I stole down the stairs barefoot, crossed the foyer with its wooden saints without looking back and softly pulled the street door shut behind me.

The little car seemed to be waiting for me at the edge of the sidewalk, like a patient dog, well-trained to the whims of his master—I hadn't driven it for three days. The motor coughed a little before it turned over, but since Jacques' window opened on the garden he couldn't have heard me starting up.

Once I got to mother's, I opened the door very cautiously and took off my shoes to go up the stairs. I listened carefully on the landing. Nothing was stirring.

I didn't turn the light in my room on right away. I sat in the darkness in front of my table for a while. My legs were weak and I was out of breath, unhappy to be there, and hurt by my own courage. I was close to tears, I could only repeat to myself: "Here's where I've got to! In three days! ..." Then I thought, to console myself, "At least, love is leaving me clear-headed. Jacques is intelligent and charming, but I love him for more than his intelligence and his charm. I know all his faults and accept them. I know he's touchy, temperamental, dissatisfied, difficult, and occasionally capable of the worst. I love him because I know he's terribly alone, horribly lost in his loneliness and exposed to every bad influence. I also know that he's capable of love even if he pretends to be a cynic. He has bursts of spontaneity and freshness, all the nobility of a youthful mind—it only took his courageous bearing in the well to show me that. But I have no illusions: loving Jacques won't always be easy; to begin with, I'll only ask him to accept my tenderness; and that will be enough, I'm sure, to revive a taste for the good in him, to drag him from his old way of life. I'll keep enough tenacity and courage from the old Claude to rescue him, and if that isn't enough, I can draw new strength from the happiness he's giving me."

During the last three days, during office hours or at a patient's bedside, my thoughts would stray ceaselessly to the future. I'd have to force myself to become strictly, professionally careful again. "And furthermore," I'd tell myself, "why think of the future when the present is so rich and wonderful?" In the afternoon, I'd escape between two patients and run to the garden, just long enough to say a few words to Jacques, to enjoy his laugh and to make him give me a kiss. Then, after the last patient had left, I would take my kit and, spurning the little car, I'd go to the garage where Jacques, who had appointed himself my chauffeur, would be waiting for me, absorbed with his car, finishing some delicate adjustment of the motor.

We felt the need—as do all who love each other—to show the world our love. We drove all over the countryside in the red sports car. Leaning against Jacques, I could have shouted from happiness, "Look! I have a lover. I have a lover!" without caring about my reputation or propriety. It's probably lucky that I didn't because it means mother has escaped a disgrace. But the few times that I've gone back to her house, dashing in and out again so Jacques wouldn't have to wait outside in the car, I could see the reproach in her eyes. Yesterday, she asked why I wasn't using the little car any more; I pointedly ignored the question and knowing me, she didn't insist. If she had, I would have told her sharply that I was twenty-five and I had the right to be free: free to have a lover, free to be seen with him, free to finally catch up on my unspent youth a little, free to take advantage of his presence day and night.

I felt guilty for a moment when I left her. But if, instead of answering sharply, I had admitted to her trustingly, daughter to mother, how deeply and totally happy I am now, she wouldn't have understood because she's only known the bare, empty life of a woman without love.

Anyway, however much mother might object, it's too late. My future is settled. I've found the man for me, whose presence makes me complete. I don't even need to fool myself by maintaining that I wouldn't have to surrender anything with Jacques. In his arms, I can forget the old war of the sexes, and my fight for false privileges; but I believe that, without wanting a Utopian experience of equality, I'll be able to keep a free and loving relationship between us.

Yesterday was stormy. As usual, yesterday's heat hangs heavily in my attic room even though dawn is near. I was thirsty. I went to fill a glass at the sink faucet, and while I was waiting for the water to get cold, I automatically looked at myself in the mirror and surprised myself by smiling at my reflection—it seemed to me that my face became more subtle, more radiant, and more gentle in the past few days. I touched my forehead, my cheeks, my eyelids—all the places that Jacques' lips have caressed. I gently touched the curve of my neck and the tender spot near my ear where his kiss almost makes me faint. I smiled at my narcissistic gesture and remembered two verses by Catullus that had intrigued me at school: "If you yield the betrothed to her lover's impatient caresses, by dawn yesterday's necklace will no longer encircle her neck." I only understood what these verses meant much later, when I read a treatise on endocrinology in medical school. Classical authors thought that the act of making love caused an inflammation of the thyroid gland.

Again, I bent toward the mirror. I looked at my neck. How wonderful it would be if my magic transformation would shine forth to the eyes of the world, if everyone could tell by looking at me that now I am a woman—a woman whose body and soul are filled with joy.

Dawn is coming. At the far edge of the plains, the sky in the east, at the tops of the apple trees in the garden, has begun to grow light. I'll lie down and try to sleep a little; I'll turn my head to the wide-open window to catch the morning breeze that's caressing Jacques' forehead.

Jacques, my love, come and join me in my dream, come and lie against my body, since I'm no longer sleepy or happy away from you. Come and lie with me, take me in that confusion of desires, of breath and of limbs, in that wild consenting, in that miraculous union of love where we are at once each other and ourselves.

Friday, August 16, 10 p.m.

Today has been the perfect model for a classical tragedy. "One action, in one day and in one place...." That describes it exactly: between this morning and tonight, everything went according to the most rigid Three Unities. I even have my confidante before me, ready to receive my laments and my tears, like a heroine of classical theater—this notebook, the humiliatingly accurate witness of my unhappiness. . . .

I'm being sarcastic about my tragedy. Since no one can help me, I'm trying to be funny to get outside of myself, to prove to myself that I'm not going mad or playing a part in a melodrama.

But can this girl shriveled up in her pain, and panting like an animal that some cruel child has tortured for fun, be the same one who lingered here alone early this morning to write about her love and her bliss?

I'm alone tonight too, but between then and now, my happiness has painfully withered away. Tonight, I choke from loneliness, not from someone's absence. It's all over for me. I'm all alone, alone forever, just as in the nights of my past.

I've decided to leave Mesnil this very night. I'll take my two suitcases with me. I didn't want to tell mother I'm going because I didn't want a painful scene. And since I'm sneaking away, I have to leave her time to fall asleep. As I wait, I think it's better to write down what happened today to make it clearer to myself, instead of throwing myself defenselessly on my bed and howling with grief.

They say that drowning people relive their lives with terrible precision in a few seconds. I want to relive the details of the day in my last moments in Mesnil. . . .

This morning I was up and out at half-past nine. I'd awakened at about eight out of habit. Still half asleep, I'd reached over for Jacques before I opened my eyes completely. It took me a minute to remember that I'd slept in my bed and that I was alone. The morning freshness wafted into my attic room just the way it did when I woke up in Jacques' room in his arms; it came in through windows that looked out over the same blue sky and let in the same smells and rural noises. With my eyes half closed, I could pretend that Jacques had just gone out. He'd come back in a few seconds, his naked body wonderfully masculine in the full light. He'd lie down next to me again, brush me gently with his fingertips and lips in a subtle caress that would be both a stimulant and a drug. I woke up completely and I smiled as I thought about our decision to talk to Vincent at lunch. From then on, I would never know the loneliness of such a chaste awakening. I sang under the shower, thinking about how soon I'd be seeing Jacques. When I went down to breakfast, mother greeted me with the hot chocolate and buttered toast she usually saved for holidays. She thought everything was all right again because her daughter had been sleeping virtuously in her own bed (as the little car in front of our door demonstrated to the whole neighborhood) and she was delighted that her respectability was secure. But she hadn't dared to thank her prodigal child directly, so she expressed it with the holiday food.

I'd been stopping at the schoolhouse morning and night. Simone Vallin's recovery was coming along well—no bleeding, only a touch of fever the first day—a typical curettage without any complications. We'd exchange a few words after I examined her but I never stayed long, because Jacques was always waiting impatiently for me at the door in his convertible. So when Simone would start to thank me, I'd interrupt and run, saying only that there was no need for thanks.

This morning when I parked the car in front of the schoolhouse, I thought that now that my time as Vincent's substitute was coming to an end, I was performing my last official visit; then I smiled at the idea of calling a visit made for an illegal abortion "official." Should I talk to Vincent today about my operation or just keep visiting Simone Vallin for a few days without telling him anything? My first idea seemed more straightforward to me. I like directness, so I was inclined to adopt it but as I pushed open the schoolhouse door, I shrugged my shoulders: why worry? Everything had been accomplished without complications, and the main thing was that the curettage had been done and Simone Vallin had been delivered from her terrible worry. As for when would be the best time to tell Vincent, Jacques would decide that.

. . .

Mme Blanchot opened the door for me, with her sleeves rolled up and her arms covered with soap. She showed me into her daughter's room. Following my recommendations, Simone was lying down and resting. When I came in, she let the magazine she was reading drop to the sheet, and as she always did, she welcomed my visit with a beautiful, confident smile.

Mme Blanchot wasn't worried about her daughter's

health any more, so she went back to her washing. When I'd finished my examination and my treatment, it occurred to me that since Jacques wasn't waiting for me I had some time for once. So I pushed the old green velvet easy chair up to the bed, the same one I'd sat in when I watched her recover consciousness after the curettage.

Except for the sunlight coming in through the drapes this morning to light the room instead of the light from the fixture, nothing in the room had changed since the night of the operation: there were dahlias in a vase on the sideboard, the same dressing gown was draped over a chair, the same red slippers lay at the end of the bed. But today's convalescent no longer looked drawn and ashen-faced as she had that night. She was propped up on her pillow, and although she still looked a little weary, she was very pretty with her long, black hair fanned out over the white pillow case. But as we chatted about nothing in particular (we hadn't yet found any point of common interest) I thought I could see the reflection of some sadness in her dark eyes, and at the same time, a bright-ness that couldn't come from a fever—I'd just taken her temperature. What was it? I went on talking, trying to figure it out. But I didn't need the flair of an old clinician to know that this unusual patient of mine was "hatching" something. Did her internal agitation, which was so much in conflict with the strong will and stubborness that is the very foundation of her chaacter, come from physical or emotional causes? And did it date from today, or from the day of the curettage? If it was the latter, I was responsi-ble. Simone hadn't wanted to complain, and I was too selfishly preoccupied with Jacques and always in too much of a rush to get back to him to notice anything.

We chatted on, but I kept thinking: no fever, no bleed-ing, no pain, nothing that could have warned me! Then it must be emotional. Maybe she was worried about her husband? I asked casually if she had any news from Algeria. She answered without hesitation:

"Thank you, mam'selle, my husband is fine. I got a letter yesterday. He's left the back country now, and he says he'll be back in France soon." What could be bother-ing her then? Was she finally paying for the terrifying amount of tension she'd been under before her abortion? If that was it, my slowness in reaching a decision had made her worry even more, so I could feel guilty for that too.

Simone fell silent again, and her eyes returned to the open magazine that lay before her. She looked even sadder now. I finally guessed. She kept looking at a two-page photograph in the magazine: some royal baby, with round cheeks full of life, gleaming pink lips, and wide-open eyes, lay between sumptuous lace curtains, clenching his tiny flowerlike fists happily and smiling with wonderful sweetness.

Did she feel me watching her? She looked up from her contemplation of that innocent face, and turned to me. I understood what was responsible for the infinite sadness, and also the bright hope in her eyes. Ever since the curette had torn that tiny bit of her flesh from her, she'd never stopped thinking about the dead child and worrying about her chances of cradling a tender, tiny, live body in her arms soon.

She could tell that I'd guessed, and she sat up and said poignantly:

"Swear to me that I won't be sterile now!"

It was exactly the same thing that Mariette had asked me in the same imploring voice at Gennevilliers, a few days after her abortion! I hadn't wanted to admit to Mariette that a badly done abortion, followed by a hemorrhage and a serious infection, almost always leads to sterility, along with other after-effects. On that day, in the small hospital room, I'd lied and promised her she'd get pregnant again, and less than five days later, as if my lie were mocking me in the end, Mariette died horribly of postabortive tetanus.

This morning I didn't have to lie out of pity. After a curettage that's been performed antiseptically and according to the rules and that's been followed by no complications or fever, the risk of sterility is infinitesimal. I told this to Simone with happy assurance. And, as if the miracle of her new child truly depended on me, she seized my hands. Her gratitude, happiness and hope shone even more clearly in her eyes than on the day when I'd promised to perform the abortion.

When I came out of the school building a little later, my heart was full of joy. I felt at peace with myself and wonderfully happy.

As I got into the car, I thought to myself that by terminating this pregnancy, I'd prevented a birth that could have been horrible both for her and for her relatives; I'd probably prevented the most cruel and unjust of

324

destinies. But by destroying this tiny link, had I criminally affected the endless chain of life? I was sure I hadn't. Surely it was future motherhood—fertile, imperious, and sovereign—that shone in her look of hope, in the way she eagerly contemplated the picture of the newborn baby; and it was life, more harmonious and more beautiful than ever, that was triumphantly taking her in its charge after my operation.

I wasn't afraid of admitting my action to Dr. Ferrières now, even if he *was* a member of the medical board and opposed to legal abortion. As a doctor, I'd been both competent and charitable. No one could maintain any longer that I'd betrayed my profession by performing an abortion on this young mother!

I drove the few hundred yards that separated me from the Ferrières house calmly and happily. But as I pulled up in front, I was stricken by another doubt—a nonprofessional one this time. Should I wait for Vincent in the office, or could I go directly up to Jacques' room the way I used to when I was nursing him? I stalled by going into the kitchen. I found Catherine preparing the crust for pear tarts—they're Vincent's and Jacques' favorite dessert.

As soon as she saw me, Catherine ran up to me and said:

"Oh, mam'selle the whole house is asleep. Monsieur Jacques didn't get up yet and Monsieur Vincent didn't get home till eight this morning because his car broke down. He looked so tired that I lied to him to make him go to bed. I told him that you said you'd do his house calls this morning and that you told me to tell him for you."

With a smile, she handed me the list of calls.

"Please forgive me, mam'selle?"

Of course I forgave her. I could have kissed her for her tact in this and also for the attention she'd lavished on me for three days. Her "little one" was so obviously happy because of me that she wanted to show me how grateful she was by her continual little kindnesses to me. The most surprising proof that she'd given me of this was that she, an old truly pious Christian, had "seen nothing" of what'd gone on between Jacques and me over the last three days. Jacques is her second god; and all he needs to do to close her eyes is to give her a kiss on her old cheek or pay her a compliment the way he used to when he was a willful, happy little boy. When I'm with Jacques in his room, Catherine avoids coming upstairs and ignores us totally.

I picked up the kit again in the office. As I crossed the foyer, I gave a friendly tap to St. Gratian's rosy cheeks—they were touched up with a bit of rouge by the medieval painter—and I joyously saluted all his coworkers of miracles, lined on top of their chests.

Most of the house calls this morning were in the country and I happily made my tour through meadows and groves. I followed the roads I'd so often traveled in the little sports car. For the last three days Jacques and I have been like two carefree children, drunk with pleasure, sun, and speed, off to some farmhouse with its slate or thatched roof, hidden somewhere over yonder in a valley. The car had purred gently along, gliding over the roads, and time had glided with it as if in a dream. But sometimes, on a sudden whim, Jacques would put on the brakes without warning, stop the car next to a ditch, and bend toward me. Under his lips, I would feel savage and dizzy with pleasure, floating between the bright depth of the heavens and the limitless brightness of the plains. When we separated, giddy and breathing hard, we'd look around us for a while, as if we'd been blinded, before we recognized each other.

This morning when I left the Ferrières house I put up the side windows and put down the top to give the humble little car the sporting look of the convertible. On my way back from my latest visit, I stopped at the edge of the road. The resemblance between the Peugeot and Jacques' car was small but as soon as I leaned my head against the seat and closed my eyes, with the sun beating down on my face, the cherished, very special face appeared to me instantly in the vague redness of my eyelids. I stayed for quite a while like that: relaxed and happy. Around me I heard the innumerable small noises of the warm summer countryside. I smiled and thought: "That old hemiplegic woman I just examined is my next to last house call. Now all my days will be Sundays ... no phone calls, no ringing bells, no emergencies or difficult consultations. Now, every time Jacques wants something I can answer him obediently: 'Whatever you want!' "

The joy that surged through me at the thought was so violent that I quickly opened my eyes as if I were really going to find his beautiful face leaning over me.

Only one name remained on my list: Mme Lemailleux, on the Perrée road. The Perrée road is a short path just to the west of Mesnil so I kept this last visit for the way back. I had no trouble finding the Lemailleux home—it's a modest one-story brick house with a slate roof and a neat little garden in front. Its two windows are hung with sparkling clean curtains. In a corner of the garden, a large wash load of shirts, socks and aprons of all sizes was out to dry on the clothesline.

I pushed open the wooden gate. Two rows of dahlias separated the cement walk from the beds of tomatoes, beans and cabbages and led me straight to the door. It was wide open. From the threshold, I could see five children between about two and seven years old sitting around a long table. They were waiting for their meal—their napkins tucked way up to the edge of their necks under their healthy cheeks, pounding happily on their plates with their spoons.

As soon as they saw me, they stopped their noise and looked at me curiously. In the corner of the kitchen, a young woman was bending over a crib; she hadn't heard me come in. She was astonished by the sudden silence, and she pulled herself up quickly but not before I was able to see the tenderness in the curve of her breast and her arms as she leaned toward the baby lying in his little bed.

Mme Lemailleux came over to me at once, excusing herself for letting me see her house in such a mess.

"When you have young children, and only two rooms, mam'selle, it's very hard. . . ."

She seemed sincerely ashamed. I looked around me. The kitchen wasn't very large but in spite of everything that was crowded into it, including the large table and a second iron-framed child's bed, it seemed to me perfectly well-kept in comparison with so many other country kitchens I'd seen that morning. I told her so and she thanked me with a somewhat timid smile.

She stood facing the door; the outside light illuminated her face. She had regular but not very clearly defined features, milky white skin, light blue eyes and pale blonde hair. Her neck was thin, her shoulders narrow, and under the linen smock her whole body looked frail and weightless.

She waited for me to speak, still smiling shyly at me; her smile was full of an unexpected grace, but in it there was something worn and forced—a deep sadness which was underlined by the blue circles under her eyes and the wrinkles that marked the corners of her lips and her eyes.

327

"Exhaustion and possible anemia," I thought. "I ought to take a blood count."

Around the table the five children, bursting with so much energy that their curiosity couldn't restrain them for long, began the racket again. The young woman tried to make them be quiet but she didn't succeed, so she ordered them to go out and play so the noise they made wouldn't interfere with my listening to their little brother with a stethoscope.

The next to youngest one was perched on a high chair. She put him on the floor, pulled a handkerchief out of her apron pocket to wipe a few noses, tucked a few shirt tails back in place as they passed by, and all the children went out, shoving each other and laughing and looking back as they left.

Once the door was closed again, she explained to me quietly:

"My youngest is going on eight months. He's had diarrhea and a little fever for three days. First I thought he was teething. Then I started to worry because the diarrhea didn't stop."

We went closer to the little bed. The child was well built and his rosy skin glowed with health. He was awake, playing with his tiny feet. As I asked my questions and began my examination, I glanced around in search of the milk pan and the bottle that I so often find all covered with flies. I didn't see anything. I was puzzled, so I asked the mother which brand of condensed milk she was using:

"I'm breast feeding him," she answered.

I continued my examination, a little less worried now, since it wasn't a question of the milk.

I made her show me the last diapers and I went through all the rites that were likely to soothe her worry. I examined the stool thoroughly—even sniffing it. Then I filled out a prescription, explaining that it was only a simple indisposition, quite certainly brought on by teething and the heat.

She looked calmer, and shyly happy at my explanation.

When I gave her the prescription, I said:

"And do keep breast feeding the child for as long as the heat lasts. That's his best protection against a serious digestive upset."

The mother nodded her head, but when I noticed how pale she was and saw all the marks of tiredness that were so clearly written on her face, I felt overwhelmed with

328

pity for her and ashamed to force her to do anything demanding.

I asked: "It isn't too hard for you to keep feeding this big boy?"

"Oh, mam'selle, if it's necessary . . ."

She looked serious. Her face showed both her acceptance of the burdens of motherhood, however painful, and her hope that they wouldn't crush her in the end. But suddenly her thin, somewhat unformed face became hard and taut, and she exclaimed with a look of fierce resolution:

"I'll breast feed as long as I have a drop of milk!"

I must have looked astonished because she said, suddenly excited:

"I'll feed him as long as I have the milk so I won't get pregnant again."

She stood straight and determined for a few seconds, so enraged that I was startled. Then she asked, in a hoarse voice that showed how worried she was:

"As long as you breast feed, you can't get pregnant, can you?"

She looked so hopeful and so worried that I didn't have the courage to completely disenchant her.

"In most cases, yes, certainly . . . But this doesn't mean you shouldn't take certain precautions just to be sure."

She didn't seem to hear me. I could see the merciless terror in her face. In a toneless voice, as if she were talking to herself, she began talking without even looking at me.

"I'm twenty-six. I got married at seventeen. When I was twenty, I already had two children. Today I have six. I always said I wanted several children because I was an only child and I know, as they say around here, that 'if you have one child, you have no child.' But six children in eight years is too much—it's just too much for me! I'm getting nervous and irritable. Young healthy children are active; they always make noise, especially in the winter when they're cooped up in two rooms. I lose my patience over every little thing. I slap them, and they look at me without understanding that I can't go on any more, that I'm done in. Never a minute of rest! There's always work, especially because of the little ones. But I love them; I do my best to bring them up right, to keep them clean, to see that they don't lack anything. When it's too hard, when I'm really exhausted from it all, I look at them and just seeing them happy and healthy gives me the courage to go on."

She spoke with her eyes wide open, staring straight in front of her as if she were talking in a void. I stood still, almost frightened by this woman who was no older than I, but who'd already had such a hard life. She spoke in a mechanical monotonous voice; and her eyes were lifeless; they only brightened when she talked about her children. But as soon as she was finished, she looked so unbearably exhausted again that I half turned my head away. For a moment her hands trembled, then in a voice dulled by her troubles, she revealed her terrible secret to me:

"If I have another child right away, I'll throw myself into the pond."

She uttered this sentence without raising her voice, in the sweet tone of a well-behaved little girl. It was unspeakably more frightening than any outburst of emotion could have been. I was silent, too upset to think of a reasonable argument against her resolve to commit suicide, such a horrible idea, and expressed with such pathetic serenity.

I looked around, searching for something to use to help persuade her she was wrong. My eyes fixed on her wedding picture. It sat in the place of honor on the sideboard in an ugly gilt frame: the Lemailleux couple as they were nine years ago—he, a little self-conscious in his wedding suit, a handsome dark young man who looked well-pleased with himself; she, frail and blonde, hardly more than a girl, dressed in a gray suit with the simple white veil of brides of modest means, leaning confidently on her husband's arm in a way that expressed all the freshness of a trusting heart.

The young woman followed my glance and explained:

"I was seventeen. At that age, you believe in love. I was sure that we'd have a good life together, and that I'd be happy."

She sighed, as if she were looking back over the experience and the disillusionments of a very long life instead of nine years of marriage. She continued totally discouraged:

"My husband is a good man. He makes a decent living—he's a mason. He brings all his pay home. He doesn't drink; well, not too much because in the construction business, you know, it's hard not to drink at all: you're always being dragged along. Except for Saturday, he comes straight home after his job every night. He takes

330

care of the garden, he cuts grass for his rabbits, he putters around the house or else he listens to the radio and then he sits down for dinner. He likes the kids—he plays with them and makes toys for them with old cans and bits of wood. But he doesn't do anything to help me. I guess housework isn't for men."

I thought: "No. Making children one after another, that's their work!" And without realizing that I was being cruel, I said bitterly:

"And of course, he refuses to take precautions?"

She shrugged her shoulders in resignation.

"When we were first married, he made love to me whenever he felt like it and I was happy; I always enjoyed it. But I had a painful pregnancy with the third one and the delivery was very hard, and Dr. Ferrières said to my husband: 'You'll have to take precautions!' but he didn't say how. My husband tried to withdraw. You know, mam'selle, that's very hard for a passionate man! That didn't work and I had my fourth right away. So he got discouraged, and he began again without taking any precautions, just like before, especially on Saturday night, since he drinks a little with his friends and comes home excited. Then I tremble when he goes to bed; I pretend to have work to do so that I can go to bed after him, or else I pretend to be asleep so that he won't touch me. Afterwards, all night long I'm afraid one of the children will cry and wake him up. Luckily, he's a heavy sleeper. I can get up several times during the night and he doesn't even notice. . . ."

Several times as she talked, she'd squinted from sheer weariness, as if even her eyes were giving way along with the rest of her body. But she just looked sad; there was no protest in her eyes . . . she accepted her troubles complete-ly. Then, as if she were finally voicing the full extent of her misery, she added with a half-submissive, half-desperate air:

"I can't go on, mam'selle. I'd like to be an old woman so I wouldn't have to be afraid when he touches me. I still love my husband, but I couldn't care less now if he deceived me with anyone. I'd accept anything as long as he leaves me alone. What do I get out of it? Every time, I'm so scared I'll get pregnant that I lie in his arms like a piece of ice or a log. Then later, when I'm expecting my period, I watch and watch . . . I can't think about anything else. I have nightmares—I dream that I'm bathing in blood and when I wake up; nothing. . . ."

Her terror of pregnancy was an almost physical fear—her voice trembled and her eyes were full of tears. I felt touched to the quick, and I hoped she understood how much I wanted to help her. She spoke again in that toneless voice:

"What can I do, mam'selle, so I won't have more children?"

Despite the sound of tragic appeal in her voice, there was something childish in the way she asked me, as if what she was asking didn't seem quite nice to her or was somehow improper. She immediately said, naïvely:

"I'd never dare ask Dr. Ferrières. The doctors say that you shouldn't have more children, but they never explain how to go about it. But you're a woman doctor. If there were a lot of lady doctors, then people would probably be able to talk about it easier and things would be better."

Her forehead wrinkled, her face tensed up and she asked nervously:

"You know what I mean?"

"Yes, of course," I said sympathetically.

She smiled painfully and said:

"Tell me how the other women do it. In Mesnil, lots of them get abortions. But I've never wanted . . . An abortion is bad; it's a sin. But if you already have six children, trying not to have any more can't be a sin, can it?"

For a few seconds I couldn't answer her. Her question came from the depths of her soul.

I took her by the shoulders and told her:

"It's your absolute right to have only the children you desire. I promise you that I'll come by this evening or tomorrow to explain the methods other women use."

Her lips had been pinched and bitter. But I'd hardly finished speaking when she sighed happily and her eyes shone with joy. She exclaimed, as if I were all-powerful and she were already saved:

"Oh! Thank you, mam'selle. I knew that you'd listen to me. . . ."

Her pale cheeks suddenly flushed with hope.

On the path, the children were playing near the car. They drew back to let me get in and I patted a few sweet little tousled heads as I went past, and when I started off the smallest one waved his hand, raising two enthusiastic, sweet blue eyes to mine.

When I went back through Mesnil the clock on the front of the town hall showed twenty past one. They were probably waiting for me for lunch. I speeded up.

Just as I was pulling up in front of the Ferrières' house, the door opened and Vincent stepped out on the doorstep. He was seeing out a man in blue working clothes who had a bandaged hand.

As soon as the man had left, Vincent came over to me with a big smile. When I started apologizing for being late, he kindly put me at ease at once.

"It doesn't matter at all! Besides it gave me time to take care of that man. He was injured at work."

He took the kit from my hands.

"Here, let me take that for you! Don't stay out in the sun. . . . Come on in. . . ."

In the foyer, he added:

"I have to thank you for making house calls for me this morning."

He smiled gratefully, as if he had no doubt it was really my idea. I was about to tell him I didn't deserve his thanks, but I didn't want to betray Catherine.

Vincent went to put the case in his office and came back at once. He took my hands in a friendly way and asked:

"These ten days haven't tired you out too much? You haven't had too many sleepless nights or difficulties? You'll have to tell me all about it as soon as you've caught your breath."

He looked at me carefully to see exactly how tired I was. His eyes were shining with affectionate curiosity as if the patients, the uncertainties, the worries and the watchful nights I'd been through had unexpectedly created a kind of luminous intimacy between us; a sort of professional brotherhood. I smiled too, welcoming his frank concern. From that moment on, I was sure that the news Jacques and I had to tell him would be received without disapproval or narrow-mindedness and that when he saw how happy we were his somewhat Puritanical rigidity would disappear.

Suddenly Vincent cried:

"Here I am keeping you chatting and you must be dying of hunger."

He called upstairs, "Jacques, hurry! Lunch is ready!"

Jacques called down, "At your orders, captain!" then he gave an imitation of a bugle call.

Vincent shrugged his shoulders.

"Always the same! At half-past twelve he was still asleep. I hope that he hasn't been too insufferable these past ten days."

The look that Vincent gave me was so calm, so warm and so kind that I was tempted for a second to tell him everything right away but I held myself back so I wouldn't be disobeying Jacques' orders. I said:

"Oh, no! Jacques has been a charming companion."

But it seemed to me that when I said Jacques' name my voice had given me away; it sounded loving despite myself, so I went into the dining room so Vincent wouldn't see that I was blushing.

During the past ten days, Catherine had been putting our two table settings side by side. Today, Jacques' was on the other side of the table, and mine was next to Vincent's. You could recognize Vincent's place by a color-ful heap of pharmaceutical brochures—Catherine had forewarned me that he had the bachelor's habit of glanc-ing at mail between mouthfuls, not wanting to waste any time.

In my honor, Vincent took the heap of brochures and put them on the sideboard without even looking at them, just as Jacques came in, freshly shaven, elegant and grace-ful. He said from the door:

"I thought they would call us to soup with the sound of the bugle. . . ."

Vincent was near the door. Jacques gave him a military embrace as he passed him, then he came toward me and announced in the most natural tone:

"Today is a holiday, so I'm kissing Claude."

And leaning toward me, he brushed my cheek with a kiss.

For an instant I saw a happy, laughing, carefree, youth-ful face very close to mine, like a movie close-up. I was about to close my eyes, to press myself against Jacques and cling to his lips. But he'd already drawn back and since his back was to Vincent, he gave me a loving smile with his lips and his eyes. Immediately it reminded me of our secret.

We sat down.

Lunch started off somewhat gratingly. Jacques kept telling stories about military infirmaries and the soldiers who had cunningly tricked his father and made a mockery of the military health service.

Vincent was eating quietly, totally absorbed in his meal. He didn't answer—it was as if he were listening to an old friend's completely boring recollections. The conversations between the two cousins at mealtime are usually dull anyway, partly because of Vincent's lack of humor but mainly because their lives had been too far apart for the last ten years for them to be able to find anything in common now. So they finally stop trying to talk, Jacques because he doesn't care, Vincent because of his natural quietness.

Catherine announced when she brought in the roast that the waiting room was almost full already.

Vincent looked at his watch, and said to his cousin:

"Why don't you eat your lunch instead of holding us all up with your stories? Besides it'll make you gain weight. You need it. . . . If you've talked like this for ten days, it's understandable that you're still so thin. . . ."

This time there was real annoyance in his voice. He leaned over his plate again and began to eat in a hurry—since his patients were waiting for him, he immersed himself in his daily world of work and discipline without hesitation.

Vincent had been so clearly irritated that I threw Jacques a pleading glance across the table, hoping that he'd shut up or at least talk about something else besides his father's medico-military misadventures. But he continued with his banter and answered my repeated looks with amused winks.

I began to smile. Feeling that he had his audience well in hand, Jacques redoubled his mimicry. His face was animated and his eyes sparkled. Seeing him so relaxed and happy, I suddenly thought of the attacks of crazy laughter that would come over us in the convertible, almost as often as the desire to kiss each other. Remembering this, I had the feeling of guilt shared with Jacques in the most marvelous of sins. I felt myself going red with pleasure and without realizing it, carried away by the irresistible happiness of my accomplice in sin, I threw back my head in a long easy laugh, in a joyful burst of intimacy and amorous triumph.

But while I was looking at Jacques, I could tell that Vincent had turned toward me in surprise at my triumphant laugh. His eyes were scrutinizing me, as if this time something had just alerted him to a decisive change in my relationship to his cousin. I was ashamed that I hadn't been able to keep our secret until the exact time chosen by Jacques, and I applied myself with downcast eyes to peeling a piece of peach at the end of my fork.

Catherine came in just then and announced to the doctor:

"The police sergeant wants to see you. He came by twice this morning with some papers for you to sign. I asked him to wait in the foyer."

Vincent put his napkin on the table and got up, saying:

"You can serve the coffee. I'll be back in a minute."

As soon as Catherine had left for her kitchen and Vincent for his policeman, I asked Jacques:

"Why are you bothering your cousin like that when we have such important things to tell him?"

Jacques shrugged his shoulders carelessly.

"When I'm happy, I like to make fun of others a little. And Vincent exasperates me when I see him so constrained and so unimaginative. Besides, if I weren't making any jokes, then he'd really be surprised and he'd wonder what I'm concealing."

Then he said abruptly:

"Not too sad, my darling, at the end of the night and this morning, when you were all alone? I wanted so much to be near you again."

He smiled tenderly.

"We'll have to do something for fun this afternoon to make up for it. If you're free, we could go to Evreux, and if we leave early enough we could even get to Deauville or the Cabourg. We'll go swimming."

I'd already stopped thinking about Vincent and the somewhat difficult thing that we'd have to tell him. I was on the road with Jacques. . . . Evreux? Deauville? Cabourg? What did it matter to me! Whatever he decided would be perfect. I was ready to obey his smallest whim with pleasure, the way I tried to understand what he wanted at the slightest hint when we were making love.

I smiled at the coming night of happiness and love. To love without fear, to surrender oneself to joy in body and soul! . . . But suddenly I thought of my last house call, of the young mother's face haunted by the fear of another pregnancy. I couldn't imagine an entire life spent without the pleasure of love because of the ignorance or the selfishness of your partner.

I looked at Jacques, the attentive, wonderful lover, and I was pierced with such violent happiness that when I thought of the desperate hell the frigid woman lives her life in, I was ashamed to be so satisfied.

Now that Vincent was back, I felt it was my responsibility, as a doctor and as a woman, to talk to him immediately about the ignorance of sex matters that I'd found among his patients. But, I thought, why not ask Jacques first about the best way to broach this delicate subject with his cousin?

So I told him about my visit to Mme Lemailleux and said that I thought a real course in sex education was needed to add a little harmony to the love life of a good many of the couples in Mesnil.

"In the courses, they could explain the physiological side of the sex act, the psychological, physical and moral responsibility of each partner and, of course, they could point out the various methods that would enable the woman to have complete freedom to decide whether or not she wanted a child."

Jacques was daydreaming when I began and, as he listened, he began to nod his head with an air of abstracted approval.

"They should plan a course in sex education for young people too, because their families" (I thought of little Maria's mother) "are usually incapable of talking tactfully about things like that, and they're usually content to let their children think that anything having to do with sex is shameful. It's stupid and it can really be harmful."

As soon as I'd finished, Jacques looked as if he wanted to think seriously about my speech for a minute, but he couldn't keep a straight face for long and burst into a hearty laugh. Then he explained the reason for his hilarity:

"Ah! These young women full of apostolic zeal for the happiness of their sex! And five minutes ago, you were reproaching me for teasing Vincent too much when I was about to announce serious things to him! He'll think your idea of starting sex education courses in Mesnil is a thousand times crazier than what we have to tell him. . . ."

He sat up in his chair.

"First of all, why do you think the young people in Ouche are so ignorant? When I was twelve or thirteen years old, during my vacation in Mesnil, my little playmates taught me as much as I could learn. At the age of fifteen they'd already eagerly begun their practical labors and the girls seemed to be well satisfied. Why give them lessons? We're not in the time of Daphnis and Chloe any more. Besides, instinct is the best teacher. Rats who've been isolated since birth behave like experienced adults at the opportune moment without any lessons."

I was a little irritated by his skepticism.

"What's true for rats isn't true for men; and since you've read Valensin, you must know about that experiment they performed with mentally defective adolescents. When they're put in the presence of willing young women, they rub against them and sometimes they even ejaculate, but they have no idea that there's anything else to it. Yet—they managed to discover ways of feeding themselves without any help. If you'd listened to what I've heard from women in Gennevilliers, you wouldn't doubt that the mysteries, lies and inhibitions that narrow-minded parents impose on their children have catastrophic effects on the entire course of their sexual lives. For most educators and families sex education consists of suppressing sexuality, just like the Bantus deny sex by cutting off their little girls' external genital organs. It's heartbreaking."

Jacques laughed.

"Don't get angry! I'll leave the children to you: all you have to do is to come to an agreement with your great friend, the teacher; she certainly owes you that. But I'm still skeptical about sex education for adults. The French are individualistic by temperament, and they don't like a third party intruding into a domain where they think they have nothing to learn, since they all think they're great champions. To them, erotic improvisation is one of the most beautiful expressions of the genius of our people—a kind of national sport where we are unrivaled."

"Even the peasants in Ouche?"

"Oh! as for them, they do their male 'duty' conscientiously, they satisfy and impregnate their partners with the generosity of young bulls. But you can't ask much more of them than an uncultivated eroticism that fully satisfies them and has the additional enormous advantage, as far as they're concerned, of being a cheap pleasure, if not free. They remind you of certain rudimentary species where everything is summed up in the reproductive organs. To think of giving them a sex education is a real fantasy. . . ."

"And in your opinion, it's impossible to inject a little brain extract into their genital glands?"

Jacques looked dubious.

338

"Even outside of your agricultural laborers do you think there are many couples who are really preoccupied with enriching their sex life? Your adult courses wouldn't be attended by many people, and in any case, certainly not by those who need them most. I'm sure that's what Vincent would tell you, if he weren't too amazed to say anything."

"I'd say that that's too easy an argument, and that it's misleading to deprive several million couples who aren't indifferent or backward of the opportunity of getting information and advice under the pretext that most of the people who need sex education and birth-control information are incapable of profiting from it."

Then I had an idea. "Once I get to that point in my argument, why not let it drop to Vincent that I wouldn't have had to do a therapeutic abortion if Simone Vallin had had spermicidal jelly and a diaphragm at her disposal when her husband came home on leave? That's how to tell him! What do you think of that?"

I was very pleased but Jacques raised his hand to stop me, as if the idea terrified him.

"Oh, no, Claude. Not right now, and especially not in front of me. I hate to see Vincent in a real crisis and if you drop your little bomb on him, that's just what will happen. It would be awful! . . ."

Then he looked at me with a smile of total innocence.

"Besides, don't forget that I know nothing about all this. . . . You couldn't tell me anything. It's a professional secret! . . ."

Catherine came in bringing a tray with a coffeepot and three cups on it. She was surprised to see us alone. "Monsieur Vincent hasn't come back?"

She looked worried. "His coffee will get cold. What is he doing with the police sergeant for such a long time?"

"I'm afraid he came to arrest him," Jacques answered, very seriously.

"Sweet Jesus! Why?"

Jacques assumed a sorrowful and confidential look.

"Don't say anything, but Vincent has taken the key to the Mourmelon rifle range, and he refuses to give it back."

She looked so confused that he added very quickly, laughing:

"I'm only joking. Don't worry! But what *is* true is that your pear tarts have been a wonderful success today.

We've been feasting on them." He said coaxingly: "It's well known that yours are the best in the whole country of Ouche. You should give Claude your recipe."

At such a compliment from her "baby," Catherine turned quite red, pulled herself up proudly, and began explaining the ideal proportion of flour, butter, eggs, salt and pears to me.

"Well," Jacques said, "with all of this Claude will have good pear tarts, just like everybody else's. But what's your very own special secret?"

Catherine suddenly looked as mysterious and impressive as a village witch. She finally said, "Well mam'selle, the pears are often hard, so they take longer to cook than the rest. To make them nice and soft, you have to cook them a little first in a little bit of sugar water, before you put them in the oven."

I listened breathlessly, my heart pounding. I could only smile to thank her, because my emotion kept me from speaking. Jacques' words, "You should give Claude your recipe," were ringing in my ears. Those words were a promise: if Jacques wanted me to know how to make the pear tarts he adores, it was because he was going to make me part of his life in the future. And at the thought, my heart jumped violently in my chest. . . .

Noises from the foyer. Vincent was seeing the police sergeant out. Catherine patted the belly of the coffeepot with the back of her hand and, once she was sure that it wasn't too cold, left for the kitchen again. The doctor's hurried step sounded on the tiles. Almost at once the door opened brusquely and Vincent came into the dining room.

I sat in my seat and I didn't even turn my head to look. His return made no difference to me. I was looking at Jacques as if he were the only man in the world. But Vincent said sharply to his cousin, "I have to speak to Claude. Leave us alone!"

The tone of his voice startled me. It was harsh and hollow, shaking with ill-contained rage. I lifted my eyes toward him in surprise. Never had I seen his features so tense and hard.

Jacques got up nonchalantly and went slowly toward the door. As he left, he said lightly to me, as if he was only giving in to Vincent to keep the peace, "Okay. I'll be in the garage."

Vincent went to the window and slammed it shut, then

walked back toward me aggressively. He seemed afraid that he might get violent. He grabbed the back of his chair and his grip was so tight that his skin turned white at the knuckles.

I watched him in amazement. What had happened during the talk with the police sergeant? His features were unrecognizable. A vertical vein pulsed in his pale forehead, his lips were trembling and his eyes were fixed harshly on me. Where was the face that had looked at me with such affectionate attention only a little while ago? There were a few seconds of painful silence in the dining room—obviously the calm before the storm. Instinctively, I had stood up to wait for what was coming. I was a little nervous; I felt my heart beat faster. Vincent finally said harshly:

"The police sergeant who just left has informed me about a rumor that's been circulating in Mesnil for the last few days, that you performed an abortion on Simone Vallin. What do you have to say for yourself?"

"Oh, so that's it," I thought with relief. I was almost happy to see it come to a head by itself. I smiled. Doubtless Vincent, already irritated by Jacques' jokes, thought I was mocking him.

"It's yes, isn't it?" he said bitterly. "I was sure of it. You did a thing like that to one of my patients, with my instruments, while I was away. And when I got back and was open and trusting with you, you didn't even have the courage to let me know. . . . I had to learn about it from a policeman! I didn't think that you were capable of deceiving me like that. It makes me think that Jacques' deceitfulness is contagious. By the way, the police sergeant also told me that you two have been seen everywhere in the red convertible for the past four days."

If Vincent had accused only me, I would probably have hung my head and tried again to make him understand my reasons for my action and then I would have humbly asked him to forgive me. But what right did he have to accuse Jacques, especially since he'd made him leave the room? What right did he have to accuse him so freely of deceitfulness when Jacques had only put off our confessions out of tactfulness, so Vincent wouldn't have to face it as soon as he got home? I reacted immediately against his accusation. It was too unjust. I decided to defend both of us.

"If the police in Mesnil are so well informed," I said

acidly, "they must have told you that Jacques wasn't with me the night of the *therapeutic* abortion."

"Exactly. On August 12 you were with Simone Vallin from nine-thirty to midnight, and your drives with Jacques didn't begin until the next day."

"I didn't know that I was being watched, or rather spied on, to that degree. But how could they know that I operated on Simone Vallin? Nobody even knew that she was pregnant."

"Nobody knew ... except the neighborhood gossips who always keep an eye out for the linen napkins drying on the clothesline in the garden behind the schoolhouse every month, and who didn't fail to notice the laundries that followed your lengthy evening with the teacher. That was enough to make your little tricks—such as leaving the car a hundred yards away from the school and carrying my big emergency kit that everyone around here recognizes—totally useless. Before you perform your next village abortion, you should know that the number of eyes watching you is incredible and that if it interested me, I could get precise information, hour by hour, about everything you've done since I left."

Vincent's voice was heavy with irony. He was obviously trying to make me look ridiculous. But suddenly it was he, with his awkward sarcasm, who seemed ridiculous to me, and stubborn, and narrow-minded—just the way Jacques had always described him to me. I was furious.

"Well! The next time I decide that it's just and necessary to perform a therapeutic abortion, they won't be able to accuse me of dissimulation or deceit. I'll do it openly to set a good example for the Pharisees of the Medical Board, for all those worthy doctors with clean hands and peaceful consciences who would rather abandon a young mother to the abortionist's knitting needle and ignore the dangers they're exposing her to than do anything about it. Absolute respect for life! Those words are meaningless when *you* say them. And when you talk, one can tell that you're falling back in admiration before your own moral purity. What wonderful board members you all are, hiding behind your conventions and traditional morals, behind the conformity of a code that's been fixed since the time of Hippocrates, and that's really only an alibi to hide your lack of courage. You don't have guilty consciences— everything in them is catalogued as neatly and as efficiently as your ethical code and your files! The elimination of an inch-long fetus that's been exposed to German measles—a poor larva most likely deformed and hideous—you can't contemplate that, but every minute all over the world, there's a toll of thousands of lives—young pregnant women who could have been saved if they'd had medical help, and could later have had beautiful children. . . ."

Vincent was still watching me silently. He looked so impassive and judgelike that I got really furious.

"You've chosen the easy side to fight on, the side of abstractions and principles. But I've chosen to help the victims, because I refuse to accept the idea that the happiness of the human species should be founded on the unhappiness of women. In the last analysis, it took more courage for me to perform the abortion on Simone than it took you to refuse it. It's so much easier to obey the rules of the Medical Board and, in the name of your fanatical 'respect for life,' let all the injustices around us go on without doing a thing."

Vincent interrupted. "Have you thought about what might happen to you if this comes to court?"

It was a direct hit, and it threw me for a second. I knew that the law prohibits and penalizes an abortion performed for German measles, but I'd never really thought that a prosecutor or a lawyer or all those men in black might be mixed up in this some day, because my action seemed so legitimate to me. The question Vincent had put to me suddenly made me face my "crime": what I was risking was arrest, judicial inquiry, the scandal of a trial before a criminal court, a long prohibition to practice, even jail. . . . My heart began to pound, my knees were wobbly. I almost fell back into my chair and begged Vincent for a few minutes' grace. But he was watching me with such a hard, inquisitorial look that I was ashamed of my weakness and I tried to draw on all my resources of courage to defy him. I clenched my fists. Breathlessly, I pulled myself up and found just enough strength to shout, "Keep your threats to yourself. I'm not afraid."

Vincent shrugged his shoulders and said in the same hard, impersonal voice, "Did you stop to think before you did it that you have involved me and that I would be mixed up in the scandal if it ever came to court?"

"So that's it," I said to myself. "The virtuous Dr. Ferrières is really afraid for his reputation and his post on the Medical Board!" I was so relieved that I breathed deeply again. A comforting wave of scorn put me back on

343

my feet again. At least I had guts! I'd been able to do something exemplary and remain true to myself. I felt secure; I saw myself again as the clear-headed courageous girl who stands out among fools and cowards. I looked insolently at Vincent. I felt like throwing everything that Jacques had told me under the apple tree in his face: that rules, codes, and morals have been set up for poor souls like him, who have no critical sense, and not for free spirits who can decide for themselves what's good and what's bad. The thought that I'd discovered love and Jacques' moral worth the same evening made me suddenly want to bait and humiliate his pitiful cousin. I didn't have to search for a cutting phrase. It came all by itself.

"Bravo! I know what you're afraid of! But you don't have to worry—if it comes to court, I'll have the dignity, and the kindness, to take all the blame."

Vincent's face went white, his jaw clenched, and he moved as if he wanted to throw himself on me. But he finally mastered himself and said, "I won't go into your arguments a second time. Your romanticism and individualism are far too simplistic. A few more years of medical experience will show you that the apparent harshness of a moral law is the only safeguard of human happiness as a whole; and a medical act like yours can only be judged if it is considered as it is in reality—not taken as an isolated instance, but given its place in the network of facts that each affect each other. Then it's a different matter. You think you're very brave, but if this tiny fetus you curetted had been a newborn baby, and even if he were deformed or crippled, if you'd held him in your hands for a moment, warm and breathing, if you'd seen his little limbs move, if you'd heard him cry, would you have been able to strangle him or tear him limb from limb? Once when I was twelve years old, I found a cat near a pond that some children had been torturing for fun. She was almost dead; her eyes had been put out, and bloody foam was coming from her mouth. I decided to drown her to end her suffering, but when I plunged her into the water, she found the strength to resist for a while. For a long time I felt her little body fighting desperately for life in my hands, and for weeks the idea of her terror made me sick with horror, with instinctive and overwhelming horror. . . ."

Vincent stopped for a moment. He was obviously shaken. He put his right hand through his hair, as if chasing away a painful memory, and I realized it was trembling a little. He pulled himself together and continued a little dryly.

"You only had what you proudly call 'courage' because you were working in the darkness of the womb, in the shadow, in blackness, and because you performed your little murder blindly, without knowing anything about your victim, without even seeing it. It couldn't cry out, or beg for mercy, or plead for its right to live. Think about the news stories in the papers—besides the dangerous holdups, there are the easy jobs done by bands of crooks who attack women alone, or old people at night. Do you know what they call them? 'The gang of cowards. . . .' Your 'brave' abortion is just that: an armed attack against a defenseless innocent. . . ."

I listened in amazement. I couldn't believe my ears. Did Vincent really dare to call me conceited and cowardly? Did he want to deny me the merit of something I'd done not out of pride, but because of an irresistible urge, because of an almost mystical certainty that it was a decisive act for the liberty of women? I was furious that he understood me so badly. I screamed, "Keep your comparisons to yourself. I'll be able to defend the legitimacy and exemplary worth of my act before a judge. You must not know that there have been two cases against doctors in England arising from the campaign to reform the abortion law. In 1937 a surgeon gave himself up partly because he couldn't find the anesthetics to perform his therapeutic abortions, and in 1948 two woman doctors declared in court that they would continue to interfere with pregnancies every time that, in good conscience, they found it necessary. I think that I'm brave enough to follow the surgeon's example, and to take the full responsibility for my act, like the two woman doctors."

As I talked, I felt an intoxicating sense of heroism rise in myself. I felt free and strong in my rebellion, even if my fight against male egotism turned out to be hopeless. I said to myself, "It's worthless to believe in something without doing something to prove it. If necessary, I'll go to the judge myself, like the English surgeon."

I think Vincent could see my determination. He took a menacing step toward me and stared hard at me as if he wanted to choke all my rebellionness out of me. . . . He said furiously, "No. I won't let you play Antigone while the jury looks on. I won't let some unscrupulous lawyer make headlines because of you, and get publicity for himself by mocking medical morality in court. I'll keep you from causing a scandal at any price."

Vincent looked so enraged that I almost felt calm again. I smiled and said, "You're afraid of a trial because of the same hypocrisy and cowardice you accuse me of. Because you know that I'm right. Because, even though it's unusual, my trial will make the problem of abortion for German measles public, so it will be a precedent that the Medical Board will have to take into consideration in the future. You can come to court to contradict me on the day of the hearing. Then I'll answer and you'll have to listen to me. . . ."

He wanted to slap me, I could tell. But he crossed his arms on his chest and said angrily, "Shut up. You're crazy. Completely crazy. Do you realize that your decision won't just involve you, but Simone Vallin too? She'll be sitting on the same bench as you between two policemen. Because of lack of judgment, because of a delusion (even if it is generous), you would creat chaos, confusion, and a catastrophic tempest of such dimensions that no one could guess the consequences beforehand."

"That's really it. No scandal; above all, no scandal. The truth isn't important. It's always the same hypocritical cant, the same taboos. And all the while, let the women manage by themselves, and die of it!"

"Don't be crazy. It's not the intention that counts, but the consequences of what you do. If we didn't have what you fanatically call taboos, the whole structure of morality would crumble and society would be back in the jungle, where only the strongest survive."

Jacques was right. What a dangerous idiot he was, this poor man, with his stubborn moralism and his narrow ideals. And he dared to accuse me of fanaticism! I just laughed. Vincent looked furiously at me, but I said nothing for a while, just to provoke him. Finally the long silence became painful, so I said impertinently, "I'm beginning to think that we're not made to agree."

As soon as I said it, I was amazed to see Vincent's face suddenly change. He seemed to age in front of my eyes. Something inside him hurt him; he looked tense, and hollow, and somehow tarnished. I didn't understand the reason for his sudden pain, but he showed it with a touching openness. His shoulders seemed bent under an invisible burden. Vincent finally said, in a soft, almost begging voice, as if he had just been deeply wounded, "Do

346

stop this awful farce. Be yourself. Stop playing the part of the persecuted, misunderstood heroine. Do you really need it to make yourself seem more significant in your own eyes? It's vanity that made you think your rebellion came from strength and courage. Don't let yourself be fooled by the power you feel when you do something antisocial, by the vain need to go against the established order at any price. You can see where this perpetual rebellion has led Jacques. I'm sure he pushed you into this."

A minute ago, watching the incomprehensible sadness of his face, I'd been ready to humble myself again. But now, perhaps because the soft, pitying tone of his voice (the sort of voice you'd use to quiet a madwoman) seemed to deny even the courage of my deed, perhaps because of his new attack on Jacques and his allusion to my relationship with him, I had to defy him. His face suddenly looked ridiculous again. I shrugged my shoulders disdainfully.

"If I'm conceited and vain, do you know what *you* are, Dr. Vincent Ferrières? A smug, narrow-minded prig. Truly a pitiable prig."

Vincent went white. He looked at me a moment as if he realized for the first time how useless his effort was. He looked hurt, despairing, and infinitely weary. Then he pulled himself painfully up again, took a deep breath, and recovered an air of true dignity. His look was authoritative again, and when he spoke his voice was calm and deliberate, as usual.

"You have betrayed my trust in you. Therefore, you will do as I say until tomorrow morning. I have the right to that."

I staggered at his first words, as if he had just put a heavy, commanding hand on my shoulder. He took a while to finish gathering his thoughts, then said in an imperious voice that didn't brook refusal, "People certainly saw the police sergeant come to visit me, and they've doubtless guessed the official reason for his call. He assured me that so far there have only been vague rumors. They haven't received an anonymous letter yet—in the country an anonymous letter is the most common way of accusing someone, and a letter would necessarily have triggered an inquiry. This afternoon, you'll take the car and continue your house calls, ostensibly just as always. They know me well enough around here to think that if

347

I'm letting you go on, the rumor must be false, and I'm sure that gossip will stop immediately."

Then, without looking at me again, he turned on his heel and went out, slamming the door behind him.

Alone again in the dining room, I realized that I was frozen with rage; my jaws were clenched, my cheeks were aflame, and I felt totally furious at Vincent, at the horrible anonymous accusers, at the cowardice of the world.

I looked around bewilderedly, and met my face in the mirror above the mantel. I looked furious, and a little ridiculous now that nobody was there. I turned away and my eyes fell on the table. One cup was still half full of coffee, the one that Jacques hadn't had time to finish before he left. I remembered the way he'd left the room with supreme indifference, and I could almost hear the easy way he'd said that he'd be in the garage. He'd looked back at me from the threshold and smiled, and I suddenly knew that he'd said that to me to tell me where I could find him again without his cousin knowing.

I dashed out of the room. In the foyer, the door to the office was closed, but there was a list of house calls in full view on the sideboard near the telephone, and the black bag for town calls. I grabbed the bag and the list without stopping, and ran through the foyer as if Vincent might change his mind and forbid me to go out.

When I got to the sidewalk, the full sun was blinding, but I just blinked and dashed on to the garage. The door was wide open. I could see at a glance that the red convertible wasn't in its place. My disappointment was so violent it almost choked me. I stopped and tried to figure out where Jacques could have gone. I needed him so much that I closed my eyes as if when I opened them, I would miraculously see him coming out of some dark corner, smiling and relaxed, and smelling of grease and gasoline. "Maybe," I thought, "he went to get gas for our trip."

I ran to the little car, jumped in, made a U-turn and charged into the main street, hoping to see the shiny shape of the convertible loom up in front of my modest hood. I drove the length of Mesnil, and only stopped when I got to the gas pump. By chance, the car was almost empty and while the garageman filled it, I had time to glance into the repair shop—no convertible.

I came back to the car, and asked, "Have you seen Monsieur Jacques go by?"

"He stopped here about ten minutes ago to use the phone. Then he took off for Evreux to pick up needle bearings that he ordered from England. He wants to go to the coast today or tomorrow so I told him he might just as well get his two carburetors adjusted in Evreux—they aren't working well." He winked at me, and said as he cleaned my windshield, "You know how it is with women, mam'selle—they always have something inside that doesn't work very well. It's the same thing with sports cars."

I thought a minute: from Mesnil to Evreux and back, one hour; to have the carburetors adjusted, one hour, or maybe two because he hadn't made an appointment. Jacques wouldn't be back till five-thirty, so I had plenty of time to see the patients on my list.

The idea that Jacques was thinking about our trip to Deauville made me happy. I got back into the car and drove off to make my calls.

Never had my rounds seemed as disagreeable or as long. But when I started off, I'd smiled with pleasure when I looked at the list to plan my itinerary. The list was long, and since the calls would involve my automatic medical reactions, they'd keep me busy and also keep me from being alone with myself for three hours. I smiled too, because Vincent's intentions were so clearly expressed on the list: according to the police sergeant, the gossip about me was limited to Mesnil, so Vincent had cut out all visits to the country, forcing me to drive around the town all afternoon. "Why not beat a drum," I thought, "as in a circus parade, or have a town crier announce me around the town, to make certain I'm noticed. Or, since I'm an abortionist, perhaps it would be more appropriate to ring a leper's bell."

The first two house calls were routine. First I saw a little old lady on free medical aid. I found her in her attic room, half deaf, entirely helpless, and at the mercy of a cloud of house flies, who must have been eager for fresh food, because they immediately attacked me. My second patient considered it a waste of his time to sit in the waiting room, so he made me come to him to sign his "reporting for work again" certificate at home. (Oh, the obsession for certificates to be signed all day long, for anything, or even for nothing. In the course of nine months of pregnancy, a certain booklet of social-agricultural maternity insurance provides for no less than

349

one hundred thirty-five doctor's signatures, which consti-
tutes—at least I hope!—a record!)

The third name on my list was Mme Vasse, my mother's grocer, and my first "supporter" among the Mesnil
shopkeepers. She hadn't called on me since the consultation about her fibroid. Had she decided on the operation
as I'd advised her?

It was the quiet part of the afternoon, and Mme Vasse
was doing her accounts behind her cash register. When I
came in, she lifted her head, ready to assume a smile
nicely gauged to the importance of the visitor. When she
saw me, she looked amazed but her lips (the thin, slightly
mustached lips of a thin dark woman in her fifties)
began to relax into a commercial smile. Then her eyes fell
on the medical bag. Immediately her face hardened, and
after a brief pause, she said in the dry tone she uses to
discourage traveling salesmen, "I thought Dr. Ferrières
was back."

Abashed, I beat my retreat, mumbling, "The doctor is
very busy this afternoon. . . . If you think it can wait . . .
I'll tell him to stop by tomorrow."

Back in my car, I tried to understand the reason for her
sudden change in attitude. "Did I forget to greet her
without realizing it? And if that's the reason for my
reception, when did I last go past her shop on foot?" As I
went over my comings and goings, I realized that for the
past two days the town patients had almost disappeared
from my office and my lists of house calls. Only the rural
patients had wanted to see me, but in the happiness of
being with Jacques, I hadn't noticed the almost total
desertion of my city patients. Why had the inhabitants of
Mesnil abandoned me? I thought in vain—I couldn't find
any notorious incident, or any disastrous case they could
have blamed me for during the past two days. There was
only one possibility left: Simone Vallin's abortion. But
why this sudden hostility? I thought about the various
young girls who'd asked me to "make them have their
periods again," and who I'd refused to help. Were they
angry with me for having done this for the daughter of
Blanchotte and a foreigner—a girl who was an outsider—
when I refused to do it for true natives? Maybe, since the
people of Mesnil wouldn't connect the teacher's pregnancy
with the German measles, they thought it was a criminal
abortion, and were blaming me for destroying an unborn
child for no reason.

As I went on with my other house calls, I became more and more sure that it was a question of typically Norman cautiousness rather than of the respect due to a two-months embryo. Besides, I'd gone over enough medical charts during the past ten days to know that most women in Mesnil get abortions without any great scruples if they don't want to have a child.

In some houses where I'd already treated people, I felt, if not Mme Vasse's dryness, at least a lack of spontaneity and even some reticence. Despite their earlier gratitude, these families wanted to stay neutral; they probably thought that they were showing thanks enough by not immediately taking sides against me. With others, I didn't exactly meet ill-will, but just the somewhat cruel curiosity I'd noticed on the evening of the accident at the well. People expressed it by steady or furtive glances, depending on how polite they were. Even if the thing went no further, it would create delicious gossip for discussion in the shops and on the doorsteps. But probably Mesnil expected a public scandal, an inquiry involving police and interrogations and a trial, and who knows, maybe even news stories and pictures in the paper. . . .

In the meantime, they thought it best to be careful. Wouldn't their names in my notebook of house calls or office visits be enough to compromise them? So for the moment the wisest thing to do was to abstain from all contact with the suspect.

I almost stopped my visits at the thought that the maneuver Vincent had dreamed up to cover for me was missing its aim—I was wasting my time going into houses where they obviously would have liked to slam the door in my face. But when I thought about it, it seemed to me that Vincent must know these people much better than I—they were surprised by my unexpected visit this afternoon, so they were on their guard, but doubtless the shift of opinion would come tonight or tomorrow, after a lengthy reflection (nothing happens fast in Ouche) and then my patients would feel reassured because I was vouched for by Vincent's presence and his moral authority.

Besides, it was too late to stop; there were only two more names left on the list. My next to last patient lived in front of the town hall. I stopped my car in the square next to the café, and as I walked along the café terrace, the customers all fell silent and stared at me. Then they must have started talking about me, because when I came back that way ten minutes later they looked at me and made some jokes about me in dialect that I couldn't understand, but they caused enormous hilarity behind my back. I pretended not to hear, but as I got back into the car, I saw that passersby were turning around to look at me. I thought, "I'm really under very close supervision. What will it be like if I have to leave for Evreux between two policemen?"

I smiled as I started up. The idea of leaving Mesnil in the custody of two policemen had just reminded me that though I didn't know where the jail was in Evreux, I did at least already know the courthouse. When I was in boarding school, we'd gone there one Thursday on an outing. Our guide had explained to us that the former great seminary of Eudists (members of the Congregation of Jesus and Mary) had become part of the present law court. We visited the chapel—now the courtroom. The only thing I remembered was a magnificent wooden ceiling, arched like the bottom of an upside-down boat. "Too bad," I thought, "that I didn't look more closely at the box where the accused stands! But now I'm being stupid. If I'm indicted, I won't appear before a jury. They don't bother with magistrates in imposing red gowns any more, or with a solemn setting for a miserable embryo a few inches long and especially not for a woman who's had an abortion and who most often looks so pitiful that she'd be acquitted very quickly by a jury. Because a jury almost never condemns women for having abortions, and why should they condemn someone who seems much more a victim of circumstances than a real culprit?).

Criminal abortions have been judged in a hearing before a judge since 1923. So, no jury for me! It would have been too beautiful: even without a lawyer, an acquittal guaranteed from the start. What member of the jury—the father or mother of a family—could have condemned me for having prevented the birth of a deformed child if he thought about his own home? So, I'll have professional magistrates to condemn me. And they're bound against the promptings of their consciences or their pity by a code that has set punishments which the judge doesn't have the right to go below, as if they wanted to secure him beforehand against his own weakness by imposing injustice on him if need be. Because they're afraid of chaos, like Goethe, or scandal, like Vincent Ferrières, they might

352

even prevent me from speaking. I wouldn't be allowed my high-sounding phrases then. I couldn't proclaim, "My conscience speaks louder than your law," or "I have acted according to my deepest convictions!" No! Precise facts, irrefutable statistics: show that physicians are paralyzed by the law of 1920 which confuses abortion and contraception and end up not even performing as many therapeutic abortions as the law allows them to because they're afraid of being taken for abortionists.

I'd just got to Mme Ancelle's villa. She was the last name on my list. I stopped at the wrought iron gate, and looked at the garden and the house, but I was so involved in my imaginary pleas for my defense, that I hardly noticed what I was looking at. I was still a schoolgirl standing in front of the courthouse in Evreux, lifting my eyes to the pediment and listening to the explanations of our guide: above the portal there had been a heart of Jesus, sculptured a long time ago by the Eudists, whose symbol it was. It had been replaced by the symbols of Themis, goddess of Law. At the age of fifteen I'd listened to all this without thinking it was at all important. Today, as I looked out at the Ancelle villa, I said bitterly to myself, "Putting the code and the sword in place of the heart—what a perfect thing for the door of a courthouse. At least you know what to expect as soon as you get to the door!"

The Ancelle villa is ugly but substantial, very well suited to the widow of a minor industrialist who died shortly after retiring from business.

I pushed open the gate, and the gravel of the path crunched under my feet. I went up the steps to the front door and rang.

An old servant opened the door a crack. Since this was my first visit here, I thought I should announce myself. "I'm Dr. Ferrières' replacement." The maid hesitated, then finally opened the door wide enough to let me into the foyer. She didn't offer me a chair, but said grudgingly, "Wait here. I'll go and see."

She came back in a few minutes. Her eyes gleamed maliciously and announced:

"I couldn't find Madame Ancelle. She isn't home."

She added aggressively, pushing me toward the door:

"The doctor will have to come back!"

I crossed the garden again. I was perplexed: what did this reception mean? And the "doctor who would have to come back," was I being alluded to in the third person, in the best language of stylish chambermaids? This wasn't very likely. So she wanted to consult with Dr. Ferrières after refusing to receive me.

When I got back into the car, I mechanically lifted my eyes to the front of the house. It was in full sunlight. At a window on the second floor, Mme Ancelle, thinking that she was invisible, was savoring my shameful retreat from behind her curtains.

It was impossible to be mistaken about recognizing her: I had seen her only a few days ago. I was in Jacques' car; we were coming home from my round of house calls and we arrived at the church just when mass let out. Jacques stopped to let a middle-aged lady go by; she was dressed in severe black and held a missal in her gloved hand. As she walked by me she swept me from head to toe with a poisonous look, heavy with scornful reprobation.

That morning, disheveled by the wind of our drive, intoxicated with speed, with sun, and with Jacques' kisses, I felt so happy that without really knowing what I was doing, I let out a long peal of joyous laughter behind her thin back. The lady in black must have taken it for insolence.

"That tropical viper—they're the most venomous kind—is Madame Ancelle," Jacques explained. "She's rich, widowed, pious, and teaches evangelic goodness to the little Sunday-school children."

He started up the car and said to tease me:

"After such a virtuously indignant look, you should consider yourself a fallen woman!"

I threw my head back against the seat and laughed again. I didn't feel soiled by any stain on my reputation; on the contrary, I only felt a marvelous inner serenity.

To be happy is an insolence in itself as far as others are concerned. That morning everything proclaimed the fullness of my joy: the way I leaned against Jacques in the car, the possessive way I looked at him, my laughter.

Mme Ancelle has just taken revenge on my insolence by having me turned out by her maid. I thought, "Religion is like one of those miracle drugs that don't automatically save you. Like those drugs, these bigoted old ladies are rarely harmless."

Then I wondered whether it was the teacher's abortion or the freedom of my attitude toward Jacques that had led to my being insulted. During my second visit to the schoolhouse, Simone Vallin had said in her blind rage that people were gossiping. At the time, it was pure calumny and I'd felt myself blush with shame. But now! Always running around with Jacques and leaving the car ostentatiously in front of his house day and night—I was behaving in the neighbors' eyes like a girl of loose morals. But who had a right to reproach me? Jacques was free and so was I and I didn't care about anyone, except the patients who called on me; and I treated them to the best of my ability. So why all the malicious vigilance? Why the gossip? I should have remembered earlier that it's hard to be a woman and to be independent at the same time, because even though sexual freedom is always recognized as a man's right, it's still not entirely recognized for women by public opinion—a so-called free woman, especially in a little town in the country, is immediately looked on as a profligate, shameless woman. Besides, I didn't know how to hide, or how to be a hypocrite. I haven't followed the rules of the game like other women. What can I complain of?

I looked at my watch: 5:35. Jacques must be back. I must go to him quickly! He'd know how to comfort me for the insults of women like Mme Vasse and Mme Ancelle. Mesnil hostility didn't really matter: I had him! The two of us would face the neighborhood together and, if necessary, we'd even face Vincent and the judges.

When I started up the car, I felt calm again. By Jacques' side I was invincible.

I'd never driven up the main street so fast, trying to find the little red spot at the edge of the sidewalk at the end of the road. Vincent's car was still in front of the house. Perhaps it was hiding Jacques' convertible. I slowed down and passed the big car. The road was empty in front of it. The garage? Also empty. I didn't want to stop in case Vincent might come out, and I was so disappointed that I wouldn't have been able to say a thing to him. Where was Jacques? For a few seconds I thought he might have had an accident. But no. They would have notified his cousin immediately and he would have left in his car. ...

I drove on for about two hundred yards, then stopped and sadly made a U-turn. When I passed in front of the house again, I had an idea: the needle bearings! Jacques may have stopped at the garage on his way back from

Evreux. I drove back the length of Mesnil. The garage-man was busy pumping gas. I asked:

"Did you deliver my message?"

He looked up and answered politely:

"I haven't seen anyone, mam'selle."

I drove on. For a moment I thought of driving all the way to Evreux. I only had to drive straight on. . . . I was on the right road. The last houses of Mesnil were coming up. No. I wouldn't go any farther. I would look as if I were chasing Jacques. He'd take me for a silly little girl without any will power. Just at the edge of town, I turned around. About ten yards ahead on the right, I saw the entrance to a small lane; when I got to it I recognized the Perrée path. Instead of driving around aimlessly,why not stop for a few moments with Mme Lemailleux? . . .

As I turned into the lane, I saw the Lemailleux children playing in the middle of the road. I honked the horn. They scattered, leaving some household junk that they had made into toys on the road. But as soon as they recognized me, they started to run toward the garden fence, shouting:

"Mama! Mama! Here's the lady doctor!"

Having done their duty, they came back to the car with the innocent curiosity of childhood. The oldest stretched out his hand ceremoniously and all the others, after him, wanted to have their hand shaken, even the smallest, the tousled little redhead who refused to let go of me and proudly conducted me to the door.

When I entered the garden with my escort jumping and shouting happily around me, Mme Lemailleux left the shed where she was doing her laundry. She greeted me happily.

"I knew that you'd come back, mam'selle. I've been expecting you all afternoon."

I was a little ashamed to think that if Jacques had been back when I thought he would be, she would have had to wait for me until tomorrow morning. Before she ushered me into the house, she sent the children back out into the lane to play.

"Cars never come by here," she said. "And if they're outside you'll be able to talk to me in peace."

The little redhead didn't want to let go of my hand. He burst into tears. I had to take him in my arms, kiss him and promise that I'd come back and bring him some candy. My promise comforted him; he smiled at me and left after lifting his eyes to me one last time—the same trusting eyes his mother had welcomed me with.

I'd intended to stop for a very short visit, but once we were in the kitchen, with the door closed behind us, I couldn't disappoint her. I knew she'd been thinking about "it" all afternoon—the miraculous technique, the magic product I'd promised to tell her about. Even at the risk of making Jacques wait, I couldn't disappoint her innocent hope.

I asked for some blank paper and a calendar, then I made her sit opposite me at the table. With her two elbows on the oilcloth, she immediately composed herself like an industrious and diligent pupil.

It only took one or two questions to make it clear that my pupil knew nothing about the physiology of reproduction. Her ignorance didn't surprise me because a great number of women are incredibly ignorant about sex. So many of them would come to me, astonished at the fact that they were pregnant because, as they would explain to me ingenuously, they carefully urinated after intercourse to expel all the seed. Mme Lemailleux's knowledge about female organs wasn't much more accurate. As to her notions about contraception, they were more or less limited to the formula: "The man who does not sow his seed will not harvest," and "plowing without sowing" had proved to be impossible for her husband. First I drew some very simple anatomical sketches in the notebook. Then, beginning with physiology, I explained to her the two periods of the menstrual cycle that are separated by ovulation, which is what makes conception possible. Before I went on, I hesitated a moment: should I explain the rhythm method? Because of me, it had been fatal for Mariette, and I knew from other cases that it was only partially effective. She seemed to understand my explanations. At least she would know that there were infertile days every month, and days when the risks of conception are greater and days when it's absolutely necessary to abstain from sexual intercourse.

I took up the post office calendar, which was decorated with a photograph of the port of Concarneau. I was so enthusiastic about making her understand that I almost asked her: "When did your last period begin?" But I remembered in time that she was breast-feeding and probably hadn't menstruated after her last delivery yet. So I picked a random date in August to illustrate my demonstration.

"Let's assume that your period begins on August 6th . . ."

Suddenly I stopped—I had unconsciously picked the first day of my own period. I smiled at the thought of the psychoanalytic conclusions Lachaux would have drawn from my choice. Then I went on again.

"Ovulation could take place between August 16th and August 22nd, and the next period would begin around September 3rd. These dates of August 16-22 are very important because both before and after ovulation the woman in our example can have sexual relations without any danger of getting pregnant."

While I was talking, I crossed off the fertile periods on the calendar. I subtracted three days *before* ovulation because, I explained, the sperm might possibly survive for that length of time, and two days *after* ovulation because the egg might survive for two days after ovulation.

"In our example," I emphasized, "the dangerous period would begin on the 16th and end on the 22nd."

I smiled again, thinking that since my first night with Jacques, it hadn't occurred to me even once that something could very well happen to *me* for lack of precautions. I sat for a few moments with the pencil poised over the date of August 16th: "Tonight," I told myself, "I too will share the main worry of women."

I lifted my eyes. She was looking at me without stirring as if keeping still would help her understand better.

"Calculating like this," I said, "is only effective in preventing conception if the woman is very regular, because you have to calculate *not* on the basis of the period you've just had but on your next period, which would start, in our example, on September 3rd. Unfortunately, it takes very little to make menstruation come sooner or later than it's expected, even for women who are very regular. For example, an emotional crisis, a cold bath, or even a trip can upset the cycle, and if that happens, the calculation I've just made becomes inaccurate. So, to be completely safe, you must abstain from all intercourse for four days both before and after ovulation every month. . . ."

The young woman kept listening in silence. I looked at her. Her face was so pale, and she looked so tired and worn down. . . . At the age of twenty-six, she looked well over thirty. From all I could tell, breast-feeding her new baby after her six pregnancies was exhausting her. If only this sacrifice of her health had been worthwhile, but she could very well become pregnant again while breast-feeding. It was ironic to see this poor woman use the same technique for avoiding a new pregnancy in the middle of the twentieth century as Egyptian women did during the reign of Ramses! She might as well have been using the contraceptive vaginal tampons made of a mixture of honey, soda and crocodile dung that were described in a five thousand-year-old formula found on a papyrus. But what struck me as even more ironic was hearing myself proposing periodic chastity to her as the triumph of modern contraceptive techniques. Why give her false hopes?

"As long as you're breast-feeding," I said, "you can't use this method. We'll talk about it again after you start to menstruate regularly again."

I chose not to explain to her that it would have been easy for me to bring back her periods, but menstruating or not, with a husband who refused to "put himself out" her daily problem would be the same.

But there *was* an answer: female contraceptives—a diaphragm that she could use by herself, maybe without her husband even knowing about it. But how could I tell her that the only method of contraception that would work for her had been forbidden by the odious law of 1920?

How could I explain to her, tired out by her many pregnancies, that in England, Switzerland, Holland and the United States—almost everywhere in the whole world, in fact—women *can* control their fertility, and consequently their happiness; but that in our country, an antifeminist law that was passed to encourage population increase doesn't leave the Frenchwoman any choice between endless pregnancies at the will of her lord and master, or the disaster of repeated illegal abortions?

I was ashamed, almost as if I'd been in favor of the law, instead of being against it both in my heart and in the thesis I'm writing. I said softly:

"If your husband doesn't want to take any precautions, then it's very difficult. There's no method or medicine that you can use by yourself."

Suddenly I thought about "the pill." This would have been a perfect case for it. I was glad that I could at least promise her something. I said:

"A year from now, maybe even earlier, there will be a

pill that will protect you completely. But right now it isn't authorized in France. You'll have to wait. . . ."

She didn't say a word. Her face looked drawn and tired. Two tears appeared at the corners of her eyes. She began to weep silently, her eyes wide open, but unseeing.

What could I do to stop the suffering that she had told me about with such innocent frankness, to stop the way her youth was draining away and her face was going to pieces right under my eyes? I tried to tell her to be patient.

"Just as soon as the pills are on sale, I'll prescribe them for you. It may be only six months from now."

She didn't let me go on. She said very quietly, not rebelliously at all:

"In six months, it will be too late. I'm too tired for another pregnancy. If you can't do anything now, nothing makes any difference to me. . . ."

As she spoke, I thought I could read other words on her lips, words that repeated the horrible threat she'd made that morning: "I'm going to throw myself into the pond."

I'd found out that there are a lot of suicides in the land of Ouche. Men hang themselves, and women drown themselves in spite of their fear of death, and in spite of the strictures of morality. I cried out in horror and pity against this seemingly inevitable disaster.

"And your children, Madame Lemailleux? Who would take care of your children? Who would love them the way you love them? . . ."

She began to tremble. She collapsed on the table and sobbed violently, the way the little blue-eyed redhead would have cried if he'd been told that he'd never see his mother again.

I left the house, feeling utterly miserable. When they saw their mother's swollen red eyes, the children stopped their games and gathered nervously around her. She took the little redheaded boy in her arms. He was overcome with tenderness, and he clasped her neck tightly and covered her face with happy kisses, while she pressed him passionately close to her.

As I drove down the lane, it seemed to me that her despair had shown me the lowest depth of women's suffering. I felt that our conversation had unmasked all the hypocritical words that the law, religion and morality use to cover up the extent and atrocity of the disaster. Of course, there were tragedies that sounded worse than Mme Lemailleux's. I thought of Ginette B., who had let her eight-months-old child starve to death. Ginette B. was twenty-three and crippled in one hand when she found that she was pregnant for the fifth time in five years. She got nothing but abuse from her husband, and no help from those around her. She was depressed and exhausted; she just didn't have the strength to make up those last bottles; but despite the expert testimony of psychiatrists, who concluded that she was not responsible "because of pregnancies coming too close together under adverse conditions," she was nonetheless condemned by the court in Versailles and she bore her fifth child in prison. I thought of Mrs. G., who had gassed herself along with four of her children in Villeurbanne so she wouldn't become a mother for the seventh time, at the age of thirty-six. I thought of Monique D., married at eighteen, mother of four children, forced to share three rooms, one water faucet and one stove with her parents-in-law and her sister-in-law's family. Pregnant for the fifth time, in despair from always being told she was just getting in the way, she locked herself up in her room when she was about to give birth and strangled her newborn baby.

I'd spotted many other cases just as tragic in the papers —I remembered having noted three during the month of May alone.

I was upset by Mme Lamailleux's wan face. The young bride of seventeen had thought that she could make happiness grow by the force of her goodwill, by working, by sacrificing her health, and by continually giving of the inexhaustible treasures of her heart. And perhaps she could have, if all the institutions of society hadn't been in league against her—from her servitude to a selfish husband to the law that lets her struggle blindly against unbearable pregnancies and now keeps me from protecting her effectively against having to have children.

I'd gotten as far as the gas station. The mechanic must have been watching for me to pass by. He waved at the Ferrières house and yelled:

"He just got back . . . I gave him your message. . . ."

I smiled thankfully through the window, and immediately speeded up. Jacques was here! "When I get back," I thought, "I'll ask him for some advice for my new patient. Maybe he'll know how I can get her a diaphragm. And maybe—why not?—he could find me a supply of the pills."

The main street was jammed. I had to slow down in spite of my feverish impatience—Jacques was back and I had so much to tell him. In the middle of town, I even had to stop and let a big truck turn around. I arched myself joyfully against the back of the seat, I stretched, I threw my head back; that was all I could do to free myself a little from the exaltation that bubbled up inside me. To think that love was giving me new strength—and a new soul, too, one that, with the experience acquired in Jacques' arms, would let me understand women better from now on, the way the pleasure I've already felt from love makes me understand the sadness of frigidity.

One of my patients passed by on the sidewalk very close to the car. Luckily she didn't see me. It was the girl who had come to tell me, thinking I might do something for her, that she hadn't menstruated since doing a cold-water laundry. "When I sent her away, did she go to the abortionist? And Alexandra Jumel, had she been able to 'get rid of it' so she wouldn't become an unwed mother? But if she remembers the two miscarriages that ended up at the hospital, maybe she'll decide it's less dangerous to keep her child."

I smiled, remembering the date of August 6th that I'd pointed out on the calendar and the sterile days I'd crossed off one after the other. It was a lucky thing, because it had reminded me that from tonight on I had to take some precautions so I wouldn't run the risk of becoming another Alexandra Jumel. In case of an "accident," people would be sure to say: "She isn't very clever for a medical student. Too bad for her." What a stupid and pitiless condemnation. Just when your whole being yearns for invasion, for surrender, for absolute fusion in possession, you have to "be careful," and that destroys the magic web of caresses, the miracle of a sacred moment and the marvelous spontaneity of love's spell by rational words and actions.

To have Jacques' child—I'd never thought of that before. My love was probably too engrossing, too possessive and too new, for me to have realized that someday I might bear Jacques' child. Did the limitless trust I had in him keep me, against all good sense and medical logic, from fearing anything from such a partner in love?

Alexandra Jumel only knows about love from the most

animalistic coupling and mating; she will become an unwed mother because she yielded to instinct like a cat in heat; and I refuse to accept the social ideas about the preservation and propagation of the species that will force her to keep her child—which is likely to be defective anyway. She makes love like a cat because she isn't capable of doing better; so, logically, she should be able to dispose of the kittens she didn't "want" and was unable to avoid, just like a cat. If I became an unwed mother, my situation would be quite different. Two beings who are in love love each other in the flesh as well as in the spirit, and they know that procreation is part of that love. Love, the sublime union of spirit and body, is accompanied by natural consequences the way everything else in biology is, and that's to be expected ... and you have to accept the child as the end result of the search for communication and communion that pushes lovers toward each other. I would accept Jacques' child as the symbol and the consequence of our love. . . .

The truck had finally turned around. The road was empty. I could leave. I could see the red convertible at the edge of the sidewalk. I sighed happily: Jacques was waiting for me in the old, kind, sheltering house; everything was fine again and I was moving toward certain happiness. My excitement had miraculously subsided. I drove the last hundred yards without impatience, letting the car roll slowly along like a ship coming back into harbor. As I stopped before the door, I who had sworn to myself never to be a housewife or a mother, dreamed for a moment about a home, and children, about a sweet house like the Ferrières house where the two of us could live and die together. . . .

In spite of my impatience at the idea of seeing Jacques again, I couldn't go by his cousin's office without leaving off the kit and making it clear that I had obeyed my orders scrupulously.

I knocked on the door, ready to leave without a word as soon as I'd returned the kit. I got no answer so I went in. When he left the office, Vincent had opened the window to get rid of the traces of odor left by the afternoon patients. The good smell of polish and old furniture was beginning to permeate the room again, and reflections from the big chestnut tree whose leaves were swaying gently outside the window rippled on the old pewter.

I deposited the kit on the desk, in plain sight, and was just about to leave, when I remembered a shot of anti-tetanus serum that I'd given during the course of the afternoon. I had to note it down at once, so I wouldn't forget.

I opened the file cabinet and took out the man's chart. I noted down the shot, the amount of the dosage of serum and the date. As I put it back in its place, I saw Simone Vallin's chart. Vincent had left it in front of the others probably because he was in too much of a hurry to refile it in its proper place. What did he want to check on that chart? I took the card and realized with amazement that Vincent had noted on it in his handwriting under the date of August 6th: "Danger of miscarriage, probably due to the German measles in June. (Seen by Doctor Sauvage.)" And under the date of August 12th: "Serious hemorrhage. Necessity of an emergency curettage. (Performed by Doctor Sauvage.)"

I stood by the filing cabinet for a long time, trying to understand the reasons that might have pushed the scrupulous Vincent to make two entries that were so utterly false. From all the evidence, he wanted to make my illegal operation look like a necessary curettage; if an inquiry were ordered, this chart would constitute proof in favor of my good faith. But why was he trying to cover up for me? He was taking a very serious risk upon himself if his deceit were ever uncovered.

I thought, "He didn't do it to protect me out of generosity, he only did it to avoid a scandal."

I put the chart back in the file. I glanced out the window toward the arbor; it was empty. I left the office, and looked over toward the staircase. I thought I could hear a vague noise coming from the second floor. Was it Vincent talking to Jacques, or had Jacques turned on his little transistor radio the way he always did as soon as he walked into his room? It didn't matter—he was certainly there in any case.

I walked up the first steps so happily that I couldn't help smiling when I remembered my hesitations just before I went to Jacques on the evening of the abortion, and also my fear that he'd gone off in pursuit of Arlette.

I got to the second turn of the stairs, facing Jacques' door. It was here, that, mad with joy, I had seen the rays of light from under his door that proved to me that he'd come home. The door was closed now, but the voices came to me distinctly. What I was hearing wasn't the radio but a conversation between the two cousins. I stopped in surprise. Was Vincent taking advantage of the fact that I was late to question Jacques immediately about what was going on between us or had Jacques decided to confess without waiting for me? If so, should I interrupt? I strained to hear what they were saying. Vincent said:

"Tell me why you pushed Claude into performing the abortion instead of persuading her not to do it."

I was amazed. In spite of the question he was asking, his voice was not at all angry. On the contrary, it expressed only infinite patience, as if he were forcing himself to use sweetness and persuasion to make a stubborn child realize that he'd done something bad.

When Jacques started to speak, his voice casual and light, I could almost see him lounging nonchalantly in his chair and smiling his mocking smile.

"All right! I'll examine my conscience very scrupulously, Father Confessor. Here's the first reason—it's not the most important one, but I'll tell you because I promised to tell everything. I wanted to see your face when you found out about it; I was just curious and, as you well know, I didn't feel any less affection for you because of my curiosity. And, as predicted, I notice that you are *not* pleased. ... Second reason—and a more serious one: I returned from a world where one out of every three children dies of hunger during childhood and where the survivors will slowly be dying of hunger all the rest of their lives, a world where they perform abortions on women as fast as they can to reduce the number of births, when they aren't busy sterilizing the men and rewarding them with a consolation bonus of three thousand rupees—barely a few francs. You must realize that such things can well change one's perspective a little about the European's sacred respect for life! Claude told me that awful story of German measles and how you had refused to do anything—and it seemed to me that your refusal came from an old-fashioned, or maybe neurotic, moralism. You'll never make me admit that getting rid of a two-month-old embryo with a curette isn't better than letting a child who has a fifty per cent chance of being a monster be born. Consequently, I still think that for the mother and the child I was right to encourage Claude to do the abortion. ... Third reason—I'm going on because I promised not to hide anything from you—Claude was driving me crazy because she couldn't make up her mind. 'I want to . . . I don't want to . . . I would do it if I dared but I don't dare. . . .' At the age of twenty-five, if you want to be the Joan of Arc of female emancipation and the missionary of free contraception, you have to know how to make your own decisions and not spend your time begging: 'Go on, be nice! Give me a little push!' "

That was what Jacques had told me under the apple tree, but that evening he'd been less ironic about it. He probably didn't want Vincent to know right away how close we had become. . . .

Around me, the house seemed even quieter than usual. I heard the scratch of a match. Jacques said:

"When you play on a woman's sense of honor, you can make her do anything. That's a law of psychology that has very few exceptions, and it's very useful for knowing how to manage women more easily. Another law that comes from my experience: most of the time, the best button to push with women is their pride. As for Claude, I only had to use her terror of being taken for a horrible conformist. She decided immediately!"

I thought: "Now he's making fun of me to make Vincent look ridiculous and make him see that *he's* the narrow and hidebound conformist." But Vincent must not have caught the allusion because he asked patiently and reproachfully:

"Did you stop to think that you were throwing her into a dreadful situation; that she's in danger of a prohibition to practice, a stiff fine and perhaps even a prison sentence?"

Jacques laughed.

"First of all, she isn't in prison yet and you have all the time in the world to make up packages of oranges to send to her there. And remember that Margaret Sanger, the redheaded rebel, was jailed several times in America before she won her fight for birth control. You have to know how to take risks as well as how to make decisions, or else you shouldn't play the role of the intrepid girl who chooses a man's profession, pretends to live freely, screams at her father and mother and wants to upset the world because it's thwarting her desire for equality and her need for independence. . . ."

Vincent didn't say anything for a while. It was so quiet that even though there was a carpet in Jacques' room, I could hear him pacing back and forth across the floor. He finally stopped and said quietly:

"Why did you deliberately compromise her reputation by showing yourself off with her all over the countryside so provocatively?"

He seemed to regret having to ask such a personal question, and he did it so tactfully that I blushed. But it didn't seem to bother Jacques in the least. He spoke lightly, in the tone he always uses with Vincent.

"I have a good excuse for that. To begin with, I went through a month of absolute chastity in the hospital, with Sister Opportune as my only female companion. For the repose of her patients Providence has made her pious, mustached, and rather fat. But at that point, my privation wasn't an absolute tragedy because, as you know, though opium gives pleasure, it has the very unfortunate drawback of making its users temporarily impotent. When I got here, you could have put the most lovely young girl in the town into my bed and she wouldn't have been in any danger. But then, just when my hormones were coming to life again, instead of putting me back into the care of some Sister Opportune, you put my cure in the hands of a young nurse who isn't fat at all, who hasn't got the least trace of a mustache, and who possesses, one must admit, a pair of rather beautiful eyes. For someone who's been out of active service for months, as far as love is concerned, you must admit that we were dangerously intimate! In my state of hearty appetite, Claude looked to me like one of the most disturbing sirens who ever tempted Ulysses and his companions. But alas, you hadn't taken the precaution of tying me to my bench or stopping up my ears. Then you disappear for ten days, leaving me in permanent intimacy with her. Did you think that with this opportunity before me, I would get one of those rubber dolls that sailors use, just to respect morality and your replacement?"

Jacques had said all this very good-humoredly, just as if he were telling some college adventure story. I was astounded. At first I thought I'd misunderstood. But with every word that followed I reacted, first with worry, and then with more and more horrified amazement. I was choking and my heart was pounding with fear.

Jacques laughed smugly.

"Because of your bad judgment, I gave in, almost without wanting to, to a pleasant dissipation, spiced with a

367

bit of rustic poetry which, I must admit, was not without charm. A mixture of love and discussions of 'great cosmic forces' I assure you, is an infallible way to get yourself into shape again."

I could hardly bear the horrible incongruousness of that voice saying such monstrous words. I was almost ready to leap up the last steps, open the door and shout out, "Stop this hideous farce, stop this profanation. Be quiet, I beg of you!" But Vincent's indignant voice stopped me.

"You're disgusting. Doing nothing with your life must be what makes you so perverted. How dare you speak so cynically about a young girl?"

Jacques retreated before the oncoming storm. He said appeasingly, "And your obsession for overdramatizing is disgusting! 'A young girl.' ... The time when young ladies sewed samplers and only knew how to answer 'yes, mother' is over and done with. Besides I was perfectly honest with Claude. Ask her if you like. I didn't hide anything about my life from her—I even told her some very ugly things about myself that you don't know and that I could easily not have mentioned. I warned her. I even warned her about me. I explained to her that I'd met her in a period of failure, discouragement and uncertainty, and that I found her—unlike most women—to be refreshing, restful, and honest, and that her presence and her friendship were doing me good. I practice lying to women as if it were a sport, but I didn't lie to her one single minute. I can swear to you that I was really frank."

I felt the choking anxiety that was knotted around my throat begin to loosen slightly. Here was the real Jacques again—the one who had said such wonderful things to me under the arbor.

"Your frankness is made up of double meanings and evasions. You've always been so comfortable in your lies that now you don't even know that you're lying."

It seemed as if Vincent was trying to get at his cousin's sense of honor and integrity and Jacques did seem touched because he exclaimed plaintively:

"Please, Vincent, don't overwhelm me. You don't realize how overpoweringly depressing your perfectionism and your sense of duty can be for a poor bastard like me. Just the way there are women of pleasure in this world, I'm a man of pleasure. It's not my fault if I'm a coward in the face of temptation and if I love life a little too much."

As his beloved voice rose and fell, I felt the warmth of

life flooding back into me, as if I were waking from a horrible nightmare. Just a minute ago, I thought I saw my love crumbling away, but now I wished that Jacques would never stop talking. But Vincent was too irritated to be able to see the full value of his cousin's guilt and honesty as clearly as I could. He interrupted him sharply.

"No! You only love yourself, because if you really loved life, you wouldn't play games with the lives of other people. What is hardest to believe is that you can make other people suffer without feeling any guilt at all. ..."

Jacques said, "Now you're starting to overdramatize again. You'd never believe to hear you talk that you listen to young girls' confessions every day in your office, and you make it sound as if you don't even know how far today's emancipated little girls go when they've barely reached puberty. Your experience in legal medicine should have taught you long ago that in so-called morals cases, it's almost always the 'victim' who's guiltiest in the last analysis. So don't start using high-sounding phrases like: 'That coward who attacks young girls.' I didn't need to attack Claude. I almost had to defend myself. Let's say, to divide the responsibility more fairly, that I let things happen without defending myself but without attacking."

"Am I dreaming?" I thought. "Is he mad? Or have I gone mad? Why is he destroying everything by saying such monstrous things? As if our love, from the very first evening, hadn't been an unceasing communion!" I wanted to scream, or shout out the protestations I was slowly and painfully forming within myself but I was so upset that the words stopped on my lips.

I passed my hand mechanically over my eyes to make sure that I wasn't having hallucinations, that I was really here, that I was really hearing such horrible things coming from Jacques. Every word reached me distinctly through the closed door, and even though it was breaking my heart, I kept listening, because I had to find the full extent of my wound.

"The only way to be of service to these intellectuals of prolonged virginity—and in our day virginity has become so rare that I swear I really didn't expect it in Claude ... As I say, the only way to be of service to them and save them from becoming real neurotics is to sleep with them. And as far as that's concerned, I swear I've managed things well: the dramatic scenes, the photogenic kisses, the passionate embraces, the moonlight and one night even the song of a nightingale. . . . Claude can't complain about her initiation; she's been perfectly broken in."

I listened to every sentence in disgust and horror. I closed my eyes and stood numbed, as if gathering all my strength before I collapsed. I stood on the step; I couldn't turn and run; I couldn't even move. I kept begging silently, "If only Vincent would shut him up. It doesn't matter how. If he has to, he should beat him into silence." But Vincent seemed unable to respond to Jacques' deliberate challenge. Why didn't he try to stop it? In my frenzy, I couldn't understand anything any more. Finally he spoke— slowly and deliberately.

"Don't you realize how disgusting it is to compare Claude to a new car that needs breaking in? Haven't you even considered that she's in love with you?"

He hadn't raised his voice, but his speech seemed to take on an almost metallic sonority; and although it was deeply changed, his voice was still calm. In an effort of almost tragic intensity to control himself and to reason with Jacques, he was begging him to be better than his cynical mask, he was trying one last time to reach that part of Jacques that he thought was still capable of human feelings. He seemed to want to avoid a final rupture between Jacques and me at any price—he was still trying to plead for my love.

Was Jacques touched by the dignity and nobility in Vincent that dominated him in spite of himself? He asked very simply and for once without irony:

"Have you known that Claude was in love with me for a long time?"

"Ever since the Sunday when I came home from Bernay, and found you playing with the puzzle."

"Congratulations!" Jacques cried. "You have sharp eyes. It was just beginning then. You can guess that I remember too. That evening Claude was being very silly, maybe because of the puzzle. She kept 'ohing' and 'ahing' and giggling inanely. She was talking nonsense and acting like a child. She was trying to be flirtatious and impulsive but unhappily she was putting on an act—she was making too much of an effort. . . . Brainy girls are terrible: they despise sex for years, and then all of a sudden they discover love and they want to start improvising without realizing that they've decided to play the game a little late and that they don't have the talent for it. It's funny that that sort of girl, who's so perceptive and intelligent about

370

everything else, can't understand that a man might desire a woman just out of curiosity and might get tired of her after a while. You're very lucky if the woman you've just slept with isn't immediately certain that you're dying to set up a household with her!"

I looked around. I was terrified. Were those really my hands on the banister, and my feet making the step creak? Was I really living through this horrible nightmare?

I heard Vincent's voice as if in a dream. He was speaking softly. I was listening to him through one of those thick fogs that muffle every sound. He was as kind and decent as if he knew I was standing listening at the door, and wanted to fight to the very end in the most brotherly way for my happiness and honor. He asked the question that was on my lips, but that I would have proudly forbidden myself to ask, even at the price of my life.

"You won't marry her then, in any case?"

"Me?" Jacques exclaimed. "No! Never."

"What do you intend to do?"

"I don't know. Or rather, I do know: get the hell out of here as soon as possible! For the last two days I've had the feeling that if I stayed here too long, something disastrous was going to happen to me. I didn't worry at the time. I always get that feeling when I stay in the same place for a little while. But you see, it's high time for me to leave. The difficulty is going to be slipping away without a painful parting scene. Tears, melting mascara, snuffling voice, sniveling—that makes me feel guilty, and then it exasperates me. I'm in danger of being really nasty just to get away."

Jacques was going to leave! I wouldn't see Jacques any more. . . . If I'd known that an hour earlier, I would have thought I was going to die on the spot. But now, as if my despair had suddenly reached its limit, I felt strangely calm and horribly peaceful. Had I gone past the threshold of pain? At the hospital, I'd seen injured people who were totally oblivious of the most terrible mutilations for a while. Now that everything had been said and the truth had been crystallized into definitive, final words, I could listen without suffering any more, as if it hadn't anything to do with me. I only felt a kind of numb curiosity as Jacques went on.

"I must find some way to get out of having to destroy the poor girl's illusions myself!"

Was I really the "poor girl" who was being so deceived by love, and who would now be lost in her loneliness?

Jacques fell silent. I could see him, looking at the ceiling, absorbed in his search for some way out. I wished I could let him know that he didn't have to worry now that I knew what he was—an overgrown perverted child who told himself make-believe stories, instead of the man I had loved, a man who was responsible for his words. Suddenly Jacques said persuasively:

"You must admit that in the last analysis everything that's happening to me is largely your fault. . . . Be reasonable, Vincent! Help me get out of this mess. . . . You're not involved; it would be easier for you. Just tell Claude for me that it's all over!"

Vincent was shocked into silence. Then he shouted:

"No! I won't do it!"

He sounded thoroughly angry but then he sighed as if he'd been thrown into some dramatic conflict of conscience. In a voice full of pain—the voice of a man who is defending what is most essential within him, who is defending his very life—he said in a muffled voice:

"No! You can't ask that of me!"

A silence fell between them, a long oppressive silence that seemed as if it would never end. It was Jacques who broke it. His voice was affectionate and he asked very gently and cautiously as if he were talking to a shy child:

"Tell me! Vincent . . . it took a while . . . but I think I'm beginning to understand . . . Claude . . . you couldn't be . . . you aren't in love with her?"

The silence that followed seemed to last forever. Vincent said nothing. Finally Jacques cried out in desperate sincerity:

"Forgive me! I'm a fool, such a fool."

There was no reason for me to listen to any more of this.

My dress was pasted to my body with cold sweat. My hands were shaking and my heart was pounding. I staggered down the stairs. I only wanted one thing—to escape from the house where everything had suddenly collapsed in ruins around me. Impassively, the healing saints watched my flight through the foyer I'd crossed happily and impatiently twenty minutes ago.

The car was in front of the door. Without even thinking that I didn't have the right to drive it now, I opened the door, started up, put it into gear and left, going straight ahead without thinking.

I drove automatically. I could only repeat over and over to myself: "It's all over!" and my brain stumbled at the words like a wasp flying against a window; I couldn't think any further ahead. I lifted my eyes to the rear-view mirror and saw my face—to my amazement, all my features were tense but very calm and it took me a moment to understand that my apparent calm really expressed emptiness and barrenness beyond all thought. Again, I murmured, "It's all over!" and only felt the echo of a vague pain, a deep diffuse pain that I didn't even try to push away. Now that Jacques was gone from my life, everything within me was collapsing, I was a ruined wasteland, a desert, a void.

I drove on mechanically, aimlessly, as if I were trying to escape from myself after fleeing from the Ferrières house.

I was still on the main highway when I saw a signpost standing on my left at an intersection. It said, "Grandhoux, 4 miles." Had I been driving toward this post all the way from Mesnil without realizing it? As if I were obeying a command, I turned to my left on a secondary road and easily retraced the path Jacques had followed to the well. After I passed the hill, I took the same little path across the meadows, then the mud road that led between barbed wire fences to the construction site.

I recognized the apple trees from a distance, and the hut with its green tarpaulin, the shaft of the winch and the yellowish loam of the rubbish from the excavation. It was nearly eight o'clock, and the site was deserted. I stopped the car near the well. The tool chest was in the same place in the hut under the tarp. I went to sit on it. "I'll be comfortable there," I thought, "without anyone to talk to me, without anyone to see me. I'll be alone in the heavy silence of defeat."

Nothing had changed around the well. The heaps of dark brown earth—the earth that comes before the chalk-clay—were a little larger, but beyond them, the same smells of hay and earth blew in off the plains, carried by the breeze that brought the freshness of evening. Impossible to believe that a tragedy had almost taken place here: three men had almost died! Everything was infinitely calm and peaceful. But tonight the sweetness of the evening was ironic for me and the August sky, which would soon look like a fishpond filled with stars, would have a mocking splendor.

I sat slumped on the tool chest. I felt crushed by a dull unending ache, an indescribable weariness at the difficult realization that my life would go on anyway. Where could I find the courage to go on living tomorrow and the day after tomorrow, and not let myself slowly die of disgust and loneliness?

I sat quietly and peacefully in the back of the hut, watching the shadows of the coming night reach toward the horizon. I was eager for the night to come and bring the darkness that would hide the outstretched plains from me. For ten days, those meadows, those fields of stubble, those small winding roads, and those hamlets had been my enclosed protective world.

I looked at the mouth of the well. It was only two steps away. When the workmen left, they'd covered it with sheets of corrugated metal to keep the farm animals from falling into it in the darkness. The brown rust-colored metal contrasted with the gray of the cement curb. "On the night of the accident," I thought, "everything fell into place with implacable logic. Seeing Jacques go down like a knight riding off to dangerous adventures, I let myself be caught up in the old myth of the hero. When he came triumphantly out of the well, why didn't I realize that he was only feeling proud of his recovered strength and his muscles? When I knew I was completely defenseless before him, why did I forget that the male of our species is carnivorous, cruel, and well-versed in lies? In the innocence of my new love, I thought I was fulfilling my physical and intellectual potential and experiencing the greatest moment of my life, freely chosen, in keeping with my nature and my vocation. But I'll really have missed everything because it was all lies."

Night was beginning to fall—a moonless night. The darkness was thick and oppressive. I couldn't stay in the hut forever. I murmured: "I must take the car back to Vincent," and then I smiled. Poor Vincent! My thoughts went back to him for the first time since I'd left his house. Because he loves me, I thought for an instant about going back to Mesnil and knocking on his door so I could cling to his goodness, his sureness and his strength. I was sure that if I confessed my despair it would touch him deeply enough so he'd forget his own sorrow and comfort me.

I imagined his open untroubled face, and his unmocking

smile. He was in love with me, but he'd never tried any clever schemes to better his chances of winning me. Even in our sharpest discussions, he always kept a tone of friendly, almost brotherly, kindness. He realized that I was in love with his cousin but he'd tried very hard to hide his love out of his wonderful sense of fairness. But now I knew how his generosity of spirit, untouched by pettiness or jealousy, must have made it a continuous ordeal for him.

"No," I thought, "I won't go to Vincent. I won't bring him a poor, humiliated, betrayed girl to comfort. He doesn't know that I know his secret. If I cry, he might try to take me in his arms, in a way that he might think was still only affectionate and brotherly. But I'd have to push him away because the deepest part of me refuses his love, love that he'll beg me to accept, sooner or later, just like Lachaux. I will not be touched by his mouth, or his hands, or his body. I never want a man to touch me again."

Before my eyes, the darkness was gradually erasing the outline of the cement edge and the rusty iron sheets. If Jacques had been buried by a cave-in, I would have waited for his body to be brought up here, and then, like a widow, I would have come back here over and over again to search for the tiniest memory, for the dazzling sound of his last laugh. Tonight the impulse to come back had been stronger than the nausea that had overcome me. Here I was again, almost unconsciously, on the exact spot where Jacques had taken me into his arms for the first time. Was I going to keep insanely searching for his ghost? And even if I decided to avoid the Ferrières house so I wouldn't keep meeting a ghost, could I resist the ghost of our love that lingered in every hollow, at every cross road, in every farmyard, in every corner of the woods?

The only way to break the spell of despair and make a healthy recovery was to leave Mesnil. But where could I go? I couldn't go very far away, or live without work, because it was out of the question to ask Vincent to pay me for substituting for him. I couldn't even borrow money from mother; I'd have to confess my troubles to her to explain my sudden departure. She'd never understand why I couldn't immediately replace Jacques with Vincent, "such a good match." The hopital in Gennevilliers? If I went there, Lachaux would try to comfort me by taking me in his arms just like Vincent. Another period as a doctor's replacement in the country? No. I couldn't bear any more sad fields, squat villages or earthy, sultry nights. And I couldn't bear the heavy gloomy silence that was now thickening the darkness around me! I wanted a town where I would find smooth sidewalks echoing under my feet instead of ditches; where I could see other faces than those of the villagers I'd once thought were rather dense but sincere and who now horrified me because of their selfishness and their ingratitude. But where should I try my luck?

I thought. Evreux? I didn't know anyone there but Alberte. Bernay? Too near. Caen? Perhaps, but how could I find someone who'd give me a job? All of a sudden I remembered an ad that I'd read in a medical journal, yesterday or the day before. It had struck me because when I glanced at it I'd thought: "This is exactly what I'd have wanted if I were looking for work!" A doctor in Caen badly needed a medical student who had almost finished her studies, who was well acquainted with gynecology, and who would be able to replace his wife. She was a doctor, and had to stop working temporarily because she was pregnant.

After I read the magazine, I'd thrown it out—in any case, I couldn't go to Vincent now to ask for it. Of course, I didn't remember the address but I'd noticed the name, even though it was commonplace. The doctor was called Legallois, like my biological sciences professor in my last year at school. He had awakened my passionate interest in biology and it was partly because of him that I'd decided to become a doctor. I could never forget his name. It was a very recent issue of the magazine. In August, replacements who were ready to arrive at a moment's notice must be scarce: here was my chance. I had to check at once to see if the job was still open!

I left the hut. As I passed by the well, I kicked one of the corrugated iron sheets. It echoed lugubriously over the emptiness below. I was tempted to take off the cover, lean over, and let myself go! A twenty-five-yard fall should do it. Down there would be the end of the story, the final blackness, the great end of everything! . . .

I shrugged my shoulders. The idea had come a few minutes too late. Even though my strength, my confidence, and my youth were shattered now, I wasn't going to die at twenty-five like a young girl devastated by her first heartbreak. Just when this job might help me recover my balance—even a very precarious one—it would have been cheating myself. I would reconsider it later on, if my life seemed to be too slow and empty.

I got back into the car. Again the headlights glanced off the big heaps of yellow and brown earth, and I left, bouncing up and down in the seat at every clod of earth.

As I drove through the fields, I planned what I'd do. It wasn't yet ten o'clock. If I called right away, I might well find Dr. Legallois at home. I didn't know his phone number, but there couldn't be many physicians of that name in Caen.

When I got to the road, I hesitated. Should I go to Grandhoux? I might be recognized there. That wasn't really important any more, but the idea that I might become an object of curiosity again made me bristle. I took the opposite direction, toward Anzeray. I got there just in time. The proprietor of the café in the center of the village was only waiting for the last two customers, who were sitting over their drinks, to leave so he could close up. Luckily, there was an old Calvados phone directory in the shed that served as a phone booth. Five minutes later, I was talking to Dr. Legallois. He said that he was indeed the author of the ad. His voice sounded young and decisive. I lied to him, saying that I'd chanced to read his ad just when my job as a substitute in Mesnil was finishing and I was getting ready to go back to Paris.

"That's really a piece of good luck," he exclaimed. "I was beginning to lose hope. My wife was thinking that she could keep on with her consultations and her duties in the dispensary for a little while longer but she's having a difficult pregnancy and it would really be unwise. It would be much better if she could stop working. Since you're free, come right away."

I said I'd come on one of the morning trains from Evreux the next day and hung up happily. Until now, I'd felt as if I was trapped in a cage, or had fallen into a trap that would never open again. Suddenly, I felt that maybe I had a chance to get out of the numbness that was worse than death; to get out of the horrible mental pacing back and forth of a caged animal, continually going over, minute by minute, the story of my abandonment.

Now that I was sure of where I was going I planned my escape as I drove back to Mesnil. Should I take the bus to Evreux tomorrow morning? I'd have to wait for it, suitcase in hand, at the bus stop in the town hall square; the whole town would watch me leave—and it would look as if I'd been dismissed or was going because of the rumors. I could ask Vincent to drive me to the station, but then I'd have to see him again and give him my reasons for leaving, all the while trying not to talk about Jacques.

As I drove on, another plan for leaving Mesnil began to form in my mind. "I'll go home to pack, I'll write two letters, one for mother, the other for Vincent. In the one to Vincent, I'll explain that I'm leaving to spare him any trouble that might arise from the abortion; and I'll apologize for having kept the car without his permission. Then I can catch the train tonight in Evreux. I'll mail that letter when I leave Mesnil. Vincent will get it tomorrow morning in the first postal delivery, before he has time to worry. One drawback: my going this way will mean he'll have to send the mechanic to get the Peugeot at the Evreux station, but when I've already used a physician's curette and instruments to perform an illegal abortion in his absence, using his car without telling him beforehand seems unimportant."

Except for involving another unkindness toward Vincent, my plan seemed perfect. Tonight, I'll sleep in Evreux; tomorrow morning I'll leave for Caen and start my new job.

The two letters are ready. Soon, when I leave, I'll put the one for mother in an obvious spot on the little table in the entrance hall. Then I'll walk out and close the door quietly behind me. I wrote it in the most natural style, inventing another story. "This evening, Doctor Legallois from Caen called me at Dr. Ferrières' and asked me to come quickly to substitute for his doctor wife. I hadn't planned to go until late August." I'd never suggested anything like this to mother, but she knows that I'm strange and this pretext is sufficiently plausible to make her believe me—or at least pretend to believe me to save her dignity. Tomorrow morning, Mme Vasse and all the other Mesnil shopkeepers will know that my medical competence was the reason for an urgent call to replace an eminent "lady doctor in Caen." If my unannounced departure tonight hurts mother a little and underlines my lack of affection and trust in her again, I'm sure she'll console herself by thinking that this substitution will at least cut short all the gossip by forcing me to leave Jacques.

The letter for Vincent is ready too. I tried very hard to write it with dignity, in the general style of: "Our paths crossed for a moment and now they are separating, but above and beyond all our differences of opinion on many questions, I'll remember your intellectual honesty and your uprightness just as I will never forget the worries I've caused you, nor your generosity in covering up for me." I used another story in his letter, inventing a telegram that I'd found at my mother's this evening forcing me to leave quickly for Evreux in his car. In conclusion, I expressed, besides my apologies and my gratitude, the hope that he would keep his feeling of friendship for me. Vincent won't understand my flight any better than mother. And even if he believed for a while that Jacques' betrayal gave him a chance to win my love, after he reads this letter he'll know he'll never have a place in my life.

Poor Vincent! You never know anything about other people. . . . You hurt them without knowing it and without wanting to. . . . Which of us will recover more quickly? Will it be Vincent who has had no love at all or I, who so firmly believed that I'd found it? What will the remedies of time, work, and patience mean for both of us? Old people who've had hard lives maintain that everything turns out for the best. How? . . . they never say. But since they're still here, it must mean that you don't die from your suffering. That kind of discussion never has any end, or any answer. So let's believe that in the long run everything will turn out for the best! . . .

Mother is sleeping deeply—I can hear her regular, heavy breathing through the wall. There's no danger of waking her up by opening drawers. In ten minutes my suitcases will be ready and I'll leave. In ten minutes I'll say good-bye to all the things—my narrow couch, my little desk, my knickknacks—that still tie me to my youth. Between the time when I came to Mesnil after Mariette's death and Simone Vallin's abortion, a thousand things have been destroyed, and my adolescence is over. Again I'm alone, alone as at the beginning of my life. My past is a great circle that's now completed. Tonight, I'll begin at the beginning again.

But to sustain me, I'll carry with me the revelation that came to me as I waited by the well—that all women are bound together by a common cause. Even if my love was nothing but deception, even if my innocence made me

379

more vulnerable, even if my sincerity made me make every possible mistake, I don't have the right to regret my experience. What I knew about love only by hearsay until now, I have felt in every part of my mind and my body. Even if my unhappiness has nothing very extraordinary or very special about it in comparison with all my patients' stories, now I'll know exactly what women mean when they talk about their loneliness, their disillusionment, and their fears.

In these last twenty-four hours there have been close to a hundred thousand births throughout the world, and in the same period of time, millions of women have been scoffed at, humiliated, betrayed and degraded. Some of these victims of men's selfishness—like Mariette, like Simone Vallin, like Mme Lemailleux—will come to me in the future and tearfully ask me to help them. And I will have to try to heal them, and give them some confidence, even in the face of the injustice of men and the law. But how can I give other women the irreplaceable treasures of peace and happiness when I myself am so bereft?

I think of the miracles of long ago ... in the heart of winter old women would suddenly find their work-worn aprons filled with bread and roses. The abundance that was so miraculously given to the poor and disinherited is doubtless one manifestation of what Christians call "divine grace." But I am not a believer, and if my calling cannot heal me, who will give me the human grace and the strength to go on?

". . . It's not a question of condemning but of understanding . . . of putting yourself in the place of thousands of women faced with the problem of pregnancy, living their anxieties and their worries, and realizing that for every unfeeling woman who refuses motherhood, there are dozens of unhappy women who can never know its joys.

"That is the constructive and humane attitude. And therefore fiction is a better witness and a more faithful reflection of society than books on ethics and a richer and more valid source of facts than medical, legal or sociological literature. The modern novelist, from Zola to Sartre, from Colette to Simone de Beauvoir, deals with the problem of abortions better than the physician, the magistrate or the sociologist. . . ."

—Jacques Derogy, *Des enfants malgré nous*

"... Did Jacques Derogy realize the severity of his statement when he asserted: 'The modern novelist deals with abortion better than the physician'?"

—Dr. M. A. Lagroua Weill-Hallé,
in the Preface to *Des enfants malgré nous*

"... At a time when the progress of man's conquest of nature is ever more staggering, it is a peculiar aberration that on a point as important as birth and birth control the password among us is still 'let nature take her course.' ... It is monstrous that in such a great number of cases the birth of a child represents a catastrophe. The explanation of this passivity is the silence that surrounds this forbidden subject; only a few psychiatrists, physicians and social workers are aware of the extent of the harm, and almost no one discusses it. ... We must put an end to so much unnecessary unhappiness as quickly as possible. An answer must be found to the anxious question: 'How do other women do it?' "

—Simone de Beauvoir,
in the Preface to *La grand' peur d'aimer*
by Lagroua Weill-Hallé

THE BIG BESTSELLERS
ARE AVON BOOKS!

A Different Woman Jane Howard	19075	$1.95
The Alchemist Les Whitten	19919	$1.75
Rule Britannia Daphne Du Maurier	19547	$1.50
Play of Darkness Irving A. Greenfield	19877	$1.50
Facing the Lions Tom Wicker	19307	$1.75
High Empire Clyde M. Brundy	18994	$1.75
The Kingdom L. W. Henderson	18978	$1.75
The Last of the Southern Girls Willie Morris	18614	$1.50
The Hungarian Game Roy Hayes	18986	$1.75
The Wolf and the Dove Kathleen E. Woodiwiss	18457	$1.75
The Priest Ralph McInerny	18192	$1.75
Sweet Savage Love Rosemary Rogers	17988	$1.75
How I Found Freedom *In An Unfree World* Harry Browne	17772	$1.95
I'm OK—You're OK Thomas A. Harris, M.D.	14662	$1.95
Jonathan Livingston Seagull Richard Bach	14316	$1.50

Where better paperbacks are sold, or directly from the publisher. Include 15¢ per copy for mailing; allow three weeks for delivery.

Avon Books, Mail Odrer Dept., 250 West 55th Street, New York, N.Y. 10019